VOLU

Gifted

KINGFISHER
LONDON & NEW YORK

Text copyright © 2012 by Marilyn Kaye
Published in the United States by Kingfisher,
175 Fifth Ave., New York, NY 10010
Kingfisher is an imprint of Macmillan Children's Books, London.
All rights reserved.

Distributed in the U.S. and Canada by Macmillan,
175 Fifth Ave., New York, NY 10010

Library of Congress Cataloging-in-Publication data
has been applied for.

ISBN: 978-0-7534-6788-6

Kingfisher books are available for special promotions and premiums.
For details contact: Special Markets Department,
Macmillan, 175 Fifth Ave., New York, NY 10010.

For more information, please visit www.kingfisherbooks.com

Printed and bound by CPI Group (UK) Ltd, Croydon, CR0 4YY

10 9 8 7 6 5 4 3 2 1

VOLUME 1

Gifted

MARILYN KAYE

KINGFISHER
NEW YORK

contents:

For my friends who first heard this story on the beach at Bandol: Thomas and Augustin Clerc; Emilie and Marion Grimaud; Jeanne, Angèle, and Baptiste Latil; Liona, Fanny, and Alice Lutz—je vous embrasse!

For my goddaughter, Iris, her brother Octave, and their parents, Muriel Berthelot and Jean-François Marti

Gifted

Out of Sight,
Out of Mind

PROLOGUE

Sometimes I look in a mirror and there's nobody looking back. I know I have a reflection.

I just don't see it.

Maybe it's all in my mind.

Maybe I've got bad eyesight.

Or maybe it's something else.

My name is Tracey. Tracey Devon. Did you get that? TRACEY DEVON. I'm writing this all in capital letters because it's like talking really loudly. People might pay more attention.

I never speak loudly. In fact, I make very little noise at all. I'm a quiet person. When I talk, I whisper. When I laugh—which isn't very often—it's a silent laugh. When I cry, I can feel the tears on my face, but there's no sound.

I'm not a ghost. I'm a living, breathing, flesh-and-blood 13-year-old girl. All my senses are intact. I have two arms, two legs, a heart, a brain—all the usual stuff. I've got two eyes, two ears, one nose, one mouth—and they're all in the right places.

1

I eat, drink, sleep, and use the toilet, just like everyone else.

But sometimes I look in a mirror and I don't see anyone looking back.

Maybe it's my imagination.

Maybe I'm going blind.

Or maybe I'm not really here at all.

CHAPTER ONE

THERE WERE 342 STUDENTS at Meadowbrook Middle School and three lunch periods each day. This meant that during any one lunch period there could be no more than 114 students in the cafeteria. The noise and commotion, however, suggested that half the population of mainland China was eating lunch together.

Students roamed the cavernous space, shouting, racing from one end to the other, knocking over chairs, banging trays down on tables. There were a couple of teachers who were supposed to be supervising the scene and maintaining order, but they couldn't stop the occasional flying meatball from that day's Spaghetti Special or the far-reaching spray from a soda bottle that had been intentionally shaken before being opened.

From her prime seat at the best table, Amanda Beeson surveyed the chaotic scene with a sense of well-being. The cafeteria was noisy and messy and not very attractive,

3

but it was part of her little kingdom—or queendom, if such a word existed. She wasn't wearing any kind of crown, of course, but she felt secure in the knowledge that in this particular hive, she was generally acknowledged as the queen bee.

On either side of her sat two princesses—Sophie Greene and Britney Teller. The three of them were about to begin their daily assessment of classmates.

As always, Amanda kicked off the conversation. "Ohmigod, check out Caroline's sweater! It's way too tight."

"No kidding," Sophie said. "It's like she's begging for the boys to look at her."

"And it's not like she's got anything on top to look at," Britney added.

Amanda looked around for more victims. "Someone should tell Shannon Fields that girls with fat knees shouldn't wear short skirts."

"Terri Boyd has a new bag," Britney pointed out. "Is it a Coach?"

Amanda shook her head. "No way. It's a fake."

"How can you tell from this far away?" Sophie wanted to know.

Amanda gave her a withering look. "Oh, puh-leeze! Coach doesn't make hobo bags in that shade of green."

Spotting imitation designer goods was a favorite game, and Amanda surveyed the crowd for another example. "Look at Cara Winters's sweater."

"Juicy Couture?" Sophie wondered.

"*Not.*You can tell by the buttons."

Sophie gazed at her with admiration.Amanda responded by looking pointedly at the item in Sophie's hand."Sophie, are you actually going to eat that cupcake? I thought you were on a diet."

Sophie sighed and pushed the cupcake to the edge of her tray. Amanda turned to her other side.

"Why are you staring at me like that?" Britney asked.

"You've got a major zit coming out on your chin."

Britney whipped a mirror out of her bag.

"It's not that big," Sophie assured her. "No one can see it."

"*I* can," Amanda declared.

"Really?" Britney stared harder into the mirror.Amanda thought she saw her lower lip tremble, and for a moment she almost felt sorry for her. Everyone knew that Britney was obsessed with her complexion. She was constantly searching her reflection for any evidence of an imminent breakout, she spent half her allowance on face creams, and she even saw a dermatologist once a month. Not that she really needed to give her skin all that attention. If

Britney's face had been half as bad as she thought it was, she wouldn't be sitting at Amanda's table. But she was still staring into her little mirror, and now Amanda could see her eyes getting watery.

Oh no, don't let her cry, she thought. Amanda didn't like public displays of emotion. She was always afraid that she'd get caught up in them herself.

Three more of their friends—Emma, Katie, and Nina—joined them at the table, and Britney got more reassurance on the state of her skin. Finally, Amanda gave in. "You know, I think there's a smudge on one of my contact lenses. Everybody looks like they've got zits."

Britney looked relieved, and Amanda made a mental note not to waste insults on friends. She didn't want to have to feel bad about anything she said. Feelings could be so dangerous.

Luckily, Emma brought up a new subject. "Heather Todd got a haircut."

"From Budget Scissors," Amanda declared, referring to a chain of cheap hair whackers.

"Really?"

"That's what it looks like."

Katie giggled. "Amanda, you're terrible!"

Amanda knew this was intended as a compliment, and she accepted it by smiling graciously. Katie beamed in the

6

aura of the smile, and Amanda decided not to mention the fact that Katie's tinted lip-gloss had smeared.

Besides, there were so many others who were more deserving of her critical attention. Like the girl who was walking toward their table right now: Tracey Devon, the dreariest girl in the eighth grade, the most pathetic creature in the entire class—maybe even in the whole school.

In Amanda's experience, in all honesty, she knew that even the most deeply flawed individuals had something of value about them. A complete social nerd might be a brain, an ugly guy could be a great athlete, and an enormously fat girl might have a nice singing voice. But Tracey Devon had absolutely nothing going for her.

She was thin—not in a top-model way, but so scrawny and bony that her elbows and knees looked abnormally large. No hips and, worse, no boobs.

She didn't shave her legs. The fact that she was blond and the hairs barely showed was beside the point. Every girl Amanda knew had started shaving her legs at the age of 11. Then there was the hair on her head—flat, stringy, and always looking in need of a wash. Her face was bland and colorless, she had no eyebrows to speak of, and her lips were so thin that she looked like she didn't have a mouth either. The best anyone could say about her face was that she didn't have zits—but she had enough freckles to make up for that.

As for her clothes, forget designer stuff—Tracey's outfits went beyond terrible. Mismatched tops and bottoms, puffed-sleeve dresses that looked like they were made for five-year-olds, shoes with laces, and ankle socks. Socks!

And that wasn't all. Tracey's special and unique ickiness went way beyond the surface. She walked around with her shoulders hunched and her head bowed. She talked in whispers—people could barely hear her, and when they did, she never seemed to say anything worth hearing. It was as if she wasn't even *there*, wherever she was.

But at that very moment she was definitely at their table, and Amanda stiffened. "What do *you* want?" she demanded.

Tracey mumbled something, but the only word Amanda caught was *Katie*. She called to the other end of the table. "Katie, your new best friend, Tracey Devon, needs to talk to you."

Katie's brow furrowed. "Who?"

"Tracey Devon! Are you blind? She's standing right here."

Katie glanced vaguely at the unwelcome visitor. "Oh, right. What do you want?"

Somehow, Tracey managed to make her request audible. "Could I borrow your notes from yesterday?"

Katie still looked puzzled. "Notes for what? Are you in one of my classes?"

"History," Tracey said in a whisper.

"Oh yeah, right. Why do you need my notes?"

"I wasn't in class. I was sick."

"Sick," Amanda repeated. "That's interesting.
I didn't know ugliness was a disease."

It wasn't one of her best wisecracks, but it got a response from Tracey. She raised her head just high enough for Amanda and the others to see the flush that crossed her face and the tears welling up in her eyes. Then she turned and scurried away.

"I just remembered—she's borrowed my notes before," Katie remarked.

A flicker of concern crossed Britney's face. "Is she sick a lot?"

Katie shrugged. "Who knows? I never notice if she's there or not. It's like she's one of those people you don't see." She took a bite of her sandwich, and the others followed.

But Amanda couldn't eat. She was too—too something. Angry? Maybe. Because it was so infuriating, the way Tracey was. It was her own fault that Amanda could mock her so easily. It was as though she *wanted* to be picked on. She didn't make the slightest effort to improve herself, and she just took Amanda's insults without making any attempt at retaliation. There were plenty of other creepy types at Meadowbrook, but at least they stood up for themselves. Like Jenna Kelley, the girl who dressed in black and had a terrible reputation. If you accused her of being a vampire, she'd tell you where to go. Why didn't Tracey ever fight back?

Amanda's friends had gone back to eating and chatting by now. Clearly, they'd forgotten all about Tracey's interruption. They probably considered Tracey beneath their contempt, not even worth an insult. Only Amanda was still seething.

She clenched her fists. Uh-oh! This wasn't good. She could feel her face getting warm and her heartbeat quickening. *Too much feeling.*

"I've got to get something from my locker," she muttered to the others. Before anyone could respond, she turned and hurried to the exit. She didn't have a hall pass, and if a monitor spotted her, she could be hauled to the principal's office, but she had to risk it.

Luckily, she was able to make it to the end of the hall and down two flights of stairs to the school basement without being caught. There was a rarely used restroom there, and she ducked into it. Splashing some water onto her face, she gripped the sides of the sink, stared into the mirror, and concentrated on pushing any sympathy, any anger—any feelings at all for Tracey Devon—out of her mind.

Do not feel sorry for her, she ordered herself. *She doesn't deserve any sympathy.*

Actually, Amanda wouldn't have minded if someone *wanted* to take pity on Tracey Devon. But that someone could not be Amanda Beeson. She knew too well the terrible consequences of caring. And to make sure she remembered, she allowed the memories to play out in her head.

The very first time . . . she couldn't have been more than five. She saw herself on a cold winter afternoon, walking along a busy shopping street, clutching her mother's hand, and looking at the people they passed. One in particular grabbed her attention.

She was huddled in the entrance of an old abandoned building, her back against the boarded door. A bowl with a few coins in it lay beside her, and there was a hand-scrawled sign propped up against the wall. Wispy gray hair poked out of a dirty bandanna that was wrapped around her head. Her body was clothed in filthy rags, and even though Amanda wasn't close enough to smell her, she somehow knew that the woman exuded a nasty odor. And even though Amanda couldn't read the sign, she knew the woman was hungry.

Amanda's mother hadn't noticed her, but she had paused in front of the store window next to the building. Something in the display must have caught her eye, because she spent some time looking at it, which gave little Amanda more time to look at the poor woman.

Now, eight years later, Amanda could still remember how she had felt—sad, unbearably sad, sadder than she'd felt when her pet goldfish had died. Why did this woman have to sit there in the cold, all alone? Didn't she have any family? Didn't anyone love her? That poor woman! What was she feeling?

Then, suddenly, Amanda knew what the woman was feeling. Because she *was* the woman. Cold and hungry, and confused, too. And she was looking at a little girl—a pretty five-year-old, with long, glossy hair topped by a woolly hat. Sturdy, bright-eyed, and wrapped in a puffy jacket. Holding the hand of a well-dressed, elegant woman in a fur coat.

And if Amanda had turned into the old lady, who was the little girl staring at her?

Her mother spoke. "Amanda, where are your gloves?"

"They're in my pocket," the little girl replied in Amanda's very own voice.

"Put them on. It's getting cold," her mother said.

"Okay." She took her gloves out of her pocket and put them on, just as Amanda would have done. Amanda-the-old-lady was bewildered. So, she was here—and she was there. How could that be?

In the turmoil of her confused mind, there were feelings that stood out—envy, longing, loneliness. Oh, it was so awful being this woman that Amanda couldn't bear it!

It took only a jerk of her mother's hand to pull her back into herself. In the next moment, she was on a street corner at her mother's side, waiting for the light to change. She knew the sad woman was just behind her, but she didn't dare turn back to look.

The next time it happened, she was older—eight or nine. It must have been summertime, because she was in the backyard, wearing shorts and a halter-top, having a picnic with a couple of friends. From the house next door came the sound of two people shouting at each other. Amanda recognized the voices even before the man and woman emerged—Mr. Blakely first, followed by Mrs. Blakely. Amanda liked Mrs. Blakely—she had a little baby boy, and sometimes she let Amanda hold him. Mr. Blakely wasn't as friendly. Just then, Mr. Blakely looked very angry, and Mrs. Blakely looked scared. Then, to Amanda's horror, Mr. Blakely hit Mrs. Blakely—he slapped her right across the face—and Mrs. Blakely started to cry.

It was awful—Amanda had never seen an adult cry like that before. How could that mean Mr. Blakely do that? And why didn't Mrs. Blakely hit him back? Nice Mrs. Blakely, who baked chocolate-chip cookies and sang to her baby and promised Amanda that she could baby-sit for him when she was old enough! Why was this happening? What could she do? What was Mrs. Blakely going to do?

Nothing. Because her husband was stronger, and angry, and even though he hit her sometimes, she loved him so much and she was so afraid he'd leave her alone with the baby . . . Amanda knew all this because she had become Mrs. Blakely, and when Mr. Blakely hit her again, it was Amanda who felt the sting on her cheek. It was terrible; she was in pain, and just over the hedge she could see two little girls watching in horror along with Amanda, who didn't look upset in the least. It was as if she didn't have any feelings at all. Which made a weird kind of sense, because the Amanda-with-feelings was in the body of Mrs. Blakely.

The rest of the memory was a blur, but somehow Amanda got back inside her own body. Soon after that, Mr. and Mrs. Blakely moved away.

There were other experiences. Two stood out—that time in the fourth grade when she saw a classmate get hit by a car in front of the school and then felt herself lying on the street, frightened and in pain and hearing the sound of the ambulance. And another time, just three years ago, when she became a *boy*—a skinny, nerdy, whiny boy named Martin, younger than her, who had lived across the street. Nobody in the neighborhood liked Martin, and his mother was always complaining to other mothers about the way their kids treated him. But then one day she saw him surrounded by bigger boys, who were pushing him back and forth and laughing at him, and she felt sorry for him . . .

That was the last one. Because by then, she'd figured it out. Feeling too much—that was the problem. When she felt bad for someone else, that was when it happened. Now, at the age of 13, she knew the words: sympathy, compassion, pity. Those were the emotions that triggered the bizarre bodysnatching, that transported her into other people and made her feel what they were feeling.

Once she understood, she knew what she had to do to prevent it from happening again. She had to stop feeling these emotions. If she didn't care about someone, she wouldn't become that person.

So she stopped caring. It wasn't easy, and often she had to struggle, but it was worth it so that she never had to suffer the experience again. At first, she just tried to block the feelings of sympathy, but then she realized it would be useful to actually fight them. She focused on behavior that would work contrary to compassion—mockery, ridicule, creative insults. And in the process she discovered a strange truth—people admired her meanness, or else they were just frightened of her. In any case, it worked to her advantage.

And now she had a fabulous life. She was the Queen of Mean and she ruled the school—or at least the eighth grade, though she felt pretty sure that her fame extended to the younger grades. She was never alone; classmates sought her approval and she was held in awe. She knew there were people who claimed to hate her, but she had no doubt that what they really wanted was to *be* her.

After a few deep breaths, another splash of water on the face, and a quick makeup repair, she was ready to go back to the cafeteria and pick up where she'd left off. And she made it through the day without feeling sorry for anyone again.

★ ★ ★

But later that night, in her beautiful pink and white bedroom, lying in her four-poster bed under a lacy canopy, Amanda thought about the strange event of the day and wondered how it had come to pass. Why had she felt a glimmer of pity for Tracey Devon? True, Tracey was pathetic, but she wasn't a victim like Mrs. Blakely or the girl who had been hit by the car.

What did she know about Tracey anyway? Not much. She knew that Tracey was one of those "gifted" kids who attended a special class at Meadowbrook. Which was sort of hard to believe, because she didn't strike Amanda as being any kind of genius. They'd gone to the same elementary school, and Tracey had been in Amanda's second-grade class. They hadn't been best friends—she was just another classmate—but there had been nothing especially awful about her. Tracey had been okay back then.

In fact, she had been almost famous. Everyone in town was talking about Tracey's family that year—her mother had just given birth to septuplets, seven identical baby girls. They were on TV, on the news. The "Devon Seven"—that's what the reporters called them. The babies were in commercials, and they posed for ads, and every year after that a TV news program included a special segment showing them on their birthday. The Devon Seven were famous.

But not Tracey Devon. She wasn't on those special TV shows. That wasn't surprising, in Amanda's opinion. Who would want to see a nerd like Tracey on TV?

Amanda realized then what really annoyed her—the fact that Tracey didn't *have* to be a nerd. She didn't have to dress so badly or act so nervous. Why didn't she stand up for herself? Why did she take all the abuse that everyone heaped on her? She was more than a nerd—she was a wimp, never fighting back, not even *trying*. She was a total, complete, absolute *loser* . . .

Amanda was aware of beads of sweat forming on her forehead. She was getting all worked up again. This wouldn't do at all. She couldn't let Tracey bother her. Everyone else just ignored her, so why couldn't Amanda?

She had to calm down or she'd never get to sleep.

She did sleep finally. When she next opened her eyes,

there was sunlight pouring in the window . . . which was odd, because her mother always woke her up when she came in to open the shutters on Amanda's windows. But there was no one else in the room . . .

She blinked. Where was her canopy? Why was she looking at a ceiling? Had she fallen off her bed? Because this didn't feel like her bed—it was harder. As her eyes began to focus, the first real stirrings of fear began. She noticed the chest of drawers in front of her. It was yellow, not pink. And what were those flowered curtains doing at the sides of her window? No . . . not *her* window. Not her room.

She sat up suddenly, and that was when she noticed her hands. What had happened to her manicure—the nice rosy polish? Whose stubby, bitten fingernails were these?

Her heart was pounding furiously, but her body moved in slow motion. Lifting legs that weren't her legs. Putting feet onto the floor, experiencing the new sensation of a carpet instead of a fluffy rug. Walking toward a mirror that hung above the unfamiliar chest of drawers. Looking in the mirror and seeing . . .

Tracey Devon.

Chapter Two

THE REFLECTION STARED BACK at her, frozen and uncomprehending. The same pale freckled face, greasy hair, and thin lips that she'd scorned the day before in the cafeteria. The scrawny body, barely concealed by a thin, babyish nightgown covered in faded pink flowers. There was no question about it—Amanda Beeson was Tracey Devon.

Her body couldn't move, but her insides were shaking. Amanda closed her eyes. *Think of who you really are,* she commanded herself. Amanda Beeson, five foot two, 110 pounds, light brown hair, blue eyes, turned-up nose. Amanda Beeson, the coolest girl at Meadowbrook Middle School, the Queen of Mean. Frantically, she tried to remember what she'd worn to bed the previous night: an extra-large T-shirt with "I heart New York" written on it that her father had brought back for her from his last business trip. When she had the image firmly imprinted in her mind, she opened her eyes again. The shock she was feeling was still visible on the face of Tracey Devon.

The silence of the room was broken by a series of harsh beeps. It took Amanda a moment to realize that the noises were coming from an alarm clock on the nightstand. She turned it off and sat down on the bed.

Stay calm, she told herself. *You know what's happening. It's happened before and it will pass.* She was actually more angry than frightened. Curse that Tracey Devon for demanding pity! If Amanda had disliked the girl before, she positively hated her now. *Hate, hate, hate,* she repeated silently.

Surely you couldn't feel sympathy for someone you hated. If she concentrated on her real feelings for Tracey, she'd get out of Tracey's body and back into her own.

But it was hard to focus on hate when what she was really feeling at the moment was hunger. It occurred to her that maybe her hunger was making her too weak to get back into herself. She could do something about that.

Moving awkwardly on unfamiliar feet, she went to the door and out into the hallway. So this was Tracey's house—or at least, the upstairs part of it.

She heard voices coming from another room and edged along the wall to peek in and see what was going on inside.

She recognized the seven little girls immediately from pictures in magazines. The Devon Seven were getting dressed, assisted by a weary-looking woman—Tracey's mother?—

and a teenage girl. Did Tracey have an older sister?

"Lizzie, help Sandie with her buttons," the woman said.

The teenager looked helpless. "Which one is Sandie?"

"Lizzie, for what I'm paying you, the least you could do is learn to tell them apart," the woman replied testily. She pointed to one of the septuplets.

So the teenager was some sort of mother's helper, Amanda realized. While they were both occupied with dressing the girls, she could creep downstairs, find the kitchen, and get something to eat.

Unfortunately, one of the children spotted her. "Mama, there's Tracey!"

Startled, the woman looked up. For a second she seemed puzzled, and then her expression changed to irritation. "Tracey, why aren't you dressed yet? You're going to be late for the bus, and I am not driving you to school."

Fine, Amanda thought, because she had no intention of *going* to school, not as Tracey Devon. She did like the idea of getting out of that horrible nightgown, though, and decided to put off scrounging for food until after she'd changed. Besides, maybe by then she'd be out of Tracey's body. She might be eating a bowl of her very own Special K in her very own kitchen.

But while she was in this body, she figured she might as well improve the way Tracey dressed for school. Examining

21

the contents of Tracey's closet, however, didn't offer much in the way of anything decent to wear. There was certainly nothing in there that Amanda would want to be seen in. Was the family too poor to buy her clothes? No, that couldn't be it. The house looked okay, and those little clones were wearing cute matching dresses. Once again, it was Tracey's fault—the girl had no taste. Another reason not to feel sorry for her.

Not enough of a reason to get Amanda out of her body, though. She opened a drawer and hunted in vain through the piles of plain white underpants for a bra—and then she remembered something about Tracey. They were in the same gym class and changed in the same locker room. Tracey didn't wear a bra. This was another reason to make fun of her.

With a sigh, Amanda began to search for the least offensive items of clothing. She ended up with a plain denim skirt—no label, of course—and the only T-shirt that didn't have stains on the armpits. The shirt was way too baggy, but she found a brown belt and cinched it in at her waist. Burrowing through drawers, she couldn't find any makeup—not even a tube of lip-gloss—but she did manage to uncover a rubber band, which she used to pull the dirty hair away from Tracey's face and up into a high ponytail.

By now she was *starving*. Noise from the room down the hall indicated that everyone was still occupied with the septuplets, so she hurried downstairs and found the kitchen. She spotted a box of granola bars on the counter and took one. She unwrapped it and managed one bite before mother's helper Lizzie came in.

"What are you doing? Those are for the girls!"

Amanda chewed and swallowed. "I'm a girl."

"You know what I mean." Lizzie went to the counter and looked inside the box. "Oh no, there are only six left," she wailed. "What's your mother going to say?"

Amanda didn't want to know. Suddenly, school didn't seem like such a bad idea.

She recalled seeing a backpack in Tracey's room and hurried back upstairs. A quick look inside revealed textbooks, so she slung it over her shoulder and ran back downstairs and out the door.

It wasn't hard to spot the bus stop—the school bus was coming up the road and a couple of kids were waiting at the corner. She didn't know any of them, and clearly Tracey didn't either, since none of them acknowledged her arrival. And when the bus stopped and the doors opened just in front of Tracey, they pushed ahead of her to get on. So *rude*. But the bus driver was even ruder—after the boy just in front of her scampered up the steps, the doors closed. As if she wasn't even there!

"Hey!" Amanda yelled, banging on the bus door. "Open up!"

The driver seemed mildly surprised when she boarded. "Sorry, I didn't see you," he muttered.

She was still fuming as she went down the aisle of the bus, which was probably why she didn't see someone's foot sticking out. She tripped over it. Sprawled on the floor, all she could think was—*so this is Tracey's life.* Nobody tried to help her get up, and the guy whose foot was responsible for her fall didn't even bother to apologize. At least no one was laughing—mostly because no one was paying any attention to her. And as she struggled to her feet, she could only pray that she'd be back in her own life very soon. As she made her way to the back of the bus, she decided that the first thing she'd do when she got to school was find herself. Maybe that would provide the jolt to end this transformation.

As soon as she got off the bus, Amanda hurried to her own locker. There the other Amanda was, fiddling with the combination and talking to Britney, who had the locker next to hers. Amanda had had the experience before of seeing herself out of someone else's eyes. It was always eerie—but very interesting.

She looked *good*. The striped skirt over the leggings

worked—she hadn't been too sure when she'd first contemplated the combination. She wasn't thrilled with the ankle boots, though—next time, she'd wear ballerina flats.

"Amanda," she said.

The other Amanda turned, and Amanda-Tracey immediately recognized her own expression—which was exactly the way she would have expected to react to any attempt at communication from Tracey Devon. "*What?*"

Amanda-Tracey had no idea how to respond. She'd been hoping that simple face-to-face contact would put her back inside her own body.

"Um . . . just wanted to say hi."

The other Amanda stared at her in disbelief. Then she turned to Britney, rolled her eyes, and said, "Let's go."

Amanda-Tracey was disappointed, but she was also relieved. That had definitely been genuine Amanda behavior. As she'd expected, she and Tracey had not swapped bodies—but it was good to have confirmation. She wouldn't have to worry about Tracey saying stupid things, acting nerdy, or otherwise ruining Amanda's reputation.

The warning bell rang, indicating that there were two minutes left before students had to be in their homerooms. It dawned on Amanda that she had no idea where Tracey was supposed to be.

She fumbled through Tracey's backpack and pulled out

a three-ring binder—*that* made sense. Amanda hadn't seen a binder like that since elementary school. Everyone in middle school used spiral notebooks, one per class. But luckily, on the inside cover of the binder Tracey had pasted a copy of her schedule. Her classroom was at the other end of the building, on the second floor.

She hurried down the rapidly emptying hallway. Halfway up the stairs the final bell rang, and she sprinted the rest of the way. *Darn!* Homeroom teachers took roll and made a big fuss about tardiness, and the last thing she wanted to do today was draw attention to herself.

But when she slipped into the classroom, the teacher didn't even glance up. None of the other students took any notice of her either—at least, not until she slid into one of the empty seats. The girl in front of her turned around.

"That's Heather's seat."

"Sorry," Amanda said. Then she wanted to kick herself— or better yet, the girl who'd spoken to her. So what if she was sitting in Heather's seat? Heather wasn't there. And *why* had she apologized? Was she actually *becoming* Tracey? She looked around. Should she take a chance or ask the girl where Tracey usually sat? No, she couldn't ask—that would be too weird. The girl probably didn't know where Tracey sat anyway, since no one noticed Tracey.

Amanda moved to the other empty seat, and it must

have been Tracey's, since no one objected. Clearly, everyone believed that she was Tracey Devon in Tracey Devon's seat. The mere notion was so horrific that she forgot to respond when the teacher took attendance.

"Tracey!" the teacher barked. "You're actually here for a change. You might consider answering to your name." The class giggled knowingly, as if this was some sort of common event.

"Sorry," Amanda said again and then mentally kicked herself and vowed not to repeat the word for the rest of the day.

After roll call came the usual boring announcements over the intercom. Amanda took advantage of the time to consider her situation.

Obviously, this body-transfer experience was different from the previous ones. She'd never spent this long inside any other body. On the other hand, the other experiences hadn't been consistent in length—some had lasted seconds, others hours. She'd always come back inside herself eventually. She wasn't worried—not yet.

Something else was bothering her, though—something that she'd never given any thought to before. While she was in another person's body, where was that person? Her memory of being the poor old lady had given her an inkling as to how the other Amanda was functioning—like

27

a robot programmed as Amanda. But where was Tracey?

"Hey, dork, the bell's ringing."

She looked blankly at the boy passing her desk and realized that homeroom was over. She jumped up and grabbed her backpack. *Get a grip,* she warned herself. *You might have to look like Tracey for a while, but you don't have to be her.*

Tracey's next class was math, which was not one of Amanda's better subjects. Tracey had the same teacher as Amanda, and they were using the same textbook, but Tracey's class was a couple of days behind Amanda's. Which was kind of cool—for once Amanda knew the answer to the equation that the teacher was writing on the board. When the teacher asked for responses, she raised her hand.

The teacher gazed out over the class. "Doesn't anyone want to take a stab at this?"

Amanda waved her hand. Then another girl tentatively put up her hand.

"Yes, Jade?"

Amanda lowered her hand. Wow! Was Tracey such a loser that even *teachers* ignored her?

She considered volunteering an answer in Tracey's next class, English, but decided against it. She was better off sticking to her original plan not to call attention to herself. She should just let things run their course until she could get back inside herself and let Tracey pick up where she had left off. It was the least she could do for the poor girl. Oh no! Was a note of pity coming through there?

She checked the schedule in Tracey's binder and saw that her next class was gym. Good—at least she'd be moving around, not just sitting and thinking. But it occurred to her that the gym was just below the classroom that she was currently in. It wouldn't take her more than a minute and a half to get there, and there were six minutes to kill between classes. What could she do with them?

In her normal life, she knew exactly what she'd do— go to the closest restroom and spend the four and a half extra minutes fixing her hair and reapplying lip-gloss. She seriously doubted that Tracey visited the restroom for any reason other than to use the toilet. She'd certainly never seen her lingering to put on makeup.

On the other hand, lingering in the hall wasn't appealing, and there was no law that kept Tracey out of public restrooms. So when the bell rang, she headed straight for the girls' restroom across the hall.

She was the first one there. Even though she knew what she'd see when she looked in the mirror, it was still sickening to face Tracey's reflection. No wonder Tracey never stayed long in the restrooms—who'd want to look at *that* every day? It was just too awful. And even though it wasn't really her,

Amanda felt an automatic urge to make some improvement.

Only she had no tools whatsoever. As she'd expected, a search of Tracey's backpack turned up nothing in the way of cosmetics.

The restroom door opened. In the mirror, Amanda watched as her friends Katie and Emma sauntered in, followed by the Amanda-robot, or whatever she was. They all lined up in front of the mirror, emptied their little makeup bags into the sinks, and went to work.

Amanda couldn't take her eyes off herself, and Other-Amanda noticed this. "What are *you* looking at?"

Wow! If she only knew whom she was really speaking to. Amanda held her tongue and said what she assumed Tracey would have said in the same situation: "Nothing." But when she saw Other-Amanda apply her own Pearls of Rose lip-gloss—the very same lip-gloss that Amanda had bought for herself just last weekend—she spoke impulsively.

"Amanda . . ."

"*What?*"

"Can I borrow your lip-gloss?"

Other-Amanda made no attempt to disguise her horrified reaction. "No!"

Amanda wasn't surprised. If she'd been back inside her own body, this was just how she would have responded to a request like that from Tracey. After all, she didn't want to get cooties, or whatever other kind of disgusting germs someone like Tracey would have.

What did surprise Amanda was the way Other-Amanda's response made her feel. She could actually sense something burning behind her eyes. This was ridiculous—she wasn't Tracey, so why should she care if anyone made fun of her? Even so, Amanda decided to make a fast escape from the restroom before Tracey's tears made an appearance. She hurried out, down the stairs and into the girls' locker room next to the gym. At least this was one of Amanda's own classes, so she knew what would be going on. They were playing volleyball this month. She picked up a clean-but-ugly one-size-fits-all gym uniform and went into the changing room.

All around her, girls were undressing and talking. With her head down, Amanda made her way to an empty locker, hoping to keep a low profile. She particularly wanted to stay away from Other-Amanda. Maybe by now she'd be tired of teasing Tracey about not wearing a bra.

No such luck. As soon as she pulled off the T-shirt, a cry went up.

"Hey, Tracey, have you ever tried this?" Other-Amanda posed with her elbows extended and began to chant while jerking her arms back and forth in an exercise:

We must, we must, we must increase our bust.

31

It's better, it's better, it's better for the sweater.

It was such an old, stale rhyme—how could anyone find it funny anymore? But Katie and the others laughed dutifully, and Amanda experienced a strange hot sensation on her face. Ohmigod, was she *blushing*? She'd never blushed before in her life!

The shrill whistle of the teacher called them into the gym. Amanda had actually been enjoying gym this month—she was good at volleyball, and it brought out her competitive streak. She was always so focused that she'd never noticed how Tracey played, but she decided she could safely assume that Tracey was a klutz, and she was pretty sure that there was no secret competitive streak hidden behind Tracey's meek demeanor.

Once they were all in the gym, Ms. Barnes in her white shorts and shirt blew the whistle again. "Captains today are Britney and Lorie." A coin was flipped to see which of the girls would go first, and then team selection began.

If she'd been herself, she'd have been Britney's first choice, Amanda thought sadly. No matter who was the captain, she was always the first or second one chosen. But it didn't come as any surprise to find herself still standing between the teams as the selection went on. How humiliating to be the last one left! Again, Amanda had to remind herself that she wasn't herself, that it wasn't really

Amanda who had to slink over to Britney's side when there was no one else left to choose. Other-Amanda had of course been Britney's first pick.

The game began, and it was a nightmare. Amanda had been half hoping that her own personality might override Tracey's natural meekness and physical limitations, but no such luck. Even when she tried her hardest to reach the ball, someone lunged in front of her. Other players pushed her aside like she was an annoying fly that had invaded the gym. Like she didn't belong there at all. A thought hit her: Tracey didn't belong anywhere! She didn't even exist for most people.

Except for you, she told herself grimly. *You* cared. *And look where it got you!*

A ball hitting her on the head brought her back to the game. Not that it did the team any good. It was her turn to serve—and Tracey's best was like Amanda's worst.

The ball hit the net, the game was over, and the team on the other side was cheering.

"Tracey, are you nuts?" Britney shrieked. "You lost the game, you idiot!"

"Now, now, it's a team sport—we don't blame individuals," Ms. Barnes murmured, but even she was looking at Amanda in despair.

At least Amanda wasn't teased back in the locker room.

Her classmates seemed to be satisfied with simply shooting dirty looks at her every time they caught her eye. Or at least, that was how it felt. The only person who didn't look angry was Sarah Miller, but that was no comfort. Sarah was the kind of smiley girl who was always nice to everyone, so as far as Amanda was concerned, she didn't count.

Lunch was next on the schedule—Tracey had the same lunch period as Amanda. But walking into the cafeteria today was a whole new experience for her. Yesterday it was her kingdom; now she felt like she was walking into a war zone, with enemies at every table. It was scary.

With her head down, she went to the end of the food line. Waiting there, she couldn't resist taking a look at her own table. How strange—to see herself sitting there with Katie and all her friends, laughing and talking . . .

"Hey, are you going to move or what?" the boy behind her demanded.

It was becoming automatic to mumble "sorry," and she caught up with the line. Normally she would have bought herself only a yogurt and a salad, but the special actually looked good, and the only happiness she was going to get that day would come from eating. But when she reached the cashier, she realized that she'd never checked to see how much money Tracey carried.

Not enough. And so she had to endure more annoyed

looks as she backed up and returned the lunch. She ended up with a candy bar and a bag of chips from the vending machine. She found a seat at an unoccupied table and started to eat. She'd never eaten a lunch alone before. Next time, she'd remember to bring a book or a magazine. *But there won't be a next time,* she assured herself. Surely by this time tomorrow she'd be herself again.

With nothing to do but eat her candy and chips, she opened Tracey's binder to see what the rest of the day was going to be like. For the next class, there was no subject like history or English listed—just a room number: 209.

It dawned on her that this could be Tracey's so-called gifted class. And for the first time since that horrible day had begun, she actually felt a little spark of curiosity.

What was that class all about, anyway? People called it "gifted," but there were other classes for brains at Meadowbrook, and they all had names like Advanced Placement English or Advanced Placement Math.

Maybe it was some kind of special-ed class. But no, Tracey was just a nerd, a loser, not someone who needed extra help with learning. So maybe that's what it was—a class for social misfits. In the back of her mind, though, Amanda knew that wasn't possible. While the other students would easily classify Tracey as a loser, it wasn't a category that Meadowbrook Middle School would ever acknowledge. Amanda had a feeling that all middle schools were like that. Teachers, principals, guidance counselors— they never knew what was really going on.

Chapter Three

I T WAS AN ORDINARY classroom, no different from most of the others in the building. There was a large map on one wall, bookshelves on another, rows of desks, and a larger desk at the front of the room, behind which sat a woman.

"Tracey! How nice to *see* you."

Amanda thought it was an odd greeting from a teacher, especially with the emphasis she had put on the word see. Did this have something to do with being "seen and not heard"? Was Tracey actually noisy in this class? That was hard to believe.

Since Amanda had no idea what the teacher's name was, she responded with, "Nice to see you, too," and then turned to see who else was there. The bell hadn't rung yet, and there were only two other students seated in the room. One was a small, round-faced boy with unfashionably short hair and a solemn expression. He looked very young—a sixth grader maybe? In any case, she'd never seen him before.

But the other face was definitely familiar. It was funny, in a way, because she'd been thinking about her the other day—Jenna Kelley. Ordinarily, Amanda wouldn't know the names of seventh graders, but Jenna was famous—or maybe *infamous* was the right word. And it wasn't just because she always wore black and rimmed her eyes with kohl.

There were stories about Jenna Kelley, and they weren't just rumors. She'd transferred to Meadowbrook just after the beginning of the school year, and not from another middle school, but from some sort of jail for juvenile delinquents. Amanda had no idea why Jenna had been in that place, but she had to believe that it had been for something bigger than shoplifting. Jenna was scary looking, like someone who carried a switchblade and wouldn't mind cutting the face of anyone who annoyed her. What was impossible to believe was the notion that Jenna might be gifted, unless *gifted* was a polite term for something else. Like criminally insane?

But that notion vanished with the next arrival.

"Ken!" Amanda exclaimed.

Ken Preston looked at her blankly. "Yeah?"

Then she remembered that Ken wasn't responding to Amanda Beeson, the girl he'd pecked under the water at Sophie's pool party last spring. He was addressing Tracey Devon, who would never have had the nerve to speak to a hot guy like him, and he was now looking quizzically at Amanda-Tracey, wondering what she wanted.

"Uh, nothing," Amanda mumbled. "Sorry." For once, she uttered that word intentionally. She had just decided that in this class she actually needed to behave like Tracey. The last thing in the world she wanted was for anyone here—meaning Ken—to find out who she really was. If Ken knew what was going on, she had an awful feeling that he would never be able to look at her again without seeing Tracey's face.

"Hello, Ken," the teacher said as he ambled to a seat.

"Hi, Madame," Ken replied.

Madame. That was interesting, Amanda thought. Maybe she was a French teacher at Meadowbrook. That would explain why Amanda had never seen her before.

The next person to join the class was another surprise— Sarah Miller, the super-sweet girl who was in her gym class. Why was *she* here? Because she was too good to be true? Was *that* a gift?

But Amanda was more intrigued by the fact that Ken Preston, too cute and so *not* a criminal or a smiley type, was here. He was super popular, and he'd been the star of the school soccer team till he had that awful accident the previous month. And even though he wasn't on the team anymore, he was still considered one of the coolest guys at Meadowbrook. So why was *he* in this class? She didn't think being cool counted as being gifted. If that had been the case, she, the real Amanda, would have been there.

The next student to enter was a young-looking girl with a glazed expression. The teacher greeted her as "Emily," and she took the seat next to Amanda. Then in came a boy whom Amanda had noticed before because he was the only student at Meadowbrook in a wheelchair. He was followed by yet another boy, and this time Amanda drew in her breath sharply.

She recognized him immediately even though she hadn't seen him in ages—Martin Cooper, who used to live across the street. The boy whose body she'd briefly occupied so long ago. He must be in the sixth grade now .. . but he still looked exactly the way he'd looked back when he was the most picked-on boy in the neighborhood.

Maybe Tracey got picked on a lot and that was a reason to be in this class. On the other hand, no one would ever pick on Jenna—not if they wanted to live. And who would pick on Ken Preston?

The bell rang, and Amanda counted eight students in the class. The average class at Meadowbrook had between 20 and 30 students. This was getting more and more mysterious.

Madame rose from her chair and came around to the

front of the desk. She was a petite, dark-haired woman with bright, dark eyes and a friendly smile. "Charles, would you like to begin your report?"

"No," replied the boy in the wheelchair.

Amanda was slightly taken aback. No one ever wanted to give reports, but no one ever actually said no. You made excuses—you claimed you'd left your notes at home, you pretended to have laryngitis—but you didn't just say no.

Madame didn't seem surprised, just disappointed. "This is your day to report, Charles."

"I'm not ready," Charles said flatly.

"The assignment was given more than a week ago—you've had plenty of time to prepare."

"I've been busy."

Jenna spoke suddenly. "Liar."

Charles turned his head. "What did you say?"

"You're lying," Jenna said. "You haven't been busy. You just don't *want* to give your report."

"How would *you* know?" Charles snapped. Laughter swept across the classroom and Charles reddened.

Amanda didn't get it, and she figured this had to be some sort of inside joke. She could see that Madame didn't appreciate it.

"That was an inappropriate remark, Jenna. You have to respect the privacy of Charles's thoughts."

41

Jenna shrugged. "It just slipped out."

Madame looked at her pointedly. "We've talked about this before, Jenna. You have to learn to control your gift. You all do. Now, Charles, you do need to give us a report today. If you haven't prepared anything, you still have to respond to the assignment. You'll just need to speak off the cuff."

Charles's lips were set in a tight line, and he stared at his desk. Amanda wondered why Madame didn't do what any other teacher would have done in this kind of situation—send him to the principal's office, give him a zero for the assignment, that sort of thing. This teacher didn't even seem upset.

She continued to speak calmly. "Would someone like to remind Charles of this week's assignment?"

The spacy-looking girl spoke. "Give an example of how you misused your gift during the past month. Like, when I knew it was going to rain on Saturday, so I told Heather not to have a picnic, and—"

Madame cut her off. "That's enough, Emily. This is Charles's turn. Charles?"

Amanda watched him with some alarm. The boy in the wheelchair was getting awfully pale, like he was about to be sick or something. She was glad that *she* wasn't sitting next to him. Poor Ken . . . Was he about to get puked on?

Ken spoke to him. "Look, man, you've gotta confront

your problem, y'know?"

"Not 'problem,' Ken," Madame corrected him. "We use the word *gift*."

Charles glared at Ken. "What do *you* know about my life? You're a jock!"

"Not anymore," Ken said.

"Well, that's your choice. You're not stuck in a wheelchair!"

So that's it, Amanda thought. She'd seen something like this on TV. This was some sort of group therapy for kids with personal problems, hang-ups. Emotional stuff. No wonder people were so secretive about it. You wouldn't want your classmates to know you were some kind of basket case.

It all made sense to her now, except for one thing. Why did the teacher refer to their problems as "gifts?"

Ken continued. "Hey, all I'm saying is that you shouldn't put off talking about your prob—your *gift*. I mean, the rest of us gave our reports—why can't you?"

Now Charles's eyes were blazing. "Because I don't feel like it, okay?" His voice was rising. "And you're really annoying me, you know? Just because I'm in a wheelchair doesn't mean you can push me around! So mind your own stupid business, you—you—" He was almost shrieking now, which was creepy, but what was even creepier was

43

the way little Martin suddenly dropped to the floor and crawled under his desk . . . just before several books came flying off the bookshelf.

Everyone ducked as the books soared by. Amanda was so startled that she didn't move fast enough, and a book clipped her ear. "Ow!"

"Sarah, make him stop!" someone yelled. *But how can Sarah do anything about it?* Amanda wondered. She was sitting on the other side of the room. In any case, Madame was able to put an end to the chaos.

"Charles!" the teacher yelled sharply. "Stop it right now! Control yourself!"

The flight of the books continued, but they were moving more slowly and then began dropping to the floor.

Madame now wore a very stern expression. "That was completely unnecessary, Charles. I'm going to give you five demerits." The small potted plant on her desk began to rise.

"*Charles!*" she said in a warning tone. The plant came back down.

Amanda, in a state of shock, was still clutching her ear. Madame noticed this. "Tracey, are you all right?"

Amanda took away her hand and looked at it. There was no blood. "I—uh—yes."

The teacher went behind her desk, opened a notebook, and began jotting down something. Amanda turned to

Emily. "What was all *that* about?"

Emily's vacant eyes focused slightly. "Oh, come on, Tracey. You don't have to be able to see into the future to know what Charles does when he gets angry."

"Madame?"

"Yes, Jenna?"

"Martin has to go to the bathroom."

There were a couple of snickers, and Martin cowered in his seat.

Madame looked pained. "Jenna, Martin is fully capable of asking to be excused himself."

Jenna's innocent expression didn't mask a nasty twinkle in her eyes. "But you know how shy he is, Madame. And I swear, he's just about to wet his pants."

"Am not!" Martin squeaked, but he looked very nervous.

"Martin, you're excused," Madame said.

As Martin scurried out the door, Amanda turned to Emily again. "But how did Jenna know . . ."

"Jenna, I don't want to have to say this again," Madame declared. "You're behaving very badly. Just because you have the ability to read other people's minds doesn't mean you have the *right* to do this. Not to mention the fact that you know what Martin does when he feels picked on."

Jenna slumped back in her seat. "Yeah, okay."

Madame shook her head wearily. "Charles has already

created a mess in the room; we certainly don't need for Martin to hurt anyone. Now, class, for the rest of the period we're going to work on breathing exercises."

There was a loud groan from the students—except Sarah, of course. Amanda wondered if she ever complained about anything.

Madame frowned.

"These exercises are essential for establishing control. Now, let's go over the five basic steps." She turned and began writing on the blackboard. "Step one: Don't breathe through your nose. Concentrate on expanding your lungs . . ."

Amanda was neither listening nor looking at the blackboard. Her head was spinning so fast that she felt dizzy. What was going on here? Charles making things move, Jenna reading minds, wimpy little Martin Cooper . . . hurting someone? How? Who *were* these people?

This was a fantasy—it couldn't be happening. People like this, people with strange powers—they belonged in movies like *X-Men*, or Japanese cartoons. How could she have ever guessed that there were people like this at Meadowbrook Middle School? Forget about Meadowbrook—these people weren't supposed to exist anywhere in the real world.

Psychos. Freaks. Monsters. She didn't know what to call

them. Ken was one of them . . . and Sarah Miller. What kind of powers did *they* have?

And ohmigod! What kind of psycho freak was Tracey Devon?

CHAPTER FOUR

JENNA WAS HAVING TROUBLE keeping her eyes open. As she went through the motions of Madame's breathing exercises, she used every intake of breath as an excuse to yawn. This meant that she always breathed out a second or two after the others in the class, which resulted in a frown from Madame aimed in her direction. Not that she cared what Madame thought of her—but there was something about the teacher that always made her cringe a little. It was almost as if Madame could see what was going on inside Jenna's head, which was ridiculous, of course. Only Jenna could see what was going on inside the minds of others. Strangely enough, however, she could never completely penetrate Madame's head. Not that she ever really wanted to. After all, what sort of interesting thoughts could a *teacher* be having?

Madame took her attention away from Jenna as she offered a sullen Charles some advice about the rhythm of his breathing. Jenna took advantage of this and closed her eyes. She could fall asleep so easily . . .

There were two reasons for this. She'd been up very late the night before. She wasn't exactly sure what time she'd drifted off, but she'd thought she could see the first rays of sunshine from her bedroom window. So she hadn't had much sleep, and that alone justified her yawning.

The other reason was the fact that she was bored, but that wasn't an unusual state of mind for her, especially here. Her classes were boring, her teachers were boring, and what was the point of being there anyway? She just didn't care what went on at school.

This class was the worst. It was too small and she couldn't hide. In other classes she sat in the back, where the teacher wouldn't notice her. There, she could tune out and amuse herself by listening to her classmates' thoughts. They were never especially amusing or even mildly interesting—other people's daydreams could be as dull as dirt. But in this class, she couldn't even do that. Madame knew her gift, and she was always watching Jenna's face for telltale signs of mental eavesdropping.

Of course, there were times when Madame was occupied with other students, like right now, and Jenna could concentrate on reading the minds of others. But these so-called gifted kids weren't any more entertaining than her usual classmates. Charles, for example, thought only about stuff like what he was going to demand for dinner that evening or what he'd make everyone watch on TV. It seemed to her that he totally ruled at home.

Madame was helping Ken breathe now, so Jenna turned her attention to Emily. When she'd first learned about Emily's gift, Jenna had hoped to find something interesting inside her head. But Emily was a total space cadet—she had no control over her gift at all. At this moment, all Jenna could see was a vague image of a raging forest fire. Somewhere, at some time in the near or distant future, a bunch of trees would burn down. Maybe. It was impossible to tell whether Emily was having visions or simply daydreaming.

Jenna focused on Martin's thoughts, but she knew there would be nothing remarkable there. Martin's head was packed with memories of all the times he had felt like a victim. The only moments when it could be intriguing to read Martin occurred when he was angry. Then Jenna could see a brilliant display of sparkling lights in lots of different colors, something like fireworks.

Sarah's thoughts were pretty boring. You'd think that a girl who could control other people might have some interesting ideas in her head, but Sarah was so *not* into using her power that she refused to even think about it. It was like she was in some sort of zen state all the time.

Jenna didn't bother to try Carter, the youngest student in the group. She knew there would be nothing inside his head. Sometimes she wondered how the strange boy could walk and eat and put on his clothes when it seemed to her that he didn't even have a brain.

Tracey was almost worse than nothing. Her thoughts were formless, just a big, thick black cloud of misery. Whatever bits and pieces Jenna could decipher were usually too depressing to read . . .

She frowned. Something unfamiliar was coming from Tracey's mind. There was a light . . . Jenna stared at her and tried to concentrate, to see into the light. But before she could make any sense out of it, someone else's thoughts broke in.

She murdered me, and now she's getting away with it! She has to be arrested! Help me! Tell the police!

There was only one head that could produce a thought like this.

"Hey, Ken," she whispered. "Someone's calling you."

Madame heard her. "Jenna! What did I tell you about eavesdropping?"

"It's okay, Madame," Ken said wearily. "You can't really blame her. This guy is so *loud*."

"No kidding," Jenna said. "I didn't even have to try to listen."

"Would you like to share this problem with us, Ken?" Madame asked.

Ken sighed. "He pops in about once a week or so, and he's really annoying me. Supposedly he was killed in an accident—he fell down some stairs and hit his head. But he claims his wife murdered him, and he wants me to call the police."

"So why don't you just do what he says?" Jenna suggested. "Tell the cops, and then he'll stop bugging you."

Ken shook his head. "I don't want to get involved. Besides, what am I going to say? 'Hello, Mister Policeman. A dead man asked me to give you a message?' They'll think I'm nuts!"

"Class, we've talked about this kind of problem before," Madame said. "What do we do when our gifts intrude on our lives? Martin?"

The scrawny little wimp murmured the standard response. "We're supposed to ignore them."

"Exactly. And if they persist? Charles?"

The boy slumped in the wheelchair spoke. "I dunno."

Madame looked at him reprovingly. "Nonsense, Charles! You know what you're supposed to do, even if you don't always do it."

Charles mumbled something.

"What did you say, Charles? We can't hear you."

"You push them away!" Charles snapped. The vase on Madame's desk quivered.

Madame glared at him. "Charles!"

The vase was still.

"Thank you, Charles. Yes, you're correct. We concentrate on forcibly pushing away the gift."

"I'm trying to lose him, Madame," Ken declared, "but this guy's really persistent."

Madame nodded sympathetically and addressed the group. "Class, Ken needs our help. Let's try to come up with some ideas for him."

Jenna hadn't meant for the groan to escape from her lips quite so loudly. Now *everyone* was glaring at her.

"Jeez, Jenna! Why do you have to be such a—" Ken caught himself. "Well, you know what I mean."

"We're all in this together, Jenna," Emily added softly. "We have to care about one another."

Madame joined in. "We need one another's support."

Not me, Jenna thought, but she managed to keep this to herself and tried to stop her expression from showing what she was thinking. What a bunch of losers! I don't want to hear any of their opinions about anything.

Happily, the bell rang just then, so she didn't have to.

"We'll continue this discussion tomorrow," Madame said. "And your assignment for tomorrow's class is to report on a moment when you successfully controlled your gift."

As Jenna moved to the door, she passed Tracey, and once again she got a glimpse of something unusual from her. But when their eyes met, Tracey let out a frightened little squeak and scampered away.

Jenna didn't really care. Even if there was something new going on inside Tracey's dull little head, what difference would it make? They were all nerds, these so-called gifted kids, each of them living a sad, pathetic, boring life.

Not like *her* life . . .

Chapter Five

AMANDA WAS WATCHING THE clock. For a while now, she'd wondered if maybe, when the final bell rang, her nightmare would be over. She had no real reason to believe that this would happen. Her transformation hadn't begun with the first bell at school, so why would it end with the last bell?

Still, she harbored a hope. After all, that last bell held a lot of meaning, not only for her but for all the students at Meadowbrook, and maybe for the teachers, too. It was a big deal: it meant the end of the school day, dismissal, escape, freedom from authority. So maybe, just maybe, that bell would signify her own freedom, her escape from the prison of Tracey's wretched body.

But at 3:45 that afternoon, Amanda Beeson walked out of Meadowbrook Middle School in the same condition she'd entered it that morning: as Tracey Devon. So Amanda revised her expectations. She'd woken up that morning as Tracey, and she wouldn't be herself till she woke up the following morning. Somehow she'd have to get through the rest of the day and the night as the number-one nerd of the universe. She planned to go to bed *very* early.

Meanwhile, there was no place for her to go other than Tracey's house. So she went over to the place where the kids who took the bus were supposed to wait. This time, she recognized one of the travelers—a boy who had been in Tracey's social-studies class. Amanda couldn't remember his name, but she thought he was kind of cute, so she decided to strike up a conversation.

"Hi."

The boy didn't even turn in her direction.

She raised her voice. "*Hi.*"

He glanced at her. "What?"

Clearly, this boy had no conversation skills. So Amanda plunged in with a safe, sure-fire remark that was bound to get him to talk. "Can you *believe* how much homework Ms. Dailey gave us?"

She waited for the expected response—wholehearted agreement, a grumble, something like that. Instead, the boy backed away and started up a conversation with another girl.

Well, what did she expect? He thought she was Tracey Devon. If only that boy knew who was really standing right by him, who was actually speaking to him, he'd be thrilled;

he'd fall all over himself, showing off, trying to impress her. That knowledge gave her a tiny bit of satisfaction, but she still felt down.

Her bus arrived, and Amanda saw that the driver was the same man who had picked them up that morning. This time, she made sure she was at the front of the group so that she could get on first and grab a front seat. She didn't want to have to go down the aisle, where someone could trip her.

But once again, when the bus doors opened, she was shoved out of the way and pushed to the back of the group. And again the bus doors closed in her face.

She moved to bang on the doors, but this time she got there too late. Someone at a window saw her, but he didn't tell the driver. He just grinned and stuck out his tongue as the bus took off.

Amanda stood there, fuming. Was the man blind or something? What was he doing driving a school bus? Maybe she should tell her mother—no, Tracey's mother—to make a complaint to the school.

And now she'd have to walk to Tracey's house. She tried to recall the route that the bus had taken that morning, and she thought she had a pretty good idea how to get there. But she was unfamiliar with the neighborhood, so of course she made a couple of wrong turns and had to backtrack twice. A trip that took ten minutes by bus took her more than an hour.

As she turned onto Tracey's street, she imagined the scene that would take place when she arrived at the house. Tracey's mother would be worried. When she, Amanda, came home later than expected, she sometimes found her mother on the verge of tears, ready to call the police and report her as a missing person.

Her friends' parents were like this, too, reacting strongly, but sometimes in different ways. She remembered Britney's mother yelling at her, and Katie could even get grounded if she came home late three times in a row.

Maybe Tracey's mother wouldn't be too angry if Amanda pointed out that it wasn't her fault, that the driver just hadn't seen her. In any case, she wasn't looking forward to the confrontation. A few more minutes wouldn't make any difference, so she walked slowly and used the time to examineTracey's neighborhood.

Amanda lived in an older part of town, where the houses were huge and surrounded by big, leafy trees. This was one of the new neighborhoods, with modern-looking houses—nice, though not as grand as the ones in Amanda's area. It dawned on her that this wasn't where Tracey had lived when they'd been in elementary school together.

How did she know this? Maybe it was being in Tracey's

body that made her remember something that she'd long ago forgotten—going to Tracey's eighth birthday party, when they'd been in the same second-grade class. The Devon family was only three people then, Tracey and her two parents, and they'd lived in a two-bedroom apartment in a garden complex. They must have moved to this neighborhood when the Devon Seven were born and they'd needed more space.

It was hard to believe that she, Amanda Beeson, the queen of Meadowbrook Middle School, had ever really gone to a party for Meadowbrook's number-one nobody, Tracey Devon. Amanda couldn't remember if her mother had forced her to go. What she did remember was an ordinary birthday party, with the usual games, a cake, and candles . . . But now that she thought about it, she had the same notion she'd had earlier—that Tracey had been a regular, normal person back then. Not one of her friends, but not a hopeless weirdo either. Briefly, Amanda wondered what could have happened to Tracey between then and now. An accident? Some kind of brain injury?

She was at Tracey's door now, and she took a deep breath. Then she turned the handle, walked in, and called out, "I'm home!" That was what Amanda always did when she arrived at her house every day after school.

But apparently, this was not what Tracey did. Mrs. Devon

shot out of a room upstairs and appeared on the landing that overlooked the living room.

"Hush!" she hissed. "The girls are napping!" Then she went back into whatever room she'd come out of.

"Sorry," Amanda murmured to no one, and she ambled into the kitchen. Back at her own home, her mother would have now made her a little afterschool snack or, if she was out, the snack would have been waiting for Amanda on the counter. She brightened when she spotted a box of cupcakes on the Devons' kitchen counter, but before she could help herself to one, the teenage mother's helper came into the room.

"Don't touch those—they're for the girls!"

"What's for me?" Amanda asked, but Lizzie had already hurried out of the room.

Amanda spotted a basket of apples on the table. She did a quick count, saw that there were more than seven, and took one. Biting into it, she went back out into the living room and looked around.

Some framed photos hung in a cluster on the wall, and while she ate her apple, she went over to examine them more closely. There was a traditional bride-and-groom picture of a woman she could identify as a younger version of Tracey's nasty mother, and she assumed that the man in the picture was Tracey's father. Then there was another photo of the couple, older, beaming proudly as they stood beside an oversize crib packed with seven tiny babies. The rest of the pictures were group photos of the septuplets on their birthdays and individual shots of each septuplet at each age. *One would have been enough,* Amanda thought— the little girls looked exactly alike.

And where was Tracey? Amanda finally located another picture, which seemed to be a framed version of the previous year's family Christmas card. There they were, the seven little smiling Devon girls standing in a row in front of their parents. Looking more closely, Amanda was able to make out Tracey, half hidden behind the Christmas tree. Funny—it was a good shot of all the others, but Tracey looked kind of fuzzy.

It was clear to Amanda that Tracey wasn't the star of this family or even a featured player. There was absolutely nothing else about her in the room—nothing like the kind of stuff Amanda could see in her own home and the homes of her friends. There were no awards or citations or blue ribbons, no medals, no statuettes of gymnasts or figure skaters.

Despite her previous total lack of interest in Tracey Devon, Amanda found that she was becoming curious about the girl. She went upstairs to the room she'd woken up in that morning. Surely there she'd be able to find some clues about Tracey's life.

She remembered noting in the morning that there was nothing on the walls, and that was strange. Most girls she knew had posters—rock stars, horses, the stars of a popular TV series, stuff like that. Tracey's walls were bare. Amanda looked on shelves, in drawers, even under the bed, but after 20 minutes of searching, she was completely mystified. She'd found nothing that gave her the tiniest clue as to what Tracey Devon was all about. There were no books, no CDs, no magazines.

But ultimately, her search paid off. At the back of Tracey's cupboard, under the laundry basket, Amanda discovered a pink notebook. Scrawled on the cover, in childish handwriting, were the words *Tracey Devon, My Diary. Private, Keep Out!*

Amanda ignored the warning. Settling down on Tracey's bed, she opened the book to the first page.

"Dear Diary, I'm eight years old today! I had a party with all my friends. We had chocolate cake with pink roses on it. I got lots of presents. But Mommy and Daddy say I have to wait a whole month for my biggest present. They are going to give me real live babies! I hope they are all girls. Boys are icky."

Amanda turned to the next page.

"Dear Diary, I got 100 on my spelling test! Mommy

took me out for ice cream. Daddy says I'm the smartest girl in the world."

And on the next page:

"Dear Diary, I went to swimming class today. We are learning how to dive. It's fun."

Tracey definitely sounded like an ordinary person in her diary, Amanda thought. This was all so normal—it was boring. She wasn't going to learn anything interesting here. She closed the notebook and tossed it onto the floor.

Of course, it didn't really matter. Amanda was completely confident that she'd be out of this dismal prison cell in the morning, so it wasn't as if she really needed to know the girl well. She paused in front of the mirror and forced herself to take another look at Tracey.

This mirror can't be very clean, she thought. The reflected image seemed blurry to her. Which was just as well, she supposed, taking into consideration how awful Tracey looked.

Suddenly an idea hit her, and she almost smiled for the first time that day. She'd thought of a way to occupy her time and actually do a good deed while she was here. (Not that good deeds were a habit with her, but she figured she might be rewarded for it by positive forces and get out of Tracey's body even sooner.)

There was something very significant that she could

63

do for this poor girl—she could make Tracey look better! Now, this day, while she had control of Tracey's body, she could get the girl a decent haircut, some cool clothes, lipgloss, and maybe some bronzer to brighten up her drab complexion. She'd be helping herself, too—if Tracey wasn't so pathetic, Amanda wouldn't have to worry about feeling sorry for her and finding herself in this situation again.

She already knew that Tracey wasn't carrying any money, and she hadn't found any in her search of the room, but from the look of the house Amanda could see that the family wasn't poor. She headed off to find Tracey's mother.

She found her in a room that she hadn't seen earlier—a cozy den with a TV. Mrs. Devon was sitting on the sofa, talking on the phone as she leafed through what looked like a clothing catalog.

"Lila, these things are so cute!" she squealed. "My girls are going to look adorable this winter. I'm going to order the little pink matching hats and mittens . . ."

If this had been her own home, Amanda would have just interrupted, but here she waited for a pause in the conversation, tapping her foot impatiently, so she could break in. She had to decide how she was going to address the woman anyway. She had no idea what Tracey called her. Mom? Mommy? Mother?

"Go ahead and answer the door, Lila—I'll hold on," Mrs. Devon said, and Amanda took a chance.

"Mom?"

There was no response as the woman turned the page of the catalog.

"Mommy?" Amanda said. "Mother?"

The woman lifted her head and looked at Amanda blankly. "Did you say something?"

"I was just wondering—could we go shopping?"

"What? Go where?"

"Shopping. Like, we could go to the mall."

Mrs. Devon responded as if Amanda had suggested a trip to the moon. "The *mall*?"

"Yeah. Not the big one on the highway—the other one, across from Meadowbrook . . ." Amanda's voice trailed off as Mrs. Devon's expression went from puzzlement to disbelief to something very close to anger.

"Are you insane? Have you lost your mind? Don't be ridiculous! I don't have time to go shopping. I have seven children upstairs!"

It was on the tip of Amanda's tongue to say, "You have *eight* children," but Mrs. Devon's friend had returned to the phone.

"Yes, Lila, I'm here. I just have to run to the drugstore to pick up the girls' vitamins. Of course we could have coffee.

65

I've got the mother's helper here and the girls are napping. Okay, see you in ten minutes."

Amanda was stunned. As Mrs. Devon hung up the phone, she glared at the woman. "You've got time to meet your friend, but you can't take me shopping?"

But Mrs. Devon walked right past her like she wasn't even there.

Chapter Six

JENNA DIDN'T PARTICULARLY LIKE any day of the week, but she really hated Wednesdays. Every Wednesday, after her last class, she had to visit the school counselor.

This was a requirement that the judge had imposed when Jenna had been released after a month in reform school. If she skipped the meetings, the counselor would report her to the judge and the judge could send her back to that place, where many of the kids were even tougher than she was.

She rapped on Mr. Gonzalez's door and waited for his cheerful, booming voice to call, "Come in!" As usual, he was sitting on his desk instead of behind it.

"Hiya, Jenna!" he said with a smile.

It was very difficult for her not to smile back. She actually kind of sort of liked Mr. Gonzalez, but she couldn't let him know that. So she just muttered something that sounded like an unenthusiastic greeting and took her usual seat.

"How are you doing?" Mr. Gonzalez asked.

"Okay," Jenna mumbled.

"Just okay? Come on, give me something more interesting than that. Fabulous, excited, miserable, angry—anything's better than just okay."

"I'm a little tired," she admitted.

"Why is that? Are you having trouble sleeping?"

It was the perfect opportunity to go into her pose. "Nah, I was out late last night. Hanging with my crew." She liked that word, *crew*. She'd picked it up from a TV show, and it sounded so much cooler than gang.

Mr. Gonzalez frowned slightly. "Jenna, you know you have a curfew. You're supposed to be back at home by ten o'clock at night."

She'd forgotten that, and it was another requirement handed down by the judge. Hastily, she amended her statement. "Well, I wasn't exactly *out*. The crew was at my place."

"Did your mother approve of that?"

"Um, she didn't know. She was out."

"I see," Mr. Gonzalez said. He picked up a pen and jotted something down in the notebook that was open on his desk. Jenna stiffened.

"She wasn't out all night or anything like that," she said. "She was home before eleven."

"And she let your friends stay?"

Jenna thought quickly. "Uh, she didn't know they were there. They were in my room and the door was closed."

Was he buying it? She searched his mind and saw that it was cloudy with doubts. She had to move the conversation along, so she improvised. "Um, one of the guys in my crew, he, uh, offered me some drugs, but I said no. And I made him leave," she added.

"That's good," he said. "Were you tempted to take the drugs?"

"Oh, no," Jenna assured him. "I never touch drugs anymore." Actually, she'd never even tried drugs, but it was one of the reasons she'd been arrested six months ago— she'd been with people who were high. She didn't mind people thinking that she'd been into drugs at one time. It was good for her bad reputation.

To her relief, the topic of conversation shifted to classes and grades—much safer subjects for Jenna. Not that she was doing brilliantly, but she'd managed to keep her performance at slightly below average, doing just well enough to keep her from getting reported to anyone official. She didn't want to do any better than that—it wouldn't be good for her image.

Thank goodness Mr. Gonzalez couldn't read *her* mind. While she pretended to listen as he talked about how bright she was and how she could do so much better and maybe get a scholarship to a university someday, her thoughts hovered around the real events of the night before.

She hadn't been with her "crew." She really didn't have a crew, unless she counted the sad bunch she sometimes lingered with around the train station, when anything was better than being in her own house.

She'd actually been at home the evening before, with plans to watch a couple of things on TV and then go to bed. But her mother had arrived home with friends, they'd put on some music and started dancing, and there was no way Jenna could have slept through that in a tiny apartment. They must have been drinking, too, because her mother had gotten sick and Jenna had had to clean it up.

So it really hadn't been her fault that she hadn't gotten much sleep the night before, but she couldn't tell Mr. Gonzalez the real story. If the judge knew how her mother was behaving, that just might be another reason to send Jenna away.

It was funny, in a way. She thought the others in her so-called gifted class had crummy lives—lives completely unlike hers. Only every now and then, she had to admit that her life sucked, too.

But there was no way she'd ever let anyone else know that.

Amanda had nothing to do. She'd finished Tracey's homework and she'd even made Tracey's bed (which was something she rarely did with her own bed at home). She wondered if there were chores that Tracey was supposed to do, like set the table for dinner. She supposed she could ask Lizzie, the mother's helper. On the other hand, she didn't particularly feel like talking to the teenager, who was always scolding her for eating something that belonged to the septuplets.

Amanda picked up Tracey's diary from the floor. This time she opened it to the middle. From the date, she could see that it was two years after the last entry she'd read. Tracey would have been ten. There was only one line on the page.

"Dear Diary, Sometimes I hate them."

Hate whom? The kids at school? So why didn't Tracey do anything about it? Frustrated, Amanda tossed the notebook back onto the floor.

Maybe there was something on TV. She went back downstairs to the little room where she'd spotted a television set. But the Devon Seven were up from their naps, and they were now gathered in that room with Lizzie, sitting on the rug and watching some dumb kiddie show.

She stood in the doorway for a moment, and one of the seven actually looked at her. "Hi, Tracey."

Amanda had a feeling it was the same one who had noticed her that morning, but she couldn't be sure. And what did it matter—they weren't *her* sisters. So she didn't even bother to respond to the kid.

On the bookshelf, she saw something that looked like a photo album. She picked it up and sat down on the little sofa with it.

The first few pages contained very old photos, black and white, of people in old-fashioned clothes. She thought they might be Tracey's grandparents or great-grandparents. In any case, they weren't very interesting. She kept turning pages until she spotted someone she recognized—Mrs. Devon as a young teenager, maybe 13. At least, she assumed it was Mrs. Devon because she looked a little like Tracey. Or the way Tracey might look if she wasn't so awful.

The girl in the photo was thin, but Amanda would have described her as slender, not scrawny. And she was blond, but her hair was chin length, short, and bouncy, not hanging in flat, stringy clumps. She had pale blue eyes like Tracey's, but they were bright, not watery. There were freckles on her face, too, but they looked cute. And she had the same thin lips, but they were rosy pink and stretched into a smile. Amanda couldn't remember ever seeing Tracey smile. Maybe at that eighth birthday party . . .

Young Mrs. Devon was wearing some cute clothes, too.

Even though the photo had to be, like, 30 years old, the miniskirt she wore would have even looked okay today, though Amanda wasn't so sure about the white boots.

She turned the page. There were more photos of Mrs. Devon, becoming more and more recognizable as she grew older. There was a copy of the same wedding picture Amanda had seen on the wall in the living room. And a couple of pages later, the same couple stood in a similar pose, but this time Mrs. Devon was holding a baby.

The baby must have been Tracey, Amanda realized. She examined the picture closely. Well, Tracey had obviously been born normal—she looked like any other baby, cute and plump, and her parents seemed very happy to have her.

There were more pictures of Tracey on the following pages—Tracey in adorable little-girl ruffled and smocked dresses, Tracey wearing a swimsuit and sitting in a wading pool, Tracey on her father's shoulders. In almost every photo, Tracey was smiling or laughing, her eyes crinkling. On the next page, Amanda saw a first-day-of-school photo—there was one almost exactly like it in the Beeson family album, and it seemed to Amanda that little Tracey was carrying the same pink Hello Kitty backpack that little Amanda carried in her picture.

Then she came to a photo that made her gasp. It was Tracey's eighth birthday party, with all the guests at the table and Tracey in the center. Amanda saw herself, and she recognized her friends Sophie and Nina, who had been in the same second-grade class with Tracey, too. That wasn't such a shock—at that age, all the girls in a class were invited to one another's birthday parties. What really blew her mind was the way she and Sophie had their arms around Tracey, as if they were actually friends! It seemed completely natural, too, since Tracey looked just as cute and happy as the rest of them.

Mrs. Devon also was in the picture, standing behind Tracey, and it was clear from the size of her that she was hugely pregnant. That was the year the Devon Seven were born, Amanda remembered.

On the next page, there were no pictures of Tracey at all.

Practically every picture in the rest of the album portrayed the septuplets—together, individually, sometimes with the parents. Occasionally there was a glimpse of Tracey, but her image was always half hidden or blurred.

From the kitchen came the sound of pots and pans clattering, and Amanda guessed that Mrs. Devon must have come home. A moment later, she heard the woman's voice.

"Lizzie! Could you help me with dinner?"

Lizzie left the room, and Amanda wondered if she should help, too. But Mrs. Devon hadn't called for her . . .

"Tracey?"

This time Amanda was almost sure that the septuplet who had just spoken was the same one who had spoken to her that morning. "What?"

"Can you read us a story?"

Now seven little faces were looking at her expectantly. Amanda had to admit that they were pretty cute. But before she could respond to the request, she heard the front door open, and a man's voice called out, "I'm home!"

The Devon Seven jumped up and ran out of the room. Cries of "Daddy! Daddy!" filled the air. Slowly, Amanda got up and went into the hallway, where she could see what was happening in the living room.

"Here are my girls!" Mr. Devon sang out as he made silly efforts to gather all the children in his arms. "Hello, Sandie, Mandie, Randie, Kandie, Brandie, Tandie, and Vandie!" The septuplets were giggling like crazy as, one at a time, he lifted the girls up into the air. He didn't seem to see Tracey in the hallway, and he didn't ask for her either.

That was when Amanda knew whom Tracey sometimes hated. Her little sisters. Once they were born, Tracey was pushed aside and nobody paid any attention to her.

"Dinner's ready," Mrs. Devon called. Her husband and the Devon Seven took off in that direction.

Amanda followed, but she wondered as she went if there'd even be a place set for Tracey.

CHAPTER SEVEN

AMANDA WAS THE FIRST to arrive in the gifted class the next day, and she'd hurried there on purpose. This was probably the only place at Meadowbrook where she would get any attention—*positive* attention, that is. In gym class, the girl with her face claimed to have seen a bug crawl out of Tracey's hair. Which hadn't been true, of course. But Amanda-Tracey hadn't been able to laugh or contradict her. It was strange—her other self was getting on her nerves! Why couldn't Amanda just ignore Tracey like everyone else?

But this was the least of her problems at the moment. She was still in the state of disbelief that she'd woken up to that morning. When she'd realized she was still Tracey Devon, a full 24 hours later, she'd been engulfed by panic. Was it possible that this was a permanent situation? She couldn't bear to even contemplate the notion. It just couldn't be—this couldn't happen to her. Somehow, she'd find a way out of this body.

Madame greeted her with a smile—the first smile that had been aimed in her direction all day. "Tracey, you're here two days in a row! That's great!"

Again, Amanda was puzzled by the enthusiastic response to her appearance. Was Tracey out that much? She remembered homeroom the day before, when roll had been taken. That teacher had acted surprised to find her there. None of her other teachers made a big deal about it—but then, none of the other teachers took attendance. Those teachers probably didn't even notice if Tracey was there or not.

Maybe Tracey was in the habit of just cutting *this* class, the gifted one. But why would she cut the one class where she got treated decently? Or, at least, *noticed*. Anyway, Amanda didn't think Tracey was the type to break rules. And where would she go?

Ken walked into the classroom, and Amanda gazed at him in a whole new light. He was still cute, he was still cool, but if she'd understood what he'd said in class the day before, Ken heard the voices of dead people. Or at least, he said he did. Whether dead people really talked to him or Ken just imagined he heard them, either way it gave Amanda the creeps.

The next to walk in—well, roll in, actually—was Charles. Charles, who seemed to be able to make things

77

move just by looking at them. That could be a useful talent, Amanda thought. Sitting at the dinner table, you wouldn't have to ask anyone to pass the salt. All you'd have to do was look at the shaker. She wondered if he had to use the remote when he watched TV or if he could change the channels with his mind.

On the other hand, his "gift" was sort of scary. Yesterday, one of those flying books could have hit her right in the face. And what if she'd been sitting under a hanging lamp? Charles could have made it drop right down on her head. She made a mental note to avoid attracting his attention. She didn't really think it would be a problem—Tracey seemed to be very skilled at avoiding attention. Maybe *that* was her gift.

Emily and Sarah were the next to enter the room. Amanda hadn't quite figured out what kind of special talents they had. All she'd really noticed the day before was that Emily said strange things and Sarah was totally unreadable. Martin was right behind her. All Amanda knew about him was that he could hurt people, but she didn't know *how*.

The little round-faced boy entered. Amanda knew nothing about him, not even his name. And finally came Jenna, who knew what people were thinking.

As Amanda glanced at Jenna, she saw that Jenna was

staring directly at her, and there was the oddest expression on her face. *Ohmigod, she's trying to read my mind!* Amanda realized. Frantically, she tried to imagine what Tracey might think about in class. She would probably be depressed, thinking about all the people who had ignored her so far that day—her parents, the bus driver, kids at school. Or maybe she'd be thinking about the person who hadn't ignored her—the girl everyone thought was Amanda Beeson. It dawned on Amanda that she really deserved the title Queen of Mean . . .

Oh no, she was thinking like Amanda! Quickly, she turned her thoughts to Tracey's seven little sisters and tried to remember their names. Sandie, Mandie, Kandie . . . Blandie? No, that couldn't be right.

"Good afternoon, class," Madame said. "As you recall, yesterday we were discussing Ken's current problem. A man who believes he was murdered by his wife wants Ken to inform the police. Ken does not want to get involved, and he's right to feel that way. Why is he right?"

Martin's hand flew up, and he waved it wildly.

"Yes, Martin?"

"He's right because the police wouldn't believe him. No one believes any of us. When I tell people what I can do, they just laugh at me, so then I have to prove it to them. And everyone gets really mad at me."

79

Ken spoke. "Martin, maybe it's better if you don't tell them. Then they won't laugh, and you won't have to prove anything, and no one will get mad at you."

Madame smiled at Ken. "Very good advice, Ken. But Martin, you did answer my question. Ken is doing the right thing by not telling the police because he wouldn't be believed. You have to remember that ordinary people—people who are not gifted—don't believe in the kind of talents you have. What could happen if any of you tell people what you can do? Emily?"

There was no response.

"*Emily!*"

"Huh? I mean, excuse me, Madame, what did you ask me?"

Madame spoke sternly. "Emily, you *must* keep your mind here, in class."

"I'm sorry, Madame. It's just that, well, I keep seeing an earthquake, and I think maybe it's going to happen tomorrow, but I don't know *where.*"

Madame shook her head. "Emily, you're supposed to try to *control* your visions, not elaborate on them."

"But if I know where the earthquake's going to happen, I could warn the people there so no one would get hurt."

Charles offered a comment. "They wouldn't listen to you. It's like Martin just said—they wouldn't believe you.

They'd just think you were nuts."

Emily persisted. "But they'd find out later that I was right."

"And then what would happen to you, Emily?" Madame addressed the entire class. "What would happen to any of you if people accepted the fact that you have a gift? Sarah, what do you think could happen to you?"

Sarah's permanent smile actually wavered. "Someone might ask me to do terrible things for them."

"You could always say no," Charles said. "That's what I'd do."

Jenna piped up. "Oh yeah? What if that person was holding a gun to your head while he asked you?"

"Easy," Charles replied. "I'd make the gun fly right out of his hands. And Sarah could do better than that. She could make the person put the gun to his own head and blow his own brains out!"

"I would never do that!" Sarah cried out.

"Maybe you *wouldn't*," Jenna said, "but you *could*."

Madame took over. "The point is, if people found out what you can do, they'd try to use you for their own purposes. You'd be taken away somewhere and studied, tested, examined. Imprisoned, possibly. Tracey, do you have an opinion about this?"

Amanda didn't know what to say. She was still trying to

come to terms with what she'd just learned—that Emily could see into the future. That Sarah could control what people did. And she was bewildered by the way Madame was talking to them—she sounded like a parent reminding children why they shouldn't talk to strangers. It was a strange attitude for a teacher to have. And Amanda still didn't know what she herself—no, what *Tracey*—could do.

Madame was waiting for an answer, and she was gazing at Tracey with a slight pucker on her forehead.

"Uh, no, I don't have an opinion, Madame."

"Typical!" Charles snorted.

From his reaction, Amanda gathered that Tracey didn't say much in this class. That was fine with her.

Madame continued. "Let's get back to Ken's situation. Yesterday I asked you to think about a moment when you successfully controlled your gift. It's possible that Ken could benefit from your experience. Who wants to tell us about a particular incident? Emily? *Emily!*"

"Yes, Madame, I had a good experience last weekend. My aunt and her boyfriend were having dinner with us. They're getting married in a couple of months, and they were talking about where to go on their honeymoon. My aunt wants to go to Bermuda, and I don't even know where that is, exactly, but I closed my eyes and concentrated, and I saw a tropical storm going on there in two months, just around the same time as their honeymoon!"

Madame appeared concerned, but Amanda didn't think this had anything to do with the aunt's honeymoon. "Did you tell your aunt?"

"Not exactly. I told them that I knew some people who went to Jamaica for their honeymoon, and they liked it a lot. So then they started talking about Jamaica. And it turns out that my aunt's boyfriend has always wanted to go to Jamaica, so they're changing their honeymoon plans!"

"Hey, that's pretty cool," Ken commented. "You got them out of the tropical storm, but you didn't have to reveal anything about yourself."

Madame nodded slowly. "Yes, that was creative thinking, Emily. But you were still taking a risk. You might have raised suspicions."

"But she's my aunt, Madame! She wouldn't want to hurt me."

"Not intentionally, perhaps," Madame said. "But the danger is there, Emily, and you must always be aware—"

"Wait a minute," Jenna broke in. "How about all those other people in Bermuda? Some of them might be on their honeymoons, too."

"But I can't help everyone!" Emily cried out.

"Why not?" Charles challenged her. "If you had seen the future before I was born, you could have told my parents that the doctor was going to make a stupid mistake when he delivered me, and they could have changed doctors, and I wouldn't be in a wheelchair!"

"I wasn't even a year old when you were born!" Emily wailed.

Madame clapped her hands. "Class, class! That's enough. We're supposed to be talking about Ken's situation today."

But just then the classroom door opened, and in walked the principal, Mr. Jackson, with a young woman Amanda had never seen before. Madame frowned slightly at the interruption.

"Good afternoon, Mr. Jackson," she said politely, but there was an edge to her voice that Amanda found interesting. Whenever the principal came into classrooms, teachers behaved very respectfully and made a big deal out of welcoming him. Something about Madame's voice and expression told Amanda that she wasn't too crazy about Mr. Jackson. Maybe other teachers didn't like the principal, but they certainly never showed it. And once again, Amanda was intrigued by how different Madame was from other teachers.

"What can we do for you, Mr. Jackson?" Madame asked, but she sounded like she didn't want to do anything at all for him.

The principal's normally solemn face was unusually

cheerful. "It's what *I* can do for *you*, Madame. *And* for your entire class. I would like to introduce you all to Serena Hancock, your new student teacher."

Madame was clearly taken aback. "Student teacher? I didn't request a student teacher, Mr. Jackson. We've never had a student teacher in this class."

The principal's face hardened slightly. "Well, you do now. And I would think you'd be grateful to have the help. Your students are supposedly gifted, isn't that right?"

Madame looked at him cautiously. "Yes."

"Well, Ms. Hancock has a gift, too. She can perform hypnosis."

To Amanda's eyes, Madame seemed alarmed now. "And why would my students need to be hypnotized?"

The principal shrugged. "Special children, special needs, special solutions. I'll leave Ms. Hancock with you now." And he left the room.

Along with the others, Amanda gazed at Ms. Hancock curiously. She was actually pretty impressed with this new addition to their classroom. Like most student teachers, Ms. Hancock was young, probably in her 20s. Unlike most student teachers, she looked very cool. She had long, thick blond hair that hung down her back in perfect waves and a scarlet mouth. Her dress was amazing—short, figure hugging, and printed in bold colors, turquoise and deep violet. Being a loyal reader of *Teen Vogue*, Amanda knew that turquoise and deep violet were very big this season.

"Please take a seat, Ms. Hancock," Madame commanded. "I'm sure you'll just want to observe today."

The younger woman smiled, revealing perfectly brilliant white teeth. "Thank you, Madame. But please, call me Serena." She turned to the students. "All of you can call me Serena."

Amanda could completely understand the startled expression that crossed Madame's face. No teachers, not even student teachers, were ever called by their first name at Meadowbrook.

Everyone watched as Serena took a seat at the back of the room. Then they turned back to Madame.

Amanda thought she looked flustered, as if she wasn't sure how to proceed. It was an odd expression for Madame—after only two classes, Amanda could tell that the teacher normally had an air of complete confidence. What was she worried about? Did she think she'd lose control of the class to a student teacher? No one ever paid much attention to student teachers.

Finally, Madame spoke again. "I think this is a good time to do some silent reading. I'm sure you've all got books with you. Please take them out now." She, too, went to her desk and opened a book.

This was very odd, Amanda thought. It was as if Madame didn't want to continue discussing their gifts in front of the student teacher. But surely the other teachers must know about the weird stuff these students could do? At least Mr. Jackson had to know about them—he was the principal! And surely he must have told this student teacher, Serena, before sending her into this room to work with these weirdos.

So why couldn't they go back to what they were talking about? If they did, maybe Amanda could finally learn what Tracey's gift was. Why was Madame suddenly acting like she wanted them all to be quiet? It seemed to her like Madame was always trying to protect them. But protect them from what—or from whom?

They didn't have to read for long. Moments later, the bell rang, and Madame dismissed them without even giving them homework to do for the next day.

Amanda gathered her books and walked out into the hall. She headed down the corridor toward her next class, and she didn't realize that Jenna was following her until Jenna whispered in her ear.

"You're not Tracey."

Chapter Eight

F OR ONE BRIEF MOMENT, Jenna thought
she might have made a mistake. The reaction to
her accusation was typical Tracey. The girl who
now gazed back at her looked nervous, fearful, and almost
ready to cry.

But any doubts in Jenna's head disappeared as "Tracey's"
expression quickly changed. She stared right back at Jenna
with a challenging look.

"You're crazy," the girl said. "Of course I'm Tracey. Who
else could I be?"

This response only confirmed Jenna's suspicion. Tracey
would never have been confrontational like that.

"You're Amanda Beeson."

"I am *not*," she declared hotly, but Jenna didn't have to
be a mind reader to see the panic in her eyes.

"Oh yes, you are. You're Little Miss I'm-Too-Cool-for-
Words Amanda Beeson. I remember when you and your
prissy friends called me a vampire. Huh—I wish! I would

have drained your blood by now."

"You're disgusting and crazy," the girl-who-wasn't-Tracey said, and she turned away. Jenna grabbed her arm.

"Do your snotty friends know you're a body snatcher? What would they say if they found out you're gifted, like the other freaks in the class?"

"They'd never believe you!"

"Let's try it." Jenna looked around. "There's Sophie Greene—isn't she one of your friends?"

"And look who she's meeting at her locker," her classmate retorted. "Amanda Beeson."

Jenna's brow puckered as she watched Sophie and Amanda walk down the hall together. "I don't know who that is. Your clone, maybe. Or a robot. It's not Tracey, that's obvious. She looks too sure of herself." She looked at Amanda-Tracey appraisingly. "So you and Tracey didn't change places?"

"No. *That's* me and *I'm* me and I don't know how it works, but . . ." Amanda-Tracey stopped suddenly, and Jenna grinned.

"So it's true. I was just guessing, but you really *are* a body snatcher. I've heard of people like you, but I've never met one before."

She recognized the flash of anger on Amanda-Tracey's face. She'd seen it before once, in the cafeteria, when someone spilled orange juice on Amanda's white jeans.

"If you tell anyone," Amanda said, "if you dare, I'll—"

Jenna didn't give her the opportunity to complete her threat. "Don't worry, Amanda, I'm not going to tell anyone. Not *yet*. There's something I'm curious about, though. Why would you want to be Tracey?"

"Are you kidding? Do you think I *want* to be inside this creepy girl's body? It—it just happened. I was thinking about her, and then . . . poof!"

"Why were you thinking about her? I can't believe the great and wonderful Amanda Beeson gives a hoot about poor little Tracey Devon." Jenna was having a good time teasing Amanda. She'd never had this kind of encounter with a popular girl, and she had to admit it was fun, even if the popular girl didn't look like herself.

"Can't you just go away and mind your own business?" Amanda fumed.

"No. I want to know where Tracey is."

It was so weird to see a haughty expression on Tracey's face. Jenna had to keep reminding herself that behind the face was super snob Amanda Beeson.

"I don't know," Amanda finally admitted.

"You can't hear her thoughts or anything?"

"No."

Jenna felt a twinge of concern. "She's not . . . *dead*, is she?

Did you kill her when you took over her body?"

"No!" Amanda exclaimed. She hesitated. "I mean, I don't *think* so." She bit her lip. "Wouldn't I feel it if there was someone dead inside me?"

"You don't feel her being alive, do you?"

"No." Amanda looked up at the hall clock. "The bell's about to ring. I don't want to be late for class."

"It doesn't matter," Jenna said. "Half the time no one sees Tracey anyway."

Amanda frowned. "Yeah, what's the deal with that? Madame keeps saying it's nice to *see* me."

"You haven't figured that out yet?"

"Figured what out?"

"Tracey's special talent. Her gift."

"What *is* her gift?"

The bell rang, and the few remaining students in the hall headed off. "Meet me after school, at the mall, in front of Barnes & Noble." She couldn't resist one more insult: "That's a bookstore, in case you don't know. It's next to Style Session, and I'm sure you know where *that* is."

Feeling unusually pleased with herself, Jenna swaggered off to her next class. For the rest of the school day, her spirits were high. She didn't like anything about Meadowbrook, but she particularly despised Amanda Beeson and her crowd. She was going to enjoy watching Amanda squirm.

Amanda felt sick. To have a freak like Jenna Kelley acting superior to her was almost as bad as being a freak like Tracey Devon. Things were getting worse and worse.

But by the end of the day, she'd made the decision to meet Jenna at the mall. Jenna knew Tracey, and Jenna could read minds, so maybe, just maybe, Jenna would be able to help her get out of Tracey's body. She didn't know how Jenna could help, but she figured there was a chance that all these weird kids were connected in some way—that they had some sort of special knowledge.

Only, would Jenna *want* to help her? Obviously, Jenna despised Amanda, which was natural. Dweebs, nerds, and geeks all pretended to hate popular girls, when they actually envied them and wanted to *be* them.

But it seemed as if Jenna might care about Tracey. And maybe she'd help Amanda if she thought she was helping Tracey. In any case, Amanda didn't have anything better to do, and going to the mall was preferable to going back to Tracey's house and being ignored.

So when the last bell rang, she hurried out of the school and went directly to the corner where she could safely cross the highway and head to the mall on the other side. And, despite Jenna's snide remark, she knew exactly where Barnes & Noble was. Stupid Jenna didn't realize that just because a girl was pretty and cool and popular didn't mean she'd never read a book.

Just moments after she arrived at the bookstore, Sophie, Nina, and Other-Amanda strolled into the mall. For a second, Amanda froze—what if they saw her with Jenna? And then she almost laughed at her silly thought.

"Why do you look so happy, Tracey?" Nina asked as the group passed her. "You've got nothing to smile about."

Now that was interesting, Amanda thought. Usually, Nina ignored Tracey like everyone else. Maybe she was just trying to impress Other-Amanda with her nastiness. Or maybe she was about to challenge Amanda's status as the Queen of Mean! Amanda made a mental note to keep a close eye on Nina.

She was distracted by the arrival of Jenna, who must have overheard Nina's remark.

"Nice friends you've got," she commented.

"Oh, shut up," Amanda-Tracey replied. "The only reason I'm meeting you here is because maybe you can help me get back inside my body. And get Tracey back inside hers," she added quickly. She guessed Jenna would be more likely to help if she thought it was for Tracey's sake.

"We've got to find her first," Jenna said. "Which might not be so easy, when you think about her gift."

"Which is?" Amanda asked eagerly.

But now Jenna was distracted by a group down at the

other end of the mall, in front of Target. "Want to meet some of *my* friends?" she asked Amanda.

"Not particularly," Amanda replied, but Jenna took off, and Amanda had no option but to follow her. As they got closer to the group, she began to have serious misgivings. Jenna's friends looked like a very creepy bunch.

An older, skinny guy with dyed green hair and a cigarette dangling from his mouth said, "Hiya, Janie."

They couldn't have been great friends if he didn't even know her name, Amanda thought. But Jenna didn't seem dismayed. "Jenna," she corrected him. "Yo, Slug."

Slug? Who had a name like Slug? Amanda couldn't wait to find out what the others were called. The sleazy-looking goth girl in black with blood-red lipstick was called Bubbles, while another girl with a shaved head and tattoos up and down her arms was Skank. Jenna introduced the heavyset guy with the half-closed eyes as Harry. Amanda thought they all looked older, at least 18. And they were all extremely ugly.

"This is my friend Am—I mean, Tracey."

Not since this bodysnatching experience had begun had Amanda felt so grateful to look like Tracey. She'd absolutely die if anyone saw her real self with people like this.

"What are you up to?" Jenna asked them.

"Gonna hit Target," Slug said, nodding toward the store.

"You ever seen one of these?" From his pocket he pulled out an oddly shaped metal gadget.

"What is it, some kind of weapon?" Jenna asked.

Slug made a snorting sound, which Amanda guessed was his version of a laugh. "Nah. You know those plastic things they stick on stuff so you can't steal it?" He was looking at Amanda now, so she felt obliged to answer.

"It's a security device. The cashier takes it off after you pay for something. Otherwise it sets off an alarm when you leave the store."

"Yeah, right. Well, this handy little number takes that plastic thing off. You can walk right out with half the store in your pocket."

"You'd have to have pretty deep pockets," Jenna said, and Amanda couldn't help laughing, but no one else got the joke.

"I only got two of these things," Slug continued, "but we'll pass 'em around. Then afterward we'll split the stash. I'm going in to check out the place first, see where the good stuff is. I'll be right back." Sticking the gadget back in his pocket, Slug strolled into the store.

Amanda turned to Jenna. "They're going to steal things?"

"Yeah," Jenna replied, in a voice that was just a little bit too cocky. "You have a problem with that?"

"Well, it's against the law, for one thing."

That comment got the rest of Jenna's friends laughing, and Amanda could feel Tracey's face turning red. "Well, you can leave me out," she said.

"Chicken?" Jenna taunted.

Amanda couldn't care less if Jenna thought she was a coward. What worried her was the idea that this enterprise could end any kind of collaboration between them.

"There's Slug," Bubbles said. He was just outside Target's door, and he beckoned them closer. Bubbles, Skank, and Harry started toward him, but Jenna hung back for a moment.

"You sure you're not up for this?" she asked Amanda.

Before Amanda could reply, she heard another familiar voice behind her.

"Hi, guys! What are you doing?"

It was Emily, from their gifted class. She was alone and carrying a bag from the bookstore.

"Just messing around," Jenna said.

Emily smiled vaguely. "I didn't know you two hung out together."

Amanda wanted to correct that assumption, but she held her tongue. "What did you buy?" she asked instead.

Emily reached into her bag and pulled out a book. Jenna read the title out loud. "*I Was Marie Antoinette.*"

"She was the last queen of France," Emily told them.

"Her head was cut off during the French Revolution."

Jenna snickered. "Who wrote the book? Her ghost?"

"No, a woman named Lavinia Pushnik. She claims that she was Marie Antoinette in an earlier life."

Amanda rolled her eyes. "You don't believe that stuff, do you?"

Emily shrugged. "I see the future. Maybe she sees the past."

Now it was Jenna's turn to do some eye rolling. "Emily, anyone can see the past. It's called history. You can read about it in books."

"Mmm." Emily seemed to have stopped listening. Her eyes were glazed over.

"Are you seeing something in the future now?" Amanda asked.

Emily nodded. "Someone who's just about to win the lottery."

"Oh yeah?" Now Jenna looked interested. "My mother plays the lottery every week."

"Someone in Canada," Emily murmured. "Toronto . . . no, Montreal."

Jenna's face fell. "Oh. Well, I have to get into Target before all the good stuff is gone."

"What do you mean?" Emily asked.

"Jenna and her buddies are about to do some shoplifting,"

Amanda told her.

Emily's expression changed. "Don't do it, Jenna."

Jenna groaned. "Oh, great! Another goody-goody who's afraid to break the law."

Emily shook her head. "Your friends . . . they're going to get caught."

"You see that?" Amanda asked. "For real?"

Emily nodded.

Jenna looked skeptical. "You're just saying that so I won't steal anything."

"No," Emily said. "It's going to happen."

"I'd better warn them." Jenna started toward the store.

"No!" Emily cried out. "You'll get caught, too. It's just about to happen."

Jenna hesitated, and that was a good thing. Because only seconds later, a uniformed guard emerged with Jenna's pals, all in handcuffs. They disappeared behind a door marked *Security*.

"Wow," Amanda said in awe. "How did you know?"

"That's my gift," Emily said, but she didn't sound particularly proud of it. "I see things. Only I never know what to do about them."

"Well, thanks for telling me about that," Jenna said. "I would have had a one-way ticket back to reform school."

"I'm glad I helped you," Emily said, but now her voice

was sad. "I don't get to help people much, mostly because my visions aren't usually very clear. And then—well, it's like Madame says, who's going to believe me? They'll just think I'm nuts."

Amanda knew that if she wanted everyone to believe that she was Tracey, she should keep her mouth shut. But she couldn't resist a question. "Could you always do this? See the future?"

"When I was five, I had my first vision. My father was leaving the house to go to work. And I saw that when he got to the end of the driveway, another car was going to come around the corner really fast and hit him hard. But I didn't tell him."

"Did it happen?" Amanda asked.

Emily nodded. "He was killed. Don't you remember? I told this story in class."

"I, uh, must have been out that day," Amanda said. Emily's story was awful, really depressing, and Amanda wanted to change the subject. Luckily, she spotted someone in the mall whom they might find interesting. "Isn't that the new student teacher?"

Just as they all turned to look at her, the young woman saw them. She waved and started toward them.

"Oh, great! A teacher," Jenna groaned.

But the young woman seemed very happy to see them.

"Hi, girls! What a coincidence, running into you here!"

Emily said, "Hello, Miss . . . uh . . ."

"Serena," the teacher prompted. "This is so cool! What are you up to?"

Personally, Amanda thought she was overdoing the "I'm-your-buddy-not-your-teacher" thing. Jenna also looked doubtful. But Emily seemed intrigued.

"We're just hanging out," she said.

"I am so excited about this job!" Serena told them.

Jenna's eyebrows went up. "Really? Why?"

"Well, it's not just student teaching, is it? I mean, you are really different."

Jenna still looked wary. "What do you mean, 'different'?"

"It's okay," Serena assured her. "I know that you guys are, you know, *special*. And I really want to know you. As friends, not students."

"But that's what we are," Emily said. "Students."

Serena tossed her head back and laughed, as if Emily had said something uproariously funny. "Really, guys, I'm not like your other teachers. Madame, she's very nice and all that, but she's *old*. It's not like you can confide in her. I want you to think of me as someone you can really talk to. You can tell me your secrets, your feelings."

"Madame doesn't like us to talk about ourselves to others too much," Emily said.

Serena nodded. "Yeah, that's kind of sad, isn't it? It must be sort of lonely for you guys, not being able to talk about what's important to you."

Emily nodded fervently. "It is."

Serena was awfully eager, Amanda thought. Why would anyone want to tell their secrets to someone they'd just met? The woman was so pushy; it was making Amanda feel uncomfortable.

Jenna seemed to be having a similar reaction. "I'm out of here," she announced and then took off.

"I have to go, too, Miss—uh, I mean, Serena," Amanda said. "Bye, Emily."

She hurried after Jenna and caught up with her. "Wait! You still haven't told me."

"Told you what?" Jenna asked.

"About Tracey. About her gift."

"You still haven't figured it out?"

"No."

Jenna grinned. "Tracey can disappear."

Walking home, Jenna was in pretty good spirits for a change. It hadn't been a bad day—not bad at all. In her mind, she kept seeing the look on the face of Amanda-Tracey when she'd told her she'd figured out who she was. Of course, it would have been more fun to see that stunned expression on the real face of that conceited Amanda Beeson, but this was the next best thing—knowing she'd freaked out the snottiest girl at Meadowbrook. And that incident at the mall had been pretty cool, too.

She didn't like Slug and Skank and the rest of them, even though she'd called them her "crew" when she talked to Mr. Gonzalez and she'd told Amanda that they were her friends. Actually, she thought they were a bunch of miserable lowlifes. They didn't do anything real, like go to school or work. They just hung around all day, begging on street corners or picking pockets or shoplifting. They were filthy and not too intelligent, though she had to admit that she liked Bubbles's goth look, which was an extreme version of her own.

They didn't really live anywhere, though sometimes they'd squat in an abandoned house or apartment until someone moved in or the police threw them out. Lots of times they slept on the benches in the train station, and that's how Jenna knew them. There were times when she also hung around the train station, when she couldn't bear to go home.

But she probably would have gone into Target with them if Emily hadn't come along and predicted what was going to happen. Like the rest of the kids in the class, Emily didn't have a whole lot of control over her gift, so Jenna had truly lucked out.

A light rain began to fall, but that wasn't what suddenly dampened her spirits. She'd turned onto the street where she lived.

The three tall brick apartment buildings took up the whole street. Brookside Towers, they were called, which was a joke—there was no brook alongside the structures, and "Towers" made them sound like castles or something. In reality, Brookside Towers was public housing, packed with all kinds of people who had only one thing in common— not much money.

Jenna suspected that the buildings had been ugly when they were built, and they were even uglier now, covered with graffiti and gang symbols. There were a lot of cracked windows, and cardboard had replaced the glass in some of them. The surrounding grounds weren't exactly gardens: any grass that might be there was covered with junk—trash bags, an old refrigerator, a broken bicycle.

There were some good people at Brookside Towers. Jenna thought of Mrs. Wong down the hall, who had put up window boxes full of geraniums. Then some nasty boys had managed to climb up to her window and destroy them. Mrs. Wong had cried . . .

No, Brookside Towers wasn't a very nice place to live. Sometimes, when her mother was sober and feeling optimistic, she'd make promises to Jenna.

"No matter how broke I am, I'm going to buy a lottery ticket every week. And one of these days, baby, our ship will come in, and I'll buy us a nice house in a nice neighborhood. If I keep buying tickets, I've got to win sooner or later, right? I mean, it's like that law of averages, or whatever it's called." Jenna never bothered to tell her mother that she was wrong, that the law of averages meant that it was highly unlikely she'd ever win at all.

Jenna didn't despise her mother. She was just a poor, weak woman whose husband—Jenna's father—had walked out on her when she'd gotten pregnant. And she could feel better about herself only by getting drunk or high. She wasn't hateful—just very, very sad.

Jenna thought you could *feel* the sadness when you walked into the apartment, even when her mother wasn't home, like now. She took advantage of her mother's absence to pick up the empty bottles, sweep the floors, and wash the dirty dishes in the sink. Hunting in a cabinet, she found a jar of peanut butter and some stale crackers to spread it on. The cable bill hadn't been paid, so the TV was worthless. With nothing else to do, she got out her homework. She had a lot of reading to do, but that was okay. Jenna liked to read.

Of course, she couldn't tell anyone that. It was too bad for her image . . .

Chapter Nine

A T FIRST, AMANDA DIDN'T think it sounded so bad, and on the way home she contemplated this piece of news. So, Tracey could turn invisible. That explained why she seemed to be absent a lot and why Madame kept saying it was nice to see her. And maybe that also explained why Tracey looked blurry in her mirror reflection and fuzzy in photographs.

Now, the question was, what could Amanda do with this knowledge? This gift opened up a whole new range of possibilities.

What if she just disappeared and took off until all this was over? Maybe she could sneak onto an airplane, go to an exotic vacation place, and lie on the beach doing nothing. Could invisible people get a tan?

She could stay in the fanciest hotels without paying. She wondered what happened when an invisible person ate— did the food just disappear? Or could you see it digesting in an invisible stomach? That would be pretty gross.

Or she could hang around some famous people, like actors or rock stars, and see what they were really like. Or even just go to her very own house and see what her other self was up to . . .

But ultimately, she had to remember the sad truth of the matter. These gifted kids—they couldn't control their gifts. Dead people seemed to speak to Ken whether he wanted them to or not, and Emily's visions of the future weren't always clear. For Tracey, disappearing probably just happened—she couldn't just snap her fingers and disappear.

So Amanda went back to Tracey's house and spent another yucky Tracey-style evening. At dinner, she pushed the food around her plate while each of the Devon Seven were asked about their day and the parents exclaimed how adorable they were. No one noticed that Tracey wasn't even eating.

After dinner, she went to Tracey's room, where she did some homework and read a book that she'd brought home from the school library. And then she remembered Tracey's diary. Maybe Tracey had gone on some interesting adventures while she was invisible.

Amanda retrieved the notebook and opened it at random.

"Dear Diary, Everybody thinks the Devon Seven are so cute. I'm not cute."

That was certainly true, Amanda thought. She turned a few more pages.

"Dear Diary, My little sisters turned three today. They're getting bigger. I feel as if I'm getting smaller."

Now that sounded interesting, Amanda thought. Was this when she started disappearing? She turned a page.

"Dear Diary, Mom and Dad don't look at me anymore. They see only the Seven. I might as well be invisible."

So it definitely was the septuplets that Tracey had written about when she wrote "Sometimes I hate them." Amanda couldn't blame her. They took all the attention away from Tracey. But now Tracey was about to become invisible, which should make up for it all.

Eagerly, Amanda turned to the next page.

"Dear Diary, Sometimes I think I'd like to get a haircut. And some new clothes. But what's the point? Nobody would notice. Nobody sees me now. I'm nothing."

Amanda was infuriated. Without even bothering to shut the notebook, she tossed it across the room. So Tracey felt sorry for herself. In all fairness, Amanda knew she was probably entitled to a little self-pity. But Amanda certainly didn't want to have to read about it.

At least Tracey was starting to make sense. From the photos she'd seen, Amanda knew Tracey must have been the center of her parents' life when she was born, as most babies were. But once the seven girls were born, she grew less and less important in her parents' eyes. She must have felt that. And if you felt like nothing at home, you'd feel like nothing at school, too. It wasn't just shyness that made Tracey disappear—Tracey faded away from lack of attention. And all because of those wretched little septuplets.

Later, lying in Tracey's bed, Amanda thought about her own home, her own parents. Being an only child, she always complained that her mother and father made too much of a fuss over her, watched her too closely, and wanted to know everything about her. She was a star at home, which was nice, but it could also get a little tiresome—there was such a thing as too much attention. Surely there had to be a happy medium between what she had and what Tracey had.

The next day, Friday, started off as a typical Tracey day. The bus doors closed in her face and she had to walk to school. That made her late arriving at homeroom for roll call, but no one even noticed.

In Tracey's English class they were reading *Romeo and Juliet,* and Amanda had something she wanted to say, about how Romeo should have felt for Juliet's pulse and then he'd know she wasn't really dead and he wouldn't kill himself and she wouldn't kill herself and they could live happily ever after. But no matter how many times she raised her hand, the teacher didn't call on her, not even when she flapped her arm wildly in the air.

It was at lunchtime that she realized what was going on. She was looking for a place to sit, an empty table. As she looked around the crowded, noisy cafeteria, she realized that she had accidentally paused right next to her own special table where Britney and Sophie and her other self were gathered. She was close enough to touch, but nobody insulted her, not even Amanda herself. That was when she knew she had become invisible.

She hurried out of the cafeteria to go to the restroom and confirm this in a mirror. How strange it felt, to be looking at yourself and seeing nothing. And how long would it last?

She left the restroom and ambled down the corridor. It was kind of cool, to stroll right in front of a hall monitor and not be asked to show a pass. She could walk right out of the building and no one would stop her. But where could she go? In a way, it was too bad that she wasn't a gangster like Jenna. She could do a lot of shoplifting in this condition.

She decided to stop at the library and pick out some books. But on the way there, she passed the principal's office. The door was slightly ajar, and she heard Madame talking to Mr. Jackson. She sounded upset, and Amanda paused to listen.

"I don't like this arrangement at all, Mr. Jackson. We have discussions of a highly personal nature in that class. My students will not be comfortable talking in front of a total stranger."

"Serena won't be a stranger for long," the principal countered. "And they'll learn to be comfortable with her. To be perfectly honest, Madame, I'm not comfortable with the way you conduct that class. I realize your students are, uh, *unusual*, but that doesn't mean they shouldn't have the usual classroom experiences."

Madame's voice rose a notch. "But surely you can understand that their special circumstances require an element of privacy!"

"What exactly makes them so special, Madame?"

There was a moment of silence. Amanda wished she could see Madame's expression.

"You know I'm not at liberty to discuss the details of these children," she said finally.

Mr. Jackson made a grunting noise. "All I know is that two years ago you showed up here with a letter from the superintendent of schools, a mandate authorizing you to start a special class, with very little information as to what kind of special students would be invited to join the class.

Obviously your students are not particularly brilliant, nor are they mentally challenged. All I can see is the fact that they have problems."

"Gifts."

"Yes, I know that's what you call them. Others might call them delusions. All I know is that someone believes these kids have—" he paused, as if he was searching for the right words "—unusual capabilities. Strange powers or something. Mind reading, fortunetelling. Am I correct?"

Amanda couldn't hear Madame's response. Maybe she didn't respond at all, because the next sound Amanda heard was the principal's long sigh.

"And I know that you are not required to share all the information with me. But whatever bizarre *gifts* these kids have, I think you're becoming overprotective of them, Madame. Perhaps a little . . . possessive?"

Madame replied to this. "I have to be possessive. They need to be protected."

"But protected from whom? From other students? From teachers? From me? Surely you're not suggesting that they're in danger here at Meadowbrook?"

"Danger can come in many forms, Mr. Jackson. My job is to prepare these students to defend themselves." Her voice rose again. "No, it's more than a job—it's a mission. I'm trying to teach these children how to cope. And you have no authority over me!"

"If you're going to yell, Madame, please shut the door." Madame obeyed quickly, and Amanda didn't have enough time to slip inside before the door closed. Too bad, because this was getting interesting. Madame certainly took her job seriously. And Amanda still wasn't completely sure what that job was.

She forgot about the library and roamed the halls looking for something else of interest to listen to or observe unnoticed. When she saw Katie and Britney with hall passes, she followed them to the restroom. At least she could catch up on the latest gossip.

She watched longingly as her two friends went through the ritual that they always performed after lunch. They emptied their makeup bags into sinks and then scrutinized their faces in the mirrors to see what elements were in need of repair. And, of course, they gossiped.

But it was a shock to hear what they were talking about today. "Amanda is really getting on my nerves lately," Britney said.

Amanda was stunned. Britney turned and looked around the restroom. "Is anyone in here?"

Katie moved over to the stalls and looked under the doors. "No one's here."

"I just had a feeling someone was listening to us."

Britney resumed the conversation. "Amanda just thinks she's all that, you know? Okay, so she got some new red ballerina flats. Did she really have to keep telling us how much they cost?"

"She does that all the time," Katie said. "It's like she wants to make sure we know she's got more money than we do. That is so uncool."

Amanda was aghast, and completely bewildered. What was the point of getting new things if everyone didn't know they were expensive? She'd always thought her friends were impressed by the cost of her clothes.

"And the way she was making fun of Shannon's shirt, the one with the flowers on it, just because her mother embroidered the flowers herself," Britney continued. "Just between you and me, I thought it was kind of cute."

"So did I," Katie said.

So this was how her good friends talked about her when she wasn't around! Just then, her other self came into the restroom.

"Guys, I forgot to show you," she said. "Look what I got at Sephora yesterday."

Amanda felt like she was watching a home movie as this Amanda opened her bag and pulled out a little case. "It's a makeup travel kit, with everything you need all in one place. Look, it's even got little brushes and everything. It was super expensive, but I just had to have it."

"Oh, I love it!" Britney exclaimed.

"It's so cute!" Katie gushed.

Two-faced creeps, Amanda thought. Another girl came into the restroom, and she took advantage of the open door to escape. With nothing else to do, she headed to the gifted class.

She was the first student to arrive, but Madame was there with the student teacher.

"I'd like to start the hypnosis sessions today," Serena was saying.

"I'm sorry," Madame said, though she didn't sound sorry at all. "I've got a complicated lesson plan. There won't be time today."

Serena smiled. "Mr. Jackson said I could take the students individually out of the classroom and work with each one in the empty room next door. So it won't disrupt the entire class."

"But the student you take out will miss what the rest of the class does," Madame objected.

"But think of the potential benefits, Madame. Your objective is to teach your students to deal with their . . . their peculiarities. There's been a lot of research that indicates that hypnosis can have a real impact on a person's ability to control bad habits."

Amanda took advantage of her invisibility to scoot around the desk and take a good long look at Serena. Personally, she couldn't see why Madame was so nervous around her. Okay, Serena was pushy, but why did Madame look so suspicious? Was she afraid that the students would like Serena as a teacher more than they liked her? But Madame didn't seem like the kind of person who cared about popularity.

The other students were arriving, and Madame spoke more softly to Serena. "Their *habits*, as you call them, are not necessarily bad."

"Well, you know what I mean," the student teacher said. "And I do have Mr. Jackson's permission to carry out these sessions."

Madame's lips tightened. Then she nodded. "All right, Ms. Hancock."

"Call me Serena."

Madame turned and surveyed the room. "Charles, please go with Ms. Hancock to the room next door."

"I don't want to go with her," Charles muttered.

"Now, Charles, there's nothing to be afraid of," Serena said brightly. "This will be fun!" She grabbed the handles of Charles's wheelchair and pushed him out of the room.

"Is she going to hypnotize Charles?" Emily asked when they were out of the room.

"She's going to try," Madame said. "Not all people can be hypnotized. Unique people may have . . . unique reactions."

Amanda thought she could see a little smile on the teacher's face, but it disappeared too fast for her to be sure.

"Now, let's see," Madame continued, surveying the room again. "We have some absentees today. Martin has the flu—his mother called the office. And Tracey—"

Jenna interrupted. "Tracey's here, Madame. I can tell."

"Thank you, Jenna, but I must remind you that it isn't appropriate to read Tracey's mind without her permission. Or anyone else's, for that matter. Now—"

But once again she was interrupted, this time by a crash that practically made the whole room vibrate. "Oh dear," Madame said. "I think hypnosis has brought out some anger in Charles."

Sure enough, seconds later the door swung open and a furious Serena stormed in, followed by Charles, who was wheeling himself this time.

"That—that brat made my chair fall over!" the student teacher fumed.

"Oh my, that wasn't very nice, Charles," Madame scolded, but her tone was mild, and Amanda could have sworn she saw a glint of satisfaction in the teacher's eyes. "Ms. Hancock—I mean, Serena—why don't you take Ken today instead?"

Serena glared at her. "No, I think I'll have *her*." She pointed to Emily.

"As you wish," Madame said coolly.

Serena's expression changed dramatically, and she smiled sweetly at Emily. "Is that all right with you, Emily?"

Amanda watched them leave and wondered if Serena's hypnosis might help *her*. Maybe if she was unconscious, Serena could reach the real Tracey inside her and get her to come back out . . .

There was a voice at her ear. "Or maybe hypnosis would turn you into Tracey for good. Wouldn't you just love that?"

Shut up, Jenna, she thought fiercely. *And don't make fun of me. Help me!* After a second, she concentrated as hard as possible on one additional word. *Please?*

It seemed to take forever before the girl sitting behind her whispered in her ear again.

"Okay."

Chapter Ten

I'M NOT DOING THIS for you," Jenna said. "I want to help Tracey. I'm sure she's not thrilled about having you inside her body."

She read Amanda's mind. *Yeah, right, whatever. Just do it.*

"And don't give me orders! I don't care if you're Miss All-That Amanda Beeson—you can't boss me around."

Jenna was almost surprised to hear the tiniest touch of meekness in Amanda's mental response. *Okay, sorry. Where are we going?*

"My place."

I hope none of her scummy friends are there.

"Don't worry, nobody's home," Jenna snapped. This was the day the new lottery tickets went on sale, and the jackpot was huge. Her mother was always willing to stand in line for hours if necessary. She thought putting in the effort would bring her more luck.

Could you please turn off your little gift? I'm entitled to the privacy of my own thoughts.

"Like I'd be interested in anything going on inside your feeble little mind."

Then stop reading it!

Jenna tried. But there was no missing Amanda's reaction when they turned the corner.

Ohmigod, she lives in Brookside Towers! Yuck!

Jenna gritted her teeth. It was too bad Amanda couldn't read *her* mind—she would hear herself being called every nasty, dirty name ever invented. But Jenna kept telling herself—just as she'd told Amanda—that she was doing this for Tracey, and she kept her mouth shut.

But why was she so intent on helping Tracey? It wasn't as if they were great friends; they knew each other only through the gifted class. And she didn't know anything about Tracey, since the girl didn't say much at all, even when she was visible.

Unsure as to whether Amanda was alongside her or behind her, Jenna held the door to her apartment open. She knew Amanda was inside when she sensed her discomfort at finding herself in such shabby conditions.

"It's not the kind of castle you're used to," she declared, "but it's clean."

What's her problem? I wasn't even thinking anything.

Well, maybe it was just what she expected Amanda to feel. "Sit down," Jenna ordered, pointing to the sofa. She pulled up a chair. "Are you facing me?"

Is she going to try to hypnotize me?

"No, I'm not into that." She caught a glimpse of something else in Amanda's head and couldn't help nodding. "Yeah, I think Serena's kind of weird, too." Then she frowned. Was she actually finding something in common with this snob?

"How did you get inside Tracey in the first place?" she asked. She caught a glimpse of a response in Amanda's mind, but it was obvious to her that Amanda was trying to put one over on her.

"You *cared* about her? Ha! Amanda Beeson cares only about Amanda Beeson." Jenna concentrated on getting deeper into Amanda's thoughts, but there wasn't much to learn. Amanda was now mentally counting backward from one thousand. Obviously, she was trying to keep Jenna from learning more about her.

"Okay, okay, I get it," Jenna said. "And I don't want to know you either. Like I said, this is for Tracey." She took a deep breath.

"Tracey, I know you're in there. It's not your fault that this—that Amanda took over your body. But you've got to be strong now. Come out, get rid of her, take over."

Does she have to make it sound so violent?

"Stop thinking!" Jenna barked. "I can't reach Tracey if

120

you keep interrupting. Tracey, I'll bet you can hear me. I don't know why you become invisible like you do. Maybe you're just shy or something. But now it's like you've completely disappeared, and that's worse. Now, if you come out, Amanda can go back into her little princess world and you can come back into yours and everything will be normal, okay? Tracey? *Tracey!*"

Jenna concentrated as hard as she could, but all she could sense was Amanda trying very hard to think of nothing.

"I give up. I can't hear her at all."

You can't give up—I have to get out of here! Bring her back!

"I just said I can't! Look, did it ever occur to you that maybe she doesn't want to come back?"

You mean I could be stuck inside Tracey forever?

Jenna was spared from answering when the door to the apartment opened. "Hi, honey pie!" her mother squealed.

"Hi, Mom." Jenna glanced nervously in the direction where Amanda was sitting.

"Guess what? I bought fifty lottery tickets!"

It was clear to Jenna that her mom must have had a few drinks before making the decision to buy more than her usual one.

"Why, Mom?"

"Honey, I just had this *feeling*. This is it! This is our week!"

"Sure, Mom." She glanced back at the sofa and knew Amanda was still there. *Get out of here*, she thought fiercely, but of course Amanda wasn't a mind reader. All Jenna got in return was Amanda's reaction to her mother.

"I'm starving, Jenna, honey. Is there anything to eat?"

"No, Mom. I was waiting for you to come home with some money so I could go to the store. I'll go now."

Her mother's face crumpled. "But I don't have any more money, Jenna. I spent it all on lottery tickets."

Jenna sighed. "It's okay—I think I've got five bucks stashed away. I'll get us something." Then she stiffened as she became aware of something very different coming from Amanda. It wasn't disgust that Amanda was feeling, or even distaste. It was pity. Amanda was feeling sorry for her.

Jenna clenched her fists in rage. Even in her foggy state, her mother could see that something was wrong.

"Honey, you okay?"

What could Jenna say? That she desperately wanted her mother out of the room so she could tell Amanda what she could do with her pity?

Then yet another realization hit her. How could she be reading pity in Amanda's mind? Girls like Amanda Beeson never thought about anyone but themselves. It was impossible that Amanda could be feeling sorry for her. So maybe, maybe, she was actually making contact with

Tracey!

And then she realized that Amanda was leaving. "Wait!" she cried out.

Her mother looked at her strangely. "What did you say, honey?"

Jenna sighed and tried to hold onto Amanda-Tracey's thoughts as she went out the door. The pity was still there, but another feeling had joined it—something that didn't make sense at all to Jenna. It seemed to her like . . . fear.

Now what was *that* all about?

Chapter Eleven

AMANDA DIDN'T PAUSE FOR a breath until Brookside Towers was way out of sight and she felt reasonably safe. She couldn't believe how close she'd come to even more serious trouble back there. The last thing she needed was to feel sorry for Jenna. Becoming Jenna Kelley was no more appealing to her than being Tracey Devon. Jenna certainly didn't have a better life than Tracey. At least Tracey lived in a nice house where there was food in the kitchen. And at least Tracey had a pair of normal parents.

Well, sort of normal. They were normal to the septuplets. But for Tracey . . . Amanda couldn't quite figure it out. Okay, Tracey was a nerd and she didn't have any friends, but weren't parents supposed to love their kids unconditionally, even if they were pathetic? The more she thought about it, the more she realized that it wasn't the fault of the Devon Seven that Tracey was such a mess. It was her parents' fault.

At that moment she wasn't in any mood to face those

parents, even if they couldn't see her. And she decided to take advantage of her invisibility by paying a visit to a place that she'd been trying not to think about.

Had it really been less than a week since she'd been in her own home? It felt like forever. It was funny how she'd forgotten what a pretty house it was. She stood there, at the end of the driveway, and just admired it.

Then she caught her breath. There she was—Amanda Beeson, accompanied by Katie and Britney, walking right by her. *Boy, if she only knew what they'd been saying about her in the restroom,* Amanda thought. She picked up her pace so that she could enter the house with them.

Her very own mother came into the vestibule to greet them. "Hello, darling. Hi, girls."

Other-Amanda didn't bother with greetings. "Mom, we're starving. Is there anything to eat?"

"Of course there is! I made chocolate-chip cookies for you."

"Yum," Katie and Britney chorused, but Other-Amanda stamped her foot.

"Mom! You know I'm on a diet! Why did you have to go make cookies?"

"Amanda, darling, there's no need for you to be on a diet," her mother protested as she followed them into the kitchen.

"Oh, what would you know?" Other-Amanda muttered.

Jeez, was she rude or what? Amanda thought. But wasn't that what she normally would have said?

"Girls, would you like some milk with those cookies?" Amanda's mother asked, opening the refrigerator and taking out a carton.

"*Mom!* Could we have some privacy, puh-leeze?"

Amanda could see the annoyance on her mother's face, but the woman didn't say anything. She probably didn't want to embarrass her daughter by scolding her in front of her friends. That was the kind of thoughtful person she was.

As soon as her mother left, Other-Amanda said, "Guys, did I tell you what I did to Tracey Devon in gym class? I told her I saw a bug crawling out of her hair!"

Britney and Katie burst out laughing. After what she'd heard her friends say in the restroom that day, Amanda-Tracey knew they were faking their enthusiasm for Amanda's meanness. They were such hypocrites! And she didn't want to listen to it anymore. She started for the door and then had another thought. She ran up the stairs to her very own room, went into the closet, and grabbed her favorite red ballerina flats. It wasn't really stealing, she told herself. After all, they were hers.

By the time she got back to Tracey's house, it was after six, and since she was still invisible, nobody could see that

126

she was home. But her absence clearly wasn't having any effect on the household. In fact, there was an event going on—a reporter and a film crew were there. The Devon Seven were all wearing identical pink dresses. Tracey's mother had obviously been to the beauty salon, and even Tracey's father had come home early from work.

They were all gathered in the living room, and Amanda hovered in the corner to see what was going on. An attractive woman was standing in front of a camera and speaking.

"The impact of multiple births on a family is enormous, financially and emotionally. Mrs. Devon, what did the arrival of septuplets do to your life?"

Tracey's mother uttered a tinkling little laugh. "Well, as you can imagine, our lifestyle certainly changed. George and I used to go out to dinner frequently and to the theater. We can't do that as often now."

"We're going out tonight," Mr. Devon added, "for the first time since the girls were born."

"Do you go out less now because of the expense?" the reporter asked.

Mrs. Devon looked insulted. "No, we're quite fortunate in that sense. But it's very difficult to find a babysitter when there are seven children in the house."

Eight children, Amanda thought. *There are eight children in the house.* Maybe Tracey wasn't an adorable little kid and maybe she didn't require a babysitter, but she had to count for something.

Mr. Devon interjected a comment. "Of course, we don't mind giving up our social life. With seven daughters, it's a party in this house all the time!"

Eight *daughters! What is the matter with these people? Don't they care about Tracey at all? Have they forgotten her?* Amanda was really beginning to get irritated with them.

"Do you ever think about having another child?"

"Heavens no," Mrs. Devon said. "Seven is plenty!"

Now Amanda was fuming, and she couldn't keep quiet. "Eight! You have eight kids!"

There was a shriek from a cameraman, and another man yelled, "Cut! What happened?"

The cameraman's eyes were huge and he was pointing in Amanda's direction. "That—that girl! She just popped up out of nowhere!"

So she was visible again. That was a relief. It wasn't a relief to the cameraman, though. His face was white and his hand was shaking as he pointed. "I'm telling you. Look at the tape—she wasn't there a second ago."

"Don't be ridiculous," the other man said. "You just didn't see her come in." He peered at Amanda. "Who are you, anyway?"

"I'm Tracey Devon. I'm the Devon Seven's older sister."

The director seemed taken aback. "Really?" To the reporter, he said, "I didn't know there was an older sibling. Did you?"

The reporter turned to the Devon parents. "I don't think you've ever mentioned another child." Then, turning back to Amanda, she said "What did you say your name is, dear?"

"Tracey." Amanda glared at Tracey's parents. "Remember me?"

Mr. Devon seemed somewhat befuddled. "Of course, don't be silly . . ."

Mrs. Devon broke in. "We thought you'd be interested only in the septuplets. Tracey is our firstborn; she's twelve."

"*Thirteen!*" Amanda corrected her. That was when it hit her—why Tracey's special gift was the ability to disappear. No one ever saw her, so she just faded away. If no one paid any attention to her, why bother being visible?

"Would you like to be interviewed, Tracey?" the reporter asked. "I'd like to know how having seven identical siblings has affected your life."

I don't have a life, Amanda thought. *I mean, Tracey doesn't have a life.* And there wasn't anything she wanted to say about the Devon Seven—she didn't even know them.

"No, I don't want to be interviewed," Amanda said. If

she'd been at her own home, her mother or father would have corrected her: "No, *thank you*." She glanced at the parents. As usual, they weren't paying attention. They both just seemed completely puzzled.

The Devon Seven were staring at her, too. They were probably amazed to hear her speaking, or to hear other people speaking to *her*. Amanda resisted the urge to stick out her tongue at the little darlings and give them a dirty look. No, it was the parents who deserved the dirty look. Somebody had to take the blame for Tracey's miserable life! Without another word, Amanda left the room and ran upstairs.

Throwing herself on Tracey's bed, she contemplated her situation—*Tracey's* situation. It wasn't right and it wasn't fair. Amanda pounded the pillow in frustration. She even began to wonder if maybe Tracey did have a worse life than Jenna. At least Jenna's mother seemed to love her.

But what really bugged Amanda was the fact that Tracey didn't do anything about it. She just let them ignore her and went along with it by disappearing.

Then Amanda sat up. Maybe it was Tracey's own fault that her life was crummy. Well, if Amanda was going to have to live as Tracey for a while longer, there was no way she'd follow in Tracey's footsteps.

A little voice inside her asked, *And what if you have to live as Tracey forever?* She forcibly pushed that horrible notion out of her mind. For as long as she did have to be this sad girl, she wasn't going to suffer like Tracey did. It was time for Tracey to take some responsibility for herself.

Amanda remained on the bed, thinking about how to go about doing that. After a while she heard the film people leave, and she came out of her room. She still wasn't sure what her first move would be, but she had to do something.

The seven little girls were now bouncing around and making a lot of noise. Mr. Devon was trying to hush them as Mrs. Devon went to answer the ringing telephone in the kitchen. From the bottom of the stairs, Amanda watched as Mr. Devon made futile efforts to get the kids under control.

"Kandie, stop jumping—you're giving me a headache."

"I'm not Kandie—I'm Mandie!" the child declared.

Mrs. Devon emerged from the kitchen with a stricken look on her face. "That was Lizzie. She can't baby-sit."

"What?" Mr. Devon yelled. "But we're meeting my boss and his wife. We can't cancel now!"

"Well, what do you want me to do?" Mrs. Devon shrieked back.

Amanda saw her opportunity. "I'll baby-sit."

Mrs. Devon continued with her tirade. "I can't find a babysitter at the last minute!"

"Yes, you can!" Amanda said more loudly. "Didn't you hear me? I said I'll baby-sit."

She must have spoken even louder than she thought, because she actually got both the parents' attention. But neither of them seemed to have understood.

"What did you say?" Tracey's father asked.

Amanda was getting impatient. "I *said*, I'll baby-sit for the girls."

Tracey's mother stared at her. "*You?*"

"Yes, me. I'm thirteen years old, remember? I can watch them. I'm not saying I'll *entertain* them, but I can make sure they don't play with matches or sharp knives. I can keep them alive till you get back."

Mr. Devon looked at Mrs. Devon. "Why not? We're not going that far. I'll leave my cell-phone number; she can call if there are any problems."

Mrs. Devon still looked uncertain. "Well . . . I suppose that would be all right."

"Absolutely," Mr. Devon assured her. "Thank you for offering, Tracey."

"Oh, I'm not doing this as a favor," Amanda corrected him. "I expect to be paid. How much do you pay Lizzie for baby-sitting?"

Mr. Devon was startled. "I don't know." He turned to his wife. "What do we pay the babysitter?"

"Five dollars an hour," Mrs. Devon said faintly.

"That will be just fine," Amanda said. "Five dollars an hour. If I'm not up when you get home, please leave the money on the kitchen table."

Still looking a little dazed, Mrs. Devon nodded.

"Good," Amanda said. "I'll be in my room. Let me know when you're ready to leave and I'll get to work." She couldn't see them as she turned to go back up the stairs, but she could conjure up the pleasant vision of two stunned parents, and it made her smile.

CHAPTER TWELVE

WHEN AMANDA-TRACEY walked into class on Monday, Jenna blinked twice. One of those two girls had been very busy that weekend. Not only was Amanda-Tracey visible, but she'd also been through some kind of transformation.

The outer person was still Tracey, but Amanda's influence was showing. The blond hair was no longer flat and stringy—it had been cut short, to her chin, and it was shining. She was wearing makeup—not a lot, but something made her eyes look bigger, and there was a slick of pink on her lips. And her clothes—they weren't Jenna's kind of clothes, but she knew that other kids at school would consider them cool. This new Tracey wore a long red tunic over cropped jeans, with a short black sweater and red ballerina shoes. She carried her books in a black canvas tote bag over her shoulder.

She was different in other ways, too. She held her head up and took long, confident strides into the room. Even Madame looked intrigued.

But before anyone could comment, student teacher Serena came into the room. "I'd like to see Jenna today," she announced.

She was addressing Madame, but Jenna responded. "Maybe I don't want to see *you*."

"Jenna, that's rude," Madame murmured.

Emily leaned over toward Jenna. "It doesn't hurt or anything, Jenna. In fact, it's kind of fun."

"That's right!" Serena said brightly. She turned to Madame. "And don't forget—I do have Principal Jackson's authorization to meet with each student independently."

"I haven't forgotten," Madame said quietly. "Jenna, would you please go with Ms. Hancock?" And at that moment, for the first time ever, Jenna thought she read a little something in Madame's mind.

And find out what this woman is really up to.

Had Jenna imagined that? Or had Madame actually allowed Jenna inside her head? Jenna decided that maybe a session with the student teacher would be more interesting than the usual boring 50 minutes in class.

"Okay." She followed Serena into the room next door. It was just another classroom, nothing special. Serena directed Jenna to sit down. She did, and then Jenna began to concentrate.

But before she could even begin to penetrate the student

teacher's mind, Serena suddenly produced a circular object the size of a dinner plate. "I want you to look at the red dot in the center, Jenna." She pressed something on the plate, and it began to rotate.

Jenna tried to look away, but for some strange reason she couldn't. She couldn't close her eyes either. And any possibility of reading Serena's mind evaporated as her own mind went blank.

No, not *blank* exactly. She was conscious—she was aware of sitting in the room and looking at Serena's plate thing—but there was something happening in her mind. It was being drained . . .

Time passed, but she had no idea how much. She couldn't take her eyes off the dot. She could hear just fine, though.

"I know all about your special gift, Jenna. But you will not be able to read my mind. If you try to read my mind, you will suffer a severe headache. The pain will become unbearable. This is a posthypnotic suggestion, Jenna. You will never be able to read my mind. Do you understand?"

Jenna didn't think she could speak or even nod her head. She was completely paralyzed. But somehow she must have communicated something, because Serena said, "Good. Now, please follow me."

Then Jenna wasn't paralyzed at all. She rose and followed Serena out of the room. That was when she realized what had been drained from her mind—her will. She would do whatever this woman said. And she didn't even have enough freedom of thought to feel afraid.

They went down some stairs, walked to the end of a corridor, and turned right. Dimly, Jenna knew they were walking into the school cafeteria.

The last lunch session was still in progress, and she was aware of the noise and the people and the general chaos, but it was as if she wasn't a part of it—more like she was watching the scene on TV. Serena led her across the room to an alcove where the teachers ate their lunch. They both stood just behind a column, so Jenna could see the teachers but they couldn't see her.

Now Serena was whispering in her ear. "There is a man at the table. He has light brown hair and he's wearing glasses. Do you see him?"

Jenna saw him, and even in her strange state she recognized him—Mr. Jones, a history teacher.

"During the next few minutes I want you to read his mind," Serena said. She left Jenna standing there and went over to the table.

With all the noise in the cafeteria, Jenna couldn't hear anything that Serena said to the other teachers. But the student teacher's lips were moving and she was smiling as she sat down next to Mr. Jones. And Jenna had no problem at all tuning in to the man; in fact, it was the easiest mind reading she'd ever done.

Wow, she's hot! Is she coming on to me? I hope so. I wonder if she's got a boyfriend. If I can get her alone later, I'm going to ask her out.

Serena returned to Jenna. "We can leave now," she said, and Jenna followed her back to the room they had been in before.

"Now," Serena said as they returned to their seats, "I want you to tell me what Mr. Jones was thinking when I spoke to him."

Jenna had no choice. Like a parrot, she repeated the thoughts she'd read. "'Wow, she's hot! Is she coming on to me? I hope so. I wonder if she's got a boyfriend. If I can get her alone later, I'm going to ask her out.'"

Serena smiled. "Excellent! Now, Jenna, I'm going to take you out of your hypnotic state. Watch the red dot again."

She held up the object, and this time it spun in the opposite direction. Again, there was the odd passage of time—seconds, minutes, she couldn't tell.

Suddenly, Jenna felt like someone had just tossed a glassful of water in her face. She wasn't wet, but she was very awake.

"That wasn't so bad, was it?" Serena asked cheerfully.

"Was I really hypnotized?" Jenna asked her.

"Absolutely," Serena assured her. "Why do you ask?"

"Because I remember everything we did."

Serena continued to smile. "Of course you do. This isn't some sort of witchcraft, Jenna—it's psychological science. I'm not attempting to change you—I simply want to understand you—all of you. You kids with your special gifts, you need special attention."

"But why did I have to—"

Serena interrupted her. "That will be all, Jenna. Please return to the classroom and send Ken in here now. We have a few minutes left."

Jenna stared at her. But now Serena had opened a notebook and was totally preoccupied with writing something. Clearly, she wasn't going to be answering any questions that Jenna might ask, so Jenna did as she was told.

But for the rest of the school day, she thought about the odd experience. She'd been with Serena for more than half a class period, 30 minutes. But the events that took place could have taken up only ten minutes or so. Had Serena made her do things she *couldn't* remember? Or had the rest of the time been occupied with staring at the spinning plate with its stupid red dot?

Jenna kept hoping to run into Emily sometime during the day so that she could compare their individual experiences with the student teacher. When school got out for the day, she hurried to the main exit and positioned herself there to wait for Emily to come out.

When she saw Amanda-Tracey emerge, she looked away, expecting that the other girl would do the same. But instead Amanda stopped and spoke.

"What did that student teacher do? Did you get hypnotized?"

"Yeah."

"What was it like?"

Jenna shrugged. "No big deal. She didn't make me quack like a duck or anything like that." She paused. She really wanted to tell *someone* what had happened. "Actually, it was kind of silly. All she wanted me to do was read another teacher's mind to find out if he wanted to date her."

"You're kidding! That's all?"

Jenna nodded. "I'll bet when she hypnotized Emily that she asked her if they have a future together."

Amanda laughed. "And she probably told Charles to push him in her direction."

Jenna started to laugh, too, and then she remembered whom she was talking to. She cocked her head to one side and pretended to be noticing something for the first time that day.

"You look different."

Amanda nodded. "Yeah, I got a haircut. And I bought some clothes and makeup."

Jenna sniffed. "Perfume, too. Must be nice having all that money to spend on stuff like that."

"You think Tracey's parents ever give her money?" Amanda countered. "They barely know she's alive."

Now Jenna was interested. "So what did you do—take the money while you were invisible?"

"*No*. I earned it. Baby-sitting for the clones. And these aren't exactly designer clothes. I got them at Target."

"Oh."

Amanda shifted her book bag to her other arm. "I have to go."

"Wait, I have to ask you something. No, I mean, I have to *tell* you something."

"What?" Amanda asked.

"Don't ever feel sorry for me."

"I don't," Amanda replied.

"You did on Friday, at my place. I read it."

"Well, you read wrong. I never feel sorry for anyone." With that, Amanda sauntered off.

Jenna stared after her. Did Amanda mean that? She tried to read her thoughts now, but the gift didn't kick in. So maybe it *was* Tracey whom she'd made a connection with.

But that didn't feel right either. If Jenna were in Tracey's situation, the only person she'd feel sorry for would be herself.

Chapter Thirteen

RRIVING AT TRACEY'S home, Amanda felt like she could have been in the Meadowbrook cafeteria. Chaos reigned. In the living room, one of the seven girls was lying on the rug, kicking and yelling. Another one was screaming. In the kitchen, one girl spilled her milk and started crying, while another snatched a cookie from her sibling's plate, and they started fighting. The mother's helper was nowhere in sight, and Tracey's mother looked to be on the verge of hysteria.

"Stop it! All of you, stop it! Go upstairs—it's time for your nap." None of the septuplets paid any attention to her, just as Tracey's mother didn't pay any attention to the fact that "Tracey" had just walked in.

Amanda moved into Mrs. Devon's line of vision and spoke loudly. "What's going on?"

"Lizzie left us!" the woman wailed. "I've called every agency in town, and there's no one available! What am I going to do?"

Amanda surveyed the pandemonium. Having spent a lot of time with the septuplets over the weekend, she had a sense of each personality. She focused on the one who was the bossiest of the group, and at the top of her lungs, she screamed, "Mandie!"

The septuplet who was taking cookies by force from the others actually looked in her direction.

"Help me," Amanda ordered her. "We have to get everyone upstairs. It's story time."

Mandie turned to the sweet one, Randie. "C'mon, we're going upstairs."

Randie was in the process of twisting Brandie's hair into sloppy braids, so those two started out together. One by one, the others followed, until there was only one crying child left in the kitchen. Amanda grabbed Tandie's hand and half walked, half dragged her out of the kitchen and up the stairs. Mrs. Devon brought up the end of the line.

Once they were all gathered in the girls' huge bedroom, Amanda asked, "Whose turn is it to pick the story?"

"Me! Me!" Vandie cried out. She was the whiny one. Amanda shook her head.

"Let me think . . . Friday night was Brandie, Saturday afternoon it was Kandie's turn, Mandie chose the story on Saturday night . . ."

"I picked the story yesterday," Randie declared.

"It's my turn! It's my turn!" Vandie shrieked.

"No, I told you yesterday—we're going in alphabetical order. Sandie picks the story today. You come last."

"That's not fair!" Vandie whined.

"Tough," Amanda said. "Life isn't fair. Sandie, go and choose a story."

As Sandie raced over to the bookcase, Amanda realized that Mrs. Devon was looking at her oddly.

"Did you cut your hair?"

"Yes," Amanda said shortly. "I had my hair cut on Saturday with the money you paid me for Friday night."

"Saturday? I didn't notice it."

"No," Amanda said. "You never do. Maybe you should take a look at me once in a while."

"Here's my story, Tracey," Sandie announced. The girls gathered in a semicircle, as Amanda had taught them over the weekend, and Amanda took her place in the center, facing them.

As she started reading, from the corner of her eye Amanda could see Mrs. Devon standing there, still looking a little dazed, as if she'd stumbled into a strange new world. As Amanda read, the septuplets were quiet, and by the time she'd finished the story, they were yawning. With the help of Tracey's mother, she got them into bed for their naps.

As they left the room together, Mrs. Devon continued

to look at Amanda as though she'd never seen her before in her life. When the doorbell rang, she seemed relieved to have something else to do and hurried to open the door. Amanda was surprised to see Jenna there.

"Um, is Aman—I mean, Tracey home?"

"I'm here," Amanda said. She joined Mrs. Devon at the door. "Come on in."

Tracey's mother seemed even more surprised than Amanda. "Tracey, who is this?"

"A friend of mine, Jenna Kelley," Amanda replied. "Come upstairs to my room, Jenna."

As they headed to the stairs, she caught another glimpse of Mrs. Devon's bewildered expression. Amanda wasn't surprised—Tracey probably hadn't had a visitor since her eighth birthday.

"What are you doing here?" Amanda asked as soon as they were inside Tracey's bedroom with the door closed. This was when she noticed that the other girl was carrying a bag.

Jenna wouldn't meet her eyes. She looked past Amanda as she spoke. "I, uh, I need a place to stay. For a couple of nights. Can I stay here?"

There were twin beds in Tracey's room. "Yeah, I suppose so. Why do you need a place to stay?"

Jenna shifted her gaze to the other side of the room. "It's

my mother . . . She's got a bunch of friends there. It looks like she's about to have another one of her parties. Which means I won't get any sleep tonight."

"Oh." Amanda looked at her curiously. "Has this ever happened before?"

Jenna nodded. "Just last week, and the noise kept me up all night. Sometimes I just go over to the train station and hang out with Slug and those guys. But this time—I don't know, I just don't feel like it."

"They're probably in jail anyway for trying to shoplift from Target," Amanda said matter-of-factly. "You know what, Jenna? I don't think you even like those people. And I'll bet you've never stolen anything in your life."

Jenna faced her indignantly. "What makes you think that?"

"Because I don't think you're as bad as you pretend you are. And if you were stealing, you'd probably have more food in your house."

Jenna's face went white. "Don't you feel sorry for me. Don't you *dare* feel sorry for me."

"Don't worry—I don't and I won't," Amanda said with feeling. "I don't want your life any more than I want Tracey's."

Jenna was taken aback. "Don't tell me you're thinking about snatching *my* body!"

Amanda got up and began pacing the room. "I don't make those decisions." Her need to confide, to talk to someone, was irresistible. And at least she didn't care what Jenna thought about her. "It just happens when I feel really sorry for someone. That's how I got inside Tracey's body."

"Yeah, I read that in your mind, and I still can't believe it," Jenna said. "You feel sorry for people?" Her brow furrowed. "You're still really Amanda Beeson, the meanest girl at school, right?"

"That's *why* I'm the meanest girl!" Amanda cried out. "I can't let myself feel sorry for people because I could end up being them! Do you think I *want* to be Tracey Devon? Or you?"

Jenna's mouth was still open. But the only word that came out was "Wow!"

"Exactly," Amanda said. "See? I'm not the perfect princess you think I am."

"I never thought you were perfect," Jenna muttered.

"And you're not the gangster I thought you were," Amanda added.

"I really was in reform school," Jenna argued.

"Why were you sent there?"

Jenna looked away again. "I was hanging out with some creeps, and they were dealing drugs. The cops raided the house where we were staying, and someone planted stuff

147

in my pocket."

Amanda nodded smugly. "I knew I was right about you. You're a big fake."

"So are you," Jenna pointed out.

Amanda shrugged, and there was a long silence. Finally, Jenna spoke. "Remember when I was telling you about Serena and the hypnotism? How she wanted me to find out if this guy was into her? Well . . . I don't think she was really interested in him. There's something else going on. I couldn't read her mind, but I got the feeling she has secrets."

Amanda nodded. "Yeah, I think she's kind of weird, too."

Jenna gazed at her quizzically. "You know what? We kind of think alike."

"Yeah, maybe," Amanda said. "But that doesn't mean we're going to be friends," she added hastily.

"Absolutely not," Jenna assured her.

"Good." Amanda stopped pacing. "Let's go to the kitchen and find something to eat. And I'll tell Tracey's mother you're staying for a while."

"What if she says no?" Jenna asked.

Amanda grinned. "She's going to have to get used to a different kind of daughter. The kind that always gets her own way."

Chapter Fourteen

THERE WERE NO ABSENTEES in the gifted class the next day, so Serena had a full group to choose from.

"Let's see," Madame said to her. "You've seen Charles, Emily, Ken, and Jenna, so there's Tracey, Martin, Sarah, and Carter to choose from."

Not me, Amanda thought. Somehow she'd have to avoid being with Serena. Who knew what she might reveal under hypnosis?

Madame wasn't giving Serena the choice. "I'd like you to spend some time with Carter, Ms. Hancock."

The student teacher had given up asking her to call her Serena. "Why him?"

Amanda was interested, too. Carter was the one student she didn't know anything about. He never spoke, and she had no idea what his special gift might be.

"We think that Carter has amnesia," Madame explained. "He was discovered a month ago, wandering the streets, by one of our teachers. We've tested him, and he seems very intelligent, but he doesn't speak or communicate in any way. We don't know anything about him."

"Why is he in the gifted class?" Serena wanted to know.

"We thought Carter might profit from being around other special young people," Madame said.

Serena didn't look terribly intrigued, but she had a question. "If he doesn't communicate, how do you know his name?"

"We don't," Madame said. "We named him after the place where he was found—Carter Street, on the west side. I think he might really benefit from hypnosis."

"Oh," Serena said, but she seemed to have lost interest and continued to gaze around the room. "Actually, I'd like to see Emily."

Madame's eyes narrowed. "But you've already worked with Emily," she protested.

"There's more work to be done," Serena insisted.

"But—"

"I do have Principal Jackson's permission," Serena reminded her.

"All right," Madame said, but there was no enthusiasm in her tone. "Emily?"

Emily obediently left the room with Serena. Madame's eyes followed them, and distrust was written all over her face. Amanda turned to look at Jenna. She didn't have to be a mind reader to know that Jenna was wondering about this, too.

Finally, Madame turned and addressed the rest of the class.

"In the past we've talked about the body-and-mind connection. Today we're going to draw on some yoga exercises, which can be helpful in learning how to control your body."

Amanda was pleased. She hoped that by concentrating on her body she wouldn't have to think about what was going on inside her head. She joined the class in pushing the desks and chairs away to clear space on the floor for the yoga exercises. Madame produced some mats and spread them out.

But yoga wasn't like doing the kind of exercises they did in gym class. Holding positions gave Amanda plenty of unwanted time to think.

My mother is really nice, she thought. And I'm not very nice to her. What's the matter with me? If I ever get back inside myself, I promise I'll be better.

That was all very well, but she'd have to be herself again before she could make good on her promise. And she had no idea when that would happen—if ever.

Where are you, Tracey? she thought. Why won't you come

*back and reclaim your body? I'm making things better for you.
You look a lot better. I've made your parents listen to you.
If you keep doing what I'm doing, you won't be a great big nothing
anymore.*

She didn't really expect any response, so she wasn't
surprised when she didn't get one. What was the matter
with the stupid girl? No, maybe stupid wasn't the right
word. Sad—that was Tracey.

Tracey, stop feeling sad. Get—get angry!

Still no response. Amanda gave up and concentrated on
her body. And she had to admit, when class was over, she
was more relaxed than she'd felt in ages.

Maybe it showed, because Madame kept looking at
her oddly. And when the bell rang, she called out, "Tracey,
could I see you for a minute?"

Amanda went to the teacher's desk, but Madame said
nothing until all the other students had left the room.

Then she gazed at Amanda with an intensity that made
Amanda uncomfortable.

"Tracey . . ."

"Yes, Madame?"

The woman shook her head. "No, you're not Tracey."

Amanda swallowed, hard. "I'm not?"

Madame smiled. "You know you're not."

Amanda bit her lip. Should she put up an argument?

Something about the confidence in Madame's expression told her there was no point. "Why—why do you think I'm not Tracey?"

"The way you walk, the way you talk, the way you look . . . I've had my suspicions for a couple days. Can you tell me if Tracey is all right?"

"I don't know," Amanda said honestly.

"Can you tell me who you really are?"

Amanda gulped. "Do I have to?"

"I can't force you," Madame said.

"Can I go now?"

Madame nodded. But as Amanda started out of the room, the teacher touched her shoulder, and she looked back.

"Whoever you are . . . be good to Tracey, okay? There's more to Tracey than meets the eye."

Amanda had a feeling that she wasn't just talking about Tracey's ability to vanish.

"I'm trying," Amanda said.

When the school day was over, Jenna was waiting for her at the school exit. "What did Madame want?"

"She knows I'm not Tracey," Amanda said glumly.

"Well, you can't blame her. You're not exactly acting like Tracey. Does she know who you really are?"

Amanda glared at her. "No, and you better not tell her."

"My lips are sealed," Jenna said. "Can you do me a favor?"

"What?"

Jenna looked uncomfortable. "This is kind of embarrassing, but . . . when I threw my stuff in my bag yesterday, I forgot something. Something kind of important."

"So you want to go home to get it?"

Jenna made a face. "The thing is . . . I don't want to go into the apartment if my mother and her friends are still hanging out. Sometimes these parties go on for days. If my mother sees me, she might start crying, and I'll feel awful."

"You want me to get it for you?"

"Would you?" Jenna asked eagerly.

Amanda shrugged. She didn't have anywhere else she had to be.

When they arrived at the door of Jenna's apartment, they could hear music and voices inside. Amanda hesitated. "What am I going to tell your mother?"

"Just say you're picking up something for me."

"But she doesn't know who I am. And she'll want to know why you can't get it yourself. What am I supposed to say?"

Jenna was silent. After a moment, she said, "Maybe you

could be invisible."

Amanda rolled her eyes. "Jenna, you know Tracey can't control that."

"But you're not Tracey," Jenna countered.

"So what?"

"You're so much stronger than she is. I'll bet if you really wanted to be invisible, you could make it happen."

Amanda didn't buy it. "Disappearing is Tracey's gift, not mine."

"But you're controlling Tracey's body," Jenna said. "Maybe you can control her gift."

Amanda still had doubts. "What is it I'm supposed to pick up for you anyway?"

Jenna gave her an abashed grin. "This is the embarrassing part. It's a teddy bear."

Amanda stared at her in disbelief. Then she burst out laughing. "See? I knew you weren't so tough!"

Then Jenna was laughing, too. "Yeah, okay, I know it's goofy, but I've always slept with him. Don't tell anyone, okay? It would be very bad for my reputation."

"No kidding," Amanda chortled. "The juvenile delinquent sleeps with her knife, her gun, and her teddy bear."

They were both giggling so hard now that they couldn't stop. And they must have been pretty loud, because suddenly a voice could be heard from inside the apartment. "Is someone out there?"

Then they heard footsteps approaching the door.

Jenna froze. "It's my mother."

"Hide," Amanda hissed.

Jenna ran into the stairwell. Amanda closed her eyes and concentrated as hard as she could. *Help me, Tracey—help me. Help me disappear.* She tried to imagine herself fading away.

She heard the door open, and she knew someone was standing there, facing her. Reluctantly, slowly, she opened her eyes.

Jenna's mother looked puzzled. She looked both ways down the hallway, and then she shrugged.

I did it! Amanda thought gleefully. She edged past Jenna's mother into the apartment, trying to avoid bumping into people. She had no idea how long she could hang on to this invisibility, so she moved fast, tearing into Jenna's bedroom. The teddy bear was on the bed.

Back out in the hallway, she ran into the stairwell. Jenna didn't look in her direction, so she knew she must still be invisible. She closed her eyes. I want to come back, *I want to come back. Tracey, let's be real.*

"You did it!"

Amanda opened her eyes to see Jenna gaping at her in admiration. She thrust the teddy bear into Jenna's arms.

"Let's get out of here."

Once they were out of Brookside Towers, Amanda turned to Jenna. "You're going to have to do something about this, you know."

"About what?"

"Your mother, how you're living—all that."

"You can't tell anyone, Amanda. This is even more important than the teddy bear. Do you know what would happen to me if people found out about my mother?"

Amanda could guess. "They'd take you away from her and put you in some kind of foster care."

Jenna nodded.

"There must be someone who can help you," Amanda said. "What about Madame? I get the feeling she really cares about us—I mean, about you guys." She couldn't believe she'd said "us," as if she was actually one of them.

Jenna shook her head. "I can't take the chance. She might feel like she has to tell the authorities." She shook her head ruefully. "Isn't this weird? You, Amanda Beeson—you're the only one who knows about my life. And I actually trust you."

"Yeah, it's pretty weird all right," Amanda replied. "You're the only one who knows my secrets, too. And I've got a favor to ask you. Could you please never try to read my mind without asking me first?"

"Okay," Jenna said.

"Thanks."

After a moment, Jenna said, "Now, you tell me something. Are we friends?"

"I wouldn't go that far," Amanda said. "But . . . we're not enemies."

Jenna nodded. "Yeah, I know what you mean."

Amanda was pleased that Jenna understood.

She really couldn't picture herself-as-herself hanging out with Jenna Kelley.

But on the other hand, she might be Tracey Devon for a long, long time. And considering Tracey's general unpopularity, she'd need all the friends she could get.

CHAPTER FIFTEEN

I T SEEMED TO JENNA that Amanda had found herself in a pretty nice place in the Devon household. She corrected herself—Amanda had made herself a nice place. From what Jenna had learned, life hadn't been like this for poor Tracey. According to Amanda, Tracey had been ignored in this family, virtually invisible even when she was visible.

Looking around now, Jenna found it difficult to believe that this had ever been the case. At the big, round breakfast table, the septuplets argued about who would get to sit on either side of their big sister. Mrs. Devon hovered over her.

"Tracey, you absolutely must have some more French toast. You need to eat; you're way too thin. Do you have your lunch money? Jenna, dear, please make sure Tracey eats her lunch at school."

"Yes, Mrs. Devon," Jenna said. Boy, was Tracey in for a shock when she got back inside her own body! she thought. Amanda had made Tracey's presence known.

She mentioned this to Amanda as they set off for the bus stop.

"It wasn't that hard," Amanda told her. "Tracey must be a complete wimp to put up with her parents behaving like that. She needs to stand up for herself and make demands. I just hope she can keep this up when she comes back and she doesn't fade away again."

"You won't let her do that," Jenna assured her.

Amanda frowned. "What's that supposed to mean? Once we're back inside our own bodies, I guarantee you I won't be involved with Tracey Devon."

"You don't feel like you're kind of connected now?"

"No!"

Her violent response almost made Jenna jump. "Jeez, I'm not saying you guys have to be best friends or anything like that, but . . ."

The bus was coming. "Watch this," Amanda said. "This bus driver never noticed her before. Sometimes he closed the door in her face." This time, when the doors opened, Amanda was the first to climb on, and the driver actually said "good morning" to her.

They sat down. "Look," Amanda said, "I'm doing what I can to make Tracey's life better. And if I say so myself, she's less of a nerd than she was before I got my hands on her. But when this business is over, don't think I'm ever going to be hanging out with Tracey Devon. We live in completely different worlds. Could you even imagine Tracey with the real me and my friends?"

"Wow, you really *are* a snob," Jenna commented.

Amanda shrugged. "Like I care what you think of me."

"I don't get it," Jenna said. "Sometimes I feel like you're really an okay person, and then you turn around and act like this."

"I'm practicing so I'll be ready when I'm myself again," Amanda informed her.

Jenna sighed and sank back into her seat. Popular girls had always been a mystery to her, and getting to know Amanda hadn't helped her understand them any better. And even though she'd promised Amanda that she wouldn't read her mind without asking first, she couldn't resist. She closed her eyes and concentrated.

I hope she finds a new mother's helper this week. I want her to take me shopping on Saturday. I don't really mind baby-sitting the kids. Sandie and Mandie are funny, and I feel especially close to Randie. I can't hate them—it's not their fault I don't get enough attention. It's my parents' fault, and my own fault, too.

Jenna was puzzled. "She" was obviously Mrs. Devon. But who was "I"? Then she gasped.

"What?" Amanda asked.

"Look, don't get angry, but I just read some thoughts."

Amanda was clearly annoyed. "Hey, you promised—"

"Wait," Jenna interrupted. "I don't think they were your thoughts. I think I was hearing Tracey!"

Amanda's eyes widened. "Really? What was she thinking? Is she getting ready to come back out?"

"It was something about how she wants her mother to take her shopping on Saturday. And some stuff about the little sisters, and how she really likes Randie."

Amanda's face fell. "Oh."

"I thought you'd be pleased! If I can read Tracey's thoughts, she's got to be closer to the surface, right?"

"They weren't Tracey's thoughts," Amanda told her glumly. "They were mine."

Jenna drew in her breath sharply. "Ohmigod! Do you know what this could mean? You and Tracey . . . maybe you're merging. You know, becoming one person together. Tracey-Amanda Devon-Beeson. Wow! What a name!"

"Shut up!" Amanda hissed furiously. "Just shut your stupid mouth."

Jenna wasn't offended by Amanda's sharp tongue. She thought she was beginning to understand now. Amanda was scared.

When they arrived at school, the two girls parted, but Jenna didn't stop thinking about Amanda. In a way, she almost hoped her suspicions would turn out to be true—that Tracey was absorbing Amanda, or vice versa. Because she had to admit, she kind of liked Amanda. She envied her confidence and she admired the way Amanda was turning Tracey's life around.

And Amanda had ignited a tiny little hope in Jenna—that in the Amanda-style Tracey she might have found a friend who could help her improve her own life.

Amanda's mood seemed to have improved somewhat when they met again in the gifted class.

"I think I'm going to volunteer to be Serena's subject today," she confided in Jenna.

"You're kidding! I told you, she doesn't give a hoot about us—she just wants to use us."

"I know," Amanda said. "She's definitely creepy. But I'm wondering if maybe hypnosis could be the answer. Like, if she went deep enough inside my unconscious, she'd have to find Tracey, right?"

"I don't know," Jenna said. "I guess it's worth a try." But she had serious doubts that the student teacher would be able to do anything meaningful. Ken came in and took the seat next to her. Jenna turned to him.

"What happened when you had your meeting with Serena?" she asked.

Amanda turned to listen, too.

He grinned. "It was total bull. She was trying to get me to contact her great-grandmother to find out where she hid her jewelry before she died."

Jenna gave Amanda a triumphant look. "See? She's only looking out for herself. She's not going to help you."

"Help you with what?" Ken asked Amanda.

"Nothing—nothing at all. Forget it and mind your own business," Amanda snapped while shooting a fierce look at Jenna. Jenna was more interested in watching Ken's reaction to Amanda's response. He was obviously startled, and Jenna couldn't blame him. That outburst was not a typical Tracey reaction.

As it turned out, Amanda didn't have the opportunity to volunteer anyway. The student teacher didn't come to class that day.

"Where's Serena?" Jenna asked Madame.

"I believe she called in sick," Madame said. She actually seemed a little concerned, which Jenna thought was odd. She tried to figure out what Madame was really thinking, but as usual, she couldn't get inside her head.

"Is she seriously sick?" Jenna asked.

"No, just a cold. At least, that's what Principal Jackson told me." The bell rang, and now Madame looked even more worried. "Where is Emily?"

Nobody knew. Madame frowned.

"She's probably dawdling in the restroom," Amanda said. "You know how she daydreams. Do you want me to go get her?"

"No, that's all right," Madame said. "I'm sure she'll be along in a minute. Now, I would like us to spend our time today sharing some personal experiences. Usually we talk about how we've tried to suppress our gifts. I know this isn't always possible, and there may be times when it's appropriate to use them. So this time, let's talk about the positive ways in which you've used your gifts this week. Who'd like to go first?"

As usual, no hands shot up. Madame sighed.

"All right, I'll decide who goes first. Martin?"

Martin looked frightened. "I didn't do anything!"

"I don't intend to punish you, Martin. I just want to know if you did anything with your gift this week that you feel good about."

Martin scrunched his little rat face as if he was thinking very hard. "Oh, yeah . . . I was in the supermarket with my mother on Monday. And I saw this woman with a little kid—I guess he was about five—and he knocked something off a shelf. And his mother slapped him!"

"Oh dear," Madame murmured. "I don't approve of punishing children physically either. But what could

165

you do about this, Martin? Did you say something to the woman?"

"Nah. I kicked her."

"Martin!"

"Well, the little kid was too small to kick her himself. So I got even for him."

Madame shook her head. "Martin, how can you think that was a positive action?"

"Because I did it for the kid, not for myself! The woman wasn't hurt too badly—she just slid all the way down the aisle and looked really embarrassed. You should've seen the kid's face. He was really happy, so I felt good about myself."

"How did you get away with it?" Charles wanted to know.

Martin beamed. "I moved really fast, when no one was looking. And who's going to think someone like me could kick a person that far?"

Madame shook her head. "I'm sorry, Martin, but I don't think this is a very good example of a positive action. Who can offer a better example?"

Sarah raised her hand, and Madame nodded in her direction.

"I saw a woman about to cross a street. Then a car came from around the corner, going way too fast, and the driver was talking on his cell phone and not paying attention. He would have hit her if I hadn't made him step on the brakes." She looked at the teacher pleadingly. "I know I'm not supposed to interfere, Madame, but I couldn't let that poor woman get injured—maybe even killed!"

"That's cool," Ken said. "You saved her life."

Jenna saw it another way. "But maybe that woman was on her way to kill her husband. You would have saved *his* life if you'd let the car hit her."

Sarah sighed and sank back in her chair.

Madame looked at Jenna reprovingly. "Do you have an interesting story, Jenna?"

She didn't, but she managed to conjure up something. "Um, the other day I was at the mall, and I knew some kids were planning to go in a store and steal stuff. They had it all worked out—they even had a gadget to take the security thingy off the items they swiped. So I told a security guard, and they were arrested."

It was only a little white lie, and she thought it would please Madame. Amanda turned around and raised her eyebrows, but Jenna ignored her.

"But how did you get the security guard to believe you?" Ken asked.

"That's a good question, Ken," Madame said. "We've talked about this before, Jenna. You all have to be very careful about revealing your abilities. What did you actually say to the guard?"

Jenna thought rapidly. "I . . . I didn't say anything about mind reading. I told him I'd overheard the kids talking."

Did Madame buy her story? Before she could respond, the classroom door opened, and the principal stuck in his head.

"Excuse me, Madame. Sorry to disturb your class," he droned. "Just a message to relay. Emily Sanders is sick today."

"Really?" Madame glanced at a sheet on her desk. "She's not on the absentee list."

"Secretary's error," he said quickly and retreated, closing the door.

Madame stared after him. Then she shook her head as if to shake out some disturbing thoughts. "Let's see, where were we? Who would like to share next? Charles?"

Jenna was relieved that Madame seemed to have forgotten her story. When Amanda-Tracey turned around, Jenna thought she wanted to congratulate her on getting away with that rewritten tale. But the girl seemed to have something else on her mind.

"Emily's not sick. I saw her in the cafeteria earlier."

"Maybe she got sick just before class," Jenna suggested.

"Then why would the principal say it was a mistake that

she wasn't on the absentee list?"

"Tracey?"

She had to turn back to face the teacher.

"Did you have a positive experience with your gift this week?"

"No."

The teacher moved on to Ken, but Jenna had tuned out. Emily was still on her mind, and she couldn't shake her. It was as if she was stuck in Jenna's head, and Jenna didn't know why. So, Emily was sick—so what? It was probably nothing serious, just a cold or something. Maybe she had thrown up that day's disgusting lunch.

Then why was she still in her head?

Jenna jerked as the answer came to her in a flash. She was thinking about Emily because Emily was trying to contact *her.*

But why would Emily want to communicate with Jenna? The answer was obvious: because Emily knew that Jenna could read minds. And she wanted Jenna to read hers, right that minute. But *why*?

Jenna shut her eyes and concentrated. Emily . . . *I'm listening. I'm trying to hear you. What do you want? Emily?*

Nothing . . . and then Emily began to fade from her mind. Another face replaced her—Serena, the student teacher.

This was getting even weirder. Why would Serena want to communicate with Jenna? Was she having a problem getting Mr. Jones to ask her out? And what did this have to do with Emily? Because now Emily was coming back inside Jenna's head.

Emily was trying to tell her something about Serena. But it was all blurry and fuzzy, because, because . . . because Emily was under hypnosis.

The bell rang, and Jenna leaned forward. "I have to tell you something," she whispered.

"I don't understand," Amanda said when she heard what had been going on in Jenna's mind. "What does it mean?"

"Emily's trying to tell me something. I think she's in trouble. And it's something to do with Serena."

"But Emily's at home sick, isn't she?"

Jenna wasn't so sure. "Do you have a cell phone?"

Amanda shook her head. "That was the next thing I was going to tell Tracey's parents to give me."

"Well, *I* don't have one." Jenna regarded the passing stream of students and stopped. "You've got one, don't you?"

"I just told you—"

"I mean, the *real* you."

Amanda looked practically offended by the question. "Of course I do. Everyone who's anyone has a phone."

Ignoring the insult, Jenna dashed down the hall and cornered Other-Amanda, who was standing at her locker with a couple of her snotty friends. "I need to use your phone," Jenna declared.

"*What?*"

Jenna repeated her demand.

"Are you *serious?* Do you actually think that *I* would lend *you* my phone?" The two girls beside her looked horrified, as if Jenna were in the process of holding them up with a weapon. Which gave Jenna an idea.

She moved in closer to Other-Amanda. "Give me your phone," she hissed, "or I'll have my crew take care of you."

One of the girls clutched Other-Amanda's arm. "You'd better do it. She knows really bad people."

But this Amanda was just as tough as the Amanda that Jenna knew. "Forget it," she snapped.

Fortunately, her friends weren't quite so gutsy. "Here, you can use mine," one said, and she thrust it into Jenna's hand.

Jenna dialed the number for directory information. There were five Sanderses in the town, and Jenna told the operator to try the first one. There was no answer. No one answered the second one either, but on the second try she got someone.

"Hello?"

"Can I speak to Emily, please?"

"Emily's at school! Who is this?"

"Uh, wrong number." She tossed the phone to its owner and ran back to Amanda-Tracey.

"She's not at home, and I should have guessed that. She has to be nearby for me to be getting a message from her."

"You think she's somewhere in this building?"

The images of Emily and Serena were coming faster and faster, and they were dark. "Yeah. Let's start in the basement."

The bell rang to signal the beginning of the next class. The two girls were heading for the stairs when a hall monitor appeared from around the corner and blocked their way.

"Where are your hall passes?"

Jenna had no patience for this nonsense. "Get out of our way."

The boy grabbed her arm with his right hand and Amanda's arm with his left. "Okay, you're both going to the office."

Jenna struggled to free herself, but he was a big kid and was strong. She turned to Amanda. "*Do something!*"

Amanda got the message. In less than a second, the hall monitor was holding nothing in his left hand. "What the heck—?"

Jenna had hoped the shock of Amanda's disappearance would cause him to loosen his grip on her arm, too, but he only tightened it. She barely felt it, though, because now her head was actually hurting. Emily was trying very hard to reach her, and she knew something had to be terribly wrong.

But Jenna didn't have Martin's strength, or Charles's ability to move things, or Tracey's gift for becoming invisible. She wasn't Sarah—she couldn't force the guy to release her. All she had was the feeling that Emily needed help.

She'd have to count on Amanda to help her. Or Tracey. Or whoever was inside that invisible body.

Chapter Sixteen

A MANDA HAD NEVER BEEN in that part of the lower level of the school. As far as she knew, it was nothing but storage rooms and plumbing and stuff like that. And she vaguely recalled signs directing a media club to meet down there, but only nerds belonged to clubs like that, so she wasn't sure.

One thing was clear—it was dark. And invisibility didn't seem to give her any special viewing powers. She edged alongside a wall, trying to feel her way.

Luckily, she had no problem with her hearing. From down the hall, she picked up a faint whisper. As she moved closer, the voice became recognizable.

"You must do this, Emily. Keep your eyes on the red dot and listen to me. Think deeper . . . deeper."

It was the student teacher. And even though Amanda had never had a session with Serena, she could guess that she was hypnotizing Emily. But why down here?

"The numbers are there, Emily. You can see them. Tell

me the numbers."

What she said didn't make any sense, but something about the tone made Amanda shiver.

"Listen to me, Emily. Can you hear me? Answer me, Emily."

And then she heard Emily's voice, flat and expressionless. "I can hear you."

"Tell me the numbers!" There was more urgency in Serena's voice now. And it led Amanda right to the door.

They were in there—she knew that. What she didn't know was how she was going to get in there with them. In all her invisible experiences so far, doors had been open. Maybe she had the ability to pass through walls.

She pressed herself against the door. Her body didn't go through it, but it turned out that the door wasn't even completely closed. The next thing she knew, she had fallen on the floor of the room.

"Who's there?" Serena asked sharply.

Still on the floor, Amanda looked up. It was a storage room, with stacks of chairs. Her eyes had become accustomed to the dark by now, and she saw Emily sitting in one of them. Amanda knew she was still invisible, because Serena wasn't looking down at her but at the open door.

Serena moved to the door to shut it, and her foot

touched Amanda's head in the process. "Darn!" Serena muttered, and she kicked the obstruction out of her way.

In her last conscious thought, Amanda learned something else about her condition. When you're invisible, you still *hurt*.

"Amanda?"

The voice seemed to be coming from very far away. Amanda strained to hear it. At least her head had stopped hurting.

"Amanda!"

The voice was sharp now. Amanda forced her eyes open. She was looking at Mr. Jones, her history teacher.

"Amanda, I asked you a question. What were the three main causes of the American Civil War?"

She'd read that chapter—she knew she had—but her brain wouldn't cooperate.

"Taxation without representation?"

Mr. Jones looked at her in exasperation. "That was the Revolutionary War, Amanda. Someone else? Britney?"

Amanda didn't hear Britney's response. She was gradually absorbing her circumstances.

Tracey had Ms. Galvin for history. Mr. Jones . . . He was *her* history teacher. Amanda's history teacher. And that was what he'd just called her. *Amanda*.

She looked at her right hand. There it was—the tiny

sapphire birthstone ring that her parents had given her on her last birthday. And her Swatch watch was on her wrist. And the nails on her fingers weren't chewed down—they were rosy pink and manicured. She stared at them for what seemed like a long time.

"Amanda?" Mr. Jones was speaking to her again.

"Yes?" she asked faintly, looking up at him.

Now he looked more concerned than annoyed. "Are you feeling all right?"

"Yes . . ." She was remembering. Emily sitting on a chair. Serena. Something about numbers. "No! I don't feel very well. I'd better go see the school nurse."

Mr. Jones tore a hall pass off the pad on his desk, and Amanda snatched it from him on her race out of the classroom. Behind her, she could hear the class buzzing. They probably thought she was about to throw up. For once, Amanda didn't care what anyone thought about her.

She ran up the stairs, flapping the slip of paper at a passing hall monitor. Then she tore down the hall and burst into the gifted classroom.

Madame was alone in the room, pacing. When she heard Amanda come in, she whirled around with an expectant look on her face. When she saw Amanda, she seemed disappointed. "Yes? Can I help you?"

"Emily's in trouble! You have to come with me!"

The teacher gasped. "Who are you?"

The words tumbled out. "I used to be Tracey. Tracey Devon. Emily's down in the basement with Serena, and—"

Madame didn't let her finish. She grabbed Amanda's arm. "Take me to her!"

Rapidly, Amanda led her down the two flights of stairs. When they reached the basement, Serena's voice could be heard.

"The numbers, Emily! The numbers! I'm in control of your mind—you have to respond. What are the numbers?"

Then they could hear Emily's voice, not as loud, but distinct. "Four . . . eighteen . . ."

"Yes, yes, keep going. I need all seven numbers."

"Twenty-four . . ."

By now, Madame had moved on ahead of Amanda, and she was the first to enter the storage room. Amanda was right behind her.

"Ms. Hancock! What are you doing?"

"Get out of here!" the student teacher yelled. "I'm working with a student!"

"Forty-six . . ." Emily murmured.

Madame strode forward and knocked the spinning disk out of Serena's hand. "Wake up, Emily. Wake up!"

"Stop it! Stop it!" Serena shrieked. "This is important! Keep going, Emily! Just three more numbers!"

But now Madame had her hands on Emily's shoulders and was shaking her. Emily opened her eyes and smiled vaguely.

"Hello, Madame."

"Emily, what's happening?"

"I'm predicting the winning lottery numbers. For next week."

Madame looked fiercely at Serena and stepped toward her. Serena glared right back. "Don't bother trying to report me. No one will believe you."

Amanda tried to block the doorway as Serena started walking out, but the student teacher pushed her aside. And Amanda didn't resist all that much. She didn't particularly want to know what might happen if she banged her head again.

It was when she stepped backward that she almost tripped on something. No, some*body*. Madame saw her, too.

"Tracey! Are you all right? What's going on?"

The thin, fair-haired girl struggled to her feet. "I—I'm not sure." She looked at Amanda, and her brow puckered. Then, a small smile appeared on her face.

"I know you . . ."

Amanda glared at her. "No, you don't." She turned to Madame, who was now propping up a dazed Emily with one arm while reaching for Tracey with the other. "I guess everything's okay here now, right?"

Without waiting for a response, she left the room, went back up to the main floor, and headed directly into a girls' restroom. It had been a long time since she'd fixed her hair and repaired her makeup.

Chapter Seventeen

L UNCH PERIOD WAS ALMOST over. From her prime seat at the best table, Amanda watched as students raced to the conveyor belt to dump their trays. She herself had no tray. *Someone* had not been watching her eating habits over the past week and had gained two pounds. Her mother had kindly prepared her a lunch of two hard-boiled eggs, carrot sticks, and an apple.

Britney spoke. "Ohmigod! Look at Terri Boyd."

Amanda looked. "What about her?"

"Her skirt's practically transparent. You can see her panties."

Amanda squinted. "Oh yeah, right."

Katie identified the next victim. "See Cara Winters? She's been telling everyone she got that sweater from a J. Crew catalog. But I saw the label when she took it off in gym, and it came from Target."

Amanda looked. "Actually, you'd be surprised," she

remarked. "They've got some pretty decent-looking clothes at Target."

Katie, Britney, Nina, Sophie, and Emma gaped at her in horror. "When were *you* in Target?" Sophie asked.

Amanda grimaced. She'd been making stupid goofs like this for a couple of days. She had to remember who she was.

"Um, my mother was buying dish towels there. And we happened to walk past some clothes."

They appeared to be satisfied with that explanation, though Amanda could still see skepticism in Britney's expression. The old Amanda Beeson might have been forced to walk past the clothing department at Target, but she wouldn't have *looked* as she passed.

She didn't want to think that she'd changed at all over the past week, and she *certainly* didn't want her friends to notice anything different about her. But it wasn't always easy. Like right now, as Tracey Devon carried her tray past their table. Amanda's eyes met Tracey's. They didn't speak, but there was definitely a silent communication.

"Why are you looking at *her*?" Katie demanded to know.

Amanda couldn't resist. "I was just wondering . . . do you think she looks different?" she ventured.

"Yeah, I noticed that, too," Nina remarked. "She's dressing a lot better. And I like her hair."

"But she's still a nerd," Britney reminded her. "Once a nerd, always a nerd. And I'm absolutely positive *her* clothes came from Target."

"Oh yes, absolutely," Nina agreed.

They were right about *that*. Amanda remembered choosing the printed top to wear with that skirt. She was actually rather proud of her work.

"Why are we even talking about her?" Katie asked. "She's nobody."

"That's not true," Amanda said. "She's somebody." Aware of how her friends were looking at her, she amended that. "Just not somebody we want to know."

She hadn't spoken to Tracey since that meeting in the basement storage room. She had to admit—she was curious. Where had Tracey been when Amanda had taken over her body? Had she been aware of what was going on? Was her relationship with her parents still improving? And what about the Devon Seven? Amanda particularly wanted to know about Randie. Maybe someday, when no one was around to see, she could corner Tracey and get the answers to some of her questions. And find out what Tracey remembered. And threaten her, or bribe her, or do whatever it took to make sure she never, ever told anyone what had happened.

Not that Amanda was really worried. Who would believe

it? Only one person other than herself knew the whole story—Jenna Kelley. And she knew Jenna would never tell. Because Jenna knew that Amanda had information that could send Jenna into foster care.

Or maybe she wouldn't tell because Jenna was actually a good person who wouldn't want to hurt Amanda . . . Amanda gritted her teeth. She hated when little thoughts like that popped inside her head. They were so *not* Amanda-style thoughts.

Britney was looking at her oddly. "You okay?"

"Fine," Amanda said briskly. Knowing what she now knew about how Britney talked about her behind her back, Amanda was especially careful not to give her any clues about how she'd changed.

And there was another stupid not-Amanda thought. *I haven't changed. I'm me again.* "I want to go to the restroom and check my hair before the bell rings," she announced.

Britney and Katie got up with their trays. "We'll meet you there," Katie announced.

Amanda thought the restroom was empty when she walked in, but then she heard a toilet flush, and Jenna Kelley came out of a stall.

She looked at Amanda, and Amanda looked at her. Amanda couldn't stop herself. "Are you still staying at Tracey's?"

"What's it to you?" Jenna snapped.

"Just wondering if that party's still going on at your place."

Jenna glowered at her. "Don't you dare feel sorry for me."

"Don't worry," Amanda said feelingly. "I won't."

Britney and Katie came in.

"How are things in vampire land, Jenna?" Britney asked, and Katie giggled. Jenna walked out. "Weirdo freak," Britney murmured. "Amanda, can I borrow your lip-gloss?"

Amanda had English for her next class. She'd just walked in when the teacher beckoned her up to his desk.

"I just received a message," he told her. "You're wanted in administration."

"Why?" Amanda asked, but the teacher didn't know. He handed her a hall pass, and she left. When she entered the reception area, the secretary told her to go directly into Mr. Jackson's office.

The principal wasn't alone.

"Hello, Amanda," Madame said.

Amanda froze.

The principal spoke. "You're being transferred out of Mr. Jones's class. Go with Madame."

"But—"

"Come along, Amanda," Madame said smoothly, and she placed a gentle hand on Amanda's arm. Feeling like she'd just stepped back into a nightmare, Amanda went along with her.

"It's not what you think," she told the teacher frantically. "You're making a mistake."

Madame smiled. "It'll be all right, Amanda. You'll see."

They walked along in silence. "Did you tell Mr. Jackson about Serena?" she asked Madame.

Madame looked at her intently. "It wouldn't make any difference, Amanda. She's disappeared."

"Well, at least she won't be bothering Emily anymore," Amanda said.

Madame smiled again, but this time there was sadness behind the smile. "Hopefully not. But there will always be another Serena."

"There's going to be another student teacher?"

Madame rolled her eyes. "No, I meant there will always be people who want something from my students. You'll have to be ready for that, Amanda. There's always going to be another threat. But I'm here to help you deal with them."

As far as Amanda was concerned, the real threat lay just beyond the door of room 209.

★ ★ ★

They were all there in the gifted classroom—the eight strange students. Charles was still slumped sullenly in his wheelchair. The amnesia boy, Carter, wore the same blank expression. Little Martin was there, and Sarah, and Ken, and so was Emily, still looking dreamy and vague. Tracey watched Amanda with interest, and Jenna had a little grin on her face. Knowing Jenna, Amanda figured it was a "nyah, nyah" smirk.

"Have a seat, Amanda," Madame said, pointing to the empty desk in front of Jenna and next to Ken. "Class, we have a new student. Amanda Beeson."

Ken looked at her in surprise. "What are *you* doing here? Are you one of us?"

No! Amanda wanted to scream. *I'm Amanda Beeson, the coolest girl at Meadowbrook, the Queen of Mean, the girl who has it all!*

But there was no point in protesting. The cold, hard truth was evident, and she responded to Ken with a short nod.

She was Amanda Beeson. Another weirdo freak.

Gifted

BETTER LATE THAN NEVER

CHAPTER ONE

J ENNA KELLEY STOOD AT her bedroom window and gazed outside without really seeing anything. Not that there was much to see—just another dull brick building, exactly like her own. Sometimes, if people left their curtains open, Jenna could see people moving around in their apartments, but they rarely did anything worth watching.

Without being able to see it, she knew there was another identical structure just beyond the one opposite. Together, the three buildings made up Brookside Towers, the l ow-income housing development where she'd moved with her mother two years before, when she was 11. It was a pretty dreary place, but it was home, and she wasn't thrilled with the prospect of leaving it. The gray sky and steady rain outside did nothing to improve her mood.

She turned away from the window and went to her chest of drawers. Taking up a stubby black pencil, she added another layer to the already thick line that circled her eyes and stepped back to admire the effect. Kohl-rimmed eyes, short spiked hair, black T-shirt, black jeans . . . No tattoos or piercings yet, but she had a stick-on fake diamond on her right nostril, and it looked real. She hoped the way she looked would startle—maybe even shock—whomever she might be meeting.

In the mirror, behind her own reflection, she could see the empty suitcase lying open on her bed. Ignoring it, she left the room.

The sound of her footsteps on the bare floor echoed in the practically empty apartment. The silence gave her the creeps. She'd spent time alone here before, of course, but she'd always known that her mother would show up before too long. This time it was different. Her mother would be staying in the hospital rehab center for two weeks. Just knowing this made Jenna feel even more alone.

She considered turning on the TV for some companionship but then remembered that all she'd hear would be static and the screen would be a blur. Her mother hadn't paid the cable bill for three months, and the service had been cut off a while ago.

Instead, she went into the kitchen and opened the refrigerator door, even though she knew there wouldn't be anything edible inside. She removed a half-empty bottle of soda. There was no fizz left in it, but it was better than nothing, and she sat down at the rickety kitchen table to drink it.

What was her mother doing right now? she wondered. Screaming at a nurse? Demanding a gin and tonic? Jenna wanted to be optimistic. Maybe her mother would make it this time, but she couldn't count on it. Her mom had tried to stop drinking before but had never made it beyond a day or two. That very morning, before she'd left, she'd drained what was left in a bottle and then announced that this was the last alcohol she'd ever drink.

Jenna had tried to read her mind, to get a more accurate picture of how serious and committed her mother was this time, but she couldn't get inside.

It was funny, when Jenna considered how easily she read minds. Young or old, male or female, smart or stupid— most people couldn't stop her from eavesdropping on their private thoughts. But there were some who were just not accessible. Like her mother.

She used to think her mother's mind was too cloudy and messed up to penetrate. Then she thought that maybe there was another reason, like a blood connection, that prevented her from reading the mind of a family member. Unfortunately, there were no other family members around, so she couldn't test that theory. She'd never known her father—according to her mother, he'd taken off before Jenna was even born. She had no brothers or sisters, and her mother had left her own family when she was young, so Jenna had never met any grandparents, aunts, uncles, or cousins.

One thing made her doubt that her inability to read her mother's mind was caused completely by the family connection. Just six months ago, when she'd been placed in the special so-called gifted class at Meadowbrook Middle School, she found that she couldn't read the mind of the teacher, a woman they called Madame. She'd tried and tried, but she was completely blocked from getting inside the teacher's head, and she'd finally given up. Maybe it was because Madame knew all their gifts so well that she was somehow able to protect herself from the special students. Gifts . . . It was a strange way to describe their unique abilities, Jenna thought. She certainly didn't feel gifted.

Having finished the flat soda, she got up and went back to her room. The suitcase on her bed reminded her that she still had a lot to do. She just didn't feel like doing it. Resolutely, she looked away and concentrated on the room that she would be bidding farewell to for at least the next two weeks.

She liked her room, and she'd spent a lot of time making it into a special place for herself—her own private, cozy cave, where she could close the door and shut out the sounds of her mother and her friends partying. The walls were a muddy gray color. She would have preferred them to be black, but beggars couldn't be choosers—the paint had been free. She'd found half-empty cans of black and white paint left on the ground behind a Dumpster, and mixing them together had given her enough to cover the walls. A dog-walking job for a neighbor had given her the resources to buy a black bedspread printed with white skulls as well as matching curtains. There were two vampire-movie posters—one showed the vampire attacking a woman, while the other was a close-up of the vampire himself with blood dripping from his mouth. And just after last Christmas, someone in her building had thrown away a perfectly good set of twinkling lights, with only a few broken bulbs. She'd arranged some garland around her door, and when she turned off the overhead light and turned on the twinkling ones, it was nicely spooky.

What kind of room would she be sleeping in tonight? A basement dungeon? Somewhere pink and white, with ruffled curtains and shelves holding a variety of Barbies? She couldn't decide which would be worse. Both images made her shudder.

Her sad fantasy was interrupted by a knock at the front door, and she groaned. For one fleeting moment, she considered not going to the door and pretending that no one was home. Eventually her visitor would go away.

Only, what was the point? She knew who was standing just outside the door, and she knew the woman wouldn't give up so easily. Even if she went away, she'd only come back, possibly with a police officer or some other official type. And they'd break down the door to get in if they had to. There was probably a law. People who were Jenna's age weren't allowed to live alone, not even for two weeks.

There was another series of knocks, more insistent this time. Reluctantly, Jenna headed to the door. She opened it to see a woman dressed in a tan suit, her fair hair pulled back neatly in a bun. The briefcase in her hand completed her professional look, and she offered Jenna a practiced smile.

"Hello, Jenna. Are you ready to go?"

"No," Jenna replied, knowing full well how rude she sounded and not caring at all. "I haven't even started packing."

The woman's expression didn't change, but now her smile looked a little strained. "Well, perhaps you'd better get going. You won't need much, you know. It's for only two weeks."

"Yeah, whatever," Jenna muttered. Two weeks in a house full of strangers. It might as well be forever. She left the social worker and went back to her bedroom. As she began tossing whatever caught her eye into the suitcase, her thoughts went back to the two temporary foster homes that she'd stayed in before.

She was eight when her mother broke her leg in a drunken fall. If Jenna had known what was going to happen, she might have left her to recover at home instead of calling an ambulance. Social services came for her while she waited in the emergency room. She was placed in a house owned by a woman who took in children for the money that the state paid her to keep them. The woman wasn't exactly cruel—she didn't whip her or anything like that—but she basically ignored Jenna and the two other little girls who were there. It really wasn't so bad compared with the second home she went to, when she was 11 and her mother was arrested for drunk driving.

She wasn't whipped there either. She was stuck in a family of do-gooders who were constantly asking her how she was feeling and encouraging her to express her true emotions. She supposed they were trying to be kind, but Jenna could read their pity, and she would have preferred to have been beaten.

Who knew what she would be stuck with this time? Glumly, she contemplated worst-case scenarios, like religious fanatics or vegetarians. Which would be worse— going to church twice a day or being deprived of Big Macs for two weeks? As she dragged her suitcase into the living room, she decided to take a quick scan of the social worker's mind, on the off chance that she might be thinking about the place where she was about to take her. Jenna wasn't hopeful—the poor woman was probably brooding over the crummy job she had, dragging miserable kids off to foster homes.

But she was in luck—Jenna read her destination loud and clear. And when she realized where she'd be spending the next two weeks, her mood improved considerably.

"Wait a second," she told the social worker. She ran back into her room and grabbed the old stuffed animal off her bed. She hadn't packed him because she was afraid that the people at the foster home would mock her for still sleeping with a teddy bear.

Or worse, there could be some little kids at the home who would put their grubby hands all over him. Now that she knew where she was going, she could stuff him in the outside pocket of the suitcase, because he'd be safe. And so would she.

Outside the building, as they got into the car, the woman looked at her suspiciously, and Jenna didn't have to read her mind to know why. She probably expected Jenna to be whining and complaining. Her sudden passive acceptance of her fate was making the social worker nervous. Maybe she thought Jenna planned to jump out of the car at the first red light and make an escape. As they approached a stop sign, Jenna couldn't resist edging toward the car door, just to see the look of alarm on the woman's face. But she stayed put until the social worker turned onto a familiar street and pulled into a driveway.

"You've been here before, haven't you?" the woman asked, but Jenna didn't bother to respond. She hopped out of the car and waved to the girl who was standing on the front steps of the house.

Tracey Devon ran toward her. Jenna took a step backward, but to her relief, Tracey stopped short and didn't envelop Jenna in a hug. Clearly, she knew Jenna well enough to realize she wasn't the huggy type.

"Surprise!" Tracey yelled. "No, I take that back; you're not surprised at all, are you? I'll bet you read that woman's mind."

"Of course I did. Hey, how did you pull this off?"

"I just informed my parents that you needed a place to stay and I wanted you to stay here. So they called social services and made the arrangements." She took Jenna's suitcase and headed back toward the house.

Amazing, Jenna thought as she followed her classmate. Just a month ago, Tracey wouldn't have dreamed of asking her parents to let her have a friend stay for two weeks. And even if she'd worked up the nerve, her parents wouldn't have heard her. Nobody listened to Tracey Devon back then. Most people didn't even see her. Because when Tracey *felt* invisible, she actually *became* invisible, fading away whenever her emotions took over. That was Tracey's "gift"—the ability to physically disappear. Even Madame, the teacher of their gifted class, was never sure if Tracey was there or not.

The Devon parents greeted Jenna warmly.

"It's so nice to have you back with us," Tracey's father said, and Tracey's mother gave her a little hug, which Jenna managed to bear without flinching. It was hard to believe that these two friendly, welcoming parents were the same people who had been the cause of Tracey's old misery. It hadn't been on purpose—they were really sorry now, and Jenna could see that they were trying to make up for it.

"It's great to be here," Jenna replied. "I mean, compared with where I could have ended up."

And then the seven other reasons for Tracey's frequent disappearances came bounding into the room.

"Jenna!"

"Hi, Jenna!"

"Jenna, can you read us a story?"

Jenna stepped back in alarm. The septuplets were covered with spots.

"Have you ever had the measles?" Tracey asked Jenna.

"I don't know," Jenna replied honestly. She didn't remember, and if she'd had the measles when she was very young, her mother had never told her. The chances were that her mother had been so out of it that she wouldn't have noticed if Jenna had been covered with spots, and Jenna would have recovered on her own.

"It's okay—they're not contagious anymore," Tracey assured her.

Jenna tried to acknowledge their enthusiastic greetings. "Hi, Sandie, Randie, Mandie . . ." She couldn't remember the rest of the names. What was the point? The girls looked alike, and there was no way she could match each with her own name. Even the rash from their measles seemed to be in exactly the same places.

It was the birth of the septuplets five years earlier that had taken Tracey's parents' attention away from their oldest daughter. It wasn't the kids' fault—not really—but Jenna couldn't blame Tracey for having feelings toward them that weren't entirely sisterly. It was only in the past month that Tracey had begun bonding with the little girls.

"Don't bother Jenna now," Mrs. Devon reprimanded them. "She's probably tired."

"And hungry," Tracey added. "Go on up to my room, Jenna, and I'll hunt down some munchies."

Jenna knew where Tracey's bedroom was because she'd

spent a few nights there before, less than a month ago, but she wasn't sure if Tracey actually remembered that. Because Tracey hadn't really been Tracey the last time Jenna was there. Their "gifted" classmate Amanda Beeson had been in complete possession of Tracey's body at the time.

Plunking herself down on one of the twin beds in Tracey's room, Jenna thought about Amanda's so-called gift. She was a body snatcher, which sounded a whole lot cooler than it really was. Unfortunately for Amanda, she couldn't just snap her fingers and become an astronaut or a rock star. She could take over someone's body only if she felt sorry for that person. If she felt an abundance of sympathy for an individual, she could find herself trapped inside the wretched person's body.

Tracey had certainly been deserving of pity back then, and not just because she was fading away. She was even more pitiful when she was visible. She was scrawny—so underdeveloped that she didn't even wear a bra. Her hair was limp and stringy, her babyish clothes didn't fit properly, and she had terrible posture. She was nervous and timid, and she always looked frightened. In the eyes of someone like Amanda Beeson, who was one of the most popular girls at Meadowbrook Middle School, Tracey Devon was seriously pathetic.

Jenna knew that Amanda had been miserable stuck

inside the body of a major nerd, and she doubted that Tracey had been happy about being possessed by Amanda. Strangely enough, though, it had all worked out for the best. Whether she had meant to or not, Amanda had actually helped the girl whose body she had snatched.

Tracey certainly wasn't pathetic anymore. The girl who came into the room bearing a bag of chips and a jar of guacamole bore little resemblance to the pre-Amanda Tracey. Her hair was shiny and had been cut and styled in a cute layered bob. Her eyes were bright, her shoulders were back, and her newly pierced ears held trendy gold hoops. She was still skinny, but now she took advantage of it, wearing super-slim jeans and a tight halter-top.

But the change in Tracey went far beyond her appearance. The girl who used to be too shy to ask anyone for the time of day sat down on the twin bed where Jenna had settled herself, dumped the treats between them, and faced Jenna squarely.

"I know you don't want to talk about it, so I'm not going to ask you how you feel about your mother being in rehab. And I've told my parents not to bring up the subject either."

"Good," Jenna said, relieved.

Tracey frowned. "That's not the response I was expecting, Jenna."

"Huh?"

"Say it," Tracey ordered her.

Jenna stared at her blankly.

"Remember the magic words? *Please* and . . ."

Jenna rolled her eyes. "Okay, okay. Thank you."

Tracey nodded with approval. "See? You *can* show appreciation." Then she smiled. "Look, Jenna, I know you're grateful. You just hate to admit it because you're afraid you'll seem like Little Orphan Annie or something."

She was right, and Jenna knew it. She had a lot of pride, and she couldn't bear the idea of anyone feeling sorry for her. And saying "thank you" seemed to be like admitting that she was needy.

This was how Tracey had really changed. All the old hurts had created in her an ability to understand other people, to know what was really going on with them. She couldn't read minds, like Jenna, but it was as if she could read *feelings*. It wasn't exactly what Madame would call a gift, but Jenna had to admit that it was pretty interesting, and a little scary, too. Tracey was getting to know her—in spite of herself—in a way that Jenna had never allowed anyone to know her before.

Tracey tore open the bag of chips. "What do you think of my room?"

Jenna looked around. She had a vague memory of

Tracey's bedroom being kind of childish and bland. Now it was decorated in bright primary colors—red curtains, red and blue plaid bedspreads, a gleaming white desk.

"Nice," she said.

"Thanks. I told my parents I wanted a completely new room, and I made them let me pick out everything myself."

"Wow!" Jenna said with admiration. "You've really got them wrapped around your little finger."

"Yeah, well, after all those years of neglect, they owed me," Tracey replied. "Hey, have you done the assignment for Monday yet?"

Her mouth stuffed with guacamole, Jenna could manage only to wrinkle her nose. That wasn't a response to the food—the guacamole was delicious—but to the reference to their homework. Madame had ordered her students to prepare a brief oral report describing when they had first become aware of their gifts.

She swallowed. "No. What about you?"

Tracey nodded. "It was easy for me. The Devon Seven were born and I was reduced to a nonentity."

"A *what*?"

"Something that doesn't exist."

That was another aspect of Tracey that was different. Once she'd started speaking up, she'd revealed something about herself that no one had ever expected—she was *smart.*

"It's not so simple for me," Jenna said. "I can't remember when I started reading minds. It seems as if I've always known what people are thinking."

"That reminds me—I've got a favor to ask." Tracey eyed her eagerly. "While you're staying here, could you *please* not read my mind?"

Jenna grinned. "Why? You got some big secret you're hiding from me?"

"No, it's just a question of privacy."

That was what Madame was always telling Jenna—that reading people's minds was like eavesdropping on private conversations or reading someone's diary.

"So do you promise you won't read my mind?"

"I don't know if I can *promise*," Jenna said. "Sometimes I can't help it. It just sort of happens. You can't control *your* gift, can you?"

Tracey sighed. "No. Ever since I got my body back from Amanda, it's harder and harder to disappear. I've been practicing, though, and I'm starting to be able to fade a little. Have you been practicing?"

"I don't need to practice. Like I said, it comes naturally."

"I mean, practice *not* mind reading. That's what Madame means about controlling our gifts—knowing when to use them and when not to."

Jenna shrugged. "Whatever. You could try to block me. I think that's what Madame does so that I can't read her thoughts. Or . . . Wait a minute—I've got a better idea. I can't read my own mother's mind, so maybe if I think of you as a sister, I won't be able to read yours either."

"Could you do that?" Tracey asked. "Think of me as a sister?"

Jenna shifted uncomfortably. "I don't know," she replied honestly. Not being a very family-oriented person, it was hard for her to imagine the kind of feelings that sisters might have for each other. On the other hand, if she had to have a sister, she supposed Tracey would be okay.

"Yeah, all right," she relented. "I'll be your sister."

The door to Tracey's bedroom burst open and seven little Devons ran in. "Can we play now?" "Will you read to us?" "Can I have some chips?"

They were all over the place. Tracey offered Jenna a halfhearted smile. "Not that I need another one."

Chapter Two

A MANDA BEESON STRUCK a pose in front of the dressing-room mirror. "What do you think?" Personally, she didn't really care whether or not Sophie or Britney or Nina approved of the dress she was trying on—*she* thought she looked hot. But you were supposed to ask your friends for their opinions, so she did.

"So cute!" Sophie exclaimed, and Britney nodded vigorously in agreement. But Nina wasn't quite so enthusiastic.

"I don't know . . . The dress is okay, but isn't it a little too tight around your hips?"

"That's how it's supposed to be," Amanda informed her. "Figure hugging." She punctuated this with a narrow-eyed glare.

In the olden days—like, a month ago—a look like that would have reduced Nina to a quivering mass of apology. But lately, Nina hadn't been quite so easy to push around. It was almost as if she was challenging Amanda's authority as

Queen Bee of the eighth grade at Meadowbrook Middle School. And this wasn't the first time.

Amanda noticed that Sophie and Britney were exchanging wary looks. She knew she needed to assert herself immediately and remind them who was in charge here. She performed a little twirl in front of the mirror and nodded in satisfaction.

"It's fabulous. It's perfect for me—I'm going to buy it," she stated firmly.

As she was making the purchase, she glanced over to where the girls were waiting for her by the door of the boutique. She couldn't hear what Nina was saying to the others, but Sophie's uneasy expression and Britney's quick glances in her direction worried her. As she handed over her mother's credit card, for the zillionth time she made a silent vow that the recent change in her life would not disrupt her social standing.

Leaving the boutique, the girls made their way through the mall and down an escalator to the food court, where eight different kinds of fast-food counters offered lunch.

"Let's get pizza," Nina declared.

Sophie and Britney looked at Amanda. Amanda took her time, letting her gaze move from the Chinese noodle place to the Burger King and beyond. "I'm going to the salad bar," she announced.

There was no reason why they couldn't each have whatever kind of food they wanted, since all the customers had to take their food away from the counters to the tables set up in the middle of the court. But it was traditional for the group to buy their lunch together as well as eat it together, and Amanda was gratified to see Sophie and Britney following her to the salad bar. A few seconds later, Nina joined them, too. Amanda mentally

racked up another point for herself.

But Nina hadn't given up. As soon as they sat down at a table with their salads, she asked the question that Amanda had been expecting—and dreading.

"How's your new class?" she inquired. "What's it called—'gifted'?"

Amanda chewed slowly on a carrot stick. Eventually, however, she had to swallow and reply.

"Fine." She knew that wouldn't be a sufficient answer for Nina, and she was right.

"Why do they call it 'gifted'?" Nina wanted to know. "I mean, no offense, Amanda, but you're not a genius."

"Actually, I don't have the slightest idea why people call it that," Amanda replied casually. "The students aren't *brilliant* or anything."

Nina persisted. "But you must be special in some way to get picked for the class. Like special ed."

Amanda stiffened. *Special ed* was the term used for classes attended by kids who weren't able to do the same work as their classmates. "No, it's nothing like that."

"But you're together as a group, so you must have something in common. Let's see . . . isn't Emily Sanders in that class?"

Britney gasped. "Emily Sanders, the space cadet? The Queen of Cloud Nine?"

Sophie giggled. "She's in my biology class, and she's so out of it. Every time the teacher calls on her, she practically jumps out of her seat. It's like she's on another planet."

Amanda almost smiled. If only they knew! When Emily looked as though she was daydreaming, she was actually having visions of the future.

Nina's eyes glittered. "So, what do you have in common with Emily Sanders, Amanda?"

"Nothing," Amanda replied sharply.

"Who else is in the class?" Nina continued. "Oh yeah, that nasty boy in the wheelchair—what's his name?"

Sophie supplied it. "Charles Temple. Is he as mean as he looks, Amanda?"

"How should I know? I've never even spoken to him." But all three of them were looking at her curiously now, so she had to come up with something to explain the group. "Look, as far as I can tell, we're just a bunch of students who were picked by chance—like out of a hat. I think they're doing a study or a survey, something like that."

"Who?" Nina asked.

"What?"

"Who's doing this survey?"

Amanda groaned. "I don't know! Mr. Jackson, maybe."

"The principal?"

"Or—or the board of education, or something like that. For crying out loud, who cares?" It was definitely time to change the subject. "Hey, did you see *American Idol* last night? I can't believe Joshua was voted off—he was my favorite."

Naturally, Nina picked up on this as another opportunity to disagree with Amanda. "He wasn't a very good singer."

"But he was so cute," Sophie said. "I just love blond-haired boys with dreadlocks."

Amanda breathed a silent sigh of relief as the TV show became the topic under discussion. She couldn't really blame her friends for being curious. After all, it didn't make sense. Amanda Beeson was cool. The gifted class was mysterious. Mysterious wasn't cool. Amanda Beeson was in the gifted class. Therefore, Amanda Beeson wasn't cool. Which just went to show how sometimes logic didn't make any sense. Amanda Beeson not cool? It was a completely unthinkable conclusion.

There was no way on earth that she was going to reveal the real reason for the gifted class—it was just too embarrassing. Very few people knew why the class existed, and the class members hoped to keep it that way. Who would want the whole world to know you're a freak?

Amanda herself still couldn't believe that *she'd* been classified as one. Okay, she'd always known she was a little different. She'd been having weird experiences since she was five years old, when she saw a shabby woman begging on a street corner. She'd felt so sad for the woman that somehow her mind took over the woman's body and she actually *felt* her suffering. It happened other times, too. Whenever she experienced a lot of sympathy for another person, she *became* that person. It was very annoying.

It wouldn't be so bad, being a body snatcher, if she could pick and choose the bodies she snatched. Unfortunately, she couldn't snap her fingers and become Miss Teen America. She had to feel pity first. And it wasn't as if she could feel sorry for someone like what's-her-name, who won the gold medal for figure skating in the last Olympics. Instead, Amanda became a girl who was hurt in an accident, a battered housewife, a boy who was picked on by bullies. Or Tracey Devon.

Yeah, it was all pretty strange, but she didn't believe she belonged in that class of weirdos. She hadn't body snatched since Tracey, and as long as she could keep herself from feeling sorry for anyone, she'd never have another experience like that again. If only she could convince Madame of that and get herself released from the World of Wackos . . .

Her thoughts were interrupted by Britney's soft shriek. "Ohmigod! Don't turn around—it's Ken Preston."

Naturally, Sophie ignored Britney's direction and turned. "He is *hot*," she remarked.

No one was going to argue with that—not even Nina. When a guy was tall and broad shouldered, when he had silky light-brown hair falling into deep blue eyes, a cute dimple, and a square jaw, he was highly desirable. He'd been a star of the Meadowbrook soccer team until he'd had some sort of accident a couple of months before, but he still looked like an athlete—and that was what counted.

Amanda watched him with interest. He hadn't noticed the girls, but if he continued walking in the same direction, he'd go straight past their table. Oh yes, Ken Preston was very hot and totally sought after by every girl at Meadowbrook Middle School. And Ken Preston was in the gifted class, too, along with Emily Sanders and Charles Temple and Amanda Beeson.

As he got closer, the girls automatically looked away from him and toward one another. When he was practically alongside them, Nina spoke loudly. "Anyone want my tomato?"

The voice drew his attention, but he didn't look at Nina. "Hey, Amanda."

"Hi, Ken," she replied.

He moved on, and she basked in the glow of her friends' admiration. "I think he likes you," Sophie said excitedly.

Nina rolled her eyes. "Because he said hello to her?"

"He didn't speak to *me,*" Britney said mournfully.

"He came to my pool party last spring, and he doesn't even remember my name," Sophie added.

"Well, I see him every day," Amanda explained. "He's in the gifted class with me."

She was gratified to see Nina's mouth drop open. "You're kidding!"

Amanda smiled. "I'll take your tomato."

It was while she was putting salt on the tomato that she noticed two other "gifted" classmates walking across the food court. This time, however, she wanted to dive under the table to avoid their seeing her. Greeting Tracey Devon and Jenna Kelley would *not* impress her friends.

Fortunately, the two girls turned in another direction, and Amanda could breathe a sigh of relief. Okay, maybe she was being snobby and shallow, but what choice did she have? Now, more than ever, she had an image to maintain.

Chapter Three

O N MONDAY AFTER lunch, Amanda hung out alone in the restroom, brushing her hair and applying layer after layer of lip-gloss until her lips were unbearably sticky. Then she used a tissue to wipe off the gunk before starting all over again. She was killing time, something she did every day at school after lunch. She would have preferred to hang out in the cafeteria, but all students were made to leave when the bell rang, to allow the kids who had the next lunch period to find seats. So she had to spend the eight minutes before the next class in the restroom.

It wasn't only because she was reluctant to go to her next class. She wanted to time her departure from the restroom so that she would enter room 209 just as the bell was ringing. She didn't want to be late—that would mean demerits and eventually staying after school for detention. But if she arrived before the bell, she'd be available for conversation with her classmates, and that was an intolerable thought.

In other classes, she enjoyed the prebell socializing that went on. But she had no desire to communicate with any of her gifted classmates. Actually, that wasn't strictly true—she wouldn't have minded talking to Ken Preston, but he always ducked in at the last minute, too. He was probably just as humiliated to be there as she was.

Today, her timing was slightly off. When she entered the classroom, she looked at the clock and noted with dismay that there was still maybe half a minute before the bell—just enough time for Tracey Devon to turn to her and try to start a conversation.

"I just thought you'd like to know—the girls are feeling a lot better now."

Amanda looked at her blankly. "Huh?"

"The Devon Seven. My sisters." Tracey grinned. "Maybe I should say *our* sisters. Remember, I told you last week that they had the measles."

"Oh yeah, right," Amanda said while thinking, *Please, bell, ring now.*

"They've got only a couple of spots each," Tracey went on.

"That's nice," Amanda mumbled, refusing to meet Tracey's eyes. Finally, the bell rang, and no one could talk.

Amanda would never admit it to Tracey—or anyone

else, for that matter—but she was actually sort of interested in the well-being of the septuplets. When she'd lived inside Tracey's body, she had almost enjoyed the time she spent with the cute little girls. But that was then and this was now, and as far as Amanda was concerned, all connections were severed when she got back to being her own self again.

Would Tracey never give up? she wondered. Just because Amanda had inhabited her body for a while, Tracey seemed to think that she and Amanda should have some sort of special bond. Ever since the girl had recovered her body, she'd been acting like they were friends—as if!

True, Tracey wasn't anywhere near as nerdy as she used to be before Amanda so kindly made her over. But she certainly wasn't in Amanda's league, and with her own status on the line, Amanda couldn't afford to be seen as friendly with Tracey Devon.

It was the same with Jenna Kelley. When she had been Tracey, Amanda had been forced to befriend Jenna. And okay, maybe she did find the rebellious girl a teeny-weeny bit interesting. But Jenna wasn't any higher on the popularity chain than Tracey—neither of them was even remotely cool—and Amanda was in no position to be charitable.

Madame had risen from her desk and was calling for

attention. The petite, dark-haired woman gazed over the class like a shepherd overseeing a flock—kindly but watchful.

"On Friday I asked you to try to recall the moment when you first became aware of your gift," she said. "Would anyone like to volunteer to go first?"

Why did she bother to ask that? Amanda wondered. That was one way in which this class was no different from any other class—nobody ever volunteered.

Madame sighed. "You will all have to report sooner or later."

But everyone preferred not starting, and Madame gave up. "Charles, you can go first. When did you first realize you had a gift?"

All eyes turned apprehensively to the boy in the wheelchair. When Charles was asked to do something he didn't want to do, he could get upset. And when Charles was upset, he could create a tornado in the classroom. Not only would he make a mess, but there was always the possibility that he would send a freshly sharpened pencil into someone's eye. It hadn't happened yet, but everyone knew it *could*.

But Madame had been working with Charles on controlling his temper, and it seemed to have had some effect. Charles didn't look happy, but at least the clock didn't drop off the wall, the light bulbs didn't explode, and he actually attempted to answer the question.

"I'm not exactly sure. I think I could always make things move. My mother says that when I was a baby and I was hungry, I could make the bottle come to me in my crib."

"But when's the first time you remember using your gift?" Madame asked.

Charles went into a long, rambling tale, something about ruining his older brother's baseball game by sending every ball he hit directly into the pitcher's mitt. Bored, Amanda wondered for the zillionth time why Madame made them talk so much about their stupid gifts. What was the point?

The teacher was always telling them that if they discussed their gifts, they would come to understand them, and if they understood them, they could learn to control them. Maybe some of the other kids needed to talk, but Amanda knew perfectly well how to control her "gift"—which she didn't consider a gift at all, but something more like a bad habit. All she had to do was avoid caring about anyone other than herself and she'd never run the risk of snatching anyone's body. Instead of feeling sorry for people, she made fun of them.

Once in a while, she'd be struck with a pang of guilt when she mocked a classmate. But whenever that happened, all she had to do was recall the awfulness of waking up as

Tracey Devon and the mean comments spilled out pretty easily.

Charles had finally finished his story, and Madame called on Sarah Miller next. Given Sarah's very special gift and the fact that she never demonstrated it, Amanda was actually curious to hear what she had to say. With her pretty heart-shaped face and short black curly hair, Sarah looked so sweet that it was hard to believe she had the most dangerous gift of all.

She was such a good student that she'd actually prepared notes for her report, and she consulted them now before she spoke.

"I was six years old, and my parents were fighting a lot. They weren't violent or anything like that—they just argued—but they were loud. One night they went on and on and on, and I kept thinking, *Stop, stop, stop* . . . And they did."

Madame raised her eyebrows. "Couldn't that have been a coincidence?"

Sarah looked sheepish. "Maybe . . . except just having them be quiet wasn't enough for me. When I realized what I could do, I made them hug each other. Then I sent my mother to the kitchen to make popcorn, and I made my father turn on the TV, and I had us all curl up together on the couch to watch *The Wizard of Oz*."

Charles spoke up. "Wow! You are so lucky. I can only make *things* move. You can make people do what you want them to do."

Amanda didn't think that Sarah looked as if she felt lucky. Madame must have been thinking the same thing, because she looked at Sarah with an expression that was unusually sympathetic.

"Were you happy about this?" Madame asked quietly.

"At first . . . and then I got scared. Because when I realized what I could do . . ." She shivered and looked pleadingly at the teacher. "Do I have to keep on talking about this?"

"No, that will be enough," Madame said. "For now. Emily, when did you first realize you could see the future?"

Emily didn't look like she particularly wanted to talk either. She took off her glasses, cleaned them with a cloth, and put them back on. Then she started twisting a lock of her long, straight brown hair as she mumbled something.

"Speak up, Emily," the teacher said.

The girl's voice was only slightly louder. "I talked about this in class before."

"Tell us again," Madame said. Her voice was kind but firm. Amanda couldn't believe she was going to force poor Emily to tell that dreary story again. Even *she* had to admit that it was pretty depressing. Did Madame really think this would make Emily feel better about her gift?

Emily did as she was told. "I was really little, only five. It was in the morning, and my father was just about to leave for work. I remember that he wore a suit and carried a briefcase. I had a vision that he was going to be hit by a car just in front of our house, and I didn't tell him. And he was struck by a speeding car and was killed."

Amanda could see the tears forming behind Emily's thick glasses. Despite herself, she felt sorry for the girl, and she became nervous. She had to do or say something right away or she might find herself inside that spacy girl's body.

"You shouldn't feel bad," she declared quickly. "I mean, it's not like it was your fault."

"I feel guilty that I didn't tell him about the vision," Emily said.

Amanda waved a hand in the air as if to brush that notion aside. "Get over it. Like you said yourself, it was the first time you had a vision. You couldn't have known you were seeing the future."

Emily whispered something.

"Speak up, Emily," Madame said again.

"What if . . . what if it wasn't the first time?"

Madame looked interested. "What do you mean?"

"I keep thinking . . . maybe I had visions before that. Like I remember one day, my mother said she was going

223

to bake a cake, and in my mind I saw a burned cake, and she forgot to take it out of the oven, and it did burn. And another time, I could see the people who would be living in the house next door even before it was sold . . ." Her voice was trembling now. "What if I had told my father what I could see in his future? I could have saved his life!"

Jenna spoke. "Emily, you were five years old! You didn't understand what was going on inside your head."

"You can't feel guilty about it," Tracey declared. "Even if you'd told your father that he was about to be hit by a car, what makes you think he would have believed you? Who listens to little kids making predictions?"

"They're right, Emily," Madame said. "You're not responsible for your father's death."

"I just wish I knew what *he* thinks," Emily said. Suddenly, she drew in her breath sharply, leaned forward, and tapped the shoulder of the boy sitting in front of her.

"Ken, you talk to dead people, don't you? Could you maybe try to find my father and ask him if he's mad at me? And tell him I'm sorry I didn't warn him?"

Ken's brow was furrowed as he turned around and faced her. "I don't talk to dead people, Emily. Dead people talk to me!"

"You don't talk back? I mean, haven't you ever had a conversation with one of them?"

"Are you nuts?" Ken exclaimed. "I don't want to encourage them—I want them to stop!"

Amanda listened to this exchange with interest. It was clear to her that Ken didn't like having a so-called gift any more than she did.

"But if you could just—"

"Emily!" Madame interrupted her. "This is inappropriate. As you well know, there are people out there who would want to exploit us if they knew about our gifts. *We* do not exploit one another. Ken, will you tell us about the first time a dead person spoke to you?"

Ken squirmed in his seat. "I really don't remember."

Charles stared at him in disbelief. "Oh, give me a break. You don't remember the first time you heard a dead person talking to you?"

Ken didn't look at him as he responded. "No. Um, I guess maybe they've been talking to me since I was born, so I never noticed."

Little Martin Cooper turned to Ken. "What does it feel like, hearing dead people? Is it like having ghosts inside your head?" His expression was fearful, as if he was afraid that the ghosts might suddenly pop out of Ken's head and start haunting *him*.

"It's not fun," Ken said shortly.

"Is a dead person talking to you right now, Ken?"

Tracey asked.

He flinched. "Jeez, you make it sound like I'm a crazy person, hearing voices. No. Maybe. I don't know— I don't listen."

Amanda was skeptical, and she could tell that Madame didn't believe him either. Personally, she didn't care one way or another. She was too busy contemplating Ken from another angle. As a boyfriend.

Why not? He was cute, he was cool, and her friends would be impressed if she hooked up with him. Even Nina would have to show her some respect. Being with someone like Ken Preston would definitely put her back on top. And it wasn't as if *she'd* suffer in the process of creating a relationship with him . . .

"Amanda? When do you first recall experiencing your gift?"

Amanda began to tell her story about the beggar she saw when she was five. As she spoke, she kept glancing at Ken. Maybe he'd be impressed with the fact that she could feel so sorry for people. But he wasn't even paying attention.

She didn't tell the part about how she had been Tracey Devon—she couldn't bear the thought of Ken picturing the old Tracey in his mind and connecting the image with Amanda. Even the new-and-improved Tracey wasn't up to her standards.

Then Tracey's hand went up, and Amanda's stomach fell. Fortunately, it was almost time for the bell.

"We'll hear from you tomorrow, Tracey," Madame said. "And from Jenna and Martin."

"What about Carter?" Charles wanted to know.

Martin started laughing, and Madame shot him a warning look. Then she looked at the boy whom no one knew.

"Carter, will you give a report on your gift tomorrow?" she asked.

There was no response to her question, and like the others, Amanda wasn't surprised. They couldn't be sure he *had* a gift. For as long as he'd been at Meadowbrook, he hadn't spoken. No one even knew his real name. A teacher had found him wandering on Carter Street. Not only mute, but he appeared to be an amnesiac, too. He was a complete and total mystery, which meant that he was very weird, and Amanda knew that was why he'd been put in this class. With the other weirdos.

Who, in a million years, would ever believe that Amanda Beeson might have anything in common with someone like Carter Street? It was truly sickening. She had to get out of here. And it certainly wouldn't hurt to have a partner to help her plan how to make her—*their*—exit.

227

Her seat was closer to the door than Ken's, so when the bell rang, she hurried out and then waited for him. As soon as he emerged, she began walking alongside him and spoke casually.

"I can totally relate, Ken."

"Huh?"

"With what you said in class today. I really do understand."

He looked at her in puzzlement. "Dead people talk to you, too?"

"No—I mean, I don't want my gift either."

"Yeah, well . . ." He looked away, and she understood. The busy, crowded hallway was no place for a discussion about something so personal.

"I was thinking, maybe we could talk about it sometime," she ventured.

There was a considerable lack of enthusiasm in his expression. "Isn't that what we do every day in class?"

"Sure, but I was thinking, just you and me . . ." Her voice trailed off as he frowned. She wasn't even sure if he'd heard her.

"I gotta go," he said abruptly. And he ducked into a boys' restroom.

She supposed he might have really needed to go to the bathroom. Because why wouldn't he want to get together with her? She was pretty, she was popular—most boys would be pleased to find her flirting with them. And Ken had actually kissed her once, at Sophie's pool party the previous spring. Of course, it hadn't *meant* anything. Some other boys at the party had probably dared him to do it—they were all acting pretty goofy that day—but still . . .

Maybe he really hadn't heard her. One of those dead people could have been trying to get his attention. But that was exactly why he *should* listen to her. If she could lose *her* gift, she might be able to help him get rid of his.

Those other "gifted" kids—they were freaks. She and Ken were cool. They belonged together—and out of that class.

Chapter Four

JENNA HAD LEFT BROOKSIDE Towers only two days before, but already the buildings looked more grim and forbidding and not like home at all. She was very glad that Tracey and Emily had offered to come along with her after school. Of course, she didn't tell them that she was grateful.

"You know, I could do this by myself," she informed them. "I don't know why you guys are tagging along."

To Emily, Tracey said, "That's Jenna's way of saying thank you."

Jenna ignored that. "And if the elevator is out of order, you'll be sorry. I'm on the fifth floor."

"You can't bring back everything by yourself," Tracey pointed out, turning to Emily. "She forgot her raincoat, her bathrobe—lots of things. Including all her school stuff."

"A Freudian slip," Emily commented.

"What's that?" Jenna asked, suspecting that it wasn't something you wore underneath your clothes.

"It's when you think you're doing something accidentally but you have a subconscious reason. Like, you *forgot* your school stuff because you don't like school."

That was one of the interesting things about Emily, Jenna thought. She might act all spacy and out of it, but then she'd come out with something really smart like that.

"And don't worry about the elevator," Emily added. "It's working."

And that was another weirdly interesting thing about Emily. "I can't believe you waste your gift predicting such stupid stuff," Jenna remarked.

"I know," Emily said mournfully. "Things like that just come to me. Then when I *try* to predict something, I get it wrong. I'm getting better, though. I got four out of seven weather forecasts right last week."

She was right about the elevator, too. But when they got off on the fifth floor, Jenna hesitated.

"What's the matter?" Tracey asked.

She couldn't tell them the truth—that she was afraid her mother had given up, had left rehab, and was now passed out on the living-room floor.

"Nothing," she said. Thank goodness *they* couldn't read *her* mind. "The apartment is at the end of the hall." Gritting her teeth, she strode forward, and the other two followed her. To her relief, the apartment was empty.

"Have you heard from your mother?" Emily asked.

Jenna shook her head as she led them into her bedroom. "People in rehab aren't allowed to be in contact with anyone on the outside. I guess she's doing all right." She heard something in Tracey's mind and turned to her. "Okay, maybe it's wishful thinking, but I can hope, can't I?"

"Hey, you promised!" Tracey exclaimed in outrage.

"Sorry, I forgot," Jenna lied. She opened her dresser drawer and began throwing stuff onto the bed.

"What are you guys talking about?" Emily wanted to know.

"Jenna promised not to read my mind while she was staying with me," Tracey told her.

"You should do what I do," Emily said.

"What do you do?" Tracey asked.

"I don't know, but Jenna never reads my mind."

Jenna grinned. "That's because I don't believe you're ever thinking anything that's worth paying attention to."

"Ha-ha, very funny." Emily picked up Jenna's slippers. "What are we going to put all this stuff in?"

Tracey produced several empty bags from her backpack, and the girls began filling them. Emily picked up a notebook and stopped.

"Are these your notes from the gifted class?"

Jenna glanced at the notebook. "Yeah. Why?"

"Because I just got a vision of our next homework assignment."

Tracey looked at her with interest. "So if you can touch something, it helps with your predictions?"

"I don't know—this has never happened before." She sighed. "There's so much I don't understand about my gift."

"Same here," Tracey said. "Now that I don't feel like a nobody, how can I make myself disappear?"

"And why can't I read everyone's mind?" Jenna wondered. She turned to Emily. "What's the assignment? Not that I care," she added hastily. "I probably won't do it anyway."

"Madame is going to ask us to think about how we could use our gifts in a career."

"Great," Jenna groaned as she picked through her underwear in search of items without holes. "I guess I could be some kind of magician. Like, 'Think of a number and I'll tell you what it is.'"

"You could be a psychologist," Tracey suggested. "It would definitely help to know what people are thinking."

"Or a police officer," Emily said. "You'd always know when people were lying, and you could solve crimes that way."

"If I could become invisible whenever I wanted, I could be a detective," Tracey remarked. "Or a spy! That would be intense!"

"I'd like to do something that helps people," Emily mused. "If I could predict natural disasters, like earthquakes, I could warn people to move before they happen."

"No one would believe you," Jenna told her. "You'd be like Chicken Little, running around yelling, 'The sky is falling.' Can you predict what's going to happen to me this week?"

"Let me think . . ." Emily scrunched her forehead and closed her eyes. After a moment, she said, "You're going to meet a tall, dark, handsome stranger."

Tracey started laughing. "You sound like one of those fake gypsy fortunetellers."

"No, really—I see that," Emily insisted. Then her expression changed.

"What?" Jenna asked.

"He's going to make you cry."

"Oh, puh-leeze!" Jenna snorted. "The day some stupid boy makes me cry . . . You know, Em, if I had your talent, I'd use it to become a professional gambler and make some money. Like, in horse races, I'd know who to bet on. Or I'd figure out the next winning lottery numbers."

Emily winced. "Like Serena."

"Oh, right." Jenna had almost forgotten about the awful student teacher who had tried to make Emily do exactly that. "Sorry." She turned to Tracey.

"If I could be invisible, I'd follow around famous people and see how they really live. Wouldn't it be awesome to hang out with Britney Spears? Or Prince William?"

"That's not exactly a career," Tracey said, "unless you're writing a gossip column."

A sudden knock on the door made them all turn in that direction. "Are you expecting anyone?" Tracey asked Jenna.

"No." Jenna went out of the bedroom and headed to the door.

"Then don't answer it!" Tracey called.

Jenna looked through the door's peephole. Unfortunately, it hadn't been cleaned since—well, it had never been cleaned, probably. So she couldn't see much—just the fact that someone sort of tall with dark hair was standing on the other side of the door.

"Hello?" she called.

"Excuse me," replied a masculine voice. "I'm looking for Barbara Kelley."

"She's not here."

Tracey was at her shoulder. "If you don't know who it is, don't let him in," she hissed.

The man at the door must have heard her. "Whoever said that is absolutely right. Never open the door to strangers. I'll come back another time."

The figure disappeared, and Jenna turned back to her curious friends. "Probably a bill collector," she said. "Or he's selling something. I've never seen him before."

"Did you get a good look at him?" Emily asked.

"Not really. He was tall, he had dark hair . . . Why are you grinning like that?"

"Because I was right with my prediction! You just met a tall, dark, handsome stranger."

"I couldn't tell if he was handsome," Jenna pointed out.

Emily sighed. "Well, he was tall and dark and he was a stranger. Three out of four isn't bad." Then, suddenly, her face changed and she shivered.

"*Now* what's the matter?" Jenna asked.

"I just got a bad feeling about him," Emily said. "Like maybe he's not a nice person."

"That doesn't make sense," Tracey said. "If he was a burglar or something like that, he wouldn't have told Jenna not to open the door."

"That's true," Emily admitted. "See? You can't rely on me. I get these visions, but a lot of the time I don't understand what they mean."

"It's too bad we can't blend our gifts and work together," Tracey commented. "Jenna could read your mind and make sense out of what you see in your head."

"She can't read my mind," Emily reminded her.

"I didn't say that," Jenna argued. "I never try."

"Try now," Emily urged. "What am I thinking?"

Jenna closed her eyes and concentrated. Then she frowned. "Nothing. You're as empty as Carter Street." Emily grinned. "I just imagined a wall in front of my thoughts."

"Ooh, let me try that!" Tracey cried out excitedly. "Jenna, try to read my mind."

"You made me promise not to."

"Well, I release you from your promise, just for one minute. Starting now."

Feeling like a circus performer, Jenna groaned, but how could she say no to someone who was putting her up for two weeks? So she closed her eyes again.

It didn't take much concentration to read Tracey's thoughts. "You're thinking about dinner tonight and hoping for spaghetti and meatballs."

Tracey made a face. "But I put up a wall, just like Emily did. A brick wall! How come it didn't work for me?"

"How should I know?" Jenna retorted. "Why are some of Emily's predictions right and others not?"

"We're mysteries," Emily said. "We're not like other people. We've got weird gifts that we don't understand, so we can't expect them to work all the time until we learn more about them."

Once again, vague, scatterbrained Emily was making an intelligent observation. They really were mysteries, all of them, Jenna thought.

And personally, she liked being a mystery. It meant that life would be full of surprises.

Chapter Five

THE NEXT DAY, WHEN she arrived at school, Amanda went up to the principal's office. There was a student working at the reception desk—a girl named Heather who'd been in Amanda's geometry class last year. Heather wasn't a nerd, but she wasn't in the top clique either, and Amanda was pretty sure she could get Heather to do her a favor.

She was right, and after graciously accepting a compliment from Heather on her new yellow platform shoes, she left the office with a copy of Ken Preston's class schedule. Then she organized her day so that she would *accidentally* bump into him at various times between classes.

The first two times, he didn't even see her. The third time, he saw her, and when she greeted him, he said hi but didn't stop to talk. And the fourth time, when she tried to start a conversation, he claimed to be busy and hurried off.

It didn't make any sense. Was it possible—really, truly possible—that he wasn't attracted to her? It was hard to believe, but she decided she would have to explore all the possibilities of getting together with him.

For the first time since she'd started the class, she hurried to room 209. She knew Ken wouldn't be there—he always showed up at the last minute. There was someone else she wanted to see—someone who just might be able to help her connect with Ken.

Being the perfect student, Sarah was already in her seat when Amanda arrived. Whoever sat in front of her wasn't there yet, so Amanda took that seat. Sarah looked up in surprise.

"Hello, Amanda."

Amanda tried to remember if she'd ever spoken directly to Sarah. She didn't think so, but she smiled brightly and tried to act as if they talked every day.

"Hi, Sarah. How're you doing?"

Sarah recovered from her shock quickly. "Fine. How are you?"

Amanda put on a doleful face. "Not too good."

Sarah had a reputation for being sweet and understanding, and she demonstrated that now. She looked concerned. "What's the matter?"

"It's Ken," Amanda said sadly. "You know—Ken Preston, in our class."

"What's wrong with Ken?"

"Well, he's so timid . . ."

"Really? I never noticed that."

Amanda continued quickly. "Well, he is, and I know he wants to ask me out, but he's too shy. Maybe you could help him."

Sarah looked confused. "What could *I* do?"

"You've got that special ability to make people do things with your mind. And I was thinking, you could make him ask me out. Nothing major—just something like a movie or miniature golf."

Sarah just stared at her, speechless. Her eyes were very wide.

"It would just be this one time," Amanda assured her. "I'm sure once I got him alone, he'd recover from his shyness. Would you do this for me? I mean, for him?"

Sarah shook her head. "I can't, Amanda."

"Of course you can. You've got the gift!"

"I suppose I should say, 'I won't.' Amanda, my gift is dangerous. And the only way I can deal with it is to not use it at all."

"But that's silly!" Amanda exclaimed. "It's just a date. How is that dangerous?"

"That's not the point, Amanda."

Amanda frowned. She didn't care about the point. She just wanted a date.

Sarah explained, "I used to have a fantasy about going to the Winter Olympics so I could help the figure skaters not fall. But I know now that doing good deeds can be just as dangerous as doing bad deeds. Because one thing could lead to another. Do you see what I mean?"

"No. Look, Sarah, if you do this for me, we could be friends. You could sit with us at lunch." Amanda knew that her table, with Britney, Sophie, Nina, Katie, and the others, was considered the best girls' table in the cafeteria. Heather-in-the-office would *kill* for a chance to sit at that table.

But Sarah wasn't Heather-in-the-office. "I'm sorry, Amanda. I just can't."

She sounded as if she meant it, too. Amanda rearranged her features into an expression that she hoped looked menacing. "Sarah, do you remember what my gift is?"

"Of course I do—you talked about it yesterday."

"Well, what if I took over your body and made Ken ask me out? I mean, me-Amanda, not me-you."

Sarah didn't seem the least bit frightened. "You'd have to feel sorry for me first, Amanda. And you don't, do you?"

She was right. Sarah wasn't the coolest, prettiest, or most popular girl at Meadowbrook, but there was nothing pathetic about her either. Amanda gave up on the idea of using Sarah. She'd have to find another way to reach Ken.

The others were coming in now, so she went back to her own seat. As usual, Ken came in last, and he still had that distracted expression on his face. She didn't even bother trying to catch his attention. What was she going to do? There had to be a way.

The bell rang, class started, and Madame called on Tracey to give her report. Amanda didn't bother listening—having been Tracey, she knew Tracey's story by heart. Tracey had been a happy only child, then her mother had septuplets, Tracey was ignored, she started to disappear, blah-blah-blah. Amanda spent the time doodling, trying to come up with a way to get Ken's attention. What if she went to his house, knocked on his door, and asked him to—

"Amanda?"

She looked up. "Yes, Madame?"

"Don't you have something to say to Tracey?"

The teacher gazed at her sternly. "Apparently you weren't listening. Tracey was thanking you for helping her learn to assert herself."

Sarah turned to look at her with a startled expression, as if she was surprised to learn that Amanda could do something nice for someone else. Jenna was looking at her, too, and grinning—she'd known when Amanda had been inside Tracey's body because of her mind-reading skills. And she knew perfectly well that Amanda hadn't

243

been trying to improve Tracey's life—only her own for as long as she was stuck being Tracey. But there was only one reaction Amanda was really interested in.

She looked at Ken. He was staring out the window, daydreaming, maybe, or listening to dead people, but in any case, he obviously hadn't been paying attention to Tracey's story. What a relief.

Madame was still staring at her. "Amanda?"

"Oh, yeah. Uh, that's okay. I mean, you're welcome. Whatever."

Madame called on Martin next. The boy—who looked to be at least two years younger than anyone else—spoke in a very annoying, whiny voice, which made it hard to listen to his story.

"It was a couple of years ago. I was shooting baskets in my driveway."

The thought of undersized Martin playing basketball was almost too much for Amanda to deal with, but she knew better than to show it. But neither Jenna nor Charles had her self-control, and they started laughing. Martin clenched his fists.

Madame rapped on her desk. "Stop it at once! Martin, remember your exercise. Close your eyes and count backward from ten."

Amanda half hoped that the exercise wouldn't work.

She'd never actually seen Martin demonstrate his gift. It would be interesting to see if he would attack a person in a wheelchair. As for Jenna, Amanda wouldn't mind seeing her get shaken up a little.

But Martin relaxed, and the animal or whatever was inside him calmed down.

"Anyway, a couple of guys came by and said they wanted to play with me. Only they kept the ball and wouldn't let me have it. I tried to get it back, but they were bigger than me. And they laughed."

He didn't have to say more. Everyone knew what happened when Martin thought people were making fun of him.

"Did you hurt them badly?" Madame asked.

"One of them got away. I broke the other one's arm, but that was all."

"So you were able to restrain yourself," Madame commented.

"Well, not exactly. It's just that he was screaming so hard that I lost the feeling."

Supposedly, it was this "feeling" that gave Martin the strength of a bear or some other type of strong animal. In any case, his power went beyond anything a normal human being could do—even a big bodybuilder.

"And that's the first time you remember getting the

feeling?" Madame asked.

"Yeah, I think so. But my mother told me that when I was three, my father took a toy away from me and I pushed him across the room. My father says she dreamed this and it never happened." He grinned. "But he never tried to take anything away from me again, so I guess he learned his lesson. I must have done a pretty good job for a three-year-old."

"This is nothing to be proud of, Martin," Madame reprimanded. "You have to learn to channel your strength and direct it appropriately."

"Maybe you could go into demolition work someday," Jenna suggested. "I'll bet you'd be great at tearing down buildings."

Martin considered this. "I'd rather tear down people."

Sarah gasped. "Martin! That's not right!"

"It's their own fault," Martin complained. "People are always picking on me. I'm small, so they think they can push me around. If they didn't pick on me, I wouldn't get the feeling and I couldn't hurt them."

"Martin, you have to take responsibility for your gift," Madame said. "We'll hear from Jenna next."

Luckily, Jenna was saved by the bell—not the usual one, but the three special chimes that signified an announcement was about to be made over the intercom. This was followed by the disembodied voice of the principal's secretary.

"Would Jenna Kelley please come to the office?"

Everyone looked at Jenna, who immediately went all defensive. "I didn't do anything!"

"Just go to the office, Jenna," Madame said. "You can give your report another day."

Lucky dog, Amanda thought. It was very likely that Madame would forget that Jenna hadn't given her report and would never call on her again to do it. Jenna didn't deserve the good fortune.

On the other hand, Jenna was on her way to Mr. Jackson's office. Amanda brightened. Nobody ever got called to the principal's office for a good reason.

Chapter Six

ENNA RACKED HER BRAIN, trying to think of a reason for being called to the office so that she could come up with a story or an excuse to get out of it. She'd done plenty of bad things in her time at Meadowbrook, but she hadn't broken any major school rules recently. She hadn't been cutting classes—not for a while, anyway. She hadn't cheated on any tests lately. Come to think of it, she'd been unusually good the past couple of weeks, not even going to the mall and hanging out with Slug and Skank, the lowlife types she'd befriended on the street. She hadn't even seen them since they'd been picked up for shoplifting.

What could be so big that she'd be called out of class? Had they looked in her locker and found something bad? Okay, it was a mess, but there weren't any cigarettes or drugs or alcohol stashed away. Surely you didn't get called to the office for a couple of Kit Kat bars.

Then another possibility occurred to her, and she felt

sick. Her mother . . . had something happened to her mother? Her legs turned to jelly and she stopped walking. That was definitely the kind of thing a person would be called out of class for—a family situation. Something really terrible, like an accident or . . . or worse.

Her mother. She was weak, she was an alcoholic, she'd never win any mother-of-the-year prizes, but Jenna loved her. And the thought of losing her . . .

"Jenna? Are you all right?"

The concerned voice belonged to Mr. Gonzalez, the school counselor. Jenna had been forced to have sessions with him after her stint in the juvenile detention center. He was nice enough, but she'd put so much effort into lying to him during their sessions that she couldn't tell him the truth now.

"Sure, I'm fine. I'm just on my way to, um . . ."

"The principal's office?" He smiled. "It's okay. I know all about it. If you need to talk later, you know where I am." And he ambled off.

He left Jenna gaping. He knew why she'd been called to the office, and he was *smiling*. So she couldn't be in trouble and it couldn't be anything terrible, like her mother being hurt. It had to be something else.

Then she wanted to kick herself. Why hadn't she read his mind? Then she'd already know!

She moved quickly now, down the hall, around the corner, and up the half flight of stairs to the administration wing. When she walked into the main office, the secretary recognized her, but for once she wasn't wearing a reproving look. She beamed at Jenna and picked up the phone.

"Jenna Kelley is here, Mr. Jackson." She put down the phone. "You can go right in, Jenna."

Still feeling shaky, Jenna went to the door and rapped. A familiar booming voice rang out. "Come in, Jenna."

She opened the door. The heavyset principal was behind his desk, and for the first time ever, he looked pleased to see Jenna. There were two chairs facing the principal's desk, and a man was sitting in one of them.

He turned as Jenna approached, and she thought he looked vaguely familiar. "Hello, Jenna," he said.

It was his voice that put the memory in focus. This was the man who had come to the door yesterday looking for her mother.

"Hello," she said uncertainly.

"Sit down," the principal said, and as she did, once again she became nervous. Had this strange man come to give her bad news about her mother? No, that couldn't be it. He, too, was smiling. And Emily had been right about something—he was definitely handsome.

The principal spoke. "I'd like you to meet

Mr. Stuart Kelley."

Jenna's eyes darted back and forth between the principal and the strange man. *Kelley* was a pretty common name, but she had to ask.

"Are you related to me?"

The man nodded and spoke gently. "I'm your father, Jenna."

His voice was soft, and Jenna was certain that she'd misheard him. "What?"

The principal repeated, "This is your father, Jenna. He's been searching for you for—how long, Mr. Kelley?"

"A long time," the man said, smiling. "But now I've finally found you, Jenna."

Jenna narrowed her eyes. She didn't know what kind of scam this guy was trying to pull, but she wasn't about to fall for it. She turned to the principal.

"This is a mistake, Mr. Jackson. I don't have a father."

Mr. Jackson gave her a jovial smile. "Everyone has a father, Jenna, even if they don't know who he is. It takes two, you know." He uttered a hoarse laugh at his silly remark.

Jenna had never much liked the principal, and now she *really* disliked him. She stood up.

"Can I go back to my class now?" Boy, those were words she'd never expected to hear herself saying. Of course, she'd never expected to be confronted by some prankster claiming to be her father.

"Sit down, Jenna!" Mr. Jackson's tone had changed—now he was his usual authoritative self. She sat down, but she didn't look at the man. She kept her wary gaze on the principal.

"This man is your father," Mr. Jackson declared. "I have checked his credentials, and I am satisfied with the evidence he has provided."

What evidence? Jenna wondered, but she didn't ask. She tried to do a quick read of the principal's mind, but all she could come up with was a confirmation that Mr. Jackson didn't like her any more than she liked him.

"Look at me, Jenna," the strange man said quietly. Despite herself, she did. He had nice eyes—a deep, rich blue, like hers. But lots of people had blue eyes.

"I can understand how you feel," Stuart Kelley went on. "What I did to you and your mother—it was a terrible thing. But I wasn't a very nice person back then. I was young and restless and I didn't want any responsibilities. I loved your mother, but when she told me she was pregnant, I couldn't deal with it. I didn't have the maturity. So I left."

Jenna steeled herself to stare right back into those blue eyes. "Where did you go?"

"California." He smiled in an almost sheepish way.

"I was a good-looking kid, and I thought I could make it in the movies."

Jenna eyed him skeptically. "Did you? Are you some famous movie star I've never heard of?"

He laughed. "Hardly. Did you ever see *Invasion of the Mile-High Martian Zombies*?"

Jenna shook her head.

"I don't think it was ever released in theaters. I'm pretty sure it went directly to DVD. I was one of three hundred Martian zombies on stilts. You can't pick me out because we all wore the same mask. And I didn't even get a credit. So no, I'm not a famous movie star. I'm an unknown DVD extra."

At least he was able to poke fun at himself, Jenna thought. But she'd watched enough crime dramas on TV to know that scam artists were usually charming.

"How did you know you had a daughter?" she challenged him.

"Your mother had a friend, Sylvia Tinsley. You wouldn't remember her—she passed away ten years ago. But we stayed in touch, and she wrote me that Barbara gave birth to a little girl."

"But you didn't come back," Jenna stated.

"No." He bowed his head. If he *was* an actor, Jenna was surprised he hadn't made it big in Hollywood. The guy looked really sad.

"How did you find me?"

"Research. The Internet." He gave her a half smile. "Your little brush with the police had one positive consequence: your name got on a database or two."

"I never did drugs, you know, no matter what you read," Jenna declared. "I was just with some people who had them." Now, why had she said that? What did she care if this total stranger thought she was a druggie?

"Perhaps I should leave you two alone so you can have a private reunion," Mr. Jackson said as he started to get out of his chair.

"No!" Jenna cried out. "I mean, that's not necessary. Nice to meet you, Mr. Kelley. Can I please go now, Mr. Jackson?'

The principal's eyes darkened, but Stuart Kelley seemed much more understanding. "I know this must come as a huge shock, Jenna. And this is a difficult time for you, with your mother in rehabilitation."

Wow! He really did know a lot about her, Jenna thought, but she said nothing.

"I can understand if you don't want to have any kind of relationship," he continued. "But would you mind if I contacted the family you're staying with? Perhaps I could visit you there, if it's okay with you."

Jenna swallowed, trying to lose what felt like a gigantic lump in her throat. She supposed there wasn't any harm in that. And the Devons were smart people. They'd be able to figure out who he was and what he was really up to.

So she shrugged. "Whatever."

This time she didn't bother to ask the principal's permission. She turned and walked out.

The secretary, still smiling, handed her a note that would allow her to show up late to whatever class she was supposed to be in now. But that wasn't where she went. Instead, she walked down a silent hall and went straight into a restroom. She needed time alone to think.

Who *was* this guy? And what did he want from her? He had to be pulling some kind of scam, but why? It wasn't as if he could kidnap her and ransom her for money.

Mr. Jackson claimed there was evidence that this Stuart Kelley really was her father. But why would he come looking for her? So he could claim her and get the welfare allowance the state gave her mother? But it wasn't much money—hardly worth the effort. None of this made any sense at all.

She was almost relieved to hear the bell ring. At least class would be a distraction. She left the restroom and practically collided with Amanda Beeson.

"There you are!" Amanda exclaimed. "I've been looking

everywhere for you!"

"What do *you* want?" Jenna asked, knowing her rudeness would have no effect whatsoever on Amanda.

She was right. Amanda practically shoved her back into the restroom. "I have a favor to ask you."

The door to one of the stalls opened, and a girl Jenna vaguely recognized came out. She was Nina something, a friend of Amanda's.

"Hi, Amanda. You're Jenna Kelley, aren't you?"

"Yeah, so what?"

"So nothing. I just didn't know you two were friends." Nina sauntered out of the restroom.

The color drained from Amanda's face. Despite everything she'd just been through, Jenna burst out laughing. Clearly, poor Amanda was devastated at having been caught talking to notorious bad girl Jenna Kelley.

She almost felt sorry for Amanda—but not quite. "Why would I do *you* a favor?"

Amanda recovered from her shock and faced her squarely. "Do you want me to tell everyone you still sleep with a teddy bear?"

"I'll just call you a liar," Jenna replied.

Amanda grinned meanly. "I have a photo."

Jenna doubted that. When Amanda had been Tracey and they'd slept in the same room, she didn't recall ever seeing a camera. And with everything else on her mind now, and her reputation not exactly squeaky clean, did she really care if people knew she slept with a teddy bear?

But she had to admit—she was curious to know what Amanda could possibly want her to do. "What kind of favor?"

"I want you to read Ken's mind. I've been flirting with him like crazy, and he's totally not responding."

Jenna cocked her head to one side. "Did it ever occur to you that maybe Ken just doesn't want to be with you?"

"No," Amanda replied. "There's got to be another reason. You have to find out what it is."

It was so annoying—the way Amanda just assumed that every girl wanted to be her friend and every boy was madly in love with her. And there was something else about this that bugged Jenna.

"Weren't you listening when Madame said we shouldn't use one another to exploit our gifts?"

Since when do you do what the teachers say?" Amanda retorted.

She had a point. But Jenna shook her head. "Look, Amanda, if he's not interested in you, then he's not thinking about you. What difference would it make if I found out that he was thinking about—I don't know— football, or soccer, or macaroni and cheese? How would that help you?"

Amanda was momentarily at a loss for words.

"I've got a better idea," Jenna said. "You're a body snatcher. Why don't you just take over his body? Then you could fall in love with yourself. It shouldn't be too difficult, considering how conceited you are."

And she walked out of the restroom, pleased that for two whole minutes she hadn't thought about the mysterious Mr. Kelley.

CHAPTER SEVEN

A S JENNA LEFT THE restroom, half a dozen girls entered, and several of them greeted Amanda. But she was barely aware of them. She walked out in a daze, with Jenna's words still ringing in her ears. Not the part about being conceited. She didn't care one little bit what Jenna thought of her. It was Jenna's idea that was stuck in her head.

Would it work? Could she really take over Ken's body and make him fall in love with her? Of course, if she was inside Ken, her physical self would be that robotic Other-Amanda who took over when she was elsewhere. But so what? That Amanda-robot-thing acted just like her. And once she-as-Ken asked Other-Amanda out, she'd get back inside herself and charm him on their date. It was just a question of getting him alone, of having his full attention.

There was only one problem—but it was a big one. How could she take over Ken's body? Body snatching worked only when she felt enormous sympathy for someone. How could she ever feel sorry for Ken? He was good-looking, he was popular, and she was pretty sure he had no problems with schoolwork. She didn't know much about his family, but she'd seen them all together at a restaurant recently. Thinking back, she recalled two parents and a little sister. They had seemed okay—a normal, ordinary family.

But maybe his parents weren't getting along—maybe they were even heading for divorce. There'd been no evidence of that when she'd seen them, but you never knew what went on behind the scenes. She'd have to ask her mother—*she* kept up to date on community gossip. Amanda knew it wasn't very kind of her to hope that Ken's parents were breaking up, but at least it would give her something to pity.

Or maybe the whole idea was absolutely stupid. First of all, she didn't have that kind of control over her gift. She could avoid body snatching by not feeling sorry for someone, but could she actually initiate a snatch? She'd never tried because she'd never wanted to, and there was no reason to think she had the ability.

On the other hand, since she'd never tried, she didn't know if she couldn't.

So what if she could make this happen? What if she could take over Ken's body, ask out robot-Amanda, and then get back inside herself just in time for the big date?

Would Ken even remember that he'd asked her out?

She thought back to her time inside Tracey's body. She'd never really talked to Tracey about it, so she wasn't sure how much Tracey remembered after she got her body back. But after she'd been inside Tracey for a while, she *had* felt some sort of connection, like Tracey knew what was going on.

So what if Ken did remember and he wasn't happy about what Amanda had made him do? She could make things even worse than they already were.

Not to mention the weirdness of being inside *Ken's* body. It was one thing to act like Tracey Devon; how could she possibly act like a boy? No, it was insane—she could never pull it off. She'd have to come up with something else.

But what? This was so frustrating—it was driving her crazy.

"Hello, hello, is anyone home? Earth to Amanda! Come in, Amanda."

She turned to see Nina, Sophie, and Britney walking alongside her. She had no idea how long they'd been there, but they were all giggling.

"What's so funny?" she demanded.

"You," Nina said. "You look so out of it! Have you been taking lessons from Emily Sanders?"

"Don't be stupid," Amanda snapped. "I've just got

something on my mind, that's all. Honestly, can't a person think about something? And don't ask me what I'm thinking about, because it's none of your business!"

Now all three girls were staring at her, and she wanted to kick herself for going all postal like that. Why had she sounded so annoyed? Getting upset like that—it was so uncool.

"Don't bite off our heads!" Nina exclaimed. "I don't know what's happened to you lately, Amanda."

Sophie nodded. "You're just not yourself."

Britney chimed in. "Ever since you got stuck in that weird class, it's like you've changed."

"I have *not*!" she declared indignantly.

The three girls exchanged looks, and Amanda knew immediately that they'd been talking about her behind her back. This was bad.

Her mind began to race. Personally, she didn't think she'd been behaving any differently, but clearly they did, so she had to do something to provide an excuse for her attitude. She needed a problem, but it had to be a cool problem, something that would give her status.

"It's Ken," she said suddenly.

They all looked puzzled. "Ken Preston?" Britney asked.

Amanda nodded. "He likes me. I can tell. He's been coming on to me like crazy—flirting at school, calling me at home, sending me instant messages . . ."

Now her friends looked confused. "What's wrong with that?" Sophie wanted to know. "Ken is *hot.*"

"Oh, sure, I know that," Amanda said carelessly. "I'm just not sure how I feel about him. And I don't want to hurt his feelings."

Uh-oh—wrong comment. The notorious Queen of Mean Amanda Beeson didn't care if she hurt someone's feelings. Was it her imagination or did all three of the girls just take a step backward, creating more of a distance between them? And ohmigod, was that Tracey Devon coming toward them? The old Tracey Devon would never have had the guts to approach Amanda Beeson. She'd created a monster!

"Amanda, hi. I just wanted to tell you that I'm sorry if I embarrassed you in class today. But I really want you to know how grateful I am—"

Amanda grabbed her arm and pulled her away from the others. "Shut up!" she hissed in Tracey's ear. "My friends don't know about me!"

Tracey's eyebrows went up. "Really? But I thought—"

"I have to get to class," Amanda said frantically, turning her back on Tracey. But her friends were already halfway down the hall. She raced to catch up with them.

"Wait up," she demanded.

"Sorry," Nina said. "We wanted to give you some privacy with your new best friend, Tracey."

Britney started to giggle and then quickly clamped her hand over her mouth. Britney Teller, who worshiped Amanda! Could her life get any worse?

It could. Because here came Ken Preston, ambling down the hall.

"Hi, Ken!" Nina called out, and she stepped aside to reveal Amanda, practically pointing at her. Ken glanced in their direction.

"Hi, Nina."

That was it. Not a word of greeting to Amanda.

"I don't think you're going to have to worry about breaking his heart, Amanda," Nina said. "He didn't even look at you. Oops! The bell's going to ring." Everyone took off in different directions.

This wasn't good. Amanda wasn't just teetering on her pinnacle anymore—she was slipping off. This couldn't be happening to her.

But throughout the rest of the school day, she saw sign after sign of her diminishing popularity. She received no compliments, not even for her new shoes. When she went into her algebra class, she saw that her friends Emma and Katie had their heads together. And when they saw her, they immediately moved apart. She knew what that meant.

They'd been talking about her, too.

The worst was yet to come. There was an assembly scheduled that day, during the next-to-last period— another one of those dull programs on the environment. They'd been having them every week—on global warming, recycling, all kinds of boring topics. Amanda had no idea what this week's subject was, and she didn't care—she had bigger things to worry about than the future of the dumb planet.

But everyone liked assemblies, even boring ones. You got out of class, and assemblies were a good excuse to spend time with your friends. You could sit wherever you wanted, so it was like the cafeteria, where the cliques could gather. Best of all, assemblies were usually held in the gym and the students sat on the bleachers. The coolest kids commandeered the highest level, where they could ignore the speakers and talk to one another without being seen by the teachers.

Amanda's gang always sat on the top row of the left side, farthest from the stage. Automatically, she went down to that end of the gym and started up the stairs. She was more than halfway to the top when she was confronted with a sight more horrifying than—well, than any massacre in any horror movie that Amanda had ever seen.

There they were: Nina, Britney, Sophie, Emma, and

Katie—and they hadn't saved a space for her. Instead, they'd allowed Cara Winters and Terri Boyd to join them. And now they were squeezing themselves together even more tightly to let in Heather Todd. Heather Todd! Who, just that very morning, had been thrilled to give Amanda a completely illegal photocopy of Ken's class schedule! How was this possible? This couldn't be happening to her. How could someone's reputation totally collapse in one crummy day?

Now Emma had seen her, and she was nudging the others. They were all looking at her, standing there all alone, with no place to sit. For what would have to be the one and only time in Amanda's life, she wished she were Tracey Devon and could just vanish.

But she was Amanda Beeson, ruler of all that was cool at Meadowbrook Middle School, and if nothing else, she could try to preserve some dignity. Refusing to meet anyone's eyes—but knowing full well that all eyes were on her—she turned and walked down the steps. Now she knew how Marie Antoinette must have felt on her way to the guillotine or how Anne Boleyn had felt when she faced her executioner. Fallen queens, all of them.

By the time she'd reached the bottom, the program was beginning and she had to take the first seat available, at the end of a row of nerdy brainiacs who probably actually cared about the environment. At least they weren't paying any attention to her. They didn't even notice her, and for once she was grateful for that.

And unlike Marie Antoinette or Anne Boleyn, she still had a head and she could use it. She would not fall apart. She would deal with this situation and she would overcome it. She would reclaim her throne.

But how? That was the big question. And so she went back to that conversation with Jenna in the restroom and began to consider Jenna's suggestion again.

From her bag, she pulled out the copy of Ken's class schedule. According to it, he had gym class after the assembly. Excellent. This meant that after the last bell, he'd need a few extra minutes to change his clothes. That would give her time to get to that end of the building and position herself somewhere unnoticeable but from where she could see him emerge. Her plan was to follow him home, and just before he arrived, she would corner him.

At that point, she had two options. She could flirt— but that hadn't worked so far. The second possibility was to discover something about him that would elicit her sympathy and, she hoped, give her the means to take over his body. She strongly suspected that this option was the better one. If she could control Ken, she could make him do what she wanted him to do: hang out with Amanda, date Amanda, make the whole school believe that he was madly in love with Amanda, and put her back up on the pedestal where she belonged. And even if it wasn't real, even if he didn't want her once she gave him back his body, so what? She'd already be back on top, and she could let everyone think she'd broken up with him, which would give her only more prestige.

Yes, the second option was definitely the one to go with. True, she'd never before tried to take over a body on purpose, but Amanda Beeson always got what she wanted. And if she wanted her life back, she'd figure out a way.

Somehow, she made it through her last class without having to pay too much attention. The second the bell rang, she was out the door, and in minutes she was at the other end of the school building. There was an exit just outside the gym from which Ken would undoubtedly emerge, and she stationed herself around the side of the building. She'd see him come out, he'd pass without seeing her, and she could follow him from a safe distance. Behind her and down a small slope was the playing field, and as she waited, she could hear the soccer team gathering out there for their afterschool practice.

She didn't have to wait long. And she was in luck—he was alone. She plastered herself against the wall to make sure he didn't see her when he passed.

Unfortunately, he didn't go in the direction that she'd anticipated. He turned and walked right past her. But fortunately, he behaved just as he'd been behaving toward her lately. He didn't even see her.

He was watching the soccer practice. His back was to her as he stood on the edge of the slope and gazed out at the boys on the field. She couldn't see his face, but something about his posture made her think that he wasn't in a very good mood.

He'd been the captain of the soccer team, she remembered. Then he'd had some kind of bad accident, and he couldn't play anymore. He probably missed his sport.

She edged along the wall to get into a position where she could have a better look at him. She wasn't any good at reading faces, and she certainly couldn't read his mind, but maybe he'd notice her and be happy to have some company. Once she could see his face, she knew he was feeling something stronger than simple regret.

She'd never seen a boy look so sad before. He must have really loved playing soccer. She could almost swear she saw a tear in his eye, which was ridiculous, of course, because cool guys like Ken didn't cry.

Or did they? Because now she could see the tear trickling down his cheek. Stunned, it took her a moment to react before she scampered out of his line of sight. He'd be so humiliated if a girl saw him crying!

She gave up on her plan to follow him and started toward home. All the way there, that image of Ken kept flashing before her eyes. What was that all about? She'd heard that guys could be seriously devoted to their sports. Her own father loved golf, and if he couldn't play for some reason, he'd probably feel kind of sad. But he wouldn't cry. Soccer must have really meant a lot to Ken. He'd looked totally depressed.

No matter how hard she tried, she couldn't get that image of him out of her mind. It was funny, in a way. Seeing a guy looking all demoralized like that certainly wasn't a turn-on. It didn't make Ken very appealing as a potential boyfriend. Some girls might like the sensitive type, but not Amanda. Public displays of emotion, particularly by boys, weren't her thing.

Lying in bed that night, she couldn't sleep. If she had to write off Ken as a possible way to get back her crown, what were her other options? She could make a huge fuss and demand that her parents get her out of that stupid gifted class, but that could also make things worse. It would be like admitting that the gifted class had been a bad place to be, and it would raise only more questions.

She tried to think of other actions she could take, but for some reason, she couldn't concentrate. This was truly bizarre, because she never had a hard time thinking about herself—she was her own favorite subject. But her mind kept going back to Ken and his expression while he watched the soccer practice.

This made no sense to her at all. She'd basically written him off as boyfriend material, so why couldn't she stop thinking about him? As she finally felt sleep begin to descend on her, she knew with despair that she'd end up dreaming about Ken Preston that night.

But as it turned out, she did more than that.

Chapter Eight

"ARE YOU NERVOUS?" Tracey asked. Sitting on the bed, Jenna pulled her knees up to her chest and wrapped her arms around her legs.

"No."

Tracey grinned. "Liar."

Jenna relented. "Okay, but you have to admit, this is all pretty weird. I'm just about to sit down to have dinner with some complete stranger who claims he's my father. Wouldn't you be nervous?"

"I'd be a wreck," Tracey said. "Something like this could make me disappear again."

"Wish I could disappear," Jenna grumbled. But since she couldn't, she went the opposite route. Hopping off the bed, she went back to Tracey's dressing table, sat down, and reapplied her makeup. She added more kohl to her eyes and a thick layer of purple stain to her lips.

"How do I look?" she asked Tracey.

"Like someone I wouldn't want to run into walking

alone through a dark alley," Tracey replied.

"Good." That was precisely the image she wanted to convey. Whoever this man was, she wanted to make sure he could see she was a tough chick, not some wimpy little girl who was craving a father figure.

"How come you weren't in class today?" Tracey asked.

"Because I didn't want Madame asking me how I felt about this Stuart Kelley guy showing up. I'm sure Mr. Jackson told her about it."

"How *do* you feel?"

"Tracey!"

"Okay! Sorry."

"Did I miss anything thrilling?"

Tracey shook her head. "Martin gave his career report. He said that with his special gift, he'd like to be a mercenary."

"He wants to be a soldier?"

"Not exactly. He thinks people would pay him to beat up their enemies."

"What about Ken? Maybe he could conduct séances to put people in contact with their dead relatives. That would make Emily happy."

"Ken wasn't there either. Emily said she could be a TV weather reporter, and Charles said he could hire himself out to couch-potato types so they'd never have to get out of their comfy chairs for another bag of chips. Madame suggested that he could help people who were like him, who couldn't get around easily, but he said he thought couch potatoes would pay more."

Jenna grinned. That was very Charles. She was enjoying this conversation—it kept her mind off the upcoming dinner. "How about Amanda? What does she think she could do with her gift?"

"Madame didn't call on her today, which was probably a good thing. She was looking even blanker than usual."

The sound of a doorbell made Jenna stiffen. "Uh-oh! Here he is. Whoever he is."

"You could always read his mind and find out."

Jenna nodded. That was exactly what she planned to do when the right moment came around. She took a deep breath. "Okay, let's go."

The Devon Seven, already fed and bathed, had been banished to their room with their babysitter so that the others could have a real grown-up dinner. When Tracey and Jenna arrived in the living room, they found Mr. Devon fixing cocktails and Mrs. Devon holding a huge bouquet of roses.

"Jenna, look what your father brought us!"

Refusing to smile, Jenna nodded. "They're very pretty."

"Tracey, would you find a vase?"

Jenna gave her friend a fierce don't-leave-me look, but

Tracey took the flowers from her mother and went off toward the kitchen.

"Hello, Jenna." The stranger was smiling at her.

"Hi," she murmured.

Now that she'd recovered from the shock she'd felt in Mr. Jackson's office, she could get a good look at this man. He was definitely what Emily had predicted—tall, dark, and handsome. He was dressed neatly in a suit and tie, and he looked perfectly at ease, as if dinner with a long-lost daughter was an ordinary, everyday event.

Tracey returned with the vase of roses, which her mother placed in the center of the dining table. Then she passed around a tray of crackers with squiggles of something on them.

"What do you think of your daughter, Mr. Kelley?" she asked gaily.

"Please, call me Stuart." He looked at Jenna. "I think she's beautiful," he said simply.

The squiggle on the cracker turned out to be cheese, but that wasn't what Jenna choked on. She stared at the man in disbelief. "*What*?"

Mr. Devon laughed jovially. "I'm sure all fathers think their daughters are beautiful. I know I do—all eight of them."

Stuart Kelley nodded, but his eyes were still on Jenna.

"And very special."

"Well, these two certainly are," Mrs. Devon said. "You do know about their special gifts, don't you?"

"The school principal did say something about Jenna having deep insights into people."

"I suppose that's one way of looking at it," Mr. Devon said. "*My* daughter can disappear."

"*Dad!*" Tracey interjected. "We're not really supposed to talk about this."

Her father brushed that aside. "Mr. Kelley—Stuart, I mean—is one of us. A gifted parent."

Stuart shook his head. "Hardly that, considering I've been missing from Jenna's life. I don't know how I'm ever going to make it up to her."

The Devon parents looked at each other. "We understand," they said in unison.

The way he was looking at her with that adoring expression was getting on Jenna's nerves. "Why did you come looking for me now?" she demanded.

He sighed and took a small sip of his cocktail. Jenna noticed that he'd barely touched it. At least he wasn't an alcoholic—that was something.

"I've been a coward," he said. "I always wanted to see you. I wanted to see your mother, too, but I assumed she'd slam the door in my face. She certainly has the right to do that. I treated her terribly."

"You sure did," Jenna blurted out. "You walked out on her when she was pregnant. No wonder she started drinking."

"Jenna," Mrs. Devon chided her gently, "people make all kinds of mistakes in their lives. At least your father is trying to make amends now."

It dawned on Jenna that they were all talking as if it was an absolute certainty that Stuart Kelley was her real father. Including herself—she'd just accused this man she'd never seen before in her life of walking out on her mother. Maybe now was the time to do a little mental exploration and try to find out who this guy really was.

But Mrs. Devon chose that moment to call them all to the table, and there was no opportunity for Jenna to stare at him and concentrate. The next few moments were taken up with accepting portions of roast beef and scooping green beans onto plates.

Jenna might not have been able to read his mind at the moment, but she hadn't finished asking questions. "Why did you just show up at the door on Monday? Why didn't you call first?"

"I couldn't find a telephone number," he replied.

That was a good point. The phone had been disconnected ages ago because the bill hadn't been paid.

"Besides," he continued, "I assumed your mother would just hang up once she knew who was calling."

"And she would have slammed the door in your face if she'd been home," Jenna countered.

"True," he admitted. "She certainly had every reason to. I just thought I'd have a better chance of talking to her if I came in person."

He probably thought he was so good-looking that she couldn't resist him, Jenna thought sourly. Unfortunately, he was probably right. He was exactly the type of guy her mother liked.

"Have you spoken to her at all?" Mrs. Devon asked.

"No. She's not allowed visitors or phone calls at the hospital. When does she come out, Jenna?"

"A week from Sunday."

"I'm very anxious to see her."

"Why?" Jenna asked bluntly.

He had a dazzling smile. "This might be hard to believe, Jenna, but I was very much in love with your mother. Even when I left her."

Tracey gazed at him curiously. "Do you think you might still be? In love with her, I mean?"

"Tracey!" Jenna glared at her. "Isn't that a little personal?"

Stuart Kelley laughed gently. "It's all right, Jenna. And who knows? All I can say is that I've never stopped thinking

278

about her. And you, Jenna."

Jenna didn't say anything. A new thought had come to her. This man was planning to stick around and see her mother when she came out of rehab. Barbara Kelley might have a foggy memory after all those years of drinking, but she wasn't stupid. Surely she'd know her own ex-husband.

Jenna looked at him now and tried to imagine him as her father. Maybe . . . *maybe* this wasn't quite as far-fetched as it seemed. An image flashed across her mind: a family, made up of a mother and a father and a daughter, living in a real house, having a normal life . . .

With effort, she pushed the picture out of her head. She was not optimistic by nature, and she wasn't going to start looking on the bright side of everything now.

There was an uncomfortable silence at the table. Stuart Kelley must have felt it, because he changed the subject. "So your father said you can disappear, Tracey?"

Jenna almost smiled. She liked the way he had said it conversationally, the way someone might say, *So your father said you play the piano?* He wasn't acting like they were freaks, the way some people would have.

"I used to," Tracey said. She looked at her parents, both of whom suddenly became terribly interested in what still lay on their plates. Jenna couldn't blame them—they must have felt awful about how they'd treated their daughter. Tracey was nice enough not to go into the whole story for Stuart.

"I'm practicing now," she went on. "What I need is to be able to *feel* invisible, and it's not so easy for me anymore. But I'm doing these meditation exercises, and they're helping." She turned to Jenna. "Right?"

Jenna agreed. "You were practically translucent last night. I could see the glow from the lamp behind you."

Tracey nodded happily. "We're in a special class, Jenna and me," she told Stuart. "And we're learning how to get in touch with our gifts and control them. Use them wisely."

Stuart turned to Jenna. "Is that working for you, too?"

Jenna shrugged. "Yeah, I guess."

Mr. Devon was looking at her with interest. "How deeply can you read minds, Jenna?"

She shrugged again. "I don't know."

"I mean, can you go beneath the surface?" he continued. "Or can you just read what people are clearly thinking?" He turned to his wife. "Just think of the benefit to therapy. People wouldn't have to be analyzed for years to find out what's going on in their subconscious minds. Jenna could tell them!"

"Let's try it right now," Mrs. Devon said excitedly. She turned to Stuart and explained, "I've been in analysis for years, and we just had a breakthrough last week—

an event that I'd buried in my subconscious. Let's see if Jenna can tell me what it was!"

"Mom!" Tracey moaned. "Don't ask Jenna to do that— it's embarrassing!"

Jenna could feel her face turning red. She *was* embarrassed, but how could she say no to the woman who was providing her with a home at the moment?

Tracey hadn't finished. "Besides, Madame says we should never exploit one another's gifts, and that includes the *parents* of the gifted."

"Who is Madame?" Stuart asked.

"Our gifted-class teacher," Jenna told him. "She says we have to be very careful about revealing our gifts. She tells us there are plenty of bad people out there who might want to use us for their own nasty purposes."

"And she's absolutely right," Stuart said firmly. "I don't know what kind of benefit people could get from using your mind-reading skills, but I'm sure they'd think of something." Turning to Tracey, he said, "And someone might try to force you to rob a bank for them. I think it's best not to let too many people know what you can do."

"I agree," Mr. Devon said. "Just keep it in the family."

"That's right." Stuart looked at Jenna. "Keep it in the family," he repeated.

Jenna suddenly became aware of a rush of feeling filling

her up. Was this happening? Could this be real?

"You're absolutely right," Mrs. Devon declared. "In fact, I'm ashamed of myself for asking you to show off your gift, Jenna."

"That's okay," Jenna mumbled.

Mrs. Devon raised her wineglass. "Let's toast our gifted daughters and vow never to take advantage of their gifts."

Stuart raised his glass, and so did Mr. Devon. "To our daughters," they intoned.

Tracey looked at Jenna, but Jenna averted her eyes. She suspected that Tracey knew exactly what she was thinking, despite not having any mind-reading skills.

Which reminded her of what she'd planned to do to Stuart Kelley. When Mrs. Devon went into the kitchen to get the dessert, Tracey left to help her, and the two men began talking about some movie they'd both seen. It was a good moment to try a little mind reading.

Since the men were talking, their topic of conversation would probably be the uppermost thing on Stuart's mind. But this would be a good opportunity to try what Mrs. Devon had suggested—to see if she could get below the surface thoughts to something deeper.

Her father's—she corrected herself—*Stuart's* back was to her, so she had no problem staring. First, she blocked out their voices, the music coming from the stereo, the sounds from the kitchen. Then she concentrated on piercing Stuart's mind.

But she couldn't. She tried again and again, but she couldn't even pick up the superficial thoughts about the movie they were discussing. Was he able to block her, like Emily? No, it was probably Emily's own weird gift that made her unable to be read. This was more like what happened when she tried to read her mother's mind. The family thing . . .

She caught her breath. Then she started coughing.

Mr. Devon poured her some water while Stuart patted her on the back. "Take deep breaths," he ordered. She did, and when the coughs died down, she drank the water.

"Are you okay?" Stuart asked.

"I'm fine," she assured her father. And in her mind, she added, *Maybe more than fine.*

Chapter Nine

AMANDA HAD NOW HAD 24 hours to practice being a boy. Well, not exactly *being* a boy—other than using the toilet, she hadn't really done anything boyish. But she'd had a day to get used to *feeling* like a boy. Which wasn't long. So she still felt very, very strange.

When she'd realized, the morning before, that she was now inside Ken Preston's body, she'd been pretty stunned. Even though that had been one of her original plans, she hadn't been aware that she'd been feeling sorry for Ken. But apparently those feelings she'd had after seeing him on Tuesday were real sympathy and pity, not simply distaste at seeing a boy cry.

So now she was in a body unlike any she'd ever known before. Thinking about it now, she *had* been a boy once— little Martin Cooper from the gifted class, years ago when he'd lived across the street from her and she'd seen him being bullied. But that had lasted only a minute or two, and at that age, she probably hadn't been all that aware of the difference between boys and girls anyway.

Now she was very much aware. When she'd climbed out of bed the day before, she couldn't even bring herself to take off her clothes to have a shower—it had been just too embarrassing to look at the body she was in. She'd realized that, other than babies and statues, she'd never seen a totally nude male before. It was all too much. So when Ken's mother appeared at the door and demanded to know why he hadn't come down for breakfast, she pretended to have an upset stomach and a sore throat. For a moment, Amanda was afraid that Mrs. Preston might call a doctor, but instead she decided he should stay in bed and see how he felt the next day. Then Mrs. Preston took Ken's little sister to school. And as it turned out, she had a job, so Amanda could be alone and had the house to herself all day.

With this body, so different from her own, nothing was easy. Talking, moving, eating—everything felt as though she were in a costume. Walking on legs that weren't her own was particularly difficult—she kept stumbling and tripping as she moved around Ken's house. When she spoke out loud and heard someone else's voice, it utterly freaked her out.

Of course, she'd had the experience of spending a

long time inside another person's body, but at least Tracey Devon was a girl. And something interesting occurred to her. Despite the fact that Tracey was a total nerd and she, Amanda, was fabulous, it hadn't been this hard being Tracey. She shuddered to think that maybe she and Tracey had more in common than she'd ever suspected.

Size made a big difference. She and Tracey were approximately the same height, but Ken was a lot taller. Going up and down stairs, reaching for things—everything like that felt awkward. There was no way she'd go back to school until she could feel—well, not normal (she couldn't hope for that), but at least not goofy.

She still felt goofy that morning, but she couldn't stay at home another day or Ken's mother would drag her to a doctor. So she got up, showered with her eyes closed, put on jeans and a T-shirt, and just hoped that Ken wouldn't have to wear a tie while she was in his body—she had no idea how guys made those knots.

Checking herself out in the mirror, she wasn't displeased. If she had to be a boy, at least she was a good-looking one. And she had to admit it was kind of nice not to have to spend the usual time fixing her hair and putting on makeup.

She went down to the kitchen. Ken's father had already left for work, and his mother was helping his little sister with her coat.

"Feeling better?" she asked Ken-Amanda.

"Yeah, fine," she replied. She took a bowl and examined the cereal boxes on the counter. "Don't we have any Special K?"

Mrs. Preston was taken aback. "Special K? Why would we have that?"

Amanda always ate Special K in the morning, because it was supposed to be good for her figure. How stupid of her—guys probably didn't worry about stuff like that. She'd have to be more careful about what she said.

"Oh, I was just curious what it tastes like," she lied.

Mrs. Preston still looked puzzled. "You've been eating Cocoa Puffs since you've had teeth, Ken. I can't believe you're interested in trying something else now."

"I'm a teenager," Amanda said lamely. "We do crazy things." She poured herself some Cocoa Puffs and was amazed to find how good they were. It occurred to her that boys always seemed to eat a lot more than girls. She'd have to take advantage of this body and indulge in the treats she was always denying her real self.

Luckily, she could remember Ken's schedule from constantly looking at that photocopy she had, so she knew where to go when she arrived at school. Unfortunately, she didn't know his locker number, so she'd have to lug his stuff around with her all day, but Ken used a backpack, so that wasn't too bad.

She'd just walked into his homeroom when she felt a hard smack on her shoulders. "Hey!" she cried out in outrage, before she remembered that guys were always slapping one another on the back.

Barry Levin looked at him in surprise. "What's the matter?"

"Oh, nothing—I, um, pulled a muscle," she said quickly. "What's up?"

"Not much. You ready for the French test?"

Her heart sank. Amanda took Spanish. "Nah, I'm toast. I'm gonna blow it."

Barry grinned. "Yeah, right. Mister Straight A is gonna blow a test."

She managed a sickly smile. With any luck, there would be a smart person sitting in front of her whose paper she could copy.

As the day went on, she discovered some interesting facts about the social life of boys. They didn't gossip about one another, they didn't compliment one another's clothes or hair, they didn't talk behind one another's backs. She didn't have to talk much at all—she just acted interested in whatever sport the other guys were discussing. Fortunately, Ken had a reputation for being pretty quiet, so nobody seemed to expect him to take the lead in conversations.

Her one slip-up came when some guy at lunch announced he'd seen a mouse run across the cafeteria floor.

"Ew, gross!" she shrieked. The other boys stared at her.

She managed a feeble grin. "I'm just making up for the fact that we don't have any chicks at the table."

It wasn't a very good excuse, and the boys still looked perplexed, but within seconds they were talking about something else and seemed to have forgotten her outburst. Which was another thing she decided was different about boys—if a girl did something uncool, her friends never let her forget it. At least, that's the way it was with *her* friends.

By the time lunch was over, she was feeling pretty satisfied with the way she'd pulled off her Ken behavior with his friends. No one was acting strangely around her or staring at her. Getting along as a boy with other boys wouldn't be all that difficult, she decided.

But getting along with girls might be. She was on her way out of the cafeteria when Cara Winters cornered her.

"Hi, Ken," she said coyly. "Are you feeling okay?"

"Sure. Why wouldn't I be?"

"You were out yesterday."

"Oh, yeah. No big deal—just didn't feel like going to school."

Cara looked surprised, and Amanda realized that Ken was not the type to cut classes whenever he was in that sort of mood.

She amended her remark. "I had a sore throat. But I'm fine now."

"Oh, good. I was just wondering ... could we get together before French today and go over some conjugations?"

So Cara was in the French class. "Uh, well, I haven't really studied."

Now she looked really surprised. "You haven't?"

"I completely forgot we were having the test today, and then I wasn't feeling good, so . . ." She let Ken's voice trail off, and Cara nodded understandingly. She moved in closer.

"I'll arrange the paper on my desk so you can see my answers," she whispered. "Of course, I know you don't like to cheat, but . . ."

"Maybe I could make an exception this time," Amanda replied.

Cara looked positively thrilled. And Amanda remembered a time when *she*'d been flattered that a guy had wanted to copy her paper. Boys really had it made.

Of course, her real test would come in the gifted class. Could she pull off her Ken act there? Last month, when she was Tracey, Madame could tell something was up after only a few days. And now she'd be sitting in the same room with her robotic other self. Would anyone sense that something was just slightly off?

She timed her entrance just like Ken did, at the last minute. And so did Other-Amanda. They practically collided at the door of room 209.

"Hi, Ken."

Could there be anything stranger than hearing your own voice speaking to you? Yes—seeing yourself through someone else's eyes. She couldn't even bring herself to look.

"Hi," she mumbled, just like Ken would have, and hurried into the room. Taking Ken's seat, she let Ken's silky hair fall into his eyes and peered out in a way that she hoped was unobtrusive.

Madame rose from her desk. "Yesterday we were talking about the ways in which you might be able to use your gift in your chosen career. Martin had just finished telling us that he wanted to hire himself out to people who wanted an enemy to be hurt. Does anyone have a question to ask him?"

Emily raised her hand. "Martin, you have to get really angry at someone before your super strength comes out. How are you going to get angry at the people you're hired to beat up if you don't have any personal connection to them?"

Amanda wasn't particularly interested in Martin's

reply, which she knew would be long and rambling. She tuned him out and spent the time looking surreptitiously at herself.

She knew some girls who actually believed they were prettier than they really were. She was not one of them. Last month she'd seen herself through Tracey's eyes, and she knew she was extremely cute. Now she looked even better. She wasn't sure if it was her last haircut or the fact that she was looking through a boy's eyes, but she was even more impressed with herself. What she couldn't understand was why Ken wasn't more interested . . .

Ken . . .

The voice seemed to come out of nowhere. Literally. Madame was giving Martin a long, stern lecture on nonviolence, and no one else in the class was speaking.

Ken?

It was in her head, she realized. The voice was coming from deep inside. She wasn't hearing it in the ordinary way, through her ears. It was something else.

Are you there? Can you hear me? It's Rick.

And suddenly, she understood. It was one of Ken's dead people, trying to communicate.

She didn't know whether to be intrigued or annoyed. On the one hand, the voice wasn't frightening at all. It was young and male and pleasant. On the other hand, she realized that *this* was why Ken always seemed so distracted.

She wasn't sure if she could talk back to the voice, but she tried. In her mind, she thought, *What do you want?*

Nothing special. Just wanted to talk.

She replied, *I don't want to talk. Go away.*

There was a moment of silence, and then the voice, softer this time, said, *Okay.* And her head was silent.

She couldn't believe it. It was so easy! All Ken had to do was tell the voices to go away, and they would obey! At least, this one did. It occurred to her that while she was inside Ken's body, she could do more than just ask herself out. She could lose Ken's gift for him! Then the two of them could unite, confront Madame, and drop out of the class together. And even if he wasn't madly in love with Amanda, he'd be eternally grateful, they could act like a couple, she'd be back on top—everything was falling into place.

And she'd be helping Ken, just like she'd helped Tracey. Not that helping other people was a high priority for her, but she had to admit (only to herself and never to anyone else) that it gave her kind of a nice feeling.

The discussion of Martin's aggressive instincts took up the whole class session, which was fine with Amanda. Madame never called on Ken or Other-Amanda, and the other students had no problem picking on Martin for 50 minutes. Amanda was beginning to understand why the little guy was an eternal victim.

She'd planned to approach herself as soon as class was over, but Other-Amanda took off the second the bell rang. It didn't really matter—she needed more time to prepare what she was going to say, and there wasn't much time between classes for a conversation. She'd meet up with Other-Amanda at her own locker after the last class.

Ken's next class was French, and even though she'd never cheated on a test before, she didn't feel the least bit guilty copying the answers from Cara. She reasoned that she wasn't really Ken or herself either, so the rules didn't count. The only problem would be if Ken got caught—but he didn't.

She got through the rest of the day without any real problems—she just never raised her hand and none of the teachers called on Ken. The only class she now had to worry about was the last one—gym. If she didn't perform well, she could blame it on having been sick the day before, but changing in and out of the gym outfit could be tricky, especially surrounded by all those boys.

But once again, she lucked out. Ken's gym class was having a lecture day on nutrition. She could sit in the back of a normal classroom and zone out.

She used the time to revise her original plan. She'd meet Amanda at her locker and set up some kind of date for after school that day or the next. Saturday at the latest. Once they were alone together, she'd take back her own body and let him have his. How she was going to do this, she wasn't quite sure, but she'd worry about that when the time came. Then she'd tell him how she'd lost the voices for him, he'd be grateful, and everything would fall into place.

Ken?

There he was again, the dead guy. *Get lost,* she said.

Ken, what's the matter with you? Why are you acting like this?

Because I'm not in the mood, she responded. *I might never be in the mood again.*

Please, Ken. Don't say that. I don't know what I'd do without you.

Despite herself and all her intentions, the voice touched her. The guy sounded so sad. Maybe it wouldn't hurt to have just one real conversation with one of Ken's dead people. She'd have a better understanding of what his gift was really like.

What do you want? she asked.

I'm feeling really down. I can't stop thinking about her.

Who?

You know! Nancy.

Amanda didn't know anyone named Nancy. It was kind

of an old-fashioned name, she thought. A grandmother-type name. Apparently, this guy—what did he say his name was? Rick—apparently, Rick had talked about this Nancy to Ken before.

Why are you thinking about Nancy?

I'm always thinking about her—you know that. I miss her so much. Like I said, I really loved her. I still can't believe she dumped me at the senior prom.

And you couldn't get her back?

How could I? That was the night I died.

This was getting interesting. So she was talking to someone who had to have been around 17 or 18 years old when he died. She wondered how that had happened. She couldn't ask—Ken probably knew.

Do you know what it feels like, Ken?

To die?

No, to love someone so much. And to have your heart broken.

No, not really.

You're lucky. It's the most unbelievable pain. You'd rather have two broken legs than a broken heart. She was everything to me: the sun, the moon, the stars. I can remember thinking I would die for her. Which is ironic, in a way. I did die, but I didn't even have the satisfaction of doing it for her.

"Ken?"

He looked up. The room was empty, and the teacher

was standing at the door.

"Class is over, Ken. I see you didn't find the topic of essential daily vitamins very exciting. But you could have tried to stay awake, just out of common courtesy." The teacher didn't wait for an apology.

Amanda got up, slung Ken's backpack over his shoulder, and hurried out. There were just a few stragglers left in the hall, heading to the exit.

She knew her own habits. Other-Amanda would be long gone. She'd been so caught up in Rick's story that she'd missed her chance to ask herself out.

It looked like she was going to have to be Ken for a while longer.

Chapter Ten

J ENNA WAS AT HER LOCKER on Friday afternoon when Tracey joined her.

"Ready to leave?" Tracey asked.

Jenna took out her jacket. "I'm not going home, remember? I'm meeting my father."

"Oh, right." Tracey smiled. "Did you hear what you just said? *My father.*"

Jenna grinned. "Yeah. And it felt so natural."

"You don't have any more doubts?"

Jenna shook her head. "It's like I told you—I couldn't read his mind, just like I can't read my mother's. We're family."

Tracey looked thoughtful. "But you can't read Madame's mind, or Emily's, and they're not family."

"That's different. Emily does something with her own gift, so I can't use mine on her. And Madame . . . she's got some weird insight. Did you notice how she was looking at Amanda today in class?"

"Yeah. What was that all about?"

"Maybe that wasn't the real Amanda."

"She seemed real enough to me," Tracey said.

Jenna slammed the locker door shut. "Yeah, and she seemed real last month, too, when she was actually occupying your body. I'll bet she's inside someone else right now."

"Who?"

"Who knows?" The girls walked to the exit together. "Who cares? But if she wasn't there, I'll bet Madame could tell."

"Could *you* tell? If you read her mind?"

Jenna shrugged. "I guess I could. But like I said, who cares?" They were outside now. "I'm meeting my father at the mall. I'll see you tonight."

As she crossed the street to reach the mall, she could feel the excitement rising inside her. She was meeting her father! It was almost too much to take in. And she wasn't just excited—she was nervous. This would be their first time alone together. Not really alone, of course—there were plenty of other people milling around the mall. But they'd have only each other to talk to. What if she couldn't think of anything to say? What if she bored him? A couple of hours alone with her and he just might decide this relationship wasn't worth the effort.

And what if he wasn't there? What if her original doubts had been on target? What if—

What if he was right there, in front of the music store, where he'd said he'd be, waiting for her?

Mentally kicking herself for having doubts, she waved to him, and he waved back.

"How was your day?" he asked.

"Fine," she replied automatically. "How was yours?"

"Fine," he said. There was a silence.

"It's not easy, is it?" he said. "You'd think that with all these years to catch up on, we wouldn't have any problem coming up with subjects for conversation."

She smiled awkwardly. She wasn't exactly ready to pour out all her feelings and experiences—not yet. She needed something not too personal to get this relationship off the ground.

She glanced at the display in the store window. "What kind of music do you like?"

"A little bit of almost everything," he replied. "Classical, jazz, rock. I'm not too crazy about folk music."

Jenna lit up. "I *hate* folk music! Do you like techno?"

"I can't say I know much about it," he admitted. "Want to introduce me?"

They went into the music store, and Jenna showed him CDs of the groups she particularly liked. There were headphones hanging on the walls so that you could listen to samples, and she showed him how to use them.

He was *cool*. He didn't pull that fake adult thing of pretending to love all the music she played for him, just to prove that he was down with the younger generation. He liked some groups, he didn't like others, and he expressed his opinions openly.

"I think I could get into this," he told her. "I'm going to write down some names so I can download them to my iPod."

She was impressed. "You have an iPod?"

"Absolutely. When you move around as much as I've been moving these past few years, it's the only way to keep your music with you. Don't you have one?"

She shook her head.

"I thought all kids had iPods."

She picked up a CD at random and pretended to study the track listing. "They're pretty expensive," she said finally.

He was silent, and she looked up.

"It's been hard on you and your mother, hasn't it?" he asked. "Financially, I mean."

Jenna shrugged. "We manage."

"Do you?"

She looked away, and he got the message.

"I could say I'm sorry," he said. "I *am* sorry. But there

wasn't much I could have done about that. I haven't been doing too well myself. Still, that's no excuse."

Jenna thought it was, and she wanted to make him feel better. "If you didn't have any money, you couldn't have sent us any."

He smiled. "You're a pragmatist. Just like your mother."

"What's a pragmatist?"

"Someone who's down-to-earth, sensible."

Jenna would never have used those words to describe her mother. But maybe Barbara Kelley had been different back when Stuart had known her.

"But I can afford to buy my daughter an iPod," he said suddenly. "Do they sell them here?"

"You don't have to do that," she said.

"I want to," he insisted.

But she had meant what she'd said. The thought of him suddenly showering her with gifts . . . It bothered her.

And to her utter amazement and delight, he understood. "You think I'm trying to buy your affection, don't you?"

She nodded.

He smiled sadly. "You're probably right. Well, you'll let me buy you a Coke, won't you?"

She could agree to that. They went into a café, and she allowed him to buy her not only a Coke but also a plate of fries to share with him. She was a little worried that he was going to start pressing her for information about herself, that he'd expect her to tell him her life story. But once again, he was cool.

He told her about his life, the adventures he'd had. He'd been living pretty much hand to mouth for the past 13 years, but he'd been doing it in interesting ways. He'd been a porter on a train that went across the country, from New York to San Francisco. He'd washed dishes on a cruise ship. He'd been a waiter in a fancy Hollywood restaurant, and he'd seen lots of famous people in person. He'd worked on a pipeline in Alaska.

He was amazing. Other kids she knew, their fathers were lawyers, teachers, salesmen. They worked in offices, factories, ugly high rises. Tracey's father had some kind of big-and-boring business. None of them were like Stuart Kelley.

And he was better looking than any father she'd ever seen. Tracey's father was practically bald. Emily's dad had a stomach that hung over his belt. Stuart Kelley could be a movie star! Jenna hadn't missed the looks he got from women they'd passed in the mall.

Like the cashier at the café. She took the bill that Stuart gave her without looking at it. She couldn't take her eyes off his face.

"I hope you enjoyed your meal, sir," she gushed.

Stuart kept a perfectly straight face as he said, "It was an absolutely delicious Coca-Cola."

He was *funny*, Jenna thought in delight. The cashier didn't get it. She just simpered as she handed him some coins.

"Excuse me," Stuart said, looking at the change in his hand. "I think you've made a mistake. I gave you a twenty-dollar bill."

"Oh no, sir, it was a ten," the cashier said.

Stuart looked at her doubtfully. "Are you sure? I'm positive it was a twenty."

Jenna couldn't resist. She focused on the cashier and read her mind.

This is the easiest ten bucks I've ever made.

"It was a twenty," Jenna announced.

The cashier pressed her lips together tightly. A man in a white shirt with a tag that read Manager came over.

"Is there a problem?" he asked.

"No problem," the cashier said and took a ten-dollar bill from the drawer. "Here's your change, sir."

"Thank you," Stuart said politely.

"Did you see me give her the money?" he asked Jenna as they went back out into the mall.

"No. But I read her mind and I could see that she was trying to cheat you."

He laughed. "That's quite a talent you have, Jenna.

I guess I won't have to worry about anyone trying to cheat *you*. Or me, while I've got you around! I think we'd better stick together. What do you think?"

"Sounds okay to me," Jenna said lightly, but she knew her smile was extending from ear to ear.

From there, they did some window-shopping, exchanging comments on fashion, books, art. Stuart had to pick up a few things at the drugstore, and they discovered they both used the same brand of toothpaste.

At one point they paused in front of a tattoo parlor, and Jenna admired the designs displayed in the window.

"Do you like tattoos?" Stuart asked.

She nodded. "I'd like to get one." She watched him carefully to gauge his reaction. Most parents she knew would go ballistic if their kids mentioned getting a tattoo.

Not Stuart. "You might want to wait a while," he said mildly. "Keep in mind that it's pretty much a permanent decision. I know they have treatments to remove them, but that's a big deal and very expensive. I thought about getting one once, a long time ago."

"What kind?" she asked.

"Nothing very original. A name in a heart." He smiled. "*Barbara.*"

"I suppose you must be glad you didn't," Jenna remarked, "considering how things worked out."

"Mmm." He smiled wistfully. "Well, you never know. I still might end up with one sometime."

Just any tattoo? Jenna wondered. Or Barbara, in a heart? But she didn't dare ask him. It was too much to hope for.

"Look," he said, "they sell temporary ones. Let's check them out."

They went inside and looked at the various types of press-on tattoos available. Jenna admired a sheet composed of letters and various borders.

"This is cool—you can design your own," she said. "And it says they last at least a week. You could try something, and after a week, if you still like it, you could get a real one tattooed over it."

"Good idea," Stuart agreed. He picked up a sheet and took it to the checkout counter. As they waited in line, he whispered to Jenna, "Keep an eye on the exchange. I don't want you to have to waste your mind-reading skills on me again!"

She grinned. Personally, she didn't think there were any gifts that would be wasted on him.

After paying for the temporary tattoos, Stuart was out of cash, so when they came to a bank, he stopped to get money out of an ATM. There was a woman in front of them, and she was taking an unusually long time. She kept putting in her card, punching numbers, and then taking out the card.

Jenna heard her utter a mild curse under her breath.

She turned to them. "I'm sorry I'm taking so long. I can't remember my PIN."

Jenna listened with interest. Here it was—an opportunity to try that subconscious mind reading Mrs. Devon had asked her about. Like an invisible power drill, she bore into the woman's mind.

"Three eight seven two," she said.

The woman stared at her, and her mouth fell open. Then her expression changed to horror. She jammed the card back into her wallet and took off in a hurry.

"That wasn't very nice of her," Stuart commented.

Jenna laughed. "She must have thought we were thieves."

Stuart started laughing, too. "I guess we make a good team, huh?"

Jenna's heart was so full that she felt like it was going to explode.

It was time for her to get back to the Devons' house. Stuart had a rental car, a cute little yellow compact, and he drove her. Parking in front, he walked her to the door.

"I'm not going to come in," he told her. "It's too close to dinnertime and it'll look like I'm scrounging for a free meal."

Jenna wanted him to stay, but she understood. He was proud, just like her.

"Well, I'll see you," she said. "You're staying in town for a while, aren't you?"

"Absolutely," he assured her. He put his hands on her shoulders, leaned forward, and kissed her lightly on the cheek. Then he pulled back and looked a little embarrassed.

"I hope I wasn't being too pushy there."

Jenna shook her head happily. "No, it's okay. I mean, I guess that's what fathers do, right?"

He smiled. "Right."

Chapter Eleven

AMANDA-KEN LAY ON KEN'S bed, staring at the ceiling, and listened. *We spent a lot of time at the beach. The sun on her blond hair—it was like gold sprinkled on gold. Her tan was golden, too. She was like that girl dipped in gold. Did you ever see* Goldfinger?

No, but I've heard of it. It's an old James Bond movie, right?

She thought Rick was laughing. *I keep forgetting you're living in another century! I was fourteen when I saw* Goldfinger. *That's how old you are, right? You should see it; it's great.*

I'll borrow it from the DVD store.

Man, I wish we'd had DVDs in my time. That must be so neat, to watch movies whenever you want.

Yeah, it's . . . neat.

Nancy and I used to go to the movies practically every Saturday night. She liked romantic films, and I liked action ones. Every Saturday, we'd argue about what to see. Not argue, really—more like debate.

Who won?

We took turns choosing. But she could have won all the time. I'd always give in to her.

By now, Amanda had figured out how to keep some thoughts to herself. So she could think about how wonderful it would be to have a boyfriend like Rick, who would cherish you and give you anything you wanted. And she didn't have to worry that he might hear that, because Rick still thought he was talking to another guy.

She communicated her next question.

What else did you guys do together?

You know the Public Gardens, near City Hall?

Sure.

That was one of her favorite places, especially when the roses were in bloom. She loved roses. When I sold my motorcycle, I used the money to give her one red rose every day till the money ran out.

Red roses and motorcycles. Wow! What a guy.

What?

She realized she hadn't kept that thought to herself.

Um, I was just wondering, why did you sell your motorcycle?

My brother joined the army and gave me his to use. There was a pause. *I don't want to talk about that, okay?*

She wondered if his brother had been killed.

Had there been a war going on when Rick was a

teenager? She still wasn't sure when that had been.

There was a knock on Ken's bedroom door.

"Come in," Amanda called.

Ken's mother stuck her head in. "Are you feeling all right?"

"Sure. Why?"

"It's Saturday afternoon, the sun's out, and you've been lying in bed all day!" She frowned. "I'm going to call a doctor. You haven't been eating much lately either. I think you need a checkup."

Amanda-Ken jumped off the bed. "I'm fine. I was just thinking about stuff. I'm going out now."

To Rick, she said, *Later.*

What she wanted to do now would require the computer, but she needed to get out of the house before she raised more suspicions in Ken's mother's mind. A teacher had told her class once that there were free online services at the public library. She'd never set foot in the public library before, but she knew where it was.

She was surprised when the librarian at the desk greeted her—greeted Ken, actually.

"Good to see you, Ken," she said with a smile.

Amanda noticed the nameplate on the desk. "Hello, Ms. Fletcher."

The woman looked startled. Then she saw that Ken was

staring at the plate, and she turned it around. She laughed softly. "Very funny, Ken. Okay, I just came on and I haven't gotten around to changing the name." She put the plate in a drawer and took out another one that read *Ms. Greenwood*.

Amanda smiled back at the librarian and inwardly breathed a sigh of relief. That was a close call.

Locating the computers, she sat down at one and turned it on. The screen lit up, and then a message appeared.

Enter Code.

She got up and went back to the librarian's desk. "The computer says I need a code to log on."

"That's right," she said with a puzzled expression. "Ken, you've used these computers before. You know what to do."

Amanda swallowed. "I, uh, forgot it."

The lines of puzzlement on the librarian's forehead deepened. But at least she answered him. "It's five zeros, Ken. Pretty easy to remember."

"Yeah, right. Of course. I'm a little out of it today."

Now the librarian looked concerned. With Amanda's luck, the woman would turn out to be a friend of Ken's mother and call her to report that Ken was behaving strangely.

Back at the computer, Amanda logged in, and in the search box she typed *Goldfinger*. What came up was a

312

description of the movie, some pictures of the actors, and a date: 1964. How old had Rick said he'd been when he saw it? Fourteen?

She didn't want to go back to Ms. Greenwood or Fletcher or whatever her name was and make a fool of herself again. So she got up and wandered around the library.

It was kind of interesting—she didn't know libraries had CDs and DVDs and video games. But she didn't take time to look at any of them. She was on a mission.

Finally, she found what she was searching for in a little room off the main area, a room that looked like it hadn't been dusted in years. On a row of shelves she found all the yearbooks of all the schools in town, going back to the dark ages or whatever. If Rick had been 14 in 1964, that meant he probably was supposed to have graduated from high school in 1967 or 1968.

There were three high schools in town. She didn't know his last name. And Rick, or Richard, turned out to be a pretty common name. Checking indexes, she found seven possible Ricks.

She started checking pictures, although she had no idea what she was looking for. In their conversations, there had been no reference to his hair color or any other identifiable characteristic.

It was extremely frustrating. Several of the Ricks looked cute, others not so much. Some of them had really long hair, which must have been the fashion at the time.

There were photos of student activities, teams, and clubs, but she didn't know what Rick had been into in high school. Except Nancy, of course. Which was why she got very excited when she accidentally hit on a picture of a boy and a girl in formal clothes with a caption that read *Rick Lasky and Nancy Chiswick*.

There was always the possibility that there had been another couple named Rick and Nancy. Even so, this felt right. She remembered Rick talking about Nancy's golden hair. This photo was in black and white, but she could see that the girl's long, straight hair was very blond.

She was more interested in the boy. He had straight hair, too, but it looked like a deep brown in the picture. It was almost as long as Nancy's—you never saw hair that long on boys nowadays, except maybe on some hippie-type rock stars. He was thin, but he didn't look unhealthy. *How did he die?* she wondered.

He was wearing a tuxedo, but not an ordinary one. It looked like there was glittery stuff on the collar and cuffs. And underneath the coat, he wasn't wearing the white shirt and black tie you'd expect to see—he had on a T-shirt. Maybe it was some kind of fashion statement. Or maybe it reflected Rick's sense of humor. He had a great smile, and even though she couldn't actually make out a twinkle in his eyes, she felt very sure it was there.

Normally, Amanda wouldn't find this whole look attractive—she preferred guys who were more manly and athletic in appearance, like Ken. But there was something very appealing about Rick Lasky, something that stirred her.

She looked at Nancy again. Amanda had to admit that she was pretty. Not as pretty as Amanda, of course, but she had a nice face. The gown was awful—all fluffy and puffy—but she could see that Nancy had a good figure. She wore a corsage of roses, which Amanda assumed were red. Naturally, Rick would have given her her favorite flowers to wear.

It must be a prom picture, she thought. Was this the prom where Nancy broke up with him?

Now she had a last name, if this really was her Rick in the picture. How funny that she was now thinking of him as "her" Rick. She went to the back of the yearbook and looked up *Lasky, Richard* in the index. There were four page numbers after his name.

The first one directed her to a group photo of some club called *Celestial Turnings*. Reading the caption under the picture, she learned that this was a literary magazine that featured creative writing by students.

She'd always thought students who were in this type of club would be nerds—brainy types who didn't know how to have fun—but these kids didn't look bad at all. Rick looked even cuter than he did in the prom picture.

The next picture was the standard senior class photo—head and shoulders, dark robe with one of those flat tasseled things on his head, fake background of blue sky and clouds. Rick had pulled his hair back into a ponytail for this one, and this gave her a better view of his face. Small ears, high cheekbones, deep-set eyes. Brown, or maybe a very dark blue. Warm, soft eyes. She felt a little flutter in her—in Ken's—stomach.

The third photo was the one taken at the prom. The fourth was the same as the class photo, but enlarged, covering almost the entire page. And bordered in black. Under the picture, she read, "In Memoriam: Richard (Rick) Lasky, 1950–1968."

She remembered he had died during his senior year, just after the prom. An overwhelming sadness came over her, and she felt an almost uncontrollable urge to cry. Which was ridiculous—all this had happened more than 40 years ago. And it wasn't as if she actually knew him—he was just a voice, that was all.

She went back to the computer and entered his name and the school's name into the search box. She was rewarded with an article from the local newspaper. An obituary.

Richard Lasky, age 18, killed in an accident on the highway. He'd been on his brother's motorcycle, she guessed. That was why he didn't like talking about it.

For the longest time, she just stared at the report. Then she went back to the dusty room. On another shelf, she found bound copies of other school publications—directories, newspapers, theater programs. And *Celestial Turnings*.

She searched the issues published between 1965 and 1968 and found two short stories and several poems by Rick. The stories were a little too wordy for her liking, but the poems were nice. One in particular.

It was called "Nancy," and it was a love poem.

I want to dive into the blue ocean of your eyes
And swim to your heart.
If you want me to stay, I will live and breathe as part
  of you and ask for nothing in return.
But even if you don't want me to stay, I will not leave.
I will simply drown in a sea of my own tears.

Now she really wanted to cry. To be loved like that— how unbelievably beautiful. Nancy couldn't appreciate this. She didn't deserve him.

I do, she thought. She took the magazine to a photocopy machine.

Later that evening, alone in Ken's room, she read the poem over and over again. And each time she read it, she felt it more and more. And she fantasized about someday when a boy would write a poem like that for her . . .

But why fantasize?

She turned on Ken's computer and opened the word-processing program. Then she retyped Rick's poem, making one change—the title. She printed it out. Then she folded it carefully, put it in an envelope, and on the envelope wrote the name that was now the title of the poem.

Amanda.

CHAPTER TWELVE

JENNA WAS HAVING SUNDAY lunch with her father in a real restaurant, the kind with cloth napkins. "How's your chicken?" Stuart asked her. "Delicious," she replied. Of course she'd eaten chicken before, many times, but she'd never had it like this, in a sauce with small mushrooms.

Her father was eating some kind of fish. There were a lot of little bones that he had to keep picking out, which would have driven Jenna crazy, but he didn't seem to mind. A man like Stuart Kelley, who had once lived alone on a beach for a month and had fished for his own meals every day, wouldn't be bothered by a few bones. His life had been so amazing!

"Did you really work on an African safari?" she asked him.

"Only for a couple of weeks," he said. "And it wasn't one of those heavy-duty hunting safaris."

This was something else she liked about him—he didn't

brag about everything he'd done. He was matter-of-fact about his adventures.

"Good," Jenna said in relief. "I don't like the idea of killing animals." She looked down at her plate. "I eat them, though. I guess that makes me kind of a hypocrite."

"I feel exactly the same way," Stuart confided, and once again, Jenna had that warm, happy feeling she'd been experiencing a lot lately. They had so much in common!

She had one worry, though. How could a man who'd been living such an exciting life suddenly move here and settle down with a regular job and a family? Because that was now her fantasy, and as hard as she tried to let her natural pessimism and distrust have an impact, the stories kept playing out in her head. A house with a yard. A mother, a father, maybe a dog, maybe even a little brother or sister . . .

"Stu? Stu Kelley?"

A red-faced man in a bright Hawaiian shirt had stopped by their table. Her father rose.

"Arnie! Good to see you!" The two men shook hands.

"What's it been—ten years? More?" the man asked. "How long are you in town for?"

"I'm not sure," Stuart said. He turned and gave Jenna a wink. "Depends on how things work out."

"What are you doing these days?"

"Not much. I'm between jobs at the moment. The money's running out, though, so I have to start looking around."

Once again, Jenna felt a rush of admiration. He didn't have much money, but he'd scraped together enough to take his daughter out to lunch in a restaurant where you didn't have to stand in line at a counter. She made a mental note not to order dessert.

The florid man nodded toward the opposite end of the restaurant. "Well, if you've still got a few bucks and you feel lucky, you might be interested in the back room."

"The back room?"

"There's a regular poker game there every Sunday afternoon. Nice guys, and the stakes aren't too high. I'm on my way there now. Want to join us?"

"No thanks," Stuart said. "I'm spending the day with my daughter." He introduced them. Stuart and the big man promised each other to stay in touch, and Arnie took off for his game in the back room.

"Is poker a hard game to play?" Jenna asked.

"Not really. It's hard to win, though. It depends a lot on the cards you're dealt, so luck is a major factor. And reading minds."

Jenna's eyes widened. "Reading minds?"

Stuart laughed. "Not literally, Jenna. Have you ever

heard the expression *poker face*?"

"No."

"It's when someone's expression tells you nothing about what they're thinking. It comes from the fact that in poker, frequently you have to bluff and pretend your cards are better or worse than they really are so that the other players will bet or raise or fold the way you want them to—so you can win."

She didn't know what he meant by raising or folding, but she got the general idea. "You have to guess what the other people are holding?"

"Exactly. And if the players have good poker faces, it's not easy. How about some dessert?"

"No thank you," Jenna said properly.

He didn't want any dessert either, so he called for the check, and the waiter brought it to the table. "Now, what would you like to do this afternoon? How about a movie?" He opened his wallet and took out some money. Jenna could see that there was very little left. She tried to think of something they could do that wouldn't cost anything.

"Do you know what I'd really like to do? See a real poker game."

Stuart was surprised. "Why?"

"I like card games, and I want to see how it works."

Stuart smiled. "I'm afraid it's not a spectator sport."

Those guys in the back room aren't going to want us watching them."

"What if you played?" Jenna asked. "Would they let me sit with you?"

He looked at her in amusement. "You really want to do that?"

She bobbed her head up and down vigorously.

He shrugged. "We can ask."

In the back room, there was a pool table, a foosball machine, and a couple of tables where people were playing cards. When Arnie looked up and saw Stuart and Jenna, he waved them over.

"Hey, we're just about to start a new round. Want to join in?"

"Do you mind if my kid sits with me?" Stuart asked.

One of the other men grinned. "As long as she's only looking at *your* cards."

Stuart pulled over two chairs and they sat down. Jenna winced as he added what little was left in his wallet to the pot, and the cards were dealt.

Jenna wasn't exactly sure what was going on—all the calling and raising meant nothing to her. But after a while, some things became clear. The cards that a player was holding were called a hand, and the best hand won the game. Sometimes, though, people would pretend to have a better hand than they really did so that the other players would give up. That was the bluffing part.

Only nobody seemed to be bluffing in this game, and it was all kind of boring. Jenna realized she had made a mistake—card games were only fun when you yourself were playing them. Like her father said, poker wasn't a spectator sport.

She found a magazine in the corner and brought it back to her chair. It was about cars and wasn't any more interesting than the poker game, so once again she indulged in fantasies about her future life. She wondered how her mother would feel about her ex-husband's return. Would she be happy? She never talked about Stuart or expressed any interest or curiosity in where he was or what he was doing. Probably because she thought she'd never see him again. She was in for a big surprise . . .

"Jenna? What do you think?"

She shoved aside her daydreams and turned to her father. "What?"

"Everyone's folded—it's just me and Mr. Clifford there. What I don't know is whether or not Mr. Clifford has a better hand than I do."

She glanced at her father's hand. It looked pretty good to her—three aces, two kings. But if Mr. Clifford had something like four aces and a king, it didn't matter—

Stuart would lose and Mr. Clifford would get that pile of money in the center of the table.

"Take a look at him," her father urged her. "Do you think he's bluffing?"

She looked at the man across the table. He seemed friendly, with bushy eyebrows and a broad smile. She didn't have the slightest idea what kind of cards he had—he held them close, like all the players, and all she could see was the back of them. Too bad she didn't have x-ray vision.

But she did, in a way. Even if she couldn't see the actual cards, Mr. Clifford was probably thinking about them.

She was pretty sure it wasn't the right thing to do, but she couldn't resist. It would be so awful for Stuart to lose the little money he had left. So she did her thing.

And she was right about what was going on in Mr. Clifford's thoughts. There they were, spread out in her mind—two aces, two jacks, and a ten. She didn't know the value for sure, but it seemed to her that her father's hand was stronger.

"I don't think you should fold."

He didn't—he raised the bet, which Jenna thought was crazy, because he didn't have any more money. But then Mr. Clifford had to show his cards, and Stuart won.

Mr. Clifford wasn't angry. He congratulated Stuart and said, "Your daughter's got good instincts."

Stuart nodded. "Yes, I think I'll keep her," he said jovially.

When Jenna saw how much money he'd won, she was pleased. "I'm glad I was right," she told him.

"But you knew you were right, didn't you? You read his mind."

She admitted she had. "But I guess that's cheating, huh? I probably shouldn't have done it."

He laughed. "That's one way to look at it."

She wasn't sure what he meant, but he wasn't mad at her, and that was all that mattered.

He insisted on getting her a little gift with some of his winnings, and she let him buy her a T-shirt—black, of course, with silver glittery stars all over it.

"Thanks," she said. "Have you tried any of those fake tattoos?"

"Not yet. How about you?"

She hesitated. Then, with an abashed smile, she took off her cardigan and revealed her upper right arm, where the word *Dad* was emblazoned in red.

Stuart put an arm around her shoulders and gave her a little squeeze. "That's my girl."

It seemed as though she'd been waiting for a moment like this all her life. Not that she'd been depressed about not having a father—like her mother, she had never given him much thought. But she had one now, and better late than never.

When they got back to the Devons' house, Mrs. Devon insisted that Stuart stay for dinner. While the adults had their cocktails, Jenna ran up to Tracey's room to show off her new T-shirt.

"Guess what?" she said to Tracey. "I'm happy!"

"You should be," Tracey said. "It's a great T-shirt."

Jenna picked up her pillow and tossed it playfully at Tracey. "Not just for that. Tracey, I really think he's going to stay! As soon as my mother comes out of the hospital, he's going to talk to her. And they might get back together!"

"Don't get carried away," Tracey cautioned her. "Your mother doesn't even know he's back in town. She might not want him."

"Are you crazy?" Jenna shrieked. She threw herself on the bed and gazed at the ceiling. "He's handsome, he's funny, he's nice . . . Who wouldn't want a man like that?"

"He doesn't have a job, does he?"

"He can *get* one. You wouldn't believe all the interesting jobs he's had. He worked on a ship, he worked at a safari camp, he had a job in Alaska—"

"Really? That's what he said?"

Jenna sat up. "You think he's lying?"

"Oh no," Tracey said quickly. "It's just interesting that he's had such a variety of jobs. What did you two do today?"

"We had lunch in a restaurant, and then we played poker. Well, my father played—I just watched. And he won!"

"Lucky him," Tracey said.

"It wasn't luck," Jenna confessed, and she told Tracey about reading the other player's mind.

It probably wasn't the right thing to do—Tracey was big on honesty. Jenna wasn't surprised when Tracey scolded her.

"That wasn't smart," she said reprovingly. "I'm sure Stuart wouldn't be happy to know you did that."

"He knows," Jenna admitted. "I told him."

Tracey looked at her curiously. "What did he say?"

"He laughed."

Tracey looked appalled. "You're kidding!"

"My father is very cool," Jenna informed her. "He doesn't lecture or give lessons on how to behave."

Tracey murmured something that Jenna couldn't hear.

"What did you say?"

"I just said . . . that doesn't sound very fatherly."

Jenna stared at her. "What's that supposed to mean?"

"Nothing."

But there was an uneasy silence in the air, which Jenna finally broke. "Don't you like my father?"

"He's okay," Tracey said. "It's just that . . ."

"What?"

"Well, he just shows up out of nowhere, says he's your father, and all of a sudden your whole life is going to change. I just don't want you to be too disappointed."

"Why would I be disappointed?" Jenna asked in bewilderment. Then, something else Tracey had said echoed in her ears. "What do you mean, he *says* he's my father? Don't you *believe* he's my father?"

"I don't know,"Tracey replied."Maybe. But your mother hasn't seen him yet. And you believe him because you can't read his mind. Which isn't much to go on."

"My mother could have been at home when he came to Brookside Towers," Jenna pointed out.

"But she wasn't," Tracey said. "And maybe he knew that."

"That doesn't make any sense," Jenna argued. "Why would he lie about being my father? To hang out with me? He's not some kind of sicko!"

"Oh no, I didn't mean that,"Tracey said hastily."All I'm saying is that you should take it easy. Don't jump to any conclusions."

Jenna glared at her."I *like* my conclusions."

Tracey was silent. Then she offered Jenna a half smile. "I'm sorry. I shouldn't talk like that about him—it's none of my business anyway. Let's talk about something else."

"Fine," Jenna said. "What did you do today?"

"Practiced disappearing."

"Oh yeah? How did it go?"

"I'm getting better," Tracey told her. "I was able to go completely invisible for a full minute. At least, I *think* I was completely invisible. It's hard to tell, looking in a mirror. There might have been an outline of me or something I didn't see."

"Try it now and I'll tell you if you're invisible," Jenna suggested.

Tracey's brow puckered, and she gazed at Jenna steadily for a moment. "Okay," she said finally. She went over to Jenna's side of the room, by the door. "If I disappear, time me so I'll know how long I can do it." She handed Jenna her cell phone and showed her the stopwatch feature. Then she stepped back a few paces.

Jenna watched. Tracey stood very still with her eyes closed. She breathed evenly and steadily, in a way that told Jenna she was concentrating.

And she began to fade. At first, it was practically imperceptible. Jenna thought it was her own imagination or wishful thinking that made Tracey seem less solid to her. But then she actually began to see through Tracey. She was translucent, and then she was transparent. Jenna couldn't see her at all.

She started the stopwatch. She was still feeling a little

annoyed with Tracey for not being enthusiastic about Stuart. But Tracey hadn't had an easy life until now—she'd been ignored at home and tormented at school—so it was probably hard for her to accept people or believe in them. Stuart would work his charm on her eventually.

How long had Tracey been able to stay invisible earlier? A full minute? She'd been gone longer than that already. It was a minute and 19 seconds . . .

A form started to appear, and Jenna stopped the watch. "One minute and twenty-two seconds," she announced as Tracey became solid again. "Why are you so out of breath?"

Tracey was panting, and her fists were clenched. "You think it doesn't take any energy to vanish?"

"I didn't think it was like running a marathon," Jenna commented. "Hey, I'm starving. Did your mother put out any of those nibbly things with the cocktails?"

"Go look," Tracey said. "I'll be down soon." She was still breathing a little heavily, and Jenna caught a glimpse of a strange, sort of sickly expression on her face before she turned away.

Clearly, vanishing required a lot more energy and effort than mind reading, Jenna thought as she ran downstairs. On the other hand, invisibility could be a real benefit in playing poker . . .

Chapter Thirteen

"AREN'T YOU GOING TO watch the basketball game with me?" Ken's father called to the person he thought was his son. Amanda paused at the bottom of the stairs. This was sticky. Ken was seriously into sports, and he probably watched all the games on TV with his father. But she'd prefer to be alone in his room and wait for Rick to contact her.

They'd been "talking," or whatever it was, most of the day. Amanda couldn't remember ever having spent an entire Sunday sitting alone in a bedroom doing absolutely nothing, not even leafing through a copy of *Teen Vogue*. But it was so absolutely fantastic to be able to concentrate completely on communicating with Rick without any distractions.

But now Ken's mother was looking at him-her strangely, too. "You *always* watch the Sunday-night basketball game with your father," she said in a worried voice.

Now she was going to start talking about taking him to

the doctor again. "Sure, I want to watch the game. I just wanted to go to the bathroom first."

"Why are you going upstairs?" his father asked. "Use the one in the hall."

She hadn't even noticed that there was another bathroom downstairs. She really had to get her act together if she wasn't going to raise any suspicions—especially if she was going to stay inside Ken's body for a while longer. She wasn't in any rush to get out. Not now, not with Rick in her life. She was in love with him.

When she came out of the bathroom, she went into the den and flopped down in the big, fat recliner.

"Hey," Ken's father cried in outrage. "Since when do you take my chair?"

"Just joking around," Amanda said, leaping up.

"What's gotten into you lately, boy?" Ken's father muttered. He picked up the remote control and turned on the TV. Amanda just hoped he wasn't the type who liked to have running commentaries during the game. She was praying that Rick would contact her, and she could pretend to pay attention to the TV. It was easy to figure out which team Ken and his father supported, so mostly she just needed to shout when they scored and growl or mutter when the other team sent a ball through the basket. She thought she could do this and talk to Rick at the same time.

But she didn't hear from him. She tried to keep her mind open, empty, welcoming, but she heard nothing. And she started to worry. Could Rick have figured out that she wasn't really Ken? She'd been trying very hard in their conversations not to sound girlie, but something could have crept in. Her feelings were becoming so strong that she might have given herself away. Fear clutched her heart. What if he never came back?

She waited and waited and tried not to let her despair show. She couldn't have been doing a very good job, though. Ken's father kept glancing in her direction worriedly. Then Ken's mother came in with a plate full of chocolate-chip cookies.

"Your favorite," she announced, putting the plate on the coffee table between the recliner and the sofa where Amanda was sitting. "Don't let your father have any—he's on a diet."

Chocolate-chip cookies were the last thing in the world she was interested in at that moment. She was so nervous that she thought she'd throw up if she took one bite. So when Ken's father made a move toward the plate, she murmured, "I won't tell." At least some cookies would be gone when Mrs. Preston came back.

Rick didn't show up, and by the time the game was over, she was in agony. She kept going over and over the last conversation they'd had that afternoon. She'd been thinking about the Public Gardens, the place Rick and Nancy used to go, and Rick had recited some of his poetry. Had she not been enthusiastic enough? She'd loved the poetry, and while he'd recited it, she'd imagined herself as—well, herself, listening to this sensitive soul express his love for *her*. Maybe she could have expressed her reaction in a better way, because ever since she'd become Ken, this was the longest they'd gone between conversations.

Luckily for her, the favored team lost, so she had an excuse to look unhappy.

"Don't take it so hard," Ken's father said. "Bailey's knee will be better by next week and they'll come back."

"Right," Amanda said, without the slightest idea who Bailey was. "I'm going to hit the sack—I'm wiped out."

Once again, she got that worried look from Ken's father. It was only ten o'clock, and she doubted Ken went to bed this early. But she couldn't stand it any longer.

She decided she was going to try to contact Rick. She recalled that time in class when Emily had asked Ken if he could contact her father. She couldn't remember if Ken had said he couldn't, or if he just hadn't wanted to.

Up in Ken's room, she turned off the lights and got into bed. Closing her eyes, she visualized the boy she'd seen in the photos and cleared her mind of everything else.

Rick. Are you there? Can you hear me? Talk to me, Rick.

She heard nothing.

Please, Rick. I need to talk to you. I have to tell you something. It's important.

It was at this moment that she realized she wanted him to know who she really was. It was a big risk. Maybe he'd be horrified to learn he'd been pouring his heart out to a girl. But how could she have a real relationship with him if he thought she was a boy?

How can I have a real relationship with him if he's dead? she asked herself. But she didn't have to answer that because suddenly Rick was there, inside her head.

Hi, Ken.

Rick, hi! I'm so glad you're here!

Yeah? Well, I am. You said you've got something important to tell me.

Was she imagining it or was there a distance between them? She wanted to kick herself. Of course there was a distance—he was six feet under or in heaven, or whatever there was after life.

But he felt so very, very close. She couldn't go on lying to him.

I'm not Ken, Rick.

What are you talking about? Of course you're Ken—no one else can hear me.

My name is Amanda. I'm inside Ken's body.

There was no response. She tried to explain.

I'm what's called a body snatcher. But I occupy bodies only of people I feel sorry for. I was feeling sorry for Ken, because he can't play soccer since he had an accident. And I became him. So that's why I can hear you.

Should she go into the whole story, about how she had wanted to make Ken ask her out? She was still debating this when Rick spoke.

Wow! I can't tell you how happy I am to hear this.

Why?

Because I was getting these feelings for you. The kind of feelings I didn't expect to have for a guy.

She wondered if he could hear her gasp.

Really? You mean, like the feelings you had for Nancy?

Exactly. The way you understood my poems . . . You really got them, what I was trying to say.

I love your poems. I keep pretending they're about me.

Had she really just said that? It was so not like Amanda to let a boy know how she felt! Amanda played it cool. Amanda played hard to get. She was on a pedestal. A guy had to *work* for her—he couldn't get her affection this easily.

But Rick could. Rick *had*. She didn't care if Rick thought she was too easy, too available.

They could be about you. My poems. You're better than

Nancy. She never had feelings as strong as yours. You're amazing! You feel so deeply, so strongly, for other people that you can become them!

If only he knew how hard she'd tried all her life to avoid caring and feeling for others.

I know what you look like. I saw your picture in an old yearbook. It's nice, being able to see you in my head while we're talking.

I wish I could see you.

It hit her then that he had no idea what she looked like. He didn't know how pretty Amanda Beeson was. He'd fallen for her personality—her attitude and feelings. She was momentarily dumbstruck. Never in a million years would she have thought that those would be qualities a boy would find appealing in her. She was pretty, she was popular—those were the aspects that pulled in the boys. That was how she got attention.

Do you want me to describe myself?

No, that's not important. I feel as if I know you, as if you're imprinted in my heart. That's enough.

They talked like this for hours, until Amanda started yawning and knew she was going to fall asleep.

They made a date to "meet" after school the following day. And she floated away to sleep on what felt like clouds of love.

★ ★ ★

The next morning, before homeroom, she went to her own locker and waited. A few minutes later, Other-Amanda showed up.

"Hi, Ken," she said.

Amanda recognized her own flirty voice. Other-Amanda fiddled with her locker combination but kept her eyes expectantly on Ken. What would Ken say to her at a moment like this?

She didn't care. She had something to give herself.

"I wrote something for you." It was only a little white lie. After all, she *had* typed it.

Other-Amanda looked puzzled. "What did you write? A letter?"

"No. It's a poem. For you."

Now she looked confused. "Why did you write me a poem?"

"To express my feelings." She pulled the envelope from Ken's backpack and handed it to her. Other-Amanda took it gingerly, as if she were afraid it would bite.

"I'll see you in class," Other-Amanda said, taking off.

But she saw Other-Amanda before that. She went to the school library during her study-hall period and saw her at a table in the back, with Katie and Britney. They were looking at a sheet of paper, and they were laughing.

She edged closer, staying behind a bookshelf so that they couldn't see her. Peering through a space between some books, she got a better look at what they were doing.

She couldn't really say she was surprised when she saw that the paper was her poem—Rick's poem. Other-Amanda was making fun of it and encouraging her friends to do the same.

"Is this unreal or what?" she was asking them. "Can you believe I ever wanted to hook up with him?"

"Do you think he's, like, had a nervous breakdown or something?" Britney wondered.

"I don't know and I don't care," Other-Amanda replied. "This makes my skin crawl. It's so, I don't know, *emotional*."

She made it sound like "emotional" was something disgusting.

"'I want to drown in my tears,'" she misquoted in a squeaky voice. "Ew, this is so weird! Who would have thought someone who looked like Ken Preston could be such a dork?"

Amanda was in pain. It literally hurt to hear these words, and not because she was Ken Preston. The words were difficult to hear because she knew this was exactly what she would say if any boy gave her a love poem. Or what she would have said, before Rick.

Thank goodness Rick couldn't see this Other-Amanda.

How could she be so shallow, so unfeeling?

Who was she, anyway? Was this the real her, this Other-Amanda she was watching? Or was she the girl inside Ken who was in love with a poet?

Maybe they were one and the same. Maybe Amanda or Other-Amanda or whoever the real person was just talked like that to impress her friends. Because it was the way *they* behaved. No, she couldn't blame her friends. It was the way *she* behaved. Because she was "cool."

At least Rick would never know this girl. He could talk only through Ken. But she had to go back inside herself sooner or later. That girl over there, making fun of a guy who showed his feelings—that was *her.*

For the first time in her life, she didn't like herself very much.

Chapter Fourteen

THERE WAS A SURPRISE waiting for Jenna after school on Monday. Just as she and Tracey emerged from the building, she spotted the now-familiar yellow car at the curb.

"It's my father," she cried in delight. She ran over to the car.

Stuart rolled down the window. "How's my girl?"

"Fantastic!" Even as she said the word, Jenna was thinking that this was probably the first time she'd ever responded to a question about herself with that word. On the other hand, who had ever called her "my girl" before?

"Just thought you might be interested in an afterschool snack," he said.

"Sure!" She waved to Tracey. "C'mon, my dad's taking us out for something to eat." She was pleased—this was the perfect opportunity for Tracey to get to know Stuart and see for herself what a great person he was.

Tracey seemed to be walking unusually slowly, and she

didn't look particularly thrilled at the notion.

"Jenna," her father called, beckoning for her to come closer to the window. When she did, he spoke quietly. "Listen, I'd rather this was just the two of us, okay? I need to talk to you."

He looked unusually serious, and at first she was puzzled. Then a disturbing thought occurred to her, and the pessimism she'd pushed to the back of her head returned to the forefront. He wanted to talk to her alone. Why? Because he'd changed his mind about hanging around. Because he was leaving town and he wanted to say goodbye.

She looked back at Tracey. Her friend couldn't have heard him, but she'd stopped approaching anyway.

"Thanks, but I've got tons of homework," Tracey said. "I need to go straight home. Have fun." She turned away and walked off in the opposite direction.

Jenna frowned. Tracey could at least have said hello to Stuart. It wasn't like her to be rude. Jenna joined her father in the car and they headed off. Already depressed, she watched him, waiting for the bad news. She should have known her fantasies were just that—fantasies. Ex-husbands and wives didn't reunite after 13 years—not when they hadn't had any contact at all during that time. There wasn't going to be any little house with a backyard. All those silly dreams she'd had were going to stay just that, dreams. Her father was going to leave, and another 13 years might pass before she'd see him again.

She pressed her lips together tightly. She would *not cry*. At least, not in front of him. After all the experiences in her life, why hadn't she learned that people always ended up letting you down? She wanted to be angry. But all she could feel was this enormous sense of disappointment.

Stuart pulled into a fast-food restaurant and ordered a couple of drinks from the drive-through window. "Want something to eat?" he asked her. "Some fries? A burger?"

"No thank you," she said stiffly. Five minutes ago, she'd been hungry. Now food was the last thing on her mind. Without a word, she took the drink he handed her. They left the parking lot, and he drove silently for a couple of minutes. Turning down a pretty street lined with trees and cute bungalows, he pulled alongside the curb and stopped. As he turned off the engine, Jenna asked, "What are we doing here?"

He didn't answer the question. "There's something I have to tell you," he said.

Jenna looked out the window on her side so that she wouldn't have to face him as she replied. "I know. You're leaving."

His silence confirmed her suspicions. Then he said, "I want to explain . . ."

She interrupted. "You don't have to. Could you just take me back to Tracey's?"

"Only if you're willing to leave tomorrow."

Slowly, she turned toward him. "What?"

"Listen to my plan," he said. "I'm tired of running around, and I want to settle down. And I want to make up for what I did to you and your mother. But I'm not doing this just because I feel guilty."

Jenna was more confused than ever. "Doing what?"

He took a sip of his drink before responding.

"I saw your mother this morning."

She was completely taken aback. "How? She's not allowed to have any visitors."

He grinned. "You might not have noticed this, but your father can be pretty charming. I had a little talk with one of the nurses, and she bent the rules."

Jenna was surprised. She thought hospitals were pretty strict about regulations. "How's she doing? Was she shocked to see you?"

"Very. But happy, I'm glad to say. And she looks wonderful. This treatment is working."

"That's great." With no idea what was coming next, Jenna waited uncertainly.

"She'll be leaving the hospital on Sunday," he continued. "And I don't want either of you living in that apartment anymore. I'm going to buy a house."

She blinked. "A house? For me and Mom?"

"For all three of us. To live together, as a family."

Jenna couldn't speak. The lump in her throat was almost painful, and at the same time, she'd never felt so happy.

"Your mother is going to give me another chance," he said. "I don't deserve it, but she wants this, too. I hope you feel the same way."

She felt pretty sure that her expression answered for her. But just in case, she said, "Oh, I do. I do."

He smiled. "Good. Now, we have to be practical. I don't want us spending even one night at Brookside Towers. This morning I saw a house I want to buy." He leaned across Jenna and pointed. "What do you think of it?"

It was like the house of her fantasies. White, with blue trim. Boxes at the windows spilling out red geraniums. Big hanging baskets of flowers on each side of the front door. A manicured lawn. It wasn't a mansion, or even a large house like the Devons'. It was cozy and sweet. It wasn't just a house—it was a home. The perfect little home for a family of three.

"It's beautiful," she breathed.

"I wish you could see the inside, but the owners are out for the day."

"Are you sure it's for sale?" she asked. "I don't see

any sign."

"They're nice people," he told her. "Even though I couldn't give them any money up front, they took down the sign. I have until Friday to pay them."

"Friday," she repeated. "This Friday? You mean this week?"

"Yes."

She was mystified. "But it must cost thousands and thousands of dollars. How are you going to get that kind of money? Can you borrow it from the bank?"

He smiled ruefully. "Not with my credit history. No, honey, I'm going to pay cash. And I'm hoping you'll help me."

"How?"

"I'm going to get a few bucks together today and tomorrow," he told her. "Enough for a couple of plane tickets and a little more. On Wednesday, you and I could fly to Las Vegas. The casinos there are open twenty-four hours a day. I could join a poker game, and with you by my side, I could win the cost of that house by Friday morning. We fly back, I hand the folks the money, we move in on Saturday. We pick up your mother on Sunday and bring her home. Here."

He'd completely taken her breath away. She wasn't even sure she'd comprehended what he'd just said.

"Do you think you can handle it?" he asked. "Staying up all night reading minds?"

"I don't know. I guess."

"Of course you can—you're a tough cookie. You're my girl, right?"

"Right." It wasn't the staying up all night that was bothering her, though. "But . . ."

"But what?"

She made a little face. "We'd be cheating." Deep inside she knew it was wrong.

He didn't disagree. "Yes, you're right. And as a father, I suppose I should be ashamed of myself, asking my daughter to help me cheat. But I'm looking at the big picture, Jenna. I'm thinking about saving your mother, making us all happy. Being a real family. It would take years and years for me to save up the money for this house. I don't think your mother can last years and years at that place where you've been living."

He was right, and she knew that. Brookside Towers was no place for a recovering alcoholic. There was just too much temptation to go back to her old ways.

"Do you know the expression 'The end justifies the means'?" he asked her.

She shook her head.

"It means that sometimes you have to do things that aren't one hundred percent right in order to reach a goal that's more important. We're talking about your mother's health and our future as a family. Don't you think it's worth doing something a little unethical for that?"

She still didn't feel good about it, but he was right.

"Yes."

He leaned over and gave her a quick hug. "Excellent. I'll call your principal tomorrow and make arrangements to take you out of school on Wednesday."

"I think you'd better come up with a different reason for it," she cautioned him.

He chuckled. "Not to worry, Jenna. Your old man can spin a tale. I'll say you've got a sick grandmother who wants to see you. We can use the same line with the Devons."

"Okay."

He started up the car. "Now, I have to go scrape together the money for our tickets and enough for me to get into a game. I'll drop you off at the Devons'."

It wasn't far. When they moved into this house, she'd still be in the same school zone. As he drove, Stuart talked about job possibilities for him in the town, but Jenna was in too much of a fog to listen.

It was happening. It was really happening. Her dreams, her fantasies—they were going to come true. Like in a fairy tale. She had no idea something like this could happen in real life.

At the Devons' house, he gave her a quick kiss on the

forehead and told her that he'd let her know what time they'd be leaving on Wednesday. Still feeling dazed, Jenna went inside.

"I'm in the kitchen," Tracey called out.

"I'll be there in a minute," Jenna called back. First, she needed a little time alone. She ran up the stairs to Tracey's room.

It was a funny thing about emotions, she thought. They never seemed to be precise—at least, hers weren't. She was never 100 percent happy or 100 percent miserable. Right now, for example, she'd just heard the best news she'd ever heard in her life. She should have been ecstatic.

Okay, so she'd have to do something she really didn't like doing, but so what? She just had to keep telling herself what Stuart had said about the ends and the means. And it wasn't as if she was so virtuous about her gift anyway. She'd certainly read minds for more stupid reasons than this! Madame was always scolding her for eavesdropping on people's thoughts.

She wasn't sure how the Devons would react, though. They were responsible for her, as her foster family. They might not want her flying off to Las Vegas, even if they believed it was to see a sick grandmother. They might want to get permission from social services, and then it would turn into a big deal. Stuart would have to fill out forms—

there would be little chance they could get permission by Wednesday. Which would mean they wouldn't have the money for the house on Friday. Which would mean her mother would come out of the rehab program on Sunday and go straight back to Brookside Towers.

Jenna had an idea. Instead of telling them, she'd leave them a note that they'd find only after she'd gone. Tracey would be furious with her for not telling her the truth, but when she saw how happy Jenna was in her new home with her new family, she'd have to forgive her.

Jenna needed paper. Tracey kept school supplies in a cabinet under her desk, and Jenna found a pad there. Then she opened the drawer to get something to write with.

Her eyes fell on an envelope, sealed, addressed, and apparently waiting for a stamp so that it could be mailed. *That's odd*, she thought. Tracey was a big e-mailer; she never wrote old-fashioned letters.

But this looked like something official. Jenna knew she was being nosy—it was none of her business—but so what? If she could read minds, she could look at envelopes. And it wasn't as if she was going to open it.

She picked it up and examined the address. *State Medical Laboratories. Department of DNA Testing.*

Was Tracey writing a paper about DNA? She hadn't mentioned it.

Jenna heard footsteps and dropped the envelope onto the desk. Tracey came in.

"I'm bringing the kitchen to you," she announced. In her hand was a plate of brownies. "I just made these. You're probably not hungry, though, if you just had something to eat with Stuart."

"I'm starving," Jenna said, taking a brownie. Sitting on her bed, she hoped Tracey wouldn't notice that an envelope that had been in her drawer was now on top of her desk.

Tracey did notice, but she must have thought she'd left it there herself, because she just picked it up and opened her drawer to slide it back in. That was when Jenna read her mind. She couldn't resist it. There was something furtive about Tracey's movements, something that made Jenna think she didn't want her to know about this envelope.

And for a good reason. As she was handling the envelope, Tracey thought about it, and her mind revealed what was contained inside.

Hairs. Some of Jenna's that Tracey had gathered from her hairbrush. And some that belonged to Stuart.

Tracey had plucked them from his head when she had been invisible the day before. That was why she'd been out of breath when she became visible again, just more than a minute later. During that time, she had run downstairs, pulled the hairs from an unsuspecting Stuart while he sipped his cocktail with the Devons, and hurried back to her room.

Jenna wondered if he'd felt it and what he'd thought it could have been. A mosquito?

Of course, that wasn't really relevant or important. What was important was the fact that Tracey was so convinced that Stuart wasn't Jenna's father that she was willing to take the extreme measure of having their DNA compared to see if they were actually related.

Automatically, Jenna reached for another brownie. She had to keep in motion, keep busy, so she wouldn't reveal what she knew to Tracey. At least, not until she'd figured out what she was going to do about it.

"They're good, aren't they?"

Jenna looked at Tracey blankly. "Huh?"

"The brownies. I've got another batch in the oven. In fact, I'd better go check on them." Tracey left the room. As soon as she was gone, Jenna went to the drawer. Opening it, she retrieved the envelope and went into the bathroom. There, she tore the letter up, again and again, into little tiny pieces that wouldn't clog the plumbing. Then she dropped them into the toilet and flushed it.

She'd have to find some way to tell her father that he should let her know if he ever felt anything unusual, like a mosquito bite out of season—without telling him why.

Chapter Fifteen

O KAY, THAT'S IT," MRS. Preston said. "I'm calling the doctor."Amanda looked up. "Why?"

"Because you haven't said a word since we sat down to dinner. Not to mention the fact that it's your favorite, lasagna, and you've barely touched it." The woman got up from the table and went to the phone.

Hastily, Amanda dug her fork into the lasagna. "I'm eating!" she yelled.

"Too late," Ken's mother called back. "Something's wrong with you, and I'm going to find out what it is." A moment later, she reappeared. "The doctor's office is closed. But I'm calling again first thing in the morning."

Amanda couldn't worry about that now. She had bigger things on her mind. Like raising the dead.

Not like in the movies, when zombies came up from the ground and vampires emerged from coffins. Just making someone dead be alive again, as he was before.

She wasn't stupid, and she didn't believe in magic or reincarnation, or anything like that. But look at her—she could take over bodies. That wasn't scientific—nobody could explain it. The same was true of every student in her gifted class. They could all do inexplicable things. Reading minds, seeing the future, making things move on their own—none of these skills made any sense in a logical world. So maybe one of them could bring the dead back to life but just didn't know it yet. Why not? It wasn't any freakier than anything else they did. The question was—who would be a likely candidate? Whose gifts might extend to something like that?

During her "date" with Rick that evening, she didn't mention her plan. She let the conversation go on in its usual lovely way. Rick talked about his dreams, goals, and ambitions—things that could never come true now that he was dead. He didn't sound depressed, though, and she soon found out why.

She asked a question that had been in the back of her mind since they'd met.

What's it like, where you are?

Beautiful.

Can you tell me about it?

It's hard to describe. It's just this incredibly happy place, full of love.

I'd like to see it.

You will, someday. Not for a long time, though, I think. You're not the type to get into a stupid motorcycle accident. And you have to wait till it's your time or you won't come here.

She understood. Not that she was thinking of trying to get there on her own, to be with him. No, she wanted him *here*, in her world. As beautiful as his world might be, she preferred to stay alive for the time being.

So they talked about other things. She confessed that she hadn't given much thought to her own future. He talked about college. He'd never been, of course, but his older brother had loved it. He told her he thought she'd make a wonderful teacher because she expressed herself so well. Nobody had ever told her that before, mostly because it hadn't been true.

She told him about her family, about being an only child, and how spoiled she was as the center of attention in her real home. She described her other experiences as a body snatcher.

She left out a lot of stuff about her life, too. She didn't talk about her clique—how they always sat together at lunch and criticized other girls. She didn't tell him how frequently she went shopping for clothes and makeup, shoes, and hair products.

He talked about books he'd read when he was alive.

He'd been a big reader. A couple of titles were familiar, but only because they'd been required reading for a class, and even then, she'd used only the CliffsNotes so that she wouldn't have to waste valuable television time reading. She didn't know most of the books he mentioned, but she filed the titles away in her memory for future reading. This dead guy was going to change the way she lived. And maybe, just maybe, he wouldn't have to stay dead.

In her gifted class the next day, Other-Amanda was giving her report on how her gift could influence her career choice. Real Amanda had lucked out—she wouldn't have to do it. Of course, sooner or later Ken would have to give *his* report.

Other-Amanda didn't surprise her. Amanda knew herself too well.

"I don't think there's anything positive about my gift at all, and it can't do me any good in the future. I want to have a fabulous life, and I can't have that if I can transfer only into bodies I feel sorry for. So my goal is to lose my gift, and that will help me achieve my goals."

"Which are?" Madame inquired.

"If I grow a few more inches, I could be a model. If I don't grow, I suppose I could be a movie star."

"Do you enjoy acting?" the teacher asked.

"I don't know—I've never tried it."

"You're not in the drama club here at school?"

Other-Amanda rolled her eyes. "No. They're not my kind of people."

Amanda-Ken saw something that Other-Amanda wouldn't have noticed—the way her classmates were looking at her. Emily and Tracey were exchanging exasperated looks. Sarah was shaking her head sadly. Jenna seemed preoccupied, as if she wasn't even listening to the report, but Martin and Charles were whispering, and they were both looking at Other-Amanda with expressions that weren't pleasant.

Ken probably looked the way she was feeling. Disgusted. With herself.

As Other-Amanda continued with her life goals, which essentially involved being rich and beautiful and having fun all the time, Amanda-Ken looked around the room and wondered who might be capable of bringing Rick back. It seemed to her that Sarah was the most likely candidate. At least, she had the most powerful gift, even if she refused to use it. Amanda would have to talk to her . . .

What do you think, Rick? There's a girl who can make people do things, even if they don't want to. I'm wondering if maybe she's got gifts that she doesn't know she has.

Like what?

Bringing someone back. From where you are. So we could

358

be together.

There was no response.

Rick?

I'm here. I'm listening.

I'd probably have to tell her the whole story, about being Ken right now, and falling in love with you . . .

She caught herself. Had she actually used that word before, with him? Was she coming on too strong?

It won't do any good.

Why?

Because it can't happen. That kind of power doesn't exist. Not outside movies and stories.

But I can't stay inside Ken forever! His parents think he's sick—his mother's taking me to the doctor tomorrow. I don't know how or when I'll get back inside myself, but it's going to happen sooner or later.

I know.

Then what are we going to do? Once I'm myself again, we won't even be able to talk!

I know.

That's the second time you've said that! Don't you have any ideas?

Only one. We have to stop connecting. Now.

She must have gasped audibly, because everyone in the class was looking at her.

"Ken? Are you all right?"

"Um, I'm feeling nauseous. Can I be excused?"

Madame quickly handed Amanda-Ken a hall pass, and she hurried out of the room. She ran down two flights to the basement restroom that nobody used, the one where she always went when she needed complete privacy.

Okay, I'm back. Why do we have to stop connecting now? Don't you have feelings for me?

Of course I do. That's why we have to stop. Because it's going to get only more difficult for both of us.

But that's not fair! Not if you love me and I love you!

It's not fair to die in a motorcycle accident when you're eighteen years old. It's not fair that people are hungry. It's not fair that a bad person can succeed and a good person fails.

I don't care about anyone else—I'm talking about us!

You don't mean what you just said. Of course you care about other people. You're that kind of person.

Was she? She wasn't so sure.

I don't want to lose you!

I'll be in your memory. You'll be in mine.

That's not enough. I want more.

Oh, Amanda, you can't have it all. You must know that.

But she didn't know that. She'd always had everything she wanted, and she wasn't about to stop now. Not when she'd found someone she wanted to be with more than anyone else in the world. This couldn't be happening to her, Amanda Beeson! She would not allow her heart to break! They belonged together, she and Rick. They had to be together . . .

But from some place far away, in the deepest recesses of her mind, she heard a faint voice.

Goodbye, my love.

And she wasn't in the restroom anymore.

She was in her seat in the gifted class. Her usual seat— Amanda's seat. Madame was looking at her with interest. Amanda didn't think it was because of her report.

But all Madame said was, "Thank you, Amanda. Sarah, would you like to go next?"

Amanda didn't hear a word Sarah said. Her head was spinning and she was trying to get a grip on herself.

How did she get here? Was it the strength of her emotions that had pushed her back inside her own body? Emotions she'd never admitted to herself before?

The classroom door opened and a dazed-looking Ken entered.

"Feeling better?" Madame asked, eyeing him keenly.

He nodded and took his seat. He glanced at Amanda and then looked quickly away.

He's embarrassed, Amanda thought. *He knows I was using him and he's feeling awkward. Not to mention the fact that he came to in a girls' restroom.*

She waited for the bell to ring and went to his seat before he could even get up.

"Hi . . ." she said, uncertain as to how he would respond.

He finally looked directly at her. "What happened?"

So he knew he hadn't been himself and he knew she had something to do with it. She realized honesty was the only way to go.

"I was inside your body. I saw you watching the soccer team practice. You looked so sad, and I felt sorry for you, and then, well, it just happened."

Okay, she wasn't being *completely* honest. But he didn't have to know her real motives. Mostly because those motives had disappeared once Rick had come into her life.

"How did it feel?" she asked. "Having me inside you?"

"I don't know," he said. "I mean, it was like a dream, all blurry and . . . and not real. Like I was here and I wasn't here . . ." He looked at her helplessly.

She could almost understand how he felt. It had to be so personal, having someone else inside you. Funny how she had never considered what Tracey felt when she had left *her* body. But then, Amanda Beeson didn't ever consider other people's feelings.

"What did you make me do?" he asked suddenly.

"You gave me a poem," she admitted. Even as she spoke,

she knew it was a mistake to tell him this. Because, of course, there was only one thing he could say.

"Why?"

She confessed, "I wanted you to like me."

It wasn't a very flattering reaction. He looked confused and then embarrassed again. He also seemed curious.

"Was it a good poem?" he asked.

"Yeah. But I didn't appreciate it."

He nodded and then rose. "I have to go."

She watched him leave and wondered if she'd ever have any kind of relationship with him again. Of course he wasn't surprised to learn that she hadn't appreciated a poem. The Amanda Beeson he knew wouldn't care.

If she'd known then what she knew now—about people and feelings. About herself. About pain and hurt and sadness.

But now she understood. And like the old poster proclaimed, this could be the first day of the rest of her life. She could be a different person, a better person.

Without Rick. And she had to call on the resources of the old Amanda, the Amanda who didn't care, to keep herself from bursting into tears right there and then.

Because she didn't think the memory would be enough.

Chapter Sixteen

SOMETHING WEIRD WAS GOING on with Amanda, Jenna thought as she half listened to Sarah's report. She could tell, just from the snotty girl's expression. She could explore her mind and find out what was happening.

But she had too many other things to think about. She was excited and she was scared.

Her father had called the principal to get her excused. He was picking her up right after this class, in less than 30 minutes. They'd be going directly to the airport, where he'd return the little rental car and they'd board a flight to Las Vegas. That was the exciting part.

She hadn't told Tracey, and she hadn't left a note for the Devons. But that wasn't the scary part. She wasn't sure what the scary part was. Flying for the first time? She didn't *think* that was it.

Sarah had finished her report, and Madame called on Ken. Ken was reluctant.

"Could I put this off till tomorrow?" he asked. "I'm kind of not in the mood."

That wasn't the sort of excuse that Madame usually accepted, but for some strange reason, she smiled at Ken and nodded. "Yes, that's all right. Let's see . . . has everyone given their reports?"

Emily's hand shot up. Madame looked puzzled.

"You gave your report last week, Emily."

"I just have a question to ask Ken, Madame. I was wondering if maybe he's had a chance to think about what I asked him. If he could contact my father."

Madame frowned. "Emily—"

But before she could go on, Amanda spoke.

"Knock it off, Emily! Leave him alone!"

Jenna was stunned, and she assumed that everyone else in the room was having the same reaction. This wasn't like Amanda. She was way too emotional.

And she didn't stop. "You don't know what it's like for Ken—to get involved with people like this, people he can't see or do anything for. It's hard enough for him to cope with the ones who contact him—he shouldn't have to go out and seek them. He suffers. Don't you understand that?"

Was there another body snatcher around? Jenna wondered. Had someone taken over Amanda? She'd never heard Amanda speak with such passion before, not even about herself.

Ken was looking at Amanda, but he didn't seem quite as shocked as everyone else. And strangely enough, Madame was almost smiling.

Suddenly, Ken clutched his head. Madame looked at him in alarm. "Are you all right, Ken?" she asked for the second time that day.

"I'm getting a message," Ken blurted out.

"From my father?" Emily asked excitedly.

"No." He turned to Jenna. "From yours."

Jenna stared at him. "My father isn't dead."

Ken held up one hand and rubbed his forehead with the other. "Wait . . . yes. Okay. I will."

No one had ever actually seen or heard Ken talk to dead people before. The room was hushed and expectant.

His face cleared, and he spoke to Jenna. "He died eight years ago, Jenna. From a gunshot wound, in a fight. He wants me to give you a message."

"This is crazy," Jenna declared hotly. "I don't know who's talking to you, Ken, but it's not my father. Stuart Kelley is alive and well, and he's picking me up in less than thirty minutes."

"He's an impostor," Ken told her. "Your father says that guy found out about you, but he doesn't know how. He's a professional gambler. He wants to use you for your mind-reading gift so he can win at poker."

"That's not true! He saw my mother at the hospital. She'd know if he was an impostor."

"Are you sure he saw your mother, Jenna?" Madame asked quietly.

Amanda reached inside her handbag. "Here, use my cell phone. Call the hospital and find out if she's had any visitors."

"No!" Jenna cried out.

Ken was rubbing his head again. "He's a scam artist, Jenna. He's got a friend working with him. Someone named Arnie. Have you ever heard of him?"

Arnie. The guy in the restaurant who knew him from way back when. The poker game in the back room. Jenna's stomach turned over.

"This isn't true!" she screamed. But it came out as a whisper.

"Your father, your real father—he wants to save you from him, Jenna," Ken told her. "He's trying to protect you. He's had a hard time reaching me, but he wouldn't give up."

Jenna burst into tears.

She couldn't remember the last time she'd done this. Jenna Kelley didn't cry. That's what she'd told Emily when Emily had made that prediction about the tall, dark, handsome stranger. Who gave off bad vibes. Who would make her cry.

Tracey came over and hugged her. Jenna didn't pull away. She was aware of other people leaving their seats, coming over to her, surrounding her. Even Charles wheeled himself over. Madame came, too. Only Carter Street remained in his seat, oblivious to what was going on as usual.

Everyone else made a wall of support around her, keeping her safe, keeping her strong. Still, she couldn't stop crying.

She buried her face in her hands. "It's okay," came a soft voice. "Let it out." It sounded like Amanda, but of course that was impossible.

Slowly, the tears began to subside, and she could hear Madame's voice over them. "This is why we have to watch out for one another. People will try to use us. And who knows what this man really wants? He could be part of something bigger, some conspiracy. We are always in danger from the outside world, class. What's happened to Jenna— it's a lesson for all of us. We're in this together."

"Why couldn't I read his mind?" Jenna asked in a whisper.

"Who knows?" Madame said simply. "He might have gifts of his own."

"And how could he have known that my mother

wouldn't be home when he came to my apartment?"

Madame gently touched her head. "As I said, Jenna, other people could be involved."

Charles spoke. "What a jerk! Hey, Jenna, do you want me to drop a house on him?"

"I'm getting the feeling," Martin said excitedly. "I could go beat him up."

Jenna took her hands away from her wet face. Tracey silently passed her a tissue.

"It's okay," she said, her voice trembling. "I can handle this myself."

"No, Jenna," Madame said. "We need one another."

The bell rang. Jenna looked at Madame. "He's picking me up in front of the school."

Madame nodded. She made a gesture, and everyone moved away, giving her room to stand up. Carter Street walked out of the room. Everyone else waited around Jenna. When she started to move toward the door, they encircled her, walking with her. Charles rolled along by her side.

Outside, the little yellow compact was waiting by the curb. The circle parted, letting Jenna see the car clearly. And the driver.

The handsome man was smiling. There was no question about it—he had a charming smile. It felt like a knife stabbing her in the heart.

Their eyes met. She still couldn't read his mind, but maybe he read hers. Or maybe it was just written all over her face.

His smile faded. She could see his hand go to the gearshift. Then, suddenly, he sped away.

Dimly, Jenna heard Madame suggesting to Tracey that she take her home. Emily was saying she'd wait with Jenna while Tracey collected their things. She was aware of a hug, a pat on the shoulder, a hand briefly clutching hers. She wasn't sure who was hugging, who was patting ... but they were friends, she thought. Maybe.

The only thing she was really sure of was the fake tattoo on her arm. *Dad*. It was already starting to fade. She'd just have to wear long sleeves until it was gone completely.

Gifted

HERE TODAY,
GONE TOMORROW

Chapter One

S OMETIMES EMILY WASN'T sure if she was dreaming or having one of her visions. Usually it happened in the early morning, just before her alarm went off.

On this particular Monday morning, she was pretty sure she was awake. She knew her eyes were open because she could see her chest of drawers, her desk, and her bookcase, with her old collection of dolls from many lands lining the top shelf. Dim sunlight was coming through the muslin curtains on her window, and she could even see the sweater she'd left hanging on the bedpost the day before.

But at the same time, she saw something else, something that didn't belong in her bedroom—an image, sort of translucent, that floated before her eyes. Even though it wasn't very distinct, she recognized the image immediately—it was one of her classes at school, her so-called gifted class.

There was the teacher, Madame, sitting at her desk.

In their usual seats sat her classmates: Ken, Amanda, Tracey, Martin, and the others. She could even see herself . . . but wait, there were only eight students—someone wasn't there.

It was funny, in a way: they all complained about the class—some of the students even hated it—but they rarely missed it. And with only nine students in the class, no one could skip it without being noticed. But who was missing in her vision? Jenna was there; she could see Sarah; and there was Charles in his wheelchair . . .

Carter was missing. It made sense that she hadn't realized this immediately. Since Carter didn't speak, he didn't call attention to himself, and it was easy to forget he was even in the room. But normally, he was there, physically at least, so this was odd.

Then her alarm clock rang, and the classroom disappeared. She sat up, reached out to her nightstand and turned it off. The image was gone, and she still wasn't absolutely sure if it had been a dream or a vision. She'd dreamed about her class before, but the dreams had been like most of the dreams she had, full of silly things, like Ken swinging from a light fixture or Charles dancing on Madame's desk. The image she'd just experienced had seemed so real . . . yes, it must have been a vision.

It probably wasn't a big deal though. Carter might act like a zombie, but he was a human being and just as susceptible to getting the flu or an upset stomach as anyone else.

"Emily! Are you up?"

Her mother's voice sounded testy, as if this was the second or third time she'd called to Emily—which was entirely possible. Emily's visions, even the trivial ones, always seemed to require all her senses, so she might not have heard her mother's earlier calls. Or maybe she'd really been sleeping. It was so hard to tell . . .

"I'm up," she called back. Dragging herself out of bed, she left her room and went across the hall to the bathroom. While brushing her teeth, she caught a glimpse of her reflection in the mirror and almost choked on the toothpaste. Why was her face so blurry? Was this the beginning of another vision?

No, it was just that she hadn't put her contacts in yet. Having done that, she went back to her bedroom where she spent about twenty seconds selecting her clothes. This activity never took very long since she essentially wore the same thing every day, with some minor variations in her choice of T-shirt or sweater. She didn't bother with makeup. Until very recently, she'd worn glasses, and what was the point of makeup when your glasses covered half your face? And even though she had contacts now and her face was more visible, she hadn't yet bought any cosmetics. Makeup required concentration, and the way Emily daydreamed, she knew she'd end up putting lipstick on her eyelids.

So when she checked herself out in the mirror, she didn't encounter anything surprising. In fact, having examined photos of herself as a small child, she knew she'd looked pretty much the same all her life. In her class picture from first grade, she could see the same oval face, long, straight nose, and full lips she saw now. She was still wearing her long, straight brown hair in the same style, which was actually no style at all.

She wondered if she would still look like this when she was an adult. But as usual, when she really wanted to see the future, she couldn't.

"Emily! You're going to be late!"

"I'm coming!" She grabbed the sweater hanging on the bedpost and ran down the hall to the kitchen. Her mother had set out a choice of cereals on the small kitchen table, and Emily helped herself.

"Did you sleep well?" her mother asked. She asked Emily the same question every day, and usually Emily responded with an automatic "yes." But this time, thinking about her confusion that morning, she looked at her mother thoughtfully.

"Mom . . . do you ever think you're awake but you're really sleeping? Or the other way around?"

Her mother looked at her sharply. "Are you having those visions again?"

I never stopped, Emily wanted to reply, but she knew this would only upset her mother. She never liked talking about Emily's gift, but every now and then, Emily took a chance and brought up the subject. She couldn't help hoping that there would come a time when her mother would want to listen to her. But the expression on her mother's face told her that now was not the time, so she didn't even bother to respond to her mother's question.

"Is there any orange juice?" she asked instead.

Her mother was clearly relieved to have the change in subject. "Of course, it's in the refrigerator. There's grape juice, too—it was on sale at the grocery store."

Her mother was always on the lookout for items on sale. She had a good job as the office manager for a company, but since the death of Emily's father, she was the only one in the house who earned money.

A couple of other kids at Emily's school had also lost a parent, and although she'd never talked to them about it, she assumed they suffered the same kind of sadness she did. But she couldn't imagine that either of them felt as guilty about it.

"By the way, I'll be late getting home today," her mother told her. "I've got an appointment with Tony."

There was nothing unusual about that. Her mother wore her hair in a short, layered style, and every six weeks she went to see Tony at Budget Scissors for a cut. But out of nowhere, Emily had a sudden vision, and she was alarmed.

"I don't think you should do that, Mom. Not today."

"Why not?"

The vision was shockingly clear. Her mother's normally soft curls were a frizzy, snarled mess. "I can see you. After your appointment. Maybe Tony's in a bad mood or something—I don't know—but he's not going to give you a nice haircut today."

Emily watched the bewilderment on her mother's face turn to irritation, and she didn't have to be a fortuneteller to know the annoyance wasn't directed at Tony the hairdresser.

"Emily, stop it, right this minute! You're talking utter nonsense."

There was no point in arguing with her, but Emily had to make one point. "Mom, if my visions are nonsense, why do you think they put me in the class for people with special gifts?"

Her mother's lips tightened. "I don't want to discuss this now, Emily. We're leaving in two minutes."

She left the kitchen. Emily finished her cereal and

went to search for her school stuff. She wasn't angry at her mother for not understanding her gift. How could she be angry when Emily didn't understand it herself? Passing through the living room, she paused to look at the framed photograph on the wall. It was something she did whenever she thought about her so-called gift, but it never provided any answers. Only more questions.

The photo was only eight years old, but her mother looked a lot younger in it. Maybe it was because she was smiling, not just with her lips but with her eyes—an expression Emily didn't see on her face very often. She had one hand on the shoulder of five-year-old Emily. And on Emily's other side was her father.

From the angle of the photo, it seemed that no matter where Emily stood when she looked at it, his eyes were on her. And sometimes she felt that he was looking at her with disappointment, like he was reminding her that she could have saved his life.

There were times when she wished she couldn't recall the memory so easily. Was it her very first vision? She couldn't be sure, but it was the first one that had a real effect on her life. And it had happened at such an ordinary moment.

It was as detailed a memory as if it had occurred the day before. Her mother was brushing Emily's hair, getting her ready for a day at kindergarten. Her father was putting some papers in his briefcase.

The image had come to her out of nowhere, just like the vision she'd had of her class that morning. She could see her father walking out the front door, heading to the car he'd parked across the street. She could see him stepping off the curb without looking both ways. Another car, moving very fast, came screaming around the corner. And hit him.

She wanted to tell him about this frightening vision, but he was already heading to the door. She knew all she had to say was something like, "Wait, Daddy, I have something to tell you," but she didn't. Even today, she still didn't know why she hadn't spoken up. Was she afraid he'd laugh at her?

The "why" didn't really matter now. Her father was killed by a speeding car and it happened just the way she'd seen it in her vision. And maybe, just maybe, if she had told him about her vision, he would have been more careful crossing the street. If he had stopped to listen to her, maybe the speeding car would have gone down her street before he even went outside. At least her mother couldn't blame her for her father's death, since she didn't really believe Emily could see into the future. But Emily could blame herself.

Now, whenever she had serious visions that could affect

someone's life, she told that person. But they didn't always appreciate it, and usually they didn't believe her. Which was understandable . . . because sometimes the visions were wrong. Well, maybe not completely wrong, but not exactly . . . clear. Like the time she told Terri Boyd in her English class that she was going to fall off the balance beam in her gymnastics competition that day. Only Terri didn't fall— not then. But at her competition the following weekend, she tumbled off. And Terri actually blamed Emily for it, telling her *she* put the idea in her head!

"Ready?" her mother asked.

Emily picked up her backpack and followed her mother outside. But just as her mother was locking the door, she had another vision. It was funny how this could happen. She could go for days without a vision and then have a dozen in one morning.

"Mom, I forgot something. I'll be right back." Ignoring her mother's protests, she ran back inside and down the hall to her room. She found what she needed in her bookcase, stuck it in her backpack, and hurried back to join her mother.

"What did you forget?" her mother wanted to know.

"A book I have to lend Jenna," Emily replied. Which was the truth—she just didn't tell her how she knew Jenna would need the book.

The five-minute drive to Meadowbrook Middle School was free of visions, but the image of the gifted class without Carter was still in her head. When she arrived at school, she considered looking for Madame to tell her about it, but Madame was always warning her not to speak up too quickly. She'd told Emily to think about her visions, to examine them and consider them before jumping to conclusions. Emily wasn't so sure about that—she saw what she saw, and that wouldn't change just because she thought about it. But Madame seemed to think otherwise, so she decided to wait until the gifted class met. Maybe she would have a clearer vision by then.

She was still vision-free at lunchtime, when she set her tray down on the cafeteria table next to Tracey and across from Jenna. Jenna was in the process of trying to get Tracey to use *her* special gift on Jenna's behalf.

"Ms. Stanford always does her photocopying during fourth period, and you've got study period then, so you won't miss a class. Just get yourself into the teachers' lounge and look at the test while she's copying it. You don't have to memorize the whole thing—I just need to know what the essay question is going to be."

Clearly this discussion had been going on for some time. Wearily, Tracey shook her head. "That's cheating, Jenna. I can't help you."

"Of course you *can*," Jenna insisted, narrowing her kohl-rimmed eyes. "You just *won't*."

"Actually, it's both," Tracey said. "I can't always go invisible on demand."

"You're getting a lot better at it though," Emily pointed out.

"Yeah, but it's not easy. Remember why I started disappearing? It was because no one paid any attention to me. If I tried talking to people, they didn't hear me. I'd raise my hand in class and the teacher wouldn't see me. Even my own parents ignored me. I *felt* invisible, so I became invisible."

Jenna gazed at her quizzically. "But you don't feel invisible anymore, do you? How come you can still disappear?"

"I have to try and remember how it was back then, when I felt like nobody. That can be pretty depressing, so I don't like doing it. But if I'm feeling too confident or strong or really good about myself, it's *really* hard."

For Emily, it was comforting to hear that others couldn't always rely on their gifts. Tracey couldn't disappear just by snapping her fingers. And Jenna, who could read minds, couldn't read *everyone's* mind. With some people, she had no problem—their minds were an open book. But she couldn't read her own mother's mind, nor Madame's, nor Carter's. And with the other gifted students, she complained about how sometimes she could read them and sometimes she couldn't. Of course, her classmates would recommend that she shouldn't even try, but Jenna, being Jenna, didn't take advice well.

"I'm sorry, Jenna," Tracey continued. "I know you think I'm being a prig, but cheating is wrong. Why can't you just study for the test like everyone else?"

Jenna made a face. "What's the point of learning everything when you only really need to learn what you're going to be tested on?" Then she brightened. "Hey, I just had a brilliant idea. I could ask Ms. Stanford some questions about the test. Then she'll start thinking about it, and I'll read her mind!"

Emily thought that was a pretty good idea, but Tracey disapproved. "It's not right, Jenna. It's still cheating."

Jenna shrugged. "It's the teachers' fault. I wouldn't have to cheat if they didn't give us so much work. I've got an essay due on Thursday, the test tomorrow, a book report to give today—" she stopped suddenly, and snatched up her backpack. Frantically, she began to search the contents.

"What's the book?" Tracey asked.

"*The Diary of Anne Frank*. And I left it at home." She dropped the backpack and looked at the others mournfully. "Can you believe it? I actually read the whole book, I wrote the report, and I marked passages to read out loud. And now I don't have the book."

Emily reached into *her* backpack. "Surprise," she said, handing over her own copy of the book.

Jenna grabbed it out of her hands. "Wow! Thanks, Em."

"How did you know she'd need it?" Tracey asked Emily.

"Jenna told me she was reading it last weekend. Remember, Jenna? You said it made you cry."

"It made me *sad*," Jenna contradicted her. "I didn't *cry*."

Tracey shook her head impatiently. "No, how did you know she would forget to bring her copy to school?"

"I had a vision," Emily said proudly.

"Cool!" Tracey exclaimed. "You had an accurate premonition."

Jenna disagreed. "But you can't say for sure that you were predicting the future."

"Why not?" Emily asked.

"Because you know how I'm always forgetting stuff, and you knew I was giving this report today. So you brought me your copy of *Anne Frank* in case I left mine at home. Which was nice of you, and I appreciate it. But you didn't know for sure that I'd forget the book."

"But I *did* know," Emily insisted. "I saw it."

Tracey backed her up. "Emily's been getting better and better at making predictions, Jenna."

Jenna looked at Emily. "Hey, I'm not saying you don't have a gift. You just don't know how to use it very well."

It was typical of Jenna to speak like that—frankly, without always thinking about other people's feelings. Emily tried not to take it personally, but she couldn't help it.

"So you think my gift is worthless."

Tracey was much kinder. "She didn't mean that, Emily. Okay, maybe you don't have much control over your gift right now, but you're definitely improving." She glared at Jenna, demanding a confirmation.

"Yeah, I guess you're getting a little better," Jenna acknowledged.

It wasn't much of a compliment, and it didn't make Emily feel any happier. She was glad to hear Tracey change the subject.

"How are things at home?" she asked Jenna.

Jenna produced her usual nonchalant shrug, but she punctuated it with a grin and said, "Not bad." Given her resistance to sounding overly positive or optimistic, "not bad" could easily mean "excellent." Emily remembered that Jenna had stayed with Tracey's family for two weeks while her mother was in the hospital, but her mother was home now, and Jenna was back there with her. Emily ventured a question.

"And your mother, she's . . ." she hesitated, unsure of how to put this delicately. Pretty much everyone knew that Jenna's mother had been in rehab. "She's doing okay?"

Jenna rephrased this in her own blunt way. "You mean, is she sober? Yeah, so far."

"I bet she's going to make it this time," Tracey declared.

"Maybe," Jenna allowed. She shot a look at Emily. "Don't you even *think* about making any predictions."

"I have no intention of even trying," Emily assured her. She knew Jenna didn't mean to insult her, but Emily couldn't help feeling a twinge of irritation. She got up before her feelings could show on her face. "I'm going to get some water."

Beside the water fountain was a row of trash cans where students emptied their trays. Emily saw Sarah Miller, another of her classmates, poking around the contents of one of them.

"What are you doing?" Emily asked her.

Sarah looked up. Her heart-shaped face was utterly woebegone.

"I lost my ring," she wailed.

Emily winced. Being someone who often lost or misplaced things, she could totally empathize.

"Did you take it off?"

"I don't think so. I leave it on all the time, even when

I wash my hands. It must have fallen off, but I don't know where or when. I just noticed that it wasn't on my finger." She touched the ring finger on her right hand as she spoke. Emily stared at it. If she concentrated very hard, she might get a vision. Sometimes this worked, sometimes it didn't.

She was in luck—her vision began to blur and her eyes glazed over. An image began to emerge . . . "You'll find it."

Since Sarah was in the gifted class, too, she knew about Emily's ability, but unlike Jenna, she actually had some respect for it. Her eyes lit up. "Really? Where?"

"It's in your coat pocket."

Sarah's brow furrowed. "You know, that's possible. I wore a coat today, and I forgot my gloves so I kept my hands in the pockets. It could have come off there."

Emily nodded. "It was a pretty clear vision. It was in the bottom of a coat pocket."

Sarah was getting excited. "So I could find it now if I go and look."

Emily hesitated. This was the weakest area of her gift— the question of "when." She might see an event, like Terri Boyd falling off the balance beam, but she might not be sure when it would happen. But in this particular case . . .

"If that's where it fell off, it must be there now," she said decisively.

Sarah looked at the clock on the wall. "The coat's in

my locker. If I hurry, I have time to look before class. Thanks, Emily!"

Emily beamed as she watched Sarah run out of the cafeteria. But her smile faded as she noticed the girls at a nearby table staring at her. She really had to learn to think before she spoke. Britney Teller and Sophie Greene were gaping at her, with open mouths and wide eyes. Amanda Beeson, Emily's gifted classmate, was with them, but her expression was very different. She was glaring at Emily, with "urge to kill" written all over her face.

Britney spoke first. "Emily, can you see things? Like a psychic?"

Emily didn't have to respond—Amanda took care of that for her.

"Yeah, sure, Emily's a gypsy fortuneteller," she declared. "Show us your crystal ball, Emily." And just in case anyone didn't hear the sarcasm in her voice, she started giggling in an especially mean way, something she could do very well, in keeping with her reputation as one of Meadowbrook's top mean girls.

Immediately Britney and Sophie joined in, doing their best imitation of Amanda's laugh. Emily could feel her own face redden. She had about as much control of her complexion as she had over her predictions.

She made her way back to her own table, where Jenna

and Tracey gazed at her sympathetically. Obviously they'd heard everything.

"In all fairness," Tracey said, "Amanda did the right thing, covering for you like that."

"I know," Emily replied glumly. "But did she have to do it so *loudly*?"

"You can't really blame her," Jenna said. "*We* know she's not really that nasty, but she has to work at maintaining her reputation if she wants to keep her status with those kids she hangs out with."

This was all true, but Emily was still feeling embarrassed. She looked forward to the gifted class, where Sarah's gratitude might cheer her up.

But when she entered room 209, she could see at a glance that Sarah wasn't any happier than she'd been when Emily first saw her in the cafeteria. Her disconsolate classmate had her elbows on her desk and her chin in her hands, and there was no ring on her finger.

She looked up as Emily approached. "I checked all my pockets. It wasn't there." Her tone wasn't accusing—Sarah was too nice for that—but Emily tried to defend herself.

"Maybe it's in the pocket of another coat," she offered, but without much conviction.

Sarah shook her head. "I haven't worn any other coat recently."

"I'm sorry," Emily said.

Sarah gave her a sad smile, as if to assure her she didn't blame Emily, but Emily felt guilty anyway. She took her seat and mentally checked her score for the day. She'd known that Jenna would forget her book (even though Jenna refused to consider it a prediction), so she gave herself a point for that. But Sarah's missing ring put her back at zero. What other premonitions had she had? There was her mother's hair, but she wouldn't know the answer to that one till she got home.

She'd predicted something else . . . Of course! Carter Street. According to her vision, he shouldn't be in class today. It was almost time for the bell, and she surveyed the room. Martin, Jenna, and Amanda were in their seats . . . Charles rolled in, followed by Tracey, and at the last minute, Ken hurried into the room.

The bell went off. As it rang, Madame entered and closed the door. Emily felt a rush of satisfaction—Carter was missing!

Madame went to her desk and looked over the room. "Where's Carter? Has anyone seen him?"

Nobody had. Madame's brow furrowed. "I can't remember Carter ever missing a class." She looked at a piece of paper on her desk. "He's not on the approved absentee list."

"Maybe he's cutting class," Martin ventured.

Madame wouldn't even consider that, and Emily understood why. Carter was like a robot—he did what he was supposed to do and what he was told to do. Nothing more, nothing less. He didn't speak, his face showed no expressions, and according to Jenna, he had no thoughts—yet somehow he functioned, physically at least, like a regular person.

No one knew who he really was or where he came from—he'd been found a year earlier on Carter Street, and that was the name he'd been given. So far, he hadn't exhibited any particular gift, and Emily didn't know why he was in their gifted class. Maybe it was because he was just different, like the rest of them.

She could tell that Madame was concerned, and her initial joy at being correct in her premonition evaporated. Carter's absence wasn't a good thing, and Emily was ashamed for taking pleasure from it.

It was warm in the classroom, and Madame started to take off her suit jacket.

"Oh, I almost forgot." She put a hand in her pocket. "Does this belong to anyone?"

"My ring!" Sarah cried out. She went to the desk to take it. "Oh, thank you, Madame. Where did you find it?"

"On the floor," the teacher replied. "It must have slipped

off your finger and rolled away. You might want to have it made smaller so it won't be loose, Sarah."

"I will," Sarah said, and returned to her desk. She didn't look at Emily as she passed her, but Emily sank down in her seat anyway. So the ring had been found—she'd been right about that. But not in Sarah's pocket.

But wait . . . what had she envisioned, exactly? Had she actually seen *Sarah* put her hand in her pocket? All she'd seen in the vision was the ring in a pocket. And that was where it had been. It just wasn't in the pocket she'd assumed it would be in. So in a way, she'd been right. She just hadn't understood her own premonition.

But that didn't make her feel much better. She had visions—so what? She didn't know what they meant. What was the good of having a gift if you couldn't even understand it?

She didn't have any more visions at school that day, and her mood didn't improve. This wasn't helped by the fact that she went home with an unusually large amount of homework.

At least the homework required all her attention, and she didn't think about her mother and her hair appointment. But when she heard the door open and her mother's call of "I'm home," the memory of her premonition came back. She hurried out to the living room.

Her mother was just taking off her coat. "Hi, honey. How was your day?"

When Emily didn't respond right away, her mother repeated her question. "Em? Did you have a nice day?"

"Oh, yeah, it was okay. Sorry, I was looking at your hair."

Her mother patted the nicely trimmed soft curls. "Do you like it?"

Emily nodded. "Tony did a nice job."

"Actually, Tony was called away on a family emergency, so I had Lauren this time. What shall we do about dinner?" She breezed past Emily and went into the kitchen.

Emily couldn't think about dinner—she was too busy pondering the implications of another messed-up premonition. Was it just because Tony hadn't been there and another hairdresser had done the job? Would her mother's next appointment with Tony be a disaster? Or was it just a false prediction?

It was all too depressing. This talent she had—it could be so precious, so valuable. So many people would love to have her gift, and they could do wonderful things with it.

But in her own clumsy hands—no, in her own clumsy brain—it was worthless.

Chapter Two

EMILY COULD FEEL HER mother's worried eyes on her as they sat across from each other at the table.

"Emily? Are you feeling all right? You're not eating."

She was right. And on the plate in front of her was one of her absolute favorites—macaroni and cheese.

"I'm not very hungry," she replied, but she stuck her fork into the cheesy pasta anyway.

Her mother still looked concerned. She really cared, Emily knew that, and for a mother, she was usually pretty understanding. About most things, at least.

"Mom," Emily began, and then she lost her nerve. Her mother sighed.

"You *are* having those visions again, aren't you." It was a statement, not a question, but Emily answered anyway. She wanted so desperately to talk about it.

"Sort of."

"Do you talk about this in your . . . your class? Isn't your teacher supposed to help you . . . *deal* with your problem?"

That was how her mother saw her gift—as a problem. When Emily was asked to join the class, Madame had told her mother that its purpose was to help the students channel and control their talents. But somehow her mother had convinced herself that the purpose of it was to help the students get rid of their delusions.

"We talk about our *gifts*," Emily said, emphasizing the last word. "We talk about how to develop them and make the most of them."

As usual, her mother didn't hear her. "Em, honey . . . if you're not getting any help from that Madame person, maybe you should go back to see Dr. Mackle."

Emily shuddered. Her mother had dragged her to the psychologist two years ago. He'd treated her like a six-year-old with an imaginary friend and said her visions were simply the product of an overactive, creative imagination. No, Dr. Mackle couldn't help her.

She gave up. "I'm fine, Mom. I've just got a lot of homework and I'm a little stressed out."

That was something her mother could understand. "Well, you go ahead and get to work," she said briskly. "I'll take care of the dishes."

"I'll clear the table," Emily offered. While she was collecting the dishes, the phone rang. Her mother got to it first.

"Hello? Hi, Tracey. Yes, she's here, but she's got a lot of homework so don't talk too long. Oh really? Okay, here she is." She handed the cordless phone to Emily. "Tracey's having some problems with the homework and she wants to talk to you about it."

This couldn't be true—Madame hadn't given them any homework, and she and Tracey didn't have any other classes together. Emily took the phone and played along.

"Hi, I'm taking the phone to my room so I can look at the assignment." That was for her mother's benefit. Once in her own room, she closed the door and fell down on her bed with the phone.

"Hi, what's up?"

"Not much. Wait a sec, I gotta yell at the clones. Hey, you guys, out of my room! Now!"

Emily could picture Tracey's identical little sisters, the infamous Devon Seven, surrounding her and begging for stories. As an only child, Emily used to envy Tracey. But after spending some time in Tracey's house, she now understood one of the reasons why Tracey was so intent on learning to disappear at will—so she could really and truly hide from them sometimes.

"Hi, I'm back. I just called to find out how you're doing. You seemed really down today."

Emily wasn't surprised that Tracey had been so aware of her feelings. Tracey was practically an authority on being depressed, having spent around five years in that condition.

"I'm confused," Emily confessed. "My visions are so— so *messy*. Sometimes I wonder if I really have a gift at all."

"Of course you do," Tracey assured her. "Think of all the times you've told me what's going to happen! Remember when you asked me if I'd ever had measles?"

Emily recalled the strange premonition she'd had a few months earlier. She kept envisioning Tracey and thinking "measles." "Yeah, I remember."

"Well, why did you ask me that? Because you knew the clones were going to come down with measles and you were worried that I might catch it."

"But why didn't I just see your sisters with measles in my vision? It's like, every time I get a premonition, it's not clear—it's all twisted and mixed-up."

"Maybe because the future is never all that clear. I mean, it can always change, can't it?"

"I guess," Emily replied, but she wasn't so sure about that. If the future could change, then how could she see it before it happened? Like today . . . "I had a vision this morning that Carter wouldn't be in class today."

"*That* must have been a clear vision," Tracey said. "And it was accurate."

There was a rap on her door. "Em, don't stay on the phone too long. You've got homework."

"I gotta go," Emily told Tracey. "Thanks for calling."

"Want to make a quick prediction before we hang up?" Tracey asked.

"I can try," Emily said. "Ask me a question."

"Um . . . Will Carter be back in class tomorrow?"

Emily half-closed her eyes, so that her eyesight was blurred, and waited to see if any kind of image formed. She was pleased when a vision of the class began to form.

"No . . . he won't be there. Wait—someone else is missing, too."

"Who?"

Emily looked over the faces in the fuzzy image. "It's you! Are you feeling okay? Maybe you're going to be sick."

"I feel fine," Tracey assured her. "Maybe I'll be invisible."

"Are you going to try to disappear tomorrow?"

"I don't know. Maybe. I practice every day, but usually at home in my room."

"Well, don't do it just so I'll think my prediction was accurate."

Tracey laughed. "See you tomorrow."

When she saw Tracey at their usual table in the cafeteria the next day, she wasn't sure if she was relieved or disappointed. Of course she was glad Tracey wasn't sick, and that she hadn't done a disappearing act just to make Emily feel better about herself (although that was the kind of thing Tracey would do). But her presence was more evidence that Emily's predictions were half-baked at best.

Still, she forced a smile as she carried her lunch to the table. "I'm glad to see you," she assured Tracey.

Tracey sighed. "I'm sorry."

"Sorry about what?" Jenna appeared at the table, carrying a lunch tray.

"Oh, nothing," Tracey said quickly. "Hey, you bought your lunch!"

Emily had noticed that, too. Jenna always brought a sandwich from home. With her mother's problems, the family had lived on public assistance, and Jenna was always short of cash.

Jenna set the tray on the table. "Yeah, how about that? My mother got a job!"

"Wow, that's great!" Tracey exclaimed.

"Doing what?" Emily asked.

"She's going to be a secretary at the hospital! That's what she used to be, a secretary, and while she was in rehab, she told one of the nurses. And it turned out she remembers all her computer skills." She turned to Emily. "Guess you didn't see that coming, did you?"

Emily's smile faded. "No. I haven't been having many

successful premonitions lately."

"Hey, it's okay," Jenna said, taking her seat. "I wouldn't have believed you if you'd predicted it." She looked beyond them and grimaced. "Oh damn. What do *they* want?"

Emily turned to see three of Amanda's friends sauntering toward them. They were whispering and smirking, and she steeled herself for an insult.

Nina, the nastiest one, spoke. "Emily, I'm trying out for cheerleading today. Could you tell me if I'm going to make the squad?"

Emily sighed. "No."

"No, you can't tell me, or no, I'm not going to make the squad?"

Britney and Sophie started giggling furiously.

Emily considered a snappy retort, something like "I won't waste my gift on something stupid like cheerleading," but of course she couldn't let them know she really could see into the future.

Tracey saved her. "She doesn't know and she doesn't care, so leave her alone."

Nina faked a look of wide-eyed innocence. "But I thought Emily could tell the future."

Jenna rolled her eyes. "Oh, *please*. Emily doesn't even know what day it will be tomorrow."

To her horror, Emily felt her eyes well up. She knew

Jenna was just trying to convince the girls it was all a joke, that the idea of Emily being able to predict the future was ridiculous. But in a way, what Jenna said was almost true, and that was what hurt. She managed to keep her expression frozen until the girls walked away, and then a tear escaped.

Tracey saw it. "Oh, Emily, you can't care what those girls think."

"I don't," Emily said fiercely, staring at Jenna.

"Hey, I was just trying to help out," Jenna protested.

"I know," Tracey said. "But Emily's feeling pretty sensitive about her gift these days."

Jenna's expression changed. "Really? Hey, I'm sorry, Em. I was just fooling around."

"It's okay," Emily sighed. "I just feel like my gift is awfully weak. I mean, compared with the others in our class."

"What about Carter?" Jenna said. "He doesn't even have a gift. At least, he's never shown us one."

"Speaking of Carter, Emily knew he wouldn't be in class yesterday," Tracey told her. "She was right about that." She turned to Emily. "And you said he won't be there today, right? I'll bet you're right again."

"But even if I am, I thought you wouldn't be there either. So I'd only be half right."

"Have you talked to Madame about this?" Jenna wanted to know.

Tracey was taken aback. "Since when do you trust teachers?"

"I don't," Jenna said quickly. "Not regular teachers. But Madame's . . . okay. I think she's different. She understands stuff."

Tracey looked thoughtful. "Do you really think she understands our gifts?"

Jenna shrugged. "Well, she knows about them and she doesn't treat us like freaks. That's enough for me."

It was enough for Emily, too. At least Madame would be willing to listen. She pushed her barely touched tray away.

"Maybe you're right. I'm going to go see if I can talk to her now."

She was in luck—Madame was already in the classroom, going through some papers at her desk. Emily stood in the doorway and coughed loudly. The teacher looked up. She didn't smile, but she spoke kindly.

"Yes, Emily?"

Emily hesitated. Madame looked preoccupied, like she had something on her mind. Maybe this wasn't a good time. But then Madame spoke again.

"Have you had a vision?"

"I'm always having visions," Emily said. "That's the

problem. Because they're not always right. No, that's not exactly true. They're just not completely right."

"We've talked about this before," Madame reminded her. "Are you examining the visions? Are you looking for clues that could help you make sense of them, to make the most of your visions?"

Madame was right—Emily had heard all this before. But she still didn't get it. She reported the visions as she saw them—what else could she do?

"Can you give me an example?" she asked the teacher.

Madame didn't get the opportunity. Another teacher appeared at the classroom door and spoke in a rush.

"Could you come with me? It's Martin Cooper . . ."

"Of course." Madame rose quickly. "I'm sorry, Emily, I have to go."

Emily didn't need any explanation for her need to leave—she could guess what was happening in some other classroom. Skinny little Martin Cooper had a gift that only served himself. If he was teased or ridiculed— which happened frequently, since he was such a whiny, babyish nerd—he went more than a little nuts. His scrawny body was suddenly endowed with an almost superhuman strength, and he became violent. Madame was the only one who could calm him down.

Yes, like Jenna said, Madame understood the special

students. Unlike most of their parents, she accepted the reality of the gifts and she believed in her students' abilities. But unfortunately for Emily, the other students' gifts usually took up more of Madame's time.

Ken could be tormented by the voices of the deceased, and he didn't seem to have much control over them. Emily often wondered how Ken had developed such a weird gift. He never really said much about it except to complain when dead people kept trying to talk to him. He certainly wasn't happy about it, ever, and Madame always seemed to have a special sympathy for him.

Charles, like Martin, had a gift which could create big problems that demanded Madame's immediate attention. He couldn't make his legs move—he'd been paralyzed since birth—and somehow he'd developed telekinesis, being able to make things move with his mind. And if he was in a bad mood, which was pretty often, he used his gift in very destructive ways.

Amanda could take over other people's bodies. If she felt very sorry for a person, she could end up *being* that person. Tracey, who'd been occupied by Amanda for a couple of weeks, said this was why Amanda was so nasty to some people—she couldn't risk caring about them.

On the other hand, Sarah didn't demand much attention from Madame, which was interesting, since she had the greatest power of all—she could make people do whatever she wanted them to do. At least, that's what they'd all been told. It was hard to believe, since Sarah was usually so nice and easygoing. And they'd never seen any evidence of her gift, since Sarah refused to use it. That was why Madame didn't have to watch her so closely. Still, the power was there, so Madame had to find Sarah pretty intriguing.

And what could Emily do? Offer predictions that might or might not come true. Not exactly something that would make Madame jump out of her seat.

There was still some time before the bell, and Emily could have gone back to the cafeteria and rejoined her friends, but she had nothing to tell them, so what was the point? She went to her seat, sat down, and half-closed her eyes.

Show me something, she told her mind. She waited for a vision. It took a while, but finally an image began to form. To her disappointment, the image turned out to be Amanda's friend Nina. She was jumping around in front of some uniformed cheerleaders. Then she performed a cartwheel, a split, and a back handspring. Something went wrong with the last move, and she ended up flat on her butt.

So Nina wouldn't make the cheerleading squad. That was comforting but not very important. And nobody would care except Nina.

Jenna sauntered into the room and sat next to Emily. "What did Madame say?"

"Not much," Emily told her. "She got called out on a Martin emergency."

"Oh, too bad. Maybe you can talk to her after class."

And tell her what? Emily wondered dismally. That Amanda's friend Nina wouldn't make the cheerleading squad? Madame would care about that just about as much as Emily cared.

"Where's Tracey?" she asked, just to change the subject.

"She had to stop at her locker. Look, here comes Madame with Martin."

The teacher walked into the room with a hand firmly attached to Martin's shoulder. He was pouting, like a five-year-old who'd been caught with his hand in the cookie jar, and he took his seat without a word. One by one the other students came in, and the bell rang.

Madame surveyed the room. "I see Carter's still absent. Has anyone seen him?" No one had, and Madame frowned as she made a note on a paper. Then she looked up and asked the same question Emily had asked Jenna.

"Where's Tracey?"

"She went to her locker," Jenna offered, and Madame frowned again. She hated for students to be late.

But Tracey wasn't late for class. She didn't show up at all. And by the end of the hour, Emily could only think of one reason why.

Tracey meant well. She wanted Emily to cheer up, to feel confident about herself and her gift. She'd managed to make herself go invisible so Emily would believe that this particular prediction had come true. Maybe right this minute Tracey was sitting in that empty seat and hoping Emily was happy.

She looked at Tracey's usual desk, and for a second, she actually thought she could see her friend. It was all in her imagination, of course. But just in case Tracey was there, Emily offered a weak smile at the empty seat.

The bell rang. Jenna came to her side and looked at the empty seat. "She's getting pretty good at disappearing," she commented.

Before Emily could respond, Amanda paused on her way out and spoke to her. "Why are you staring at Tracey's desk with that goofy smile?"

Jenna answered for her. "Emily predicted that Tracey wouldn't be in class today."

Amanda shrugged. "Nah, she's just being invisible."

"How can you be so sure about that?" Emily asked.

"Because it's more likely than one of your visions coming true."

Jenna, who would do or say anything to contradict Amanda, responded. "It's not just Tracey. Emily predicted that Carter wouldn't be in class yesterday."

"Big deal. So she actually got two predictions right." Amanda turned to Emily. "So tell me, Miss Know-It-All, who else is going to disappear tomorrow? Me, I hope. I hate this class."

Emily knew she was being mocked, but even so, she let her eyes glaze over to see if anything would be revealed. And she had a vision.

"Martin."

"Yeah, whatever," Amanda said airily and left the room.

Jenna didn't say anything, but her skeptical expression told Emily she didn't have a whole lot more faith in Emily's prediction than Amanda had. So the next day, at least two people were pretty surprised when Martin didn't appear in class.

CHAPTER THREE

AS MADAME CLOSED THE door and Martin still hadn't appeared, Jenna turned around and gave Emily an appreciative nod. Emily didn't seem to notice—she had a dazed expression on her face. Which wasn't that unusual—she always looked a little dreamy and out of it.

Jenna hadn't meant to hurt Emily's feelings about her gift. She liked Emily. She might be a space cadet who cried a little too easily, but she was a good person, and she was a friend. And Jenna didn't have all that many friends.

That was pretty much her own fault—she knew that. She'd come to Meadowbrook Middle School after a brief stay in a program for troublemakers, and she hadn't kept that a secret. In fact, she'd acted like she was proud of her bad reputation and kept up a veneer of toughness that scared most of her classmates away. Only Tracey and Emily hadn't been put off by her attitude. They got to know the real Jenna, and they accepted her.

So Jenna really hoped she hadn't hurt Emily's feelings, and just to find out, she searched Emily's thoughts. It was never easy reading Emily's mind—with all those premonitions and visions, it was kind of cluttered. It was easier to figure out what Emily was *feeling*—Jenna could almost always get a sense of that.

Actually, Jenna sometimes found it difficult reading the minds of everyone in this class, especially Madame. Probably because none of them was completely normal.

But she got enough from Emily to reassure herself that Emily wasn't brooding on Jenna's teasing. Emily— like Jenna—was wondering where all the missing students were.

So was Madame, apparently. The teacher looked seriously disturbed as she surveyed the room.

"I'm going to the principal's office," she announced. "I want you all to spend the time writing down your own personal goals for your gifts."

This wasn't an unusual assignment. Madame frequently ordered them to ponder their gifts and note their thoughts. But this time, she looked like her own thoughts were elsewhere.

She left the room, and Jenna turned to Ken sitting next to her. The dark-haired, broad-shouldered former athlete seemed lost in his own thoughts, which wasn't unusual either. He was a friendly guy, but he always looked like something was bothering him.

"What's going on?" she asked him. "Where do you think they are?"

Ken gave his head a little shake, as if he was trying to lose whatever was occupying his mind. Or maybe he was just responding to her question.

"Not a clue," he replied. "Can you read their minds?"

Jenna didn't think so. Every now and then, if someone was trying to be heard, she could read minds from a distance. But usually she had to be in close proximity to the person.

"I'll try," she said. She closed her eyes and envisioned Carter, Tracey, and Martin. Nothing came to her.

"They're not trying to contact me," she told Ken.

"Me neither," Ken said.

Jenna was relieved to hear this, since only dead people talked to Ken. She looked around at the others in the room. Emily was still staring into space, probably trying to drum up visions, which was a good thing, Jenna suspected. She didn't want to disturb her.

Off to the side of the room in his wheelchair, Charles seemed to be trying to amuse himself. Two pencils, engaged in what looked like a sword fight and unguided by any hands, floated in the air in front of him. Clearly Charles was moving them with his mind. *He* didn't appear to be concerned about the missing students. That made sense, since Charles rarely thought about anyone but himself—which was probably why he didn't have a friend in the world.

Sarah was doing what she was supposed to be doing. She had her class notebook open on her desk and was writing studiously. Jenna didn't bother to read her mind. Sarah seemed to avoid thinking anything interesting in case she felt tempted to use her gift.

Amanda was fidgeting. She rapped her fingernails on her desk, opened and closed her notebook, and tapped a foot. Finally, she got up and went over to Ken, the one person in the class she felt was on her social level and therefore worth communicating with.

"This is creepy," she declared.

"No kidding," Jenna remarked.

Amanda shot her a quick withering look as if to say "I wasn't talking to you." Jenna didn't care. Having hung out with Amanda when Amanda was occupying Tracey's body, she knew that she was a mass of contradictions—inside, she was actually sort of decent. But her mean-girl act wasn't just on the surface. It went pretty deep, and sometimes Amanda could be sincerely nasty.

Never to Ken though. Even if he wasn't involved in sports anymore, he'd been a total jock before his accident, and that obviously counted for a lot in Amanda's book. Jenna often suspected Amanda had a crush on him.

"What do *you* think, Ken?" Amanda asked.

"Something's going on," Ken said. "If they were sick, they'd be on the absentee list. Their parents must be worried."

"Carter doesn't have any parents," Amanda pointed out. "And Tracey's parents probably think she's vanished on purpose. But if Martin's parents don't know where he is, they have to be going crazy. He used to live across the street from me, and I remember his mother always calling for him to come in if he was out playing."

Jenna couldn't resist. "So you and Martin played together as children?" she asked mischievously. "Were you like best friends?"

Amanda didn't even dignify that with a reply. "Ken, what do you think we should do?"

"I don't know," Ken said simply.

Jenna had a suggestion. "We could ask Emily who's going to vanish next." She turned to Ken. "Emily predicted that Carter and Tracey and Martin would disappear."

Ken's eyebrows went up. "Yeah? Hey, Emily." He raised his voice. "Emily!"

Slowly, Emily turned to them. "Yes?"

"Come here," Amanda said imperiously.

Don't take orders from her, Emily, Jenna thought furiously. But Emily wasn't a mind reader, and she still looked so dazed, she'd probably take orders from a squirrel.

She made her way over to Jenna, Ken, and Amanda.

"What's going on?" Amanda demanded to know.

Emily was taken aback. "How would I know?"

Ken spoke much more kindly. "Did you have a premonition that those three would disappear?"

Emily nodded. "Yes. But that's all I saw. Just them not being here."

Amanda sniffed. "That's *all*? Oh, great. You see people missing—big deal. What good is your gift, Emily, if you don't know why they're gone or where they are or anything?"

Jenna was glad to see that Emily was now getting annoyed with Miss I'm-All-That. "Sorry if my gift doesn't meet your high standards of—of *giftedness*, Amanda."

Jenna clapped her hands in glee and Ken grinned.

But Amanda was not pleased. Her voice rose. "You know what I think, Emily? You're just showing off. You didn't even have any premonitions."

"Oh yes she did," Jenna interjected.

Amanda ignored that. "You're a great big fake, Emily."

Emily drew herself up. "I am *not*."

Now Amanda's voice became shrill. "Oh yeah? Then

417

tell us who's going to disappear next!"

Now Jenna understood. Amanda was getting nervous.

Emily looked directly into Amanda's eyes. "You are."

It was all Jenna could do to keep herself from patting Emily on the back to congratulate her. This was exactly what Amanda needed to hear—something that would make her freak out. She deserved to be frightened.

And she was scared—anyone could see that. She went completely pale, and given the amount of makeup she used, that was pretty dramatic. And her thoughts were so clear to Jenna that she was surprised everyone couldn't hear them.

Ohmigod ohmigod ohmigod what am I going to do, help me, somebody, help me . . .

And then Amanda ran out of the room, looking as if she was about to throw up.

"That wasn't very nice, Emily," Ken said.

"I couldn't help it," Emily said simply. She turned and went back to her seat.

"It served Amanda right," Jenna said to Ken. "She can be pretty nasty."

Ken shrugged. He'd been distracted by a new game Charles was playing on the other side of the room. Charles was sending things into the wastebasket next to Madame's desk. First, he threw a crumpled piece of paper. It sailed through the air and landed in the basket. Then he crumpled another piece of paper and did the same thing.

"It's amazing, what that guy can do with his mind," Ken said. But Jenna thought it was a waste of a gift to use it on stupid activities like that.

When he got bored, Charles looked around for something more interesting to toss.

"Charles, stop it!" Sarah cried out as her bag suddenly left her side and went sailing through the air in the direction of the wastebasket.

Why didn't Sarah just *make* him stop? Jenna wondered. She knew why, of course. Because Sarah refused to use her power. What Jenna really wondered was why she wouldn't use it. As with Ken, there was something secretive about Sarah.

Now Sarah's bag hung in midair, upside down, and all the contents poured out into the wastebasket.

"Charles!" Sarah wailed.

"Cut it out, Charles," Ken said, but Charles ignored him. Jenna glared at him in disgust.

"You're such a jerk, Charles. No wonder you don't have any friends."

"Who says I don't have any friends?"

"It's pretty obvious," Jenna retorted. "You're always alone. I think that speaks for itself."

Luckily for Sarah, Madame returned to the room then.

She saw Sarah's bag fall into the wastebasket, and no one had to tell her what was going on.

"*Charles*," she said.

For a second, Charles faked a look of innocence. Then, with a shrug, he looked in the direction of the wastebasket. Sarah's bag rose out of it and returned to Sarah's desk.

Madame didn't say anything else to Charles. She didn't even threaten him with demerits, as she normally would have done. Jenna didn't try to read her mind—she knew from experience that it was impossible to know what Madame was thinking.

The bell rang, and Madame didn't even mention the assignment she'd given them. "Have a nice day," she said automatically as they all got up and headed for the door. But as Jenna passed Madame's desk, she thought she heard an additional remark from the teacher.

It sounded like, "Be careful."

Chapter Four

THE NEXT DAY AT school, Emily found it even harder than usual to concentrate in her classes. She was feeling just a little bit ashamed of herself. Maybe more than a little. What she'd said to Amanda— telling her she would be the next one to vanish—wasn't very nice. She knew Jenna was proud of her for having the guts to talk to Amanda like that, but it wasn't really an Emily thing to do. She wasn't the type to fight mean with mean.

Amanda had been really scared, Emily knew. She'd probably worried about it all night long. She might not even be at school today, she was so nervous. But if she wasn't there, it wouldn't be because of Emily's prediction. Because it hadn't been Amanda who was missing in Emily's most recent vision of the gifted class.

She'd had the vision before Amanda even called her over in class the previous day. It came just after Madame left the classroom to make phone calls; it came without any effort on her part. She hadn't even forced her eyes to glaze over—it happened automatically.

The vision had been the clearest one yet. There was the gifted class, on the next day—today. She was positive about the date, because she could actually make out the calendar that hung by the door. *That* was peculiar—her visions didn't usually include details like that. She could easily see that Carter still wasn't there, and neither were Tracey and Martin. And there was another person missing.

Sarah.

She confessed this to Jenna at lunch. "I don't know why I didn't warn Sarah. Maybe I just wasn't sure it was a real prediction. Or maybe I guess I just didn't want to scare her."

Jenna grinned. "Yeah, scaring Amanda is much more fun."

"*Jenna.*"

"Oh, c'mon, Em—lighten up. It was good for Amanda. She's got a little too much self-esteem. She needs to be taken down a notch."

Emily looked over at another table in the cafeteria. "She doesn't look upset today."

Amanda was with her usual snotty friends at their usual table. Nina was crying, she noticed. She must have just found out she didn't make the cheerleading squad. The other girls looked like they were comforting her. Not

Amanda though. She was busy filing her fingernails. She couldn't even show a little sympathy for her own friend! Maybe Jenna was right. Amanda deserved a scare, even if it didn't last very long.

Jenna was eating. "You know, these school lunches aren't half bad. The way you and Tracey are always complaining, I thought they'd be a lot worse."

"Speaking of Tracey," Emily said, "aren't you just a little worried about her?"

"Not really. Because I still think Tracey disappeared on purpose. You know how she's been trying for ages to stay invisible for longer periods."

"What about Carter and Martin?"

"Well, Carter's a mystery, right? He appeared out of nowhere, and now he's disappeared. I just can't get too spooked by him. And Martin, he's always whining about his home and how his mother nags him. He probably ran away. Any day now, they'll find him sleeping in a bus station."

"So you still don't believe in my predictions."

Jenna just shrugged. "You said it yourself—they're pretty screwed up."

Emily didn't get it. "But you supported me yesterday in front of Ken and Amanda."

"I'm your friend," Jenna said matter-of-factly. "I'm always loyal to my friends." She went back to her mashed potatoes. "Could you pass the salt?"

Emily couldn't believe Jenna could be so blithe about everything. She wished she could read her friend's mind. She had a pretty good feeling this was all an act Jenna was putting on, to show how tough she was.

"What about Sarah?"

Jenna did her who-cares shrug. "Let's wait and see if she shows up in class."

She didn't. The second Emily entered room 209, her heart sank when she saw the empty seat. Sarah was always there early. Madame, at her desk, was staring at Sarah's seat, too.

Ken arrived, then Amanda, then Charles. Jenna sauntered in as the bell rang. When she saw Sarah's empty seat, she turned to Emily.

"Okay, I take it back. You've got a gift."

Madame spoke sharply. "What do you mean by that, Jenna?"

Madame was one of the only people who could intimidate Jenna, and Jenna practically stammered. "Well, I, uh, meant that, you know, how Emily makes predictions of the future, and, you know . . ."

Madame broke in. "Emily! Did you know that Sarah would disappear?"

Emily shifted uneasily in her seat. "I—I sort of had a

vision. But I didn't know if it was real."

Madame stared at her. "And the others? Carter, Tracey, Martin—did you have visions about them?"

Suddenly Emily felt terrible. She nodded.

"Why didn't you say anything?"

"Because—because I didn't trust them. The visions, I mean. My predictions are always so mixed-up. They're like bits and pieces, like a puzzle, and I can't put them together to make a real picture! Like, I'll see an earthquake, but I don't know when or where it's going to happen. Or I'll see someone have an accident in gymnastics, but I don't know if it's going to be at the next competition or the one after that."

It dawned on her that she'd probably never said so much at one time in class.

Madame looked sad. "I know your premonitions are confusing, Emily. But you have a gift. You should have told me about these visions."

Not for the first time, Emily wished she could give her gift back to whomever gave it to her. The disappointment in Madame's face . . . Emily couldn't bear to look at her teacher. She felt like she'd let her down. Not to mention Carter and the other missing students.

Madame's voice became softer. "There's always an element of truth in your visions, Emily. You might not understand them, but they have meaning. You have to learn how to interpret them, to look for clues that can help you put them in context. You have to figure out what's important and weed out what's irrelevant."

Emily's head was hurting, and her eyes were stinging.

"Can you see them, Emily?" Madame asked. "The missing students ... Can you see where they are? Is anything coming to you?"

Emily shook her head. "I see the future, not the present," she whispered.

"Concentrate on the future of one of them," Madame urged. "Carter. Do you see him in the future?"

She tried very, very hard, so hard her head wasn't just hurting, it was throbbing. Something started happening. A blurry image began to form ...

In pain, she managed to say, "I see him, I see him."

"Where is he?" Madame asked.

"Here. He's here, in class, in his seat."

"And the others?" Madame persisted. "Where are they?"

Her head was about to explode. Emily burst into tears. "I don't know, I don't know."

She was dimly aware of Jenna on one side of her, Madame on the other. As they led her out of the room, Madame spoke softly.

"I'm sorry, Emily, I shouldn't have pushed you like that.

I'm going to send you to the infirmary and have your mother called. Jenna, could you go with her?"

A short time later, Emily was lying on the infirmary cot, and the school nurse was calling her mother. And it wasn't long until her mother appeared at the door.

"The school called me. Honey, are you all right?" She came to the cot and put a hand on Emily's forehead. Emily gently pushed it away.

"I don't have a fever, Mom."

"She just got upset in class," Jenna declared. "Madame thought she should go home."

Her mother's lips tightened. "Which class? The crazy class?"

"Mom!" Emily shot Jenna an apologetic look.

"It's okay," Jenna murmured. "I'd better get back."

Emily's mother didn't even bother to thank her for helping Emily. She was more than upset.

"I'm taking you out of that class," she declared in the car on the way home. "It's not doing you any good at all—it's making things worse. Now, you just close your eyes and relax. I'll give you some aspirin when we get home."

Emily was grateful to be left alone. She had a lot to think about.

She'd tried to tell Madame about her visions, and she should have tried again. But Madame just kept telling her

427

she needed to interpret them, to study them, and never told Emily *how*. Was she stupid? Or lazy? Now she was starting to feel like she'd been given a gift she didn't deserve. Carter, Tracey, Martin, and Sarah . . . With her gift, she might have been able to stop them from disappearing. If only she'd worked harder, if only she'd understood what her visions meant . . . Now her head was hurting again, but she was glad. She deserved the pain. She'd never felt so guilty in her life.

At home, she swallowed the pills her mother brought her, even though she knew they wouldn't do any good. But they did help her to relax a little, and maybe that was why the vision appeared.

She saw herself, in the dark of night, on a street corner. She could read the names on the signpost—Maple Street and Stewart Avenue. She wore jeans, a green T-shirt, and a brown sweater. She was alone.

A car pulled up. With no street lights, she couldn't see what color it was, but she could tell it was an ordinary car, nothing fancy or unusual. There was a woman in the driver's seat and a man sitting next to her. The woman's hair was blond—it must have been a very light blond for Emily to be able to notice it in the darkness.

One of them said something. She couldn't hear the words, but the Emily in her vision got into the car. And then the vision faded.

Emily sat up. *How bizarre*, she thought. She knew Stewart Avenue—it was on the other side of town, in a business district that was busy by day, empty at night. What possible reason would she have to go there? And why would she get into a car with strangers? For as long as she could remember, her mother had warned her never to talk to strangers, let alone get into a car with them. It was the wrong thing to do. Didn't all parents warn their children about this? Anyone with half a brain knew how dangerous talking to strangers could be. It was totally out of character for her to even daydream of doing something stupid like that.

She took the book she'd been reading from her nightstand and opened it. It was a good book, a mystery, and she looked forward to reading a few pages every night before going to bed. But she couldn't concentrate on it. She got up and went out to the living room.

Her mother was watching TV. She was pleased to see Emily. "Are you feeling better, honey? Do you want something to eat?"

Emily shook her head. "I'm not hungry, Mom. But I'm not sick," she added hastily.

"How about if I heat up the leftover macaroni and cheese?" her mother asked hopefully.

She knew that if she could show some enthusiasm for macaroni and cheese, her mother would feel a lot better.

"Okay, that would be great."

Soon she and her mother were curled up on the sofa with bowls of macaroni and cheese. They found a marathon of a fashion makeover reality show on TV and settled down for the evening.

Emily liked this kind of show. She enjoyed watching ugly ducklings turn into swans with the right clothes and makeup. But no matter how entertaining the episodes were, her mind kept going back to that last strange vision. Maple and Stewart. When would she find herself on the corner of Maple and Stewart? And why?

By ten thirty, both she and her mother were yawning and the marathon was finished. Her mother did something she hadn't done in years—she followed Emily into her bedroom to tuck her in.

"I know you're going to feel better in the morning," she said, kissing Emily on the forehead. "And I'm going to call your principal. You won't have to go to that gifted class anymore."

Emily was in no mood to argue. "'Night, Mom."

Once her mother left, she realized she really wasn't sleepy at all. She just lay there and thought about the events of the past week. But there, in the corner of her mind, she kept going back to that earlier vision. Maple and Stewart, Maple and Stewart . . .

She gave up on trying to sleep, got out of bed, and went to her desk. Madame was always telling her she had to interpret the visions, search for details and look for clues. So once her computer had warmed up, she typed "Maple and Stewart" into the search box on her Internet browser and hit enter.

There was an old movie starring actors named Alicia Maple and Del Stewart, and a store called Maple and Stewart that sold plumbing supplies. There was a law firm called Maple, Stewart and Jones, and a mapping service that offered to give her directions to the corner of Maple and Stewart. She clicked on that one, but it didn't tell her anything she didn't already know.

There were no clues here.

Maple and Stewart . . . She realized the street intersection wasn't far from where Jenna lived in that housing project. Maybe Jenna would know something unusual about that corner. She looked at the clock. It was after eleven, too late to call. But there was a chance Jenna might be up late surfing on her computer. Emily could send an instant message. She went into her e-mail file, where Jenna was listed as an IM friend, but she wasn't online.

She noticed something else though—a notification that

she had a new e-mail. She clicked on it.

Hi Emily, it's me, Tracey. I'm so sorry—they made me send this. They said they'd hurt us if I didn't. Can you go to the corner of Maple and Stewart tonight at midnight and wait there? Someone will pick you up.

Tracey

And then someone had added, a couple of lines down:

If you want to find your classmates, you will be there.

And find herself in the same danger her classmates were probably in. But it was her fault if her classmates were in danger. She knew what she had to do.

In the dim light, she dressed in the same clothes she'd been wearing in her vision: jeans and a green T-shirt. The brown sweater hung on the back of her chair. She threw a few things in her backpack—her contact lens case, a change of underwear, her toothbrush. And she put her watch back on.

She scribbled a note and placed it on her bed. Then she left the room, glancing anxiously at the half closed door to her mother's bedroom. She noted with relief that there was no light on—her mother wasn't up reading. Even so, she moved very quietly. Her mother was a light sleeper.

Once outside, she debated taking her bike, which was in the building's parking garage. But she had plenty of time to get there by midnight, so she went on foot. It took her forty-five minutes to reach the corner of Maple and Stewart.

There were no lights, no sounds—the area was deserted, just like in her vision. It was a little chilly—maybe she should have worn a jacket. But she hadn't been wearing a jacket in the vision.

She waited. Funnily enough, she didn't feel very nervous. In fact, she was unusually calm. She looked at her watch. It was midnight.

She heard something and looked down the street. In the distance, she could see a car coming. It wasn't going very fast.

She couldn't make out the color of the car, but it looked fairly ordinary. It slowed down as it approached her corner and then stopped. There was a blond haired woman in the driver's seat and a man next to her. Shadows obscured their faces, but the woman's platinum blond hair was too bright to ignore.

The woman spoke, calmly but firmly. "Get in, Emily."

She did. Because she knew that in this particular situation, it was the right thing to do.

Chapter Five

J ENNA WAS ANXIOUS TO talk to Ken, and when she spotted him on the steps leading to the school entrance, she hurried toward him. But when she reached the bottom of the steps, she paused. She could see who he was with, and there was no way she could talk to Ken now. He was with a couple of jocks, and not just ordinary athletes. They were stars—even Jenna, who was not into sports, recognized them as the cocaptains of Meadowbrook's basketball team. She'd been forced to go to assemblies where these guys had been introduced and cheered, along with the football, soccer, and baseball captains.

Jenna had very firm opinions about jocks—as far as she was concerned, they were all stupid and boring. Emily and Tracey always told her this was a stereotype and couldn't possibly be true of every athlete in the world, but Jenna held firmly to her beliefs. There was no way she wanted those guys to hear the news she had for Ken.

She couldn't understand why Ken hung around guys

like that, even though Ken himself had been a major jock once, before she came to Meadowbrook. Emily had told her he was captain of the soccer team, and he'd been injured in a bad accident. In fact, according to Emily, it was just after the accident that he developed his gift. And Ken was okay—not boring and definitely not stupid. So maybe her attitude toward athletes really was a stereotype.

Still, her news was private and personal and only for Ken's ears. But it was getting close to the time when they'd all have to enter the building. Ken would be off to his first class, and she'd lose this opportunity to talk to him. So she slowly mounted the steps and edged toward the boys. Somehow she had to get Ken away from his buddies.

She was close enough to hear Ken now. It sounded like he was congratulating the other two.

"That was an amazing game last night."

"Incredible," one of the boys said. He cocked his head toward the taller boy. "When Mike made that first basket, I was totally blown away. It looked like a wild throw to me."

"It was a wild throw," Mike admitted. "I was as shocked as everyone else when it cleared the net."

"You were lucky," Ken remarked.

"Yeah," Mike agreed. "And I stayed lucky all night. I didn't miss a throw."

"It couldn't be just luck," the other boy said. "You were

terrific at Monday's game, too."

"I know," Mike said, but his forehead puckered.

"I don't know what happened. I haven't been that good all season."

"No kidding," the other boy said. "You've been a disaster. I don't think you scored half a dozen points before Monday." He turned to Ken. "You should have heard the way Coach has been bawling him out."

"So that's what got you going," Ken commented.

"I guess," Mike said, but he didn't sound very sure of himself. "Hey, Ken ... you know that kid in the wheelchair?"

"Charles Temple? Yeah, what about him?"

"He was at the game last night."

"So what?" the other boy asked.

"He was at Monday's game, too. I noticed because of the wheelchair—he couldn't go up into the stands. He was on the floor, just at the edge of the court."

Ken echoed the other boy. "So what?"

Mike looked distinctly uncomfortable. "I don't know. I never saw him at a game before. And he kept giving me weird looks. There's something spooky about him."

Now Ken looked uncomfortable. "Spooky?"

"Yeah ... You know anything about him?"

"No." Ken noticed Jenna on the lower step. "Uh, I gotta go talk to that girl. See you guys."

He hurried down the stairs and joined Jenna. "Did you hear those guys? Geez, I hate when people ask me about the gifted group."

Jenna had more important things on her mind. "Listen, something's happened. Emily's gone."

He looked at her blankly. "Gone where?" Then his eyes widened. "You mean, she's disappeared like the others?"

"Not exactly. She left a note for her mother, so she didn't just disappear—she knew she was going away. Her mother called me this morning. She was completely hysterical."

"Did the note say where she went?"

Jenna shook her head. "Only something about how she had to find her friends and not to worry about her."

"But how would she know where to look for them?"

"I don't know. Maybe she had a vision. We should find Madame and tell her."

That turned out to be unnecessary. Once inside the building, they were witness to a commotion going on just outside the principal's office. Madame's calm, measured tone could be heard, but Emily's mother's angry voice was louder.

"How can you let this happen?" she cried. "Young people start disappearing from one particular class and parents aren't notified?"

Madame replied, "The parents of the missing students

437

were notified immediately, Mrs. Sanders."

Emily's mother wasn't satisfied with that. "And what about the parents of the other students? If I'd known what was happening in that so-called gifted class, I could have prevented my daughter's disappearance!"

Other kids had been attracted by the noise and were gathering around. The principal, Mr. Jackson, looked nervous. He ushered the two women into his office and closed the door.

By the time the bell rang for homeroom, word of all the missing students had spread through the school. Homeroom classmates who knew that Jenna was in the gifted class gave her uneasy looks, like they half-expected her to vanish before their very eyes. Jenna didn't care about that—with her goth makeup, black clothes, and tough-girl attitude, she was used to being stared at. But she cared about her friends, Tracey and Emily, and she was even worried about the classmates she wasn't so friendly with. She looked forward to class and the opportunity to talk with Madame and the remaining students about what they could do.

She didn't have to wait for the class. Before homeroom was over, the teacher received a note and beckoned to Jenna.

"You're to go to room 209 immediately," the teacher told her.

When Jenna arrived, Amanda was the only other of her gifted classmates in the room.

"Do you know why we're meeting now?" Jenna asked her.

Amanda shrugged.

"Is it about Emily?"

Amanda just shrugged again. Jenna gazed at her curiously.

"Have you even heard about Emily?"

"No."

"She's missing. I think she ran away to look for the other students."

"What other students?"

"The ones who disappeared from our class!"

Amanda nodded. "Okay," she said. She rose from her chair and started toward the door. Jenna blocked her. She hadn't expected Amanda to show any deep concern about this, but not getting any reaction at all surprised her.

"Amanda! C'mon, we have to talk about this, we have to do something."

Amanda looked at her blankly. "Why?"

Now Jenna was shocked. None of Amanda's friends could hear them, so there was no reason for her to put on an act. And she knew Amanda had some decent qualities, some real feelings. This total lack of interest was very, very strange.

Unless . . . unless . . . "You're the other Amanda," Jenna declared, her heart sinking.

The real Amanda would have snapped at Jenna and called her crazy. This Amanda simply stared at her blankly.

Jenna sighed. "Sit down, Amanda."

The Other-Amanda obeyed.

There was no point in trying to talk to this whatever-it-was, this thing that looked like Amanda, talked like Amanda, moved like Amanda—but wasn't Amanda, just a robotic shell of the real girl. Oh, what a crummy time for Amanda to suddenly do a body snatch! She might not have the world's best personality, but at least she was smart.

Which was probably why she'd done a body snatch. She must have really believed Emily's prediction. Which clearly didn't come true, since the body of Amanda was still here. But where was the real Amanda?

So there was only herself, Ken, and Charles left to work with Madame on this situation. Ken was the next to arrive.

"I just saw Madame," he said. "She's going to be a little late. The police are here, and she has to talk to them."

Jenna shook her head. "I don't think the police are going to be much help. You know these aren't regular kidnappings. There won't be ransom demands or anything like that."

"You're right." Ken turned to Amanda. "Hi, Amanda.

You got any theories about this?"

"About what?"

"The missing students! Jenna and I were just saying we don't think these are ordinary kidnappings."

Other-Amanda opened her handbag and brought out a cosmetic case. She set up a little mirror on her desk and began applying mascara to her eyelashes.

"Amanda!" Ken said again. "Do you have any ideas?"

"No," she replied and continued putting on her makeup.

"Don't bother with her," Jenna informed him. "She's not Amanda."

Ken understood what she meant and groaned. "Oh, no."

Madame arrived. Despite the events of the morning, she seemed calm, though Jenna thought she detected a dark glint in the teacher's eyes. She didn't waste any time on opening remarks.

"We have a situation," she said abruptly. "And we've all got to work together." She stopped. "Where's Charles?"

As if on cue, the door opened and Charles wheeled himself in. "Sorry I'm late," he said casually. "I was hanging with my friends."

"What friends?" Ken murmured.

"Could I have *everyone's* attention?" Madame demanded. "Amanda?"

"She's not Amanda, Madame," Jenna told her.

The teacher sighed and closed her eyes for a moment as if trying to absorb this new bad news. "All right, thank you, Jenna. Charles, would you please stop that immediately!"

Jenna realized that paper clips were jumping out of the tray on Madame's desk and going into the cup that held pencils and pens. But Madame had spoken more sharply than usual, and Charles stopped.

Madame continued in the same tone. "We can't afford not to take this seriously, people! I do not believe that Tracey is invisible or that Martin has run away from home. Someone—some organization—is causing members of our class to disappear, and these disappearances have something to do with who you are. We have to figure out who is behind this and why."

"Do you think they're in danger?" Ken asked the teacher.

"It's quite possible, though not in the way you think. I don't think they will be physically injured. But I do think they will be used."

Jenna knew what she meant. It was Madame's greatest fear for them—that their gifts could be utilized by people with bad intentions. Trust no one—that was her mantra. But Madame's next comment surprised her.

"I must say, though, I feel a little better knowing that Emily has gone in search of them."

Jenna's mouth fell open. "Why?"

"Because in a situation like this, I think she's our best hope," Madame said simply.

Jenna couldn't believe what she was hearing. Emily, their best hope? Emily, with her inaccurate predictions? Emily, whose gift was the weakest of them all?

If Emily was their best hope, Jenna thought, then they were in more trouble than she'd ever imagined.

Chapter Six

WHEN SHE WOKE UP, Emily had no idea where she was—geographically speaking. She could tell that she was in a bed, but that was about it.

Immediately after she'd entered the back seat of the car, the man in the passenger's seat turned around, leaned toward her, and put a blindfold over her eyes. He'd done this gently, almost apologetically, but even so it had been a frightening moment, and Emily had started to panic. This wasn't alleviated by the woman's sharp voice.

"Don't struggle, Emily. There's nothing you can do."

"What's going on?" Emily asked, without much hope of getting an answer.

"You'll find out when the time is right," the woman said.

The man spoke in a kinder tone. "Here's something to drink."

She felt a bottle being placed in her hand. Then she

444

heard a soft whirring sound. Reaching out, she felt a glass panel that now separated her from the people in the front seat, like in a limousine. She wouldn't be able to hear anything they said to each other.

There was one benefit to the silence and darkness. It might be easier to concentrate and envision her future. She took a sip from the bottle and almost immediately wanted to kick herself. *How stupid can I be?* she wondered as drowsiness swept over her.

Now, awake, she sat up in the bed. There was nothing covering her eyes, but the room was pitch-dark. She could feel a table next to her bed and something that could be a lamp on it. By touch, she located a button and pushed it in.

Light flooded the room. There wasn't much to see though. It was a plain room, with light blue walls. There was something on one wall in the shape of a window, but it was completely covered by a metal shutter. A white chest of drawers stood against the far wall.

There were two other beds in the room, but both were empty. They were unmade and looked as if they'd been slept in recently. The door started to open, and Emily stiffened.

"Good morning."

Emily let out the breath she'd been holding. "Tracey."

Tracey came over and sat on the edge of Emily's bed. "How are you feeling?"

"A little groggy," Emily admitted.

Tracey nodded. "They gave you something to make you out of it."

"Where are we?"

"I don't know," Tracey replied. "In some kind of house, but I don't know the address. And all the windows are blocked."

"How did they get you here?"

"They grabbed me inside the girls' bathroom at school and put a wet towel on my face. There must have been something in it that knocked me out. They must have put me in a car and taken me here. I woke up in this room."

"A man and a woman with blond hair?"

Tracey shook her head. "There were two men, and the woman was a redhead."

So there were at least four of them, Emily thought. "Who are they?"

"I don't know."

"What do they want us for?"

"I don't know that either."

"Tracey!" Emily exclaimed in frustration. "You've been here three days. Haven't you learned anything?"

She shook her head. "Nothing. I managed to go invisible on the first night and looked around the place, but I couldn't find any clues. There's a floor above us, but

446

the door at the top of the stairway is locked. I guess that's where they stay."

A creak above them confirmed this. Someone was up there.

"I think they know about my gift," Tracey continued. "Even when I'm invisible, they whisper to each other and I can't hear a word they're saying."

"Did you try just asking them what they want?"

"Of course I asked them," Tracey said. "They just keep saying I have to be patient. Maybe they're waiting till they have us all here before they explain what they want." She offered a half-hearted smile. "No offense, but I was hoping the next captive would be Jenna. At least she might be able to read their minds and figure out what's going on."

"I can't believe you're being so calm about this," Emily marveled.

Tracey shrugged. "Someone has to be calm. Carter's worthless, of course. He's just like he is back at school. He does what he's told, and the rest of the time he stares into space. Martin whimpers and whines. Sarah looks totally freaked and barely speaks. I think maybe she's in shock."

"I can relate to that," Emily said with feeling. "Do they know about all our gifts?"

"I don't know!" Tracey replied for the umpteenth time. Then she looked sadly at Emily. "I'm sorry I dragged you into this. They made me write that message to you."

"I didn't care. I wanted to help all of you. I felt bad that I didn't see what was going to happen in time. I could have warned you."

"Don't be such a goof. You couldn't have stopped them."

Emily's stomach rumbled loudly.

"You're hungry," Tracey declared. "Get dressed and we'll have some breakfast. I have to say, they're taking pretty good care of us here. The food's okay, and there's lots of entertainment."

"It's still a prison," Emily reminded her as she got into the sweatpants and shirt that were laid out on the bed.

"Well, at least it's an upscale one," Tracey said. "There are DVDs, an Xbox, games . . ." She was still extolling the virtues of their jail as Emily followed her out of the bedroom.

Emily wasn't fooled by Tracey's cheery tone. This was a Tracey thing to do—take charge and try to keep their spirits up. Clearly this wasn't working for Martin. Entering what appeared to be a dining room, they found him slumped in his seat, eyeing his plate of food mournfully.

"I like my eggs sunny-side up," he whined.

"Shut up and eat," Tracey ordered him. "Scrambled eggs are just as good. And look at that nice crispy bacon."

Carter ate steadily, but the expression on his face—or

lack of expression—gave no indication of whether or not he was enjoying the food. Sarah looked exactly like Tracey had described her—just plain scared.

Remembering the drink in the car, Emily eyed the food warily. But Tracey had said it was okay, and there was Carter, not showing any side effects from eating it. Along with the eggs and bacon, there was toast and orange juice that looked freshly squeezed. Emily didn't think she'd be able to eat, but she surprised herself.

Maybe it was because the place just didn't seem scary at all. Except for the lack of windows, they could have been in any normal, ordinary house. They sat around a big table on comfortable, matching chairs. The plates were decorated with a floral pattern, similar to the dinnerware Emily knew at home. There were real forks, knives, and spoons, not plastic ones.

Surreptitiously Emily touched the edge of the knife lightly. No, it wasn't sharp enough to cut anything tougher than eggs. Not that she'd ever have the guts to stab a human being . . .

From what Emily remembered from the night before, they hadn't behaved like serious bad guys. The woman wasn't friendly, but she hadn't been nasty, and the man was almost nice.

She was pretty sure it was the same man who entered

the dining room at that moment. He was thin, slightly balding, with a neatly trimmed short beard and wire-rimmed glasses perched on his nose. As he approached the table, everyone froze and looked at him.

He placed a stack of napkins on the table. "Do you need anything?" he asked the group in general. "I suppose you're too young for coffee."

He wasn't frightening at all. In fact, as he gazed around the table, he looked a little uncomfortable, almost nervous.

No one said anything. "I can make more toast if you want it," he offered. When none of them asked for any, he left the room looking relieved.

As she continued eating, Emily noticed a tear trickling down Sarah's face. Tracey must have noticed it, too. Sitting next to Sarah, she leaned over and put an arm around her shoulders.

"It's going to be okay," she said soothingly.

Sarah flinched and shrugged off Tracey's arm. "Get off."

Emily eyed her curiously. She didn't know Sarah well at all, but she was always nice in class, never rude. Clearly the situation was affecting her. She just hoped that meant Sarah would use her gift if it became absolutely necessary.

They were all finishing their breakfast now. Again Tracey took charge.

"Who wants to go into the living room and play *Grand*

Theft Auto?" she asked brightly.

No one jumped at the opportunity, and it didn't matter anyway, because at that moment the hostage-takers or kidnappers or whatever they were all entered the dining room. There was the balding guy and another guy with a lot of curly brown hair who was shorter and fat. While the skinny guy still looked nervous, the shorter one was grinning. They weren't young but they weren't old. Emily guessed they were around her mother's age.

It was the woman who really grabbed her attention. For one thing, she was very pretty, sort of glamorous looking. Emily estimated her age at around thirty, but she wore a lot of makeup so it was hard to tell. She wore fashionable tight jeans with boots and a polka-dot shirt. Her long black hair gleamed with midnight-blue highlights, and she wore hoop earrings that looked like real gold.

Her eyes were blue, but a very different shade of blue than the streaks in her hair. They were so pale they were practically transparent.

What was really amazing was her expression—or, more accurately, her lack of expression. Her perfectly sculpted features were completely blank. For a second, her lips stretched and turned up slightly at the ends, but never in a million years would Emily have called that a smile. If anything, it made her shiver.

451

"Welcome," she said, although there was nothing welcoming about her flat voice. "I hope you're all comfortable. My name is Clare." She indicated the chubby guy. "This is Howard, and the man on my other side is George."

George looked at the ground and murmured, "Hello." Howard beamed at them. "Hi, guys!"

Now she was positive George was the man who'd been in the back seat with her. But she wasn't sure about the woman. The voice sounded familiar, and she could be wearing a wig. Or last night's blond hair was a wig. Or the red hair Tracey had seen . . . Oh, why was she thinking about hair at a time like this?

Clare continued. "I know this must be strange to you, and you have to be wondering what's going on. Well, now that you're all here, we can explain."

Emily looked at Tracey and knew she had to be thinking the same thing. If the point had been to kidnap all the gifted students, then they weren't all here.

The woman might have been a mind reader. "We're not bringing in all your classmates, by the way. You're the ones we need now."

Tracey spoke up. "Why?"

"For your gifts, of course." The odd lip twitch which must have been her version of a smile appeared briefly again. "You're all exceptional young people with very special talents. Tracey, you can become invisible. Martin, you're capable of great strength. Emily, you have the ability to see the future, and Sarah . . . Sarah, you have the greatest gift of all. You can control people."

Emily shuddered. She sounded so matter-of-fact, she could have been talking about who excelled at math and who could play the piano. Maybe this was why she seemed scarier than the men. There was something unreal about her.

As scared as she was, Emily had to say something, and she said the first thing that came to mind.

"What about Carter? He doesn't have a gift."

Clare didn't seem surprised, and she only glanced at Carter, almost as if he was insignificant. "That doesn't matter. We've got the people we need."

Again, Emily was amazed at her own daring. "The people you need for what?"

The pale blue eyes rested on her. "You're going to help us rob a bank."

Chapter Seven

THIS TURNED OUT TO be all the information they were going to get for the moment. The group was dismissed, with Clare's promise that they'd learn more at lunchtime. Emily followed the others into what they called the living room.

Tracey hadn't been exaggerating when she described the amusements available in their prison. The room was like a massive media center, with a large flat-screen TV, video game equipment, computers, and iPods with headsets for anyone who wanted to listen to music. A bookcase held books (all the latest teen series), DVDs, video games, board games . . . everything and anything remotely entertaining to meet everyone's taste.

Sarah immediately curled up on a plush pillow chair with an iPod and earphones, which she clamped to her head, shutting everyone else out. Martin went over to the bookcase and studied the video game titles.

Emily was vaguely disappointed. Robbing a bank—it

seemed so . . . so ordinary. It was a felony, of course, but she'd been expecting something *bigger*.

People didn't normally try to use her gift, which was a good thing. She hated the thought of someone trying to manipulate her. Tracey had asked her for a weather prediction once, when her family was planning a beach vacation. That wasn't a big deal. But once a crazy student teacher had demanded that she predict the week's winning lottery number. That had been seriously creepy. She'd refused to do it, but the teacher had hypnotized her and tried to force the prediction out of her.

But how could her gift provide any assistance in this plan? Would they want her to predict how much money would be in a bank's vault on a particular day? She'd never been very good at math.

"Any criminal can rob a bank," she murmured to Tracey. "What do they need *us* for?"

"To make it easier, maybe," Tracey suggested. But she admitted she was puzzled by the goal. "I thought their project would be something grander."

Martin was surprised, too. Clutching a video game box, he joined them. "I don't want to rob banks," he complained.

"Neither do we," Tracey assured him.

"I'd rather do something like *this*." Martin showed them the video game cover.

Emily read the title. "*Toxic Teen Avengers.* What is it?"

"It's a video game about these kids with superpowers who save the world."

"Save the world from what?" Tracey wanted to know. She took the box and began reading the description.

"From some other kids with superpowers who want to destroy the world," Martin replied.

Emily couldn't help smiling. "Whose side are you on, Martin? The savers or the destroyers?"

"Who cares? I just think this sounds a lot more interesting than robbing banks. And we've got superpowers, too. We could be like these guys."

Tracey shook her head. "I think a lot depends on the kind of superpowers a person has, Martin. We're not fire starters, we can't fly . . ."

"Sarah's gift is better than those powers," Martin said.

"But Sarah won't use her gift," Emily reminded him. Still, in the back of her mind, she was a little comforted to know that Sarah was capable of doing amazing things. She turned to Tracey. "Don't you think if one of us was in serious danger, Sarah would call on her powers to help out?"

"I hope she would," Tracey began, but she couldn't continue. From across the room, Sarah let out a wail.

"Sarah, are you okay?" Emily asked anxiously.

Sarah didn't hear her—she was still wearing the headset.

But she was staring at her hands with horror. Emily and Tracey hurried over to her.

"What's wrong?" Tracey asked.

Sarah took the headset off. "Look at my nails," she moaned.

Emily looked, but Sarah's fingernails looked perfectly normal to her. "What's wrong with them?"

"They're all bitten! I don't bite my nails!"

"You're nervous," Tracey said, trying to comfort her. "We all are. You probably didn't even realize you were biting them."

It seemed odd to Emily that Sarah would be agonizing over her fingernails when they were all being held captive. She'd never struck Emily as being particularly vain, but of course, she didn't know her all that well.

"Maybe that woman Clare has a nail file," she suggested, but now Sarah was looking beyond her, and her eyes were wide with fear.

"Where's Carter?" she asked in a whisper.

Emily and Tracey looked around the room. Carter was so quiet and unobtrusive that people frequently didn't even notice if he was around. But he was definitely not in the room.

"In the bathroom?" Tracey suggested.

"I think he's gone," Sarah said.

"Gone where?" Emily asked.

Now Sarah was trembling. "I think . . . when you told them he doesn't have a gift . . . they just got rid of him. I mean, if he can't help them rob banks, what good is he?"

"You think they sent him back to Meadowbrook?" Emily wondered.

"I think they killed him." Sarah choked on the words, and her eyes filled with tears. Tracey sat down on the puffy chair and put an arm around her.

"Calm down," she said soothingly. "Those people didn't seem like killers to me. I'm sure Carter's all right."

Sarah pushed Tracey's arm away. "I don't care what they did to Carter. I'm worried about me!"

"Sarah!" Emily exclaimed.

"Shh," Sarah hissed and beckoned the two girls closer. She glanced over at Martin to make sure he wasn't listening, and then she spoke in a whisper. "I'm not Sarah."

For a moment, both Tracey and Emily were silent. Then they looked at each other, and Emily was pretty sure they were both drawing the same conclusion. The girl's next words confirmed it.

"I'm Amanda."

A small groan escaped Emily's lips, and she could have sworn she heard Tracey mutter something stronger.

"What else could I do?" Amanda demanded. She glared

at Emily. "It's all your fault, you know. You told me I'd be the next one to disappear, and I believed you. That's why I took over Sarah's body."

"Wait a minute," Tracey interjected. "I thought you could only do that if you felt sorry for the person."

Amanda nodded. "That's right."

"How could you feel sorry for Sarah?" Emily wanted to know. "She's smart, she's cute, she's not a nerd or anything like that."

"She's got really big feet," Amanda said. "And she doesn't have a boyfriend."

"That's all you needed to feel sorry for her?" Tracey asked. "Big feet and no boyfriend?"

Amanda nodded. "Yeah, that's kind of weird, huh? I guess my gift is getting stronger. Or maybe it's just easier for me to feel sorry for anyone who's not me."

Tracey and Emily exchanged looks again. "Amanda, this is not good news," Tracey said sternly. "We were counting on Sarah's gifts to get us out of here."

"She never uses them anyway," Amanda pointed out.

"Yeah, but we figured if we got into a bad situation, she'd give in and help us out," Emily told her. She looked at Amanda thoughtfully. "You don't have Sarah's gifts by any chance, do you?"

Amanda shook her head. "I tested myself at breakfast.

I tried to make you spill your juice."

"Thanks a lot," Emily muttered.

"Well, like I said, it's your fault I'm here. And it's not like I can just snap my fingers and get back into myself—you know it's not that easy. It's harder getting out than getting in." She looked at Tracey accusingly. "Do you think I would have stayed in your body for so long if I could have gotten out faster?" She got up and began to pace. "You know what really bugs me? That I believed you! Everyone knows your predictions are off the wall most of the time. If I'd just stayed myself, I would have been fine."

Emily wasn't even aware she was smiling until Amanda asked, "What's so funny?"

"It was Sarah I saw disappearing. I only said it was you because you were getting on my nerves and I wanted to scare you."

Amanda scowled. "So it's even more your fault than I thought. And when the kidnappers find out I don't have any talent, they'll get rid of me just like they got rid of Carter."

Emily had a feeling an apology would be appropriate at that moment, but she didn't think it would make Amanda feel any better. And Amanda was being so—so Amanda-ish that she didn't feel very sorry.

Tracey spoke. "Amanda, when you took over my body, after a while we started to bond or something." Amanda-

460

Sarah looked horrified, so Tracey quickly amended that. "Okay, not like friends, but you picked up on what I could do. And you were able to disappear, remember? So maybe the same thing will happen to you now, and you'll get Sarah's powers." She turned to Emily. "Can you see if that's going to happen?"

"I'll try," Emily said. She backed away from the two girls, half-closed her eyes and let everything go blurry. Then she concentrated on a mental picture of Amanda. Slowly, the picture took on a life of its own, and she saw Amanda–Sarah in a big space where there were desks, a counter, people waiting in a line—could it be a bank? Yes, and Emily herself was there, and Tracey, too, and other people she couldn't see very well. The person who looked like Sarah was flapping her hands worriedly and looking totally useless. Frightened, too.

Then, it was like a curtain dropped briefly over the vision. When it went back up and she could see the vision again, the Sarah figure was in a completely different role. She was in control, making people move, taking charge. She looked confident, like someone with power . . .

The picture faded, and she opened her eyes. Amanda–Sarah and Tracey looked at her expectantly. "Well?" Amanda asked. "Do I get Sarah's gift?"

"I don't know," Emily said helplessly. "I had two

completely different visions. In one of them you had power, and in the other one you didn't."

Tracey's eyes widened. "You saw two different futures?"

"I guess," Emily said. "And I don't know which one is right. That's never happened to me before."

"You really are worthless," Amanda declared in disgust.

"Amanda, that's not true," Tracey snapped. "Emily just happens to have a gift that's more complicated than ours."

Amanda's eyes narrowed. "I hope it's not too complicated for our kidnappers. Or she'll end up just like Carter." She gulped. "And me." Her eyes filled with fear again.

"Calm down," Tracey ordered. "We're all in this together, and we're all gifted, and we'll work together to figure this out." But this time, she didn't sound very sure of herself. Amanda certainly didn't look convinced.

"You disappeared yesterday and it didn't help us out," she said. "Martin can't turn his strength on by himself—something has to happen to him. I can't do anything as Sarah. And Emily . . . well, we just saw how useful she's going to be."

Tracey didn't have a comeback for her, and Emily didn't either. At that moment, she was experiencing something she could never have predicted.

She was in complete agreement with Amanda.

CHApter Eight

ENNA SAT ALONE IN the cafeteria. It was strange, in a way. Before she got to know Emily and Tracey, she'd always sat alone in the cafeteria, and it never bothered her. But maybe she wasn't as much of a loner as she thought she was. Now, she missed her friends.

She looked around for Ken, but she didn't see him. She *did* see Charles, and she was surprised to notice where he was sitting. His wheelchair was parked by one of the tables where the jocks sat. Among them were the basketball players Ken had been talking to that morning on the steps.

Poor Charles, Jenna thought. Did he really think he could break into *that* exclusive clique? But she didn't give this too much thought. She had more important things on her mind.

It wasn't time for class yet, but she decided that being alone in an empty classroom was better than being alone in a crowded cafeteria, so she sneaked out of lunch early. She could think better without all the noise. And she needed to think, hard.

She wanted to make another attempt to contact Emily. Once before, when Emily had been trapped in a storage room, Jenna had been able to read her mind from a distance and come to her rescue. Of course, Emily hadn't been very far away that time—the room was in the basement of the school. But maybe she wasn't far away now. Or maybe Jenna's gift could extend to longer distances. In any case, it was worth the effort.

She concentrated with determination in the silence of room 209. But the effort was wasted. As hard as she tried, she couldn't hear Emily. Or Sarah, Tracey, Martin, or Carter. She slumped back in her seat and wished someone else would arrive in the classroom to distract her from her own thoughts.

Someone did—but it was only Amanda-the-robot, or whatever that thing was who looked like Amanda. The pretty duplicate went to her seat and pulled out her cosmetics case. Without much hope, Jenna tried to communicate.

"Hey, Amanda."

"Amanda" tore her eyes away from her own reflection. "What?"

"You wouldn't happen to know where the real Amanda is, would you?"

The blank expression on fake Amanda's face gave Jenna her answer.

Ken came in next, followed by Charles. Ken looked glum. Charles was beaming.

Jenna started with Ken. "What's up?"

Ken scowled and rubbed his forehead. "Someone's been bugging me."

Jenna knew what he meant. Every now and then, dead people tried to send him on a mission. Ken's problem was that he was essentially a nice guy, and he hated to say no. So he kept putting them off, telling them "not now" or "maybe later," and they kept on nagging him.

"Just put your foot down and make it clear that you're not going to run their afterlife errands for them," Jenna advised. "They'll have to give up sooner or later."

Ken shook his head. "This one's a mother. I don't think she's ever going to give up." He blinked. "What's that noise? I don't think it's coming from inside my head."

"It's Charles," Jenna told him. "He's whistling." Charles had never whistled in class before, and they both turned to stare at him.

"That tune sounds kind of familiar," Jenna said.

"No kidding," Ken replied. "It's the school fight song. Don't you ever go to any games?"

"No."

"Hey, Charles, what's going on?" Ken asked. "Are you getting school spirit or something?"

"Just trying to remember the tune," Charles said cheerfully. "I'm going to the basketball game this afternoon."

Ken sighed. "Charles, if you're going to get into sports, why don't you back winners? Watch the wrestlers or the soccer guys. Our basketball team stinks this year."

"They won the past two games," Charles pointed out.

"Yeah, but they lost the ten games before that, and they lost big time," Ken said. "And it's only Mike Brady who's scoring."

Charles stopped smiling. "That's your opinion. I'll bet they make it to the finals this year."

Ken shook his head. "Nah, no way. A team can't get to the finals with only one good forward. Mike can't keep this up—he's not that great a player."

"So why do you go to all the games?" Charles demanded to know.

Ken shrugged. "Those guys are my buddies."

"Yeah, well, they're my buddies, too," Charles declared.

Ken rolled his eyes in disbelief.

"He was sitting with them at lunch today," Jenna told him.

Ken grinned, as if he assumed she was joking. "Yeah, right. Anyway, don't expect much from your buddies today, Charles. Who are we playing? St. Mark's? They've got an amazing team. They haven't lost yet this season. I hate to say it, but our guys are doomed."

"Don't talk about my friends like that," Charles yelled.

Suddenly the big fat dictionary on Madame's desk rose and took off in the direction of Ken's head, moving fast.

"Charles!" Madame was in the doorway. "Stop that at once!"

The book froze in midair. Then, at half the speed, it sailed back to Madame's desk.

"Don't waste your gift on nonsense," Madame said as she went to her desk. "That goes for all of you. Your gifts may be needed for more important purposes."

"Like what?" Charles asked.

"Charles, have you not noticed that half the class is missing?"

"Oh, that."

Madame glared at Charles and seemed about to lecture him when the door opened. Jenna gasped when she saw Carter Street walk into the room.

"Carter!" Madame exclaimed. "Where have you been? Are you all right?"

Jenna almost laughed. Did Madame really expect a response? Carter never spoke, and today was no exception.

Without making eye contact with anyone in the class, he went to his usual seat and sat down.

Madame studied him for a minute. Then she turned to Jenna.

"Jenna, read his mind. See if you can find out where he's been."

Jenna now had another reason to gasp. Madame had never asked her to read someone's mind before. In fact, she was always telling Jenna to stay out of other people's heads. She'd been scolded numerous times for invading the private thoughts of classmates.

But there was one student in the class whose mind had always been closed to her. "I've tried to read his mind before, Madame. I can't get anything."

"Try again," Madame ordered.

"Okay." She looked at the boy and concentrated. It was as she expected—nothing was revealed to her. After a moment, Madame asked, "Would it help to get closer to him?"

"Maybe," Jenna said, but without much hope.

She got up and took the vacant seat in front of Carter. Moving the chair so she could face him, she stared into his eyes. Carter stared right back. She tried to think of her gift as an x-ray, something that could see through anything. And maybe she really was penetrating Carter's mind. But all she saw was complete darkness, a black void. She didn't know if he was intentionally blocking her gift or if there was just nothing there.

"I'm sorry, Madame." She started to turn away, but something about Carter's face made her look at him again. "Madame, his eyes look funny. Like, sort of watery. The way mine get when I have a cold."

Madame approached and gazed at him thoughtfully. "Yes, I see what you mean. And he's more pale than usual." She turned.

"Amanda, would you accompany Carter to the infirmary, please?"

Obviously programmed to behave like Amanda, Other-Amanda let out a heart-rending sigh. Then, with an expression of great reluctance, she got up.

"Carter, go with Amanda," Madame said. And as always, Carter obeyed a direct command.

They had just left the classroom when Ken uttered a word that was highly frowned upon by Meadowbrook teachers. It wasn't typical of him, and Madame looked more concerned than annoyed.

"Ken? What's wrong?"

He was clutching his head with both hands. Jenna didn't even have to concentrate to read his thoughts. She thought everyone might be able to hear the shouting that was going on in poor Ken's head.

You must talk to my son. It's urgent! My boy is in big trouble, and he needs my advice.

"Leave me alone!" Ken pleaded.

This is important! Listen to me. You have to contact him, now!

"No! Get out of my head!"

Jenna jumped. She'd never heard Ken sound so angry.

Jenna and Madame watched him anxiously. A few seconds passed, and Ken's eyes widened.

"Hey, I think she's gone."

"See?" Jenna said. "I told you, you just have to be tough with these dead people."

Madame, however, still looked worried. "Ken . . . you're sure you haven't heard from, from . . . " she looked like she was having trouble saying the words ". . . from the missing students?"

Ken shook his head. "No, Madame. I'd listen to one of them. I just hope . . . " his voice trailed away.

"You hope what?" Madame asked.

"I just hope I won't have to."

By the end of the school day, Jenna's frustration level had reached an all-time high. It was pathetic—working math problems, conjugating Spanish verbs, and playing volleyball in gym class when her friends were missing and possibly in grave danger. And here she was, doing nothing about it.

Her thoughts went back to Carter. He had to know something. He was their only link to the others. If she couldn't read his mind, maybe she could get some information out of him another way.

Back in the days when she'd run with a pretty rough street crowd, she'd known some scary people. At least, they knew how to act scary. Jenna could recall a few tactics that just might shake up Carter and frighten him out of his usual zombie state. The last bell had rung, and students were leaving the building, but there were a lot of afterschool activities going on—club meetings, the basketball game—so the infirmary had to stay open. There was a good chance Carter might still be there.

Unfortunately, the school nurse was still there, too. It wasn't going to be easy to threaten Carter with her watching.

"Yes?" the nurse asked. "Can I help you?"

Jenna thought rapidly. "There was an explosion in the chemistry lab! A teacher told me to come and get you."

The nurse rose from her desk and glanced into the little room off the reception area. Whatever she saw must have reassured her because she snatched up a bag and hurried out.

Jenna berated herself—she should have sent the nurse to the gym, which was all the way on the other side of the

471

school. It wouldn't take her long to get up a flight of stairs and see that there was nobody lying on the floor of the lab. Jenna didn't have much time.

In the little room, there were four cots, but only one was occupied. Carter was sleeping.

"Carter!" Jenna said sharply. "Wake up!"

Carter didn't move. She went over to him and poked his arm. "Come on, Carter, wake up!"

There was still no response. She put her hands on both his thin arms and shook him. But the guy could really sleep. If she hadn't seen his chest going up and down, she would have thought he was dead.

But Carter was weird in so many ways. When he was awake, he was like a sleepwalker. It made sense that his actual sleep would be something else altogether.

Now what was she going to do? The nurse would be back any minute. Another idea occurred to her.

If Carter was in a really deep sleep, he could be dreaming—and there was a chance he could be dreaming about his recent experiences. And if he was really, truly unconscious, maybe he wouldn't be able to block her efforts to read his mind.

Having never tried to read the mind of a sleeping person, she wasn't sure if it would work. But it turned out to be even easier than reading a mind that was completely awake and alert. She didn't even have to concentrate very hard—an image formed almost immediately.

It was a house—a large house that looked old and abandoned. Windows were boarded up, and a door that had once been red was covered with graffiti. There was something vaguely familiar about the scene.

"Excuse me, young lady!" A very irate nurse stood in the doorway with her hands on her hips. "What's going on? There was no explosion upstairs! And what are you doing in here with my patient?"

"Gosh, I thought I heard something. It must have been my imagination. Sorry!" Jenna slipped past the nurse and scurried out of the infirmary.

She had to share this news with someone who would care. First she ran up to room 209, but Madame wasn't there. Then she remembered Charles talking about the basketball game. Had Ken said he was going, too?

Outside the gym, she could hear yelling and cheering. When she pushed the door open, it was practically deafening. *How could people get so excited about a stupid basketball game?* she wondered. Especially since, according to Ken, Meadowbrook's team wasn't so great.

Not according to the scoreboard though. Under the heading "Home," the number was 110. Under "Visitors," the score read 0. Jenna vaguely recalled Ken saying they were playing some superduper team today. It certainly didn't look that way to her.

But Jenna wasn't really interested, and she didn't waste any more time thinking about the score. She scanned the bleachers for Ken. Finally she spotted him, way up on the top level.

"Excuse me, sorry, excuse me," she chanted while squeezing by the cheering fans. When she reached the top, she practically pushed some guy off the stands in order to plant herself down next to Ken.

Ken glanced at her, but his eyes went back to the game immediately. "Can you believe this?" he exclaimed. "I don't know what happened to these guys, but they're playing brilliantly! It's not just Mike—they're all making baskets. And St. Mark's can't even score! They can't even get the ball near the net."

"Who cares?" Jenna asked impatiently. "Ken, listen, I read Carter's mind!"

That tore his attention away from the court. "What did you find out?"

"Just the image of a house. But that could be where he was being held, and where the others are now."

"Where's the house?"

"I don't know," Jenna admitted. "But I've got this feeling I've seen it before. I just need to remember . . ."

"Oh, forget about it!"

Jenna was taken aback by Ken's reaction. Then she realized that he wasn't responding to her—his eyes had strayed back to the basketball court. A boy, one of the guys Ken knew, stood at one end of the court and held a ball. He was looking at the hoop at the other end of the court.

"I can't believe Mike's going to try that," Ken said. "Why doesn't he toss it to another player? There's no way he can make a basket from that distance."

Looking at Mike's position on the court, Jenna had to agree. She knew nothing about basketball, but she couldn't imagine any normal person being able to throw a ball that far and actually meet a target. Then she realized that something far from normal was going on.

"Ken, look!" She pointed at Charles, whose wheelchair was parked at the bottom of the opposite bleachers. He was staring at the basketball with an expression that was very familiar. And when the ball left the hands of the player, it flew the length of the court and fell right into the basket, so neatly that the net didn't even rustle.

A roar went up from the crowd. But even with all the noise, Jenna didn't miss the groan that came from Ken.

"I can't believe it!" He smacked the side of his head. "Charles is moving the ball for them!"

"Do you think the team knows he's doing it?" Jenna

wondered.

"I doubt it," Ken said. "They don't know about his gift—nobody at school does, except for us." Then he frowned. "But Mike was asking me about him earlier. He called Charles spooky."

Spooky . . . The word ignited something deep in her memory. Back when she was hanging with the low-life types and staying out all night, they were always looking for shelters when the weather was bad.

She drew in her breath so sharply that Ken looked at her in alarm. "Are you okay?"

"I just remembered," she said. "I know where that house is."

Chapter Nine

ARLIER THAT SAME AFTERNOON, Emily sat with Amanda-Sarah on a sofa facing the big flat-screen TV. Amanda had chosen the DVD they were watching, a romantic comedy. It didn't matter to Emily, though, since she wasn't actually watching it. She was more interested in trying to drum up a vision.

More than ever before, she needed to see the future. She had to know what they were about to face so they could prepare themselves—to fight? To escape? How could she help them if she didn't know what was in store for them?

It was easy to zone out in front of the movie because she'd already seen it and hadn't really enjoyed the first time. Amanda was totally engrossed in it and wouldn't interrupt her. Martin was playing a video game—either saving or destroying the world—and the last time she'd looked, Tracey had been reading. She was in a decent environment for receiving visions.

And the visions came, one after another. The only

problem was, they didn't make any sense to her. She saw Martin lifting the very sofa she was sitting on and leaning back to throw it across the room. She saw Tracey disappearing and reappearing, blinking on and off like a light on a Christmas tree. She saw Charles breaking down a door with his mind . . . Wait a minute. Charles? He wasn't even here! Maybe someday, somewhere, Charles might break down a door, but what did that have to do with their own immediate future? It wasn't like he'd break down this door to rescue them—Charles wouldn't lift a finger to help anyone but himself.

Frustrated, she shook her head violently in the hope that this might clear her mind. What was it Madame had said about her visions? She had to interpret, to look for clues that would give the visions meaning.

If Martin threw the sofa really hard, and if he threw it at the door, there was a good chance the sofa would break it down. Then they could get out. Even if only one of them made it through, that one person could get help for them all. But would Martin throw the sofa toward the door? She needed to conjure up the vision again and see exactly where the sofa would go. She could be standing by the door when Martin lifted the sofa, ready to escape and run for help. Or maybe Tracey should be there instead. She could disappear—and be much harder to catch if Clare and the others went after her as she ran away.

She looked over to where she'd last seen Tracey. They needed to talk about this and get a plan organized.

Tracey wasn't there.

Emily went over to Martin, who was still playing his *Toxic Teen Avengers* video game.

"Where did Tracey go?"

Martin didn't take his eyes off the screen. "I don't know."

"Did you see her leave the room?"

"No. Whoa, did you see that? We just destroyed France!"

"Congratulations," Emily murmured.

Martin turned to her. "Hey, you know what? It's not so bad here. My mother won't let me play violent games like this. The food's better here, too, and there's lots to do. And the people aren't mean."

"Not yet," Emily said. "I'm going to look for Tracey."

But Tracey wasn't in the bathroom or the bedroom. Had she gone invisible to do some snooping? Emily went back to the living room.

"Tracey?" she called softly.

To her relief, Tracey suddenly reappeared. "I was looking around," she began, and then stopped. From behind her, Emily could hear the sound of someone clapping. She turned to see Clare standing there.

At least, she *thought* it was Clare. This time, the woman

had her hair in a short black bob, and she was wearing a sharp business suit. Only the pale blue eyes and the hard voice assured her that this was really the same woman. It was impossible to guess what she really looked like, Emily realized.

"Very good, Tracey," Clare said. "I'm pleased to see how well your gift works. I'd like to see demonstrations from all of you."

As soon as she left the room, Amanda-Sarah hurried over to Tracey and Jenna. "What am I going to do?" she asked in a panic.

A germ of a notion popped into Emily's head. "I've got an idea." She glanced at Martin to make sure he was still absorbed in his game. From the way he'd been talking earlier, she wasn't sure he should be included in any plans to foil the kidnappers.

They were called in for an afternoon snack a few minutes later and presented with a make-your-own-sandwich buffet.

"Wow, this is great," Martin enthused as he spread huge gobs of peanut butter on a slice of bread. "My mother never gives me peanut butter."

Emily wasn't very hungry, but she forced herself to eat. She knew she had to keep up her energy levels.

Clare and the two men ate with them, so the girls were

on edge. Fortunately, the adults seemed most interested in talking with Martin, and Martin was happy to answer their questions.

"Does your gift cause you problems at school, Martin?" Clare asked.

"Oh sure," Martin said. "People don't believe how strong I am. But if they mess with me, they're in for a big surprise. Once the captain of the wrestling team picked on me. He ended up out cold."

Emily remembered that. An ambulance had to be called, and the big guy was carried out of school on a stretcher.

"You must have gotten into some serious trouble," Howard commented.

Martin grinned and shook his head. "Nope. When the guy accused me of attacking him, nobody believed him!"

"So people don't know about your gift?" George asked.

"Some people know about it because they've seen me in action," Martin said. "But then later, they look at me and they think, No way he did so much damage. Once I hit someone so hard, he went out a window on the second floor. Luckily for him, he landed in a bush, or he could have had serious injuries. A couple other kids were witnesses. But when the teacher asked them about it, they said the boy fell."

"Because they were afraid of you?" Clare wanted

to know.

"Probably," Martin said proudly.

Emily doubted that. It was more likely that the kids didn't believe their own eyes. Who would believe someone as babyish and whiny as Martin could have that kind of power?

"I'll bet bigger guys are always challenging you," Howard commented.

"Oh sure, all the time," Martin said. "Everyone wants to fight the champ, right?"

Amanda-Sarah started coughing loudly, and Tracey looked down at her plate. Emily was positive they were trying very hard to keep from laughing out loud, just like her.

She had to wonder why Martin wasn't more nervous about having to demonstrate his gift to Clare and the men. Had he managed to convince himself that he was in control of his strength? That he could turn it on and off at will? In her opinion, he was going to have more problems than the fake Sarah. He didn't even have Emily and Tracey helping him out.

Control . . . Did these kidnappers have any idea how hard it was for the so-called gifted class to use their gifts effectively? Tracey was making progress, but she still had to use her memory, and sometimes her mood just wouldn't let her disappear. Jenna could be blocked by strong people who knew about her gift and had worked up enough power to protect their thoughts. Amanda had to feel pity before she could take over someone's body.

Emily wasn't sure if Ken could call on a dead person or if he had to wait until someone contacted him. Martin had to be bullied and teased before his strength emerged. And Sarah refused to use her gift at all.

As far as she could tell, Charles was the only one in the class who had complete control of his gift—which made her wonder why *he* hadn't been brought here. It seemed to her that he had the best gift for robbing banks—he could probably make all the money fly out of the bank and into the criminals' hands. And he'd be just as willing to get involved as Martin was—neither of them had any sense of loyalty.

She was pondering this question when Clare spoke to her. "Emily? Are you having a vision?"

"No," Emily replied. "I was just . . . you know, thinking."

George looked interested. "But isn't that how you see the future? By just thinking about it?"

Emily squirmed uncomfortably. "Sort of, I guess. But not really."

"Then how does it happen?" Clare demanded.

"I—I don't know."

"Personally," Howard said, "I don't care how she does it, I just want to see her do it."

"Yes," Clare said. "I told you all we wanted to see demonstrations of your gifts. Let's start now." The frosty eyes were on Emily. "With you."

Emily swallowed what felt like a peach stone in her throat. "Now? Here?"

"Yes. I want you to tell us the future of our project."

Emily took a deep breath. She looked at Tracey, and then at Amanda-Sarah, and hoped they'd remember what they hadn't had time to practice. It was mainly up to her, though, and for Amanda's sake, she had to pull it off.

"No."

Clare frowned. "What?"

"No, I won't do it. I won't try to see the future, and you can't make me."

Martin stared at her as if she were nuts. "Of course they can! They're in charge, dummy. Haven't you ever heard of torture?"

For a moment, Emily thought the snack she'd just eaten was going to come right back up. Her eyes darted between pretty, glamorous Clare; Howard who looked like a teddy bear; and serious, bespectacled George, who reminded her of a math teacher. Looks could be very deceiving.

Tracey piped up. "They don't have to torture Emily to get information, Martin. They can use Sarah to get it out of her."

Clare's eyebrows shot up. "Is this true, Sarah? I know that you're capable of making people move. Can you make them think and speak, too?"

For a moment, Sarah's face was blank, like she was totally bewildered by the conversation. Emily and Tracey both looked at her, and her expression cleared.

"Yeah, sure. I can make Emily do anything. You want to see her act like a duck?"

"No, that won't be necessary. Just make her see the future of our project and tell us about it."

"Okay," Amanda-Sarah said. Looking at Emily and speaking in a very low voice, she growled, "Listen very carefully. You will do as I say."

If she hadn't been playing a role herself, Emily would have burst out laughing. Amanda sounded like an amateur magician in a school talent show. Somehow Emily managed to keep a straight face and stare right back at her.

"We want to know what's going to happen when we rob the bank."

Martin broke in. "That's *banks*, plural. Right? We're going to rob a lot of banks."

"That's right, Martin," Clare said, and Emily could almost detect a hint of approval in those steely eyes. "But we'll be satisfied if we can just learn what's going to happen on the first mission."

Emily acted the way she would if she was truly trying to have a vision. She let her eyelids drop lightly to make her surroundings go hazy, and she tuned out all sounds.

A few seconds later, she began to speak. "I see a big room. It's—it's a bank. The Northwest National Savings and Loan Association. There's a long counter, and a few people are standing in line waiting to see the people who work there. Behind the counter, there's a locked door that leads down a corridor and into a vault. Tracey . . . Tracey's invisible. She follows a banker through the door to the vault when he unlocks it."

Clare spoke. "Tell us what Sarah is doing, Emily."

"She's . . . she's doing something so people can't move. I think. It's hard to see her. She's blurry."

"What does Martin do?"

"He breaks down the door. Behind the door, there's a safe."

"Do you know the combination of the safe, Emily?" Clare asked.

"No, I can't see it. But the banker has gone into the vault to open the safe, so Tracey will see the combination. There's a lot of money in the safe. You're waiting for Tracey, Sarah, and Martin outside in an SUV. You drive away."

"So the robbery is a success," Clare said.

"Yes," Emily replied.

"Thank you, Emily." Clare permitted herself a frosty smile. "Well, we've now seen what Tracey, Sarah, and Emily can do. That just leaves Martin. But we're not going to ask Martin to demonstrate his gift right now. We've been told by a trusted eyewitness about the havoc Martin can create, and we don't want any broken dishes. We'll think of a way he can show us his talents later. Now, you're all free to do as you please this afternoon."

"Can we leave?" Tracey asked.

Clare gave her a chilly look. "No."

Back in the living room, Martin returned to his video game. Amanda-Sarah and Tracey gathered with Emily.

"I think we pulled that off pretty well," Tracey declared.

"Oh, absolutely. We totally fooled them," Amanda-Sarah agreed.

"Not because of you," Tracey stated. "Where did you come up with that silly hypnosis voice?"

"It wasn't silly!" Amanda protested.

Tracey turned to Emily. "How did you keep from laughing?"

Emily shrugged. "I don't know."

"And that was a great story you gave them," Tracey added. "It sounded totally believable, like you were really seeing the future."

Emily tried to smile. "Thanks."

Amanda was still annoyed over Tracey's criticism of her performance. "I think I was very believable. I sounded just like Sarah."

"How would you know what Sarah sounds like?" Tracey asked. "I'll bet you've never had a single conversation with her in your whole life."

While the two of them bickered, Emily crept away. She took a book from the bookshelf without even looking at the title. Then she sat down, opened it, and stared at a page without reading a word. Maybe if she looked like she was engrossed in the book, the others wouldn't bother her. She couldn't let them get too close—they might be able to see how upset she really was.

There was a reason why she'd been able to make her story of the future sound so real. She hadn't made anything up—she wasn't that creative.

It was a very precise and realistic vision—the clearest, most detailed vision she'd ever had. It didn't require any interpretation. It was a real vision of a very real crime. What she'd just told them was exactly what would happen.

CHAPTER TEN

I T WAS ABOUT THREE months ago," Jenna told Ken. She had to yell into his ear to be heard, since the crowd was still cheering that last unbelievable basket. "I was with these friends." She hesitated. Just about everyone knew about her reputation, but she didn't want Ken getting the wrong idea about her.

"Well, they weren't exactly friends, just some people I was hanging out with because I had some problems at home, and—"

"Yeah, okay, whatever," Ken said impatiently. "What about the house?"

"We were looking for a place to sleep for the night," she confessed. "We'd been kicked out of the bus station . . ." She paused again. Thinking about her past on the streets wasn't easy. "Anyway, we saw this abandoned house, and we tried to find a way in, but it was all boarded up. I was kind of glad because the house looked so spooky to me. One of the guys, he had a can of paint, and he started spraying graffiti on the door. I don't know why. That was the house I saw in Carter's mind."

"Do you remember where it is?"

"I think so. I'll bet that's where Tracey and the rest of them are."

"There's only one way to find out for sure," Ken said. He stood up. "Is it far? Can we get there by walking?"

Jenna rose, too. "Shouldn't we go to the police and tell them?"

"Tell them what? That you read Carter's mind and now you know where the missing kids are? Come on, Jenna. They're not going to buy that."

He was right—Jenna knew that. There was also the fact that certain police officers might recognize her ... and they would be even less likely to believe any story she might tell them.

"But even if we find the house, what can we do?" she asked Ken. "Break in and rescue them? Whoever kidnapped them must be there, too, watching them. Maybe with weapons. How can we fight them?"

Ken thought for a minute. "We need Charles," he said finally. "Even if the kidnapper has a gun, Charles could get it out of his hand. Come on, let's get him."

At that moment, a whistle blew and a huge roar went up from the fans. Jenna glanced at the scoreboard and saw

490

that Meadowbrook had won by a landslide.

They pushed through the excited crowd and made their way to the gym floor. Charles was still in the same place, applauding wildly and watching the team congratulate each other, slapping hands in the air and clapping each other on the back. Ken and Jenna hurried to his side.

"We think we know where the missing kids are," Ken told him hurriedly. "You have to come with us."

Charles stopped clapping. "Why?"

"Because you can make things move!" Jenna said in exasperation. "You might have to make a gun drop out of someone's hand or make a door open."

"I can't," Charles said. "Mike and the guys are going out for pizza and they invited me to come." He smiled happily. "They think I bring them good luck."

"Oh for crying out loud!" Ken exclaimed. "Charles, your classmates could be in big trouble! Don't you want to save them?"

"I'd rather go out for pizza with the basketball team," Charles replied.

"Too bad," Ken growled. He went behind Charles and grabbed the handles of his wheelchair. Charles pushed on the brake so the chair couldn't roll.

One of the players saw them. "Hey, what do you think you're doing? Leave Charles alone!" He started to come toward them, and several teammates joined him. They didn't look happy.

"Ken, we can't force him to come with us," Jenna said hurriedly. "And I think we'd better get out of here or we won't be going anywhere either."

Once outside the gym, Ken turned to Jenna. "Which way?"

"You know the industrial park behind the bus station? It's just past that."

Across the street, in front of the mall, they had to wait almost half an hour for a bus, which let them off in front of the bus station twenty minutes later. It took them another fifteen minutes to make their way through the industrial park. But the house was right where Jenna remembered it was.

Without speaking, she and Ken went to the front of the place and looked for an entrance. She recognized the graffiti on the red door. Without much optimism, she gave it a push, but it didn't budge. They wandered around and looked for another way to get in. But the house was so boarded up, they couldn't even make out if there was a light on inside. They couldn't hear anything either.

Ken pressed his face up against a crack in a board. Seconds later he let out a cry of pain.

"What?" Jenna cried out in alarm.

"It's that woman in my head again!" Ken moaned.

Jenna could hear her. *Talk to my son! Give him a message from me! It's important!*

"Get out, get out!" Ken yelled.

"Shh," Jenna hissed. "I'll go and check out the other side of the house."

She didn't expect to find anything there that might give her a clue as to whether anyone was inside, but she needed to get away from Ken and what was going on in his head. She had an idea.

She thought about the time she'd been able to hear Emily's call for help. If Emily *was* in this house, Jenna was closer to her than she'd been that time. She pressed the side of her head against the house and concentrated.

She heard nothing—not through her ears, not through her head. She knew Emily was capable of blocking Jenna's mind-reading skills, but surely at a time like this she'd be trying to make contact.

She thought she heard something—a dull, low murmur. It could have been the wind in the nearby trees, she supposed. Or maybe her own heartbeat. But somehow, at that moment, she knew for certain that Emily was in this house. The others, too, probably, and whoever was holding them captive. But it was Emily she sensed. Emily was close by, maybe even leaning against this very same wall on the other side. If only she could understand what Emily was thinking. She was a mind reader, so why couldn't she read the mind behind this wall?

Because the mind on the other side of the wall wasn't sending a message. It was showing her a mood. Jenna could feel it. It was like a thick, dark cloud coming down over her, enveloping her in despair. Sadness. Hopelessness. That was what Emily was feeling at that minute.

Ken joined her. "I got rid of that woman. Have you seen anything?"

"Emily's in big trouble," Jenna told him. "Which means they all are. We have to get in there, Ken."

Ken nodded grimly. "Which means we have to get Charles."

Chapter Eleven

"HEY, CHECK THIS OUT! Emily, come over here!"

Emily looked up from the book she wasn't reading. Amanda-Sarah beckoned to her. Listlessly, she rose and went to the sofa where Amanda-Sarah and Tracey were sitting.

"What?"

Amanda-Sarah's eyes were bright. "Watch this." She looked at Martin, who was in front of the screen by the Xbox console, holding the controller. His thumbs moved rapidly, hitting the buttons that controlled the action of the characters on the screen. Suddenly, he let out a yelp.

"Hey! That's not what you're supposed to do!"

Emily shrugged. "Martin's talking to the TV. So what?"

"No, you don't get it," Tracey said excitedly. "Sarah—Amanda—whoever she is, she made Martin hit the wrong button! She's getting Sarah's gift!"

"So far, I can only make his thumbs move," Amanda-

Sarah said. "But I could get stronger, I think."

"That's nice," Emily murmured.

"*Nice?* Emily, don't you see what this means? If she keeps practicing, maybe she can end this crazy business!"

Emily shook her head. "I don't think so."

"You don't think I'm going to get any better?" Amanda-Sarah asked.

"I didn't say that. You'll probably get better at using Sarah's gift, but it's not going to stop the robberies."

"Why not?" Tracey asked.

"Because . . . I just don't think it can."

Amanda-Sarah looked annoyed. "You know, you're being a real downer, Emily."

Tracey agreed. "Yeah, what's wrong with you? You act like you've given up."

Emily raised her head. What was the point of hiding the truth anymore? They might as well know why she was so depressed.

"That story I told at lunch—it wasn't a made-up story. It was my real vision. We're going to be robbing banks."

Neither Tracey nor Amanda-Sarah responded immediately. They both stared at her like she'd lost her mind.

"I don't know why, but for some reason, we're all going to help them. When I had the vision, I didn't understand how this could happen because Amanda can't do what Sarah can do. But now that Amanda's getting Sarah's gift . . . well, it all makes sense."

They still didn't look convinced, so Emily went over the vision again.

"Remember what I said? Tracey would disappear and follow a banker into the vault, where she'd see the combination to the safe. Martin would break down the door leading to the vault. Amanda would stop the security guards from interfering. And Clare would drive everyone away in an SUV."

"I remember what you said," Tracey told her. "But there was something you left out. Where are you when all this is going on?"

"I'm not absolutely sure," Emily said. "I wasn't in my own vision. Maybe I'm being held hostage. That could explain why the rest of you go along with the robbery— because they'll hurt me if you don't."

Amanda-Sarah looked skeptical. "But you're just guessing, aren't you? You didn't see yourself as a hostage in your vision."

"That's right," Tracey said. "Maybe you're not in the vision because you escaped."

Emily drew in her breath as a tiny bell rang in the back of her memory. "I forgot about that!" She sat down between the two girls. "I had another vision just before lunch. It was a vision of Martin throwing this sofa across the room with so much force that it broke the door down."

"And we escape through it?" Tracey asked excitedly.

Emily tried to remember. "That wasn't part of the vision. But somebody should be able to get out the door, shouldn't they?"

"There you are!" Tracey declared triumphantly. "You escape, and you run for help. The rest of us go through with the robbery, but when Clare takes off in the SUV with us and the money, there's a roadblock and a dozen police cars to stop the car at the corner!"

Amanda-Sarah looked at her in surprise. "Are you having visions now, too?"

"No, I'm just being logical. This explains everything!" She turned to Emily. "What do you think?"

Emily could actually feel the dark cloud of depression begin to lift. "You're right. Madame said I had to learn how to interpret my visions instead of just taking them literally. This is a perfect example. I had a very clear vision of a successful bank robbery, with all of us playing our parts. But none of us *wants* to commit a bank robbery."

Amanda-Sarah glanced at Martin. "I'm not so sure about him."

Tracey disagreed. "I don't think Martin really wants to

be a criminal. He just thinks it would be exciting, like a video game. In the real world, he'd be scared out of his mind."

"Anyway," Emily went on, "it's all starting to make sense now. But there's still something we have to figure out." Now she directed her attention toward Martin. "How are we going to get him to throw the sofa?"

The three of them studied the small, thin boy. Oblivious to their interest, Martin's eyes remained glued to the screen while his thumbs tapped rapidly on the controller. The girls considered various options quietly and came to an agreement.

Recalling what had happened in her vision, Emily rose from the sofa and stationed herself beside the door. Amanda-Sarah also got off the sofa and then went to the opposite end of the room, where she positioned herself just behind Martin.

Tracey, the only one remaining on the sofa, spoke. "Martin, aren't you ever going to stop playing video games?"

"I like video games," Martin said.

"Maybe someone else would like to play that game," Tracey said.

"Too bad," Martin said.

Amanda-Sarah moved quickly. She leaned over Martin's

shoulder and snatched the controller out of his hand.

"Hey!" Martin cried in outrage.

"Too bad for *you*, Martin," Amanda-Sarah sang.

Martin jumped up. Amanda-Sarah held the controller high over her head. Martin, who came up only as far as her shoulders, hopped up and down, trying to get it.

Amanda-Sarah laughed. "Give up, Martin. You'll never be tall enough to reach this.

"Give it back!" Martin yelled.

"Does itty-bitty Martin want his toy?" Amanda-Sarah said. "Maybe Emily will give it to you." She tossed the controller across the room, and Emily caught it.

It wasn't as easy for her to tease and ridicule Martin— she just didn't have Amanda's natural gift for meanness. But she did her best.

"Come and get it, Martin, if you can." She waved the controller in the air. "What's the matter? Are you scared of me?"

Martin ran over to her. When he was within a foot of reaching her, she threw the device back to Amanda-Sarah.

Once again, Amanda-Sarah taunted him by holding it too high. By now, Martin was shrieking, and his face was red.

"Here, Martin," Amanda-Sarah said, extending the controller in his direction. But as he reached out for it, she threw it to Tracey on the sofa.

Tracey held the controller. "Martin, I'm not moving. You can come right over here and take it out of my hand."

Martin raced over to the sofa. But just as he reached Tracey, she disappeared. And since she was holding the controller, it vanished along with her.

"Come back!" Martin screamed.

She did. He reached. She disappeared again.

Emily recalled her vision of Tracey blinking on and off like a Christmas tree light. And here it was, happening in real life—another accurate vision!

Martin's screams were louder now, and Emily wasn't surprised to see George and Clare run into the living room. She was a little worried though. Would she be able to get out the door before they came after her? Could Tracey and Amanda-Sarah block them to give her some extra time?

Martin was completely frustrated now. He'd been teased to his limit, and he responded just as the girls had assumed he would. In a rage, he grabbed one end of the sofa and lifted it. He raised the large piece of furniture in the air over his head and leaned back as if to give himself the momentum to throw it. Emily tensed up and prepared herself to move. And then . . .

Martin let out a high-pitched squeal. So did Amanda-Sarah. And Emily saw why. A little gray mouse raced across the baseboard and disappeared into a little hole. It must have startled Martin so deeply that he forgot about being teased.

Which meant he lost his superstrength. The sofa dropped to the ground with a thud. There was no open door for Emily to run through. She'd screwed up the vision again.

At least Clare and George were impressed. "Martin, you *are* strong!" Claire exclaimed.

Once again the woman had changed her look. Now she looked like she could be a celebrity, a singer or an actress. Her hair was blond again, but this time it was long and *big*, all curls, very glamorous. Dangling gems hung from her ears and she wore a tight, sparkly red dress and stiletto heels. Amanda-Sarah gasped.

"Ooh, you look *hot!*" she exclaimed.

It was hard to read any expression in those transparent eyes, but Emily could have sworn the woman was pleased. "Do you think so?" she asked.

"Absolutely!" Amanda-Sarah said. "I love that dress. In my opinion, this is definitely your best look."

Emily and Tracey exchanged looks. This was so Amanda—Clare could be pure evil, and Amanda would still be impressed by her style.

Or maybe Amanda was faking her admiration, trying to buddy up with Clare so that Clare would trust her, and then she would use that trust to help her classmates.

For the zillionth time, Emily wished Jenna was there. A mind reader would be so useful—much more useful than a second-rate fortuneteller like her.

"Red is your color," Amanda continued, but now Clare had turned her attention back to Martin.

"Was it easy for you to lift the sofa?"

Martin looked smug. "No sweat. It wasn't even heavy. I could have tossed it across the room."

George was clearly intrigued. "And you don't have to do anything to prepare yourself? Go into a trance or chant something?"

"No," Martin said nonchalantly. "I'm just your run-of-the-mill superhero."

"Bull," Amanda-Sarah muttered. Clare heard her.

"What are you saying, Sarah?"

"He can't just snap his fingers and turn into Superman."

"*Amanda!*" Tracey hissed. "I mean, *Sarah!*"

But as usual, Amanda was too caught up in her own announcement to catch the warning.

"He's acting like he can just turn it on and off. He has to be teased first until he's ready to cry, and *then* he gets the power."

"Interesting," Clare said. "All right, I think it's about time to get started."

"We're going to rob a bank *now*?" Tracey asked in

dismay.

"No, not right this minute," Clare said. "We're going to have a little rehearsal first. I assume that in the past you've all used your gifts independently, to serve your own purposes. But to my knowledge, you have never worked together as a team, combining your gifts to achieve one common goal."

"How do you know that?" Tracey asked in bewilderment. "We've never seen you before—not until we were brought here."

Clare looked at her coolly. "But we've known about you for some time now, Tracey. And we know what you've all been up to."

Emily felt sick. This could only mean one thing—there was a spy among them, in their class. Charles? That could explain why he hadn't been brought here. Maybe he was already a member of this criminal team.

Then another candidate came to mind, one that made her feel even sicker. Madame . . . *She* knew them better than anyone. The students confided in her. She knew their strengths and weaknesses. She'd always claimed to be on their side. Was it possible they'd all been fooled? Had Madame betrayed them to these people?

She had no opportunity to envision Madame's future.

"Let's begin our rehearsal," Clare said. "Howard!"

The chubby guy hurried into the room. He was rubbing

his hands together in delight. "Are we going to practice now? Can I play the bank manager?"

"Yes, all right," Clare said, but Emily didn't miss the look of scorn that flashed across her face. Clearly Clare didn't have much respect for Howard. So why was he on her team?

Clare indicated the sofa. "This will serve as the bank counter. The bookcase is the bank entrance. Tracey, Martin, Sarah, go and wait in front of the bookcase. Emily, where will the security guard be standing?"

Emily just glared at her. Clare sighed.

"Sarah, make Emily tell us where the guard will be standing."

By this time, Amanda might very well be able to do that, Emily thought. *And who knows what else.*

"Okay, okay, I'll tell you. He's next to the door."

Clare eyed her keenly. "You could be lying, I suppose. Well, it doesn't matter—the guard will be in uniform. Sarah, you shouldn't have any problem identifying him. George, stand over there and be the guard. Now, Tracey, Martin, and Sarah will enter together, but Tracey will be invisible. Tracey, disappear."

"Now?" Tracey asked.

"We only have time for one rehearsal," Clare said. "We need to cover everything. Disappear."

Tracey folded her arms across her chest. "What if I don't want to?"

"Then I'll order Sarah to make you disappear."

"What if Sarah refuses?" Tracey asked.

If Clare had seemed cold before, this was nothing compared to the way she looked at Tracey right that minute. It was as if icicles were shooting out of her eyes.

"Haven't you wondered where Emily is going to be while all this is going on? She'll be waiting in the car with me. And I will be armed. Do you see where this is going?"

Emily's stomach turned over. So she'd been right. This was what her mind had refused to show her. They'd hold her hostage to ensure that the others would do what they were supposed to do.

Clearly Tracey got the message, too. She faded away. Clare spoke to the empty space where Tracey had been. "And don't even think about trying to do something now either. Your friends will suffer for it."

She turned to Martin. "Martin, go to the bank counter. If there's a line, take your place in it. Don't go to the front. You mustn't draw attention to yourself. Sarah, stand behind Martin. From there, you can see the guard *and* the tellers at the counter."

"Why do I have to be able to see the tellers?" Amanda-

Sarah asked. "I thought I only had to stop the guard from reacting."

"The tellers have alarm buttons under their side of the counter," Clare told her. "They can't be given any time to press the button and alert the police. You'll need to stop them as well as stop the guard. You can do that, can't you?"

"I . . . I don't know. I've never tried doing two things at once."

"Well, that's why we're having a rehearsal—to make sure you can," Clare said. She went over to the sofa and dragged one of the small end tables behind it. "We'll call this the door to the vault. Tracey, go behind the counter and stand by it so you can follow the first person who goes through."

Even though she couldn't see her, Emily assumed that Tracey was doing as she was told. She was too good a friend to risk Emily's life.

"Now we're all in place. The first thing that has to happen is that someone goes into the vault. It could be one of the tellers or the bank manager. Howard, you do it."

Howard took some keys from his pocket, jingled them in his hand, and spoke to an imaginary companion.

"Yes, of course, Mrs. Montague, we can get your diamond necklace out of your safe-deposit box. Come with me, please." He walked slowly toward the sofa and continued talking to his pretend client. "And may I ask where you will be wearing that lovely necklace? Ah, the opera! How very nice."

Clare looked at him with undisguised contempt. "Howard, we don't have much time."

Howard quickened his pace. Behind the sofa, he twisted the key as if he was putting it into a lock.

"Get right beside him, Tracey," Clare said. "Stay with him as he goes inside."

Howard acted as if he was opening a door. He made a big show of standing aside to allow the invisible Mrs. Montague to precede him, and presumably the invisible Tracey went through, too. He walked a few more steps and then made the movements of turning a combination dial.

"Watch this carefully, Tracey," Clare said. "You have to be able to remember the numbers. Now, Howard, leave the vault. Tracey, stay where you are."

Howard obeyed, once again pretending to open the door for the lady and locking it behind her. Clare's eyes remained on the position behind the sofa.

"Tracey, show yourself," she demanded sharply.

Emily held her breath. What if Tracey had run off in search of a weapon to combat the crooks? But she'd been right to assume that Tracey wouldn't risk being disobedient. Tracey reappeared, right where she was supposed to be.

"Very good," Clare said. "Now, Martin, this is your big moment. You're at the front of the line, facing the teller. I'll play the teller." They took their positions, and Clare continued.

"We want the teller to make you angry, so you'll be strong enough to break down the locked door leading to the vault. You'll have to create the right atmosphere so she'll upset you. Do you understand me?"

It was obvious Martin didn't have a clue. "Huh?"

Clare frowned. George approached her. "Actually, considering what we just saw, it might not be a good idea to practice teasing. You don't want him breaking any doors down in *here*."

Clare considered this. "But he needs to see what he has to do."

"I'll play his part," George offered, and Clare agreed. They held a brief, whispered conversation, and then Clare turned back to Martin.

"Martin, you have to watch very carefully and remember what George says. All right, George, you're Martin. What is the first thing you say to me, the teller?"

"I'd like some money, please," George said.

"Do you have a check you want to cash?" Clare asked.

"No."

"Do you have a debit card and a PIN?"

"No."

"Do you have a checking account or savings account at this bank?"

"No."

Clare shook her head. "I'm sorry, young man. You're not eligible to withdraw money here."

"But I want some," George said. "I want a million dollars. Right now."

Now Clare produced an artificial and condescending smile. "Don't we all. But that's not how the banking system operates."

"Please can I have some money? Pretty please?"

"I'm sorry, no. Now please step aside and let me help the next customer." Looking toward Martin, she said, "This is when you start crying."

George wasn't much of an actor. "Boo hoo," he said flatly. "Boo hoo. Give me some money."

"Now, Sarah, you start teasing him."

"Get out of the way! You're holding everyone up. What kind of idiot doesn't understand how a bank works?" Amanda-Sarah scoffed.

"Will that be enough to make you get strong, Martin?" Clare asked.

Martin actually looked offended. "I can call on my superpowers whenever I want!"

Amanda-Sarah piped up. "If it's not enough, I can do more. I'm good at annoying him—I can get him to explode."

Does she have to be so cooperative? Emily thought. Knowing Amanda, she was probably just relieved Emily was going to be the hostage instead of her. Amanda didn't care about anyone but herself, but Emily never would have thought she could sink so low . . . Could Amanda be the traitor among them? There were so many possible spies. Emily hadn't thought her spirits could go any lower, but now they were plummeting to depths she'd never before experienced, and that dark cloud enveloped her completely. She didn't even need to drum up a vision to know that they were all doomed.

The rehearsal continued. George went back to playing the guard, and Martin took over his own role. He made a big production out of breaking down an imaginary door, even adding sound effects.

"Emily, you stand in for the guard," Clare ordered. "Sarah, make her unable to move."

"Sure thing," Amanda-Sarah said. She fixed a wide-eyed stare in Emily's direction.

Emily tensed up, expecting some sort of cold tingle to creep over her as her body froze up. But nothing happened. She knew she could have moved if she'd wanted to.

So Amanda hadn't absorbed any more of Sarah's powers—not yet, at least. But Emily wasn't going to point that out. She stood very still and held her breath.

Clare gave a short nod. "That will be all. We'll leave for the bank at six o'clock."

"Banks aren't open at six o'clock," Tracey said.

"Northwest National is open till seven one night a week," Clare informed her. "Which happens to be tonight. Tracey, come with me. I want to teach you some tips on memorizing numbers. If any of you are hungry, there are cookies on the dining room table."

Emily watched as the adults and her classmates went into the dining room. She wasn't hungry, and there was another reason she wanted to be alone. She could feel the tears burning behind her eyes, and she didn't want them to see her cry.

It was going to happen just as she envisioned it. Well, at least now she knew she was really capable of seeing the future. But it wasn't much comfort. In one and a half hours, she'd be forced to rob a bank, and there wasn't anything she could do about it. They wouldn't be hurt—they were much too valuable to Clare. They'd just become lifetime criminals.

Amanda–Sarah came back into the room. Hastily Emily wiped her eyes, but it wasn't necessary—the body snatcher barely glanced at her.

"Have you seen my watch? I mean, Sarah's watch. I took it off around here somewhere."

"What does it look like?"

"Old-fashioned—there are these tacky little pearls all around the face. It's bad enough having Sarah's bitten fingernails—I don't have to wear her icky jewelry . . . Oh, here it is."

Emily watched her in amazement. "How can you act so—so casual? Aren't you upset about all this?"

Amanda-Sarah shrugged. "Oh, I'm sure I'll get back into my own body pretty soon. I won't be stuck with these people forever."

"But what about the rest of us?" Emily asked.

"Don't worry," Amanda-Sarah said. "When we're all together at the bank, I'll stop them. I didn't want to do it while we were practicing because I wasn't sure I could freeze all three of them at the same time. But once we're at the bank, I'll freeze Clare while she's in the car with you. She'll let me get close enough because she likes me. Then, once we're in the bank, I'll freeze George and Howard. See? It'll be easy."

Emily sighed. "You think you can stop Clare *and* George *and* Howard from moving?"

"I stopped you, didn't I?"

"I was faking it."

The other girl's face fell. "Oh. Well, there's a chance I'll have more of Sarah's gift by the time we get to the bank. I wouldn't count on it though. When I was Tracey, I never could stay invisible very long."

Emily dropped into a chair. In the back of her mind, she must have been clinging to the tiny hope that there was still a chance to get out of this. But it wasn't to be.

"Cheer up," Amanda–Sarah said. "Maybe we can get away at the bank. You never know what will happen."

"But I *do* know what's going to happen," Emily reminded her. "That's why I'm so depressed."

Amanda–Sarah looked thoughtful. "I don't get it. I mean, how can you ever really know exactly what's going to happen in the future? You can see what *might* happen, but you can't know for sure, can you? There's always that butterfly thing."

"What are you talking about?"

"Haven't you ever heard about the butterfly effect? I saw a movie about it. A butterfly can flap its wings in Brazil and cause an earthquake in Japan. Or something else. A typhoon, maybe."

Emily was in no mood for nonsense. "Don't be stupid."

"No, really. It's like, something really small can happen, and it has an effect that builds and builds. Like the way my parents met."

Emily sank deeper into the chair. "I really don't want to hear how your parents met, Amanda."

"No, listen, it's cool. My father was on his way to a job interview. He was early, so he took a walk through a park, and when he passed too closely by some bushes, a button on his jacket was pulled off. He didn't want to look like a slob, so he ran into the first dry cleaners he saw to see if someone could sew it back on right away, before his interview. And my mother was in there picking up some clothes. That's how they met!"

Emily wasn't impressed. "So? It's what's called a coincidence."

"But, wait, think about it. If that button hadn't fallen off, they might never have met. I wouldn't have been born. So I wouldn't have taken over Tracey's body, and she'd still be that nerdy girl she used to be. You see? Tracey's okay today because my father walked through a park. Get it?"

"Not really," Emily said. Amanda–Sarah gave up and went back into the dining room.

But even as Emily returned to her private sadness, she had to admit there might be something to what she'd just heard. Like, why hadn't her vision of Martin breaking the door down happened? Because a stupid mouse ran across the floor, and Martin turned out to be afraid of mice. If it wasn't for that mouse, the police might be here right now, freeing the kids and arresting Clare and her gang.

Then she sat up straight. That wasn't exactly right. Now that she thought about it, she remembered that her vision only included Martin throwing the sofa. She'd *hoped* it would break down the door, but that wasn't part of the vision.

Okay, maybe Amanda's story was kind of interesting. Still, it didn't make her feel any better about what they were about to do. In just over an hour, they'd be robbing a bank. And she didn't see how any butterfly was going to be able to stop it from happening.

Chapter Twelve

K EN KNEW WHERE THE basketball team would be hanging out. Gino's Pizza at the mall across the street from Meadowbrook was *the* popular place for athletes. As they approached, he pointed, and Jenna saw half a dozen players squeezed into a booth by the window.

"The big question is, how are we going to get him away from his new buddies?" Jenna wondered.

Ken rolled his eyes. "Who aren't his buddies at all. Mike's superstitious—he's always been like that. He thinks Charles is some sort of good luck charm, and he's persuaded the other guys to go along with it. I mean, how else could he explain their sudden winning streak?"

"So they're totally using him," Jenna said.

"Yeah. And as soon as the season's over, they'll dump him."

"You're sure of that, huh?"

"I know these guys. I bet they make fun of Charles

when he's not around."

Jenna thought about that. "Charles is proud. If he knew that they don't really like him, he'd leave."

Ken agreed. "I guess we could tell him. But he wouldn't believe us."

Jenna nodded. "But if he heard it from *them* . . ."

"What do you mean?"

An idea was forming in her head. "Do you have a cell phone?"

"Sure."

"Can I see it?"

He handed it over. Jenna had a quick look at it, grinned, and then told Ken her idea.

"It's worth a shot," he said. "Let's go." They went to the door of the restaurant.

"Wait a second," Jenna said. "How do I look?" She rearranged her features into what she hoped was a convincing expression.

"Seriously depressed," Ken said.

"On the verge of crying?"

He cocked his head to one side and scrutinized her. "Well . . . it would be better if you could actually work up a few tears."

Jenna tried, but it was impossible. Seriously depressed would have to do.

They entered and ambled over to the table where the basketball players and Charles were sitting. "Can we squeeze in?" Ken asked. Without waiting for a reply, he pushed his friend Mike to one side and sat down next to Charles.

Charles looked at him with something that resembled interest. "I thought you were going off to save those kids from class," he muttered, too quietly for the others around the table to hear him.

"Nah," Ken replied softly. "Too much trouble. Hey, can I have a slice?"

Jenna wasn't insulted when none of the boys made room for her. She wasn't the kind of girl the jocks went for. In fact, she had a feeling she scared half of them. That made it even harder to look pathetic and win their sympathy. But she did her best.

"I'm not staying," she said in a quavering voice. She sniffed loudly and rubbed her eyes.

"What's *her* problem?" Mike asked.

"Her ring came off her finger and fell into a storm drain outside," Ken said.

"I dropped my wallet in a storm drain once," another player said. "But I got it back. I chewed some gum, put it on the end of a stick, and fished around for it. The wallet stuck to it and I pulled it out."

"We tried that," Ken said quickly. "But we couldn't find the ring."

"Tough luck," one boy said.

"Yes," Jenna said and gave a few more sniffs. "It was a very special ring. My father gave it to me before he died."

She thought that adding a sentimental touch like that might mean something to them.

One of the boys spoke. "Did you see the look on the face of that St. Mark's guy when he tried to make that shot and his ball went into the bleachers? I still can't figure that one out. I thought it would be an easy basket for him."

"Yeah, how did that happen?" another boy wondered.

"Who knows, who cares?" Mike sang out. He tossed an arm around Charles. "We've got our good luck charm. He not only helps us win, he makes the other team lose, big time!"

Jenna had to get the conversation back to her nonexistent ring. Clearly sentiment wasn't going to work. She tried another tactic.

"It had diamonds and rubies on it," she said.

The team members looked at her blankly.

"My ring," she reminded them. "The one that fell in the sewer. Diamonds and rubies. And a great big sapphire."

That impressed them.

"Real jewels?" Mike asked. "Wow, that sucks."

Ken snapped his fingers, as if a brilliant idea had suddenly occurred to him. "I know how you can get it back! Charles, could you come outside with us?"

"Why?" Charles asked.

Ken looked at him meaningfully. "You know why, Charles. We could, uh, try the stick thing again and . . . and you'd bring us luck." To the others, he added, "He's just that kind of guy, isn't he? Lucky, I mean?"

Charles glared at him. "Yeah, well, maybe I don't want to bring *you* any luck."

"Aw, c'mon Charles," Mike said. "Ken's a pal. Why don't you see if you can help his friend?"

"Yeah, maybe there's a reward in it for you," another boy said.

Jenna thought rapidly. Charles was in her math class. "I'll do your math homework for a month," she offered.

"Hey, that's a pretty good deal," one of the boys said.

Charles seemed to think so, too. "Yeah, okay." He backed his wheelchair into the aisle, and Jenna followed him out of the restaurant. Ken stayed behind at the table.

Thank goodness there really was a drain at the edge of the road just in front of the restaurant. Charles peered down into it.

"I don't see anything," he said.

"It's in there," Jenna assured him. She glanced back at

the restaurant, where she could see Ken talking to the others. *C'mon, Ken, do it fast! I don't know how long I can keep him out here.*

"If it's got diamonds, I should see a sparkle," Charles said.

"The diamonds are dirty," Jenna said hurriedly. "I have to get the ring cleaned. Can't you just imagine it in your head and bring it up without seeing it?"

"I don't know. I never tried that."

"It's gold, and there's a big diamond, and a ruby on each side of the diamond, and lots of little diamonds on the band."

"I thought you said there was a sapphire."

"Oh, right. Absolutely. A humongous sapphire."

"I never saw you wear a ring like that," Charles said.

"Well, um, I'm not allowed to wear it to school. Look, just concentrate on that image, and I'll bet you can make it come out. You're so gifted, Charles—you've got the most amazing gift. You're so lucky. All I can do is read minds, but you can move things. That's so much cooler." She was jabbering now, but she'd do anything to keep Charles out here until Ken accomplished what he had to do.

"Shut up, I'm concentrating," Charles said. A minute passed. "Nah, this isn't working. I'm going back inside."

"Just try one more time, please!" Jenna *pleaded*. "Think

about all that homework you won't have to do!"

"Wait a minute," Charles said. "What kind of grades do you get in math, anyway? I don't want you doing my homework if you're going to do a bad job."

Fortunately, she didn't have to answer that. Ken came out of the restaurant.

"Did it work?" she asked excitedly.

He held up his cell phone. "I've got it right here."

"What are you guys talking about?" Charles demanded.

"Your so-called friends," Ken said. "We just thought you might like to know what they really think of you."

He turned on the phone's recording device and pressed Play. The first voice they heard was Ken's.

"So, Charles is hanging out with you now. He's really a pretty good guy when you get to know him."

A boy spoke. "Are you kidding? He's a total dweeb! That kid is too pathetic. He doesn't do anything at school—he just rolls around and complains about everything."

"He can't help being in a wheelchair." That was Ken's voice again.

"That's got nothing to do with it," another voice said. "If he wasn't in the wheelchair, he'd be a walking dweeb."

Mike spoke next. "Look, if he can get us into the finals, he can hang out with us. At least till the season's over."

"But he's really getting on my nerves," another boy

said. "And we've still got a month left before the finals."

"But just think how great we'll feel when we win the state championship," a boy declared.

Mike spoke. "Not to mention how great we'll feel when we can dump Charles."

Ken turned off the phone. "I'm sorry about this, Charles. But you should know what kind of creeps you're hanging out with."

Jenna was watching Charles's face. What little color he had was gone, and it wasn't hard to see that he was really on the verge of tears. In fact, one tear was already making its way down his cheek.

"You know, Charles, we would be your friends," she said, "if you'd let us. I know Emily and Tracey would be, too." She didn't include Amanda. Charles wasn't *that* gullible. "Too bad Tracey and Emily have been kidnapped. Who knows, we may never see them again."

Fiercely, Charles brushed the tear away, but he didn't say anything. Jenna did a quick scan of his thoughts. He was on the edge.

"I mean it, Charles. I don't lie. All you've got to do is be a nice guy, and you can have all the friends you want."

There was a long moment of silence. Finally Charles spoke.

"Okay."

At that moment, a car pulled up alongside them. The driver's window came down, and a familiar voice spoke.

"Get in."

"Madame!" Jenna exclaimed. "How did you know we were here?"

Ken answered for her. "Cell phones have other functions besides recording gossip, Jenna."

The trunk of the car opened. Ken helped Charles into the front seat while Jenna folded the chair and put it in the trunk. She got into the back with Ken, and they took off.

Jenna told Madame about the house and how she sensed Emily and the others were inside. "But I could only feel her mood. I couldn't read her thoughts and find out anything specific, like why they've been taken there."

"We'll find out soon enough," Madame said grimly. She followed Jenna's directions to the old abandoned house behind the industrial park.

"Think you can get the door open, Charles?" Ken asked.

"Piece of cake," Charles replied.

As they approached the house, Jenna frowned. "Something's different."

"What?" Madame asked.

"I don't know. But I'm not feeling Emily's mood."

Madame parked the car, and they all got out. Charles rolled himself to the front of the house. He stared at the red door. Nothing happened.

"It's got chains on it," he said.

"Is that a problem?" Madame asked.

"Nah. I just have to concentrate a little harder."

His brow furrowed, and seconds later the big red door flew open—Charles had unscrewed the hinges. Ken ran toward it.

"Wait," Madame cried out. "Don't go inside. Wait for the police!"

But Ken was already inside the house. Jenna wasn't sure whether to follow him or not. It looked so dark in there.

There was something else, too. She couldn't hear any thoughts at all. With the door open, she should have been able to pick up something. It was as if there were no working brains in there at all.

Ken emerged, shaking his head. "They're gone."

"Where?" Jenna cried helplessly. But she knew no one could answer that.

Suddenly Ken put his hands to his head. "Not now!" he cried out. "Leave me alone!"

Again Jenna could hear the nagging woman's voice. *Please, talk to my son, he's going to get into trouble. You have to tell him I'm very upset with him. That will make him stop.*

"I want *you* to stop!" Ken yelled. "I don't care about your stupid son!"

He's not stupid. His name is Howard. He's really a good boy—he just got involved with bad people. I've been watching him. They've kidnapped some very strange young people and now they're about to rob a bank.

Ken and Jenna looked at each other. "Young people with special gifts?" Ken asked.

Yes, there's one girl who predicts the future and another one who disappears—

"Do you know where they are?" Ken asked.

Of course I know where they are. I'm in heaven. I can see my son whenever I want—

Maybe it wasn't very nice to interrupt the deceased, but this woman could have gone on forever. "Where are they?" Ken and Jenna demanded in unison.

She told them.

Chapter Thirteen

THERE DIDN'T SEEM TO be anything unusual going on at Northwest National Savings and Loan. From the parking lot, Jenna could make out the shadows of figures inside the bank, not running or moving in any suspicious manner. She couldn't tell if any of them were her classmates. The four of them left Madame's car and started across the street.

Jenna's senses were on high alert, and she knew she'd pick up the thoughts of her classmates as soon as she was close enough. But she didn't expect to hear Emily while she was still in the parking lot.

I wish I could be inside with the rest of them. I can't even see what's going on.

"I hear Emily!" she told the others.

"Is she in the bank?" Madame asked.

"No. The others are inside, and she's thinking about how she wishes she could be with them. I'm sure she's in one of these cars." But there were at least twenty cars in the parking lot, and she couldn't tell where the thoughts were coming from.

I'm scared. Clare looks so calm and confident, like nothing can possibly go wrong. I'll bet she'd use that gun on me, too, if the others tried to get away. And they might try. They've only got Howard and George in the bank with them, and they're not the sharpest crayons in the box. I don't think they're even armed. Clare's the brains.

"Howard . . . isn't that the name of the dead woman's son?" Jenna asked Ken. "He's in the bank with the others. Emily's in a car with someone called Clare, and Clare's got a gun."

"If I knew which car they were in, I could get the gun away from her," Charles said.

"Okay, you and Madame find the car," Jenna said. "Ken and I will go into the bank."

"No," Madame said. "Wait until we get the gun. I'm not letting my students go into that place when there's someone around here with a firearm."

Jenna took the handles of Charles's wheelchair. "Maybe Emily's thoughts will get louder when we get closer," she said. She began pushing Charles between two rows of cars.

"Don't go so fast, Jenna," Madame chided her. "You don't want to attract attention. I think this Clare person just might notice someone running with a wheelchair in a parking lot. Not to mention the fact that she might recognize both of you."

"How?" Jenna wanted to know. "She hasn't seen me."

Madame spoke quietly. "You don't know that, Jenna. I have a very strong feeling that this Clare is no ordinary criminal. And this is no ordinary bank robbery."

Jenna had no idea what she was talking about, and she couldn't worry about it now. But she slowed her pace, and Ken and Madame followed closely behind. Jenna kept her eyes and ears open and hoped her special ability was in prime working order.

I wish I could see what was happening in the bank. The guard—he wouldn't shoot a kid, would he? Even if the kid was trying to rob the bank?

Emily's thoughts were definitely louder. Despite Madame's warning, Jenna quickened her pace. Was it that truck over there? Or maybe the green car with the dent in the bumper. If only the lights in the parking lot were brighter so she could see people inside the cars . . .

"It's the SUV," Ken whispered.

Jenna stopped. "How do you know?"

"Howard's mother. She just told me it used to be her car."

Jenna brought the wheelchair up behind the SUV. She bent down to speak into Charles's ear. "Can you sense the gun yet?"

"No. I have to get around to the driver's side. Let go of the chair."

Something told Jenna not to argue. She lifted her hands. Slowly, Charles began pushing himself around to the side of the vehicle. Jenna stayed behind with Madame and Ken. She held her breath, and she couldn't hear any breathing coming from the other two either.

Suddenly the driver's window rolled down. Jenna heard a woman's voice.

"What the—"

And then a gun came flying out of the window. Ken's former life as an athlete came in handy, as he ran and caught it. Then all the car doors opened. Emily leaped out, and at the same time, the car started up. Jenna and Madame leaped out of the way as the SUV backed out. With doors still open, it sped out of the parking lot.

Charles spun his wheelchair around, but it was too late. The big car was out of his sight before he could stop it.

Jenna didn't care. She was too busy hugging Emily tightly. Only for a second though. Jenna wasn't into public displays of affection.

"The others are in the bank," Emily told them.

"We know," Madame said. "Are the men with them armed?"

"I don't think so."

"We're armed," Ken said proudly, holding the gun.

"Put that down," Madame snapped. "I don't want any shooting. I'm calling the police. You stay here."

She took out her cell phone. Jenna looked at Emily with her eyebrows raised.

She told Ken to stay put. Not us.

Jenna nodded. She grabbed Emily's hand, and while Madame's back was to them, they ran to the bank.

Chapter Fourteen

"THERE'S MARTIN, TALKING TO the woman behind the counter," Emily said. "He's supposed to break down the door to the vault." She explained how Martin was supposed to demand money and unleash his superpowers when the teller treated him like a stupid little kid. A customer came out of the bank, leaving the door slightly ajar. Now they could hear Martin's shrill voice.

"But I want some money *now*!"

A man wearing a name tag approached him. "I'm the bank manager. Is there a problem here?"

The teller behind the counter spoke. "I'm trying to explain to this young man that we don't give money away."

The manager chuckled. "I see. Come with me, young man. I'll show you how banks operate."

"I just want some money," Martin whined.

"Yes, of course you do," the man said kindly. "And I'm going to show you how to open a savings account and earn interest."

"I don't want interest, I want money!" Martin screamed.

"Where's Tracey?" Jenna asked Emily.

"Well, if my vision was right, she should be invisible. She's supposed to get the money out of the vault. See the curly haired man? That's Howard. The skinny one by the door is George." She turned to Jenna. "How did you find us?"

"Howard's mother," Jenna said. "Long story, tell you later."

Emily clutched Jenna's arm. "Uh-oh, it's happening now!"

They couldn't hear anything, but they could see, and the expression on Martin's face was something they'd seen before. And then, like a tornado, he tore across the room and crashed through a door.

Emily's heart sank when she saw a security guard draw his gun. Then she saw Amanda-Sarah running for the exit before she slipped on the floor and fell, hard.

"Ohmigod!" Emily shrieked. George was reaching inside his coat. For a gun?

She'd never know. Amanda-Sarah, still sitting on the floor, looked at him. And George froze.

Emily stared at the little scene for a second, thinking, *Wow. Amanda really has got the hang of Sarah's gift.* But something was off. Something about Sarah's eyes looked different . . .

Emily gasped. "It's Sarah!"

"Well, of course it's Sarah," Jenna said. "Who else?"

Obviously, Jenna hadn't bothered to read *her* mind.

"Long story," Emily said. "Tell you later."

Then they both clapped their hands over their ears. Three police cars, sirens wailing and red lights flashing, pulled up in front of the bank. Six officers jumped out of the cars and ran in, shouting for everyone to put their hands in the air.

Now Madame, Ken, and Charles were by their side.

"What happened?" Madame asked in bewilderment. "I hadn't called the police yet."

They heard Tracey's voice before they saw her. "I pushed the alarm button." Tracey was visible and beaming happily. "It's silent in the bank, but it alerts the police that something's going on. As I sneaked into the vault, I looked over my shoulder and saw you outside. I knew Emily must be safe, so I ducked back out the vault door and hit the button under the tellers' counter before Martin even broke the door down. How did you get away from Clare, Emily?"

"Charles got the gun," Emily told her.

Tracey stared in disbelief at the boy in the wheelchair. Charles gave her a haughty look. "I'm the real hero," he said.

Emily was sure he'd never let them forget it either. But

that was okay with her.

Martin was the next to emerge from the bank. "That teller didn't bother me," he announced. "I used my strength all on my own."

Emily didn't have the heart to tell him they'd heard the whole thing—he'd definitely lost his temper.

Sarah followed him. She was the only one among them who didn't look relieved or happy. She actually seemed a little bit sad. She slipped past the others and stood beside Madame.

"I had to do it," she whispered.

"I know," Madame said and put a comforting arm around her.

Emily looked at her curiously. Had it been that awful for Sarah, using her gift? Maybe someday she'd learn why the girl was so sad.

Two police officers emerged. One had George in handcuffs, and the other had Howard. As they passed, Ken spoke.

"Howard, your mother is not very happy with you."

Howard gaped at him. George's eyes were searching the parking lot. But Clare was long gone.

Another policeman came out. "Are you all okay?"

"Yes officer, we're fine," Madame said.

He shook his head in puzzlement and looked at Martin.

"One of the tellers, she said she saw this boy break open the door to the vault."

Madame let out an odd little artificial laugh. "Well, that's hardly possible, is it, officer?"

He shrugged. "I guess one of the robbers set up an explosive charge and it went off when the kid was by the door. Good thing you weren't hurt, young man."

"Nothing hurts me," Martin bragged. Madame grabbed his arm. "Ow!"

"You didn't get all the bad guys," Emily told the policeman. She explained about Clare. The policeman took out a notebook.

"Can you give me a description of this Clare?"

Emily, Tracey, and Martin exchanged looks. What could they say?

"Blue eyes," they chorused, and then fell silent.

The officer smiled. "Don't worry, kids, I know you're still pretty upset. We'll get details from the guys we caught." He closed his notebook. "So who's the hero here?"

Emily glanced at Sarah.

"Tracey hit the alarm button," Sarah said softly.

"But this is the real hero," Tracey said, putting her hand on Charles's shoulder.

"He got the gun away from Clare," Emily added. Madame glared at her, and she bit her lip.

537

"Here's the gun, officer," Ken said quickly and handed it over.

"Good work, young man," the policeman said.

Emily looked at Charles. She wasn't surprised to see that he was pouting. She knelt by the wheelchair.

"Don't worry, Charles. We know you're the real hero. And we're going to treat you like one."

Slowly, his face cleared. His cheeks reddened. He smiled. And without even trying to look into his future, Emily suspected that it was going to be very different from what she might have predicted for him just days earlier.

Chapter Fifteen

A RE YOU SURE YOU want to go to school?" Emily's mother asked anxiously on Monday morning. "It seems to me you need more than a weekend to recover."

"I feel fine, Mom," Emily assured her. She got out of the car in front of Meadowbrook. "Don't worry. I'll see you later."

She had to admit, she felt a little tired. But she hadn't wanted to stay at home. More than anything, Emily wanted her life to get back to normal.

She still couldn't believe all the events of the past week. She'd returned home Friday night feeling as if she'd been away for a month. So many emotions . . . she'd been scared, confused, angry, depressed . . . and what was she feeling now?

She wasn't sure. But she knew it wasn't bad. And she knew she'd learned something about herself.

Madame had told them all to come to her room first

thing in the morning before school started for a debriefing. Emily was glad she wouldn't have to wait until the gifted class to see everyone. Having been through this adventure, would they be closer as a group?

She wasn't the first one to arrive at room 209. Jenna was already there. She nodded at Emily.

"How do you feel?"

"A little tired," Emily admitted. "But okay. How are you?"

"Okay," Jenna echoed. But Emily thought she looked even more tired than Emily felt. Her eyes were unusually dark.

"I'm glad it's over," Emily said.

Me, too," Jenna said. And she smiled—but to Emily, it looked a little forced.

Ken came in next, and *he* was definitely in good spirits. "I feel great," he told the girls. "You know, I always felt like I had the most worthless gift. I couldn't do anything with it. Yesterday, for the first time, it paid off!"

"How's that?" Emily asked.

"Jenna read Carter's mind, and that's how we knew about the house. But then this dead woman told me where you were! She was the mother of one of the kidnappers—Howard. She wanted me to give him a message."

"What was the message?" Emily asked.

"She wanted me to tell him he was doing a bad thing and that she was very upset with him. What was he like?"

"He was okay," Emily said. "If I'd met him somewhere else, I might even have thought he was kind of sweet."

Jenna looked surprised. "Your kidnapper was *sweet*?"

"Yeah, that one was. The other man was okay, too. I don't think either of them was very smart, but they were never mean to us. The woman, Clare . . . she was scary."

"She knew how to dress though. I mean, the woman had style." That comment came from Amanda. Back in her own body, she sauntered into the room and took her seat. Then she examined her fingernails. "Whatever takes over my body when I'm out of it does a very nice manicure."

Charles wheeled himself into the room. Emily nudged Ken, and the two of them began applauding.

"Charles, you saved my life," Emily declared. "I wish you could have seen Clare's face when that gun flew out of her hand!"

Charles looked pleased, but a little embarrassed, too. He wasn't used to anyone making a fuss over him.

Tracey arrived next, followed by Martin. Then Carter Street walked in.

Their eyes were on him as he went to his seat and sat down, but, as usual, he didn't react.

"I wonder why they just let him go," Ken mused.

"Because he didn't have a talent they could use, I guess," Tracey suggested.

"Then why did they take him in the first place?" Emily wondered. "They seemed to know everything about all of us."

No one could answer that, and the classmates sat in silence for a moment.

The last student to enter was Sarah. She went directly to Amanda.

"I want to thank you."

Amanda stared at her. "For what?"

"For taking over my body."

Emily was very surprised. "You're glad Amanda snatched your body?"

Sarah nodded. "It put me in a position where I had to use my gift. But I didn't use it before I absolutely needed to. If I'd been in control, I might have been tempted to use it earlier." And she took her seat.

Once again, Emily couldn't help wondering why Sarah was so anxious to avoid using her gift. It was one mystery that definitely hadn't been cleared up.

Finally Madame arrived. "Good morning, class. I won't keep you long, and we can spend more time talking during our regular class time. But while your memory is still fresh, I have to ask you something. What kind of an effect has this

542

experience had on you in regard to your gift? Do you feel different about it now?"

"I do," Ken said. "I actually got something useful from one of my voices."

Charles had something to say, too. "It was kind of cool, using my gift to save Emily. That lady probably wouldn't have killed her, but—"

"But you never know," Emily said. "Thank you, Charles."

Madame looked at Emily. "What about you, Emily? Have your feelings about your gift changed?"

Emily took a deep breath.

"Yes. Now I know I really have a gift, and it's just as good as everyone else's. Looking back now, everything I've envisioned has come true."

Martin interrupted. "Wait a minute. You said the bank robbery would be a success, and it wasn't."

Emily nodded. "That's because I assumed it would be because I saw Tracey get into the vault and you break the vault door. But I didn't envision the end result—I was just guessing."

"What about the two different visions you had of me?" Amanda wanted to know. "I mean, of me-as-Sarah? First you said I'd have her gift, and then you said I wouldn't have it."

"That's because you fell down," Emily said simply. "And

I didn't see that. You wouldn't have been able to freeze George. But you *did* fall, and I guess that's what pushed you out of Sarah's body. Sarah came back into herself and froze George. In my vision, I saw all the possibilities." She grinned. "Maybe the floor was waxed that day and a butterfly flew past the floor cleaner and she left too much wax on one spot."

Madame smiled. "The butterfly effect. I suppose it could have an impact on predictions."

"There's more," Emily said. "I have to learn to separate what I see in my visions from what I want to see. Like, I saw Martin would throw a sofa, and he did. But I'd only hoped he would throw it and break a door down—I didn't see that in the vision. And I have to look for details in the visions. Calendars, watches, newspapers—anything that might indicate a day or a time. I need to notice what people look like. Does someone have a suntan? That could mean the event I'm envisioning is going to happen in the summer." She went on to tell them about the vision she'd had of her mother's bad haircut, and how she thought the vision was a failure because her mother's hair came out okay.

"Looking back, I realize that in the vision, my mother was wearing her heavy quilted coat. The bad haircut will happen in the winter." She smiled. "Anyway, I know I still have to work on my gift. I need to practice examining and interpreting my visions. But at least now I know for sure that I have a gift. And it has value."

"Very good, Emily," Madame said with approval. "Now you can begin to use your gift realistically."

Emily was feeling pretty good when she left the classroom with Tracey. "I'll tell you the best thing that came out of this whole experience," she confided. "My mother's giving me a cell phone. Of course, she'll probably call me every ten minutes on it." She shivered and stopped. "I left my sweater in 209. I'd better go back and get it."

"See you at lunch," Tracey said.

Emily went back to the classroom, but she paused outside the door when she heard voices. She recognized them—Madame and Jenna were talking.

She knew it wasn't right to eavesdrop, but something about the intensity in Jenna's tone kept her there, listening.

"I read her mind, Madame. Clare—before she got away. It was just a glimpse, but I learned something. She didn't care about robbing that bank. This was a test—of us. Some of us, at least."

"I was afraid of that," Madame said. "What was she testing—the extent of their gifts?"

"Yes, but more than that. She wanted to see how much resistance the students would present—if they could be manipulated and coerced. I can understand why they didn't take me. I'd have read their minds and known what they were really up to. I don't know why they didn't take Charles or Ken. Or Amanda. Well, they did take Amanda, but it was an accident. But this whole thing, it had nothing to do with robbing a bank. It was an experiment, Madame."

"And was she pleased with the results of the experiment?" Madame asked.

Emily had to strain to hear Jenna's low voice. "Yes. And she didn't care what happened to Howard or George. There are other people involved, but not them. And the other people—they've got plans. I don't know what the plans are, Madame, but I think something big is going on. Something a lot bigger than a bank robbery."

Madame spoke calmly. "Yes, I can believe that, Jenna."

"Who *are* these people, Madame? What do they want?"

"I'm not sure. But you're right, Jenna. They're planning something. And they're very dangerous."

"What are we going to do, Madame?"

"We're going to work together, and you're going to learn how to use your gifts defensively."

"Are you worried?"

Emily wished she could see Madame's face. She had a feeling it might tell her more than her words.

"I'm not worried about you, Jenna. Or your classmates. I'm worried for the world. And how my gifted students are

546

going to have to save it."

There was a silence in the classroom. Which was fine with Emily. She didn't want to hear any more. She could leave her sweater there for the time being.

The halls were crowded now as people hurried to their first classes. Emily hurried, too, and tried not to think about the conversation she'd overheard. But she had to think about it because it was there, in her head, and it couldn't be pushed aside. And the questions went around and around.

What did those people want from them? Who were they, really? Would she be called upon to predict their motives? And how could a handful of middle school teenagers save the world? So much to think about, to worry about . . .

But oddly enough, she didn't feel panicked. She and her classmates were special. They had gifts. Maybe now they'd begin to learn the real purpose of those gifts. Hearing voices, reading minds, snatching bodies—there was a reason why they had these unique talents. Maybe now, in the face of something really big, they'd learn how to use them in the best possible way.

Emily would have her visions. She'd try to see what she could in the future and try to understand what she was seeing. She'd look for clues and read between the lines. She would interpret; she'd weed out the irrelevancies.

And always keep her eyes open for butterflies.

NINE SECRET GIFTS IN ONE CLASS—
WHAT COULD POSSIBLY GO WRONG?

Find out in an excerpt
from Volume 2 in the Gifted series:

Chapter One

KEN WAS TRYING TO ignore the voice in his head. Everyone else in the room was involved in a lively debate with Madame, their teacher. His classmates were paying attention, and they actually looked interested. Even Jenna Kelley, who generally affected an expression of boredom, was getting into it.

"What's the big deal, Madame? Okay, so maybe there are bad guys out there who want to get their hands on us. But we can take care of ourselves. We're gifted, for crying out loud!"

"Yes, you have gifts," Madame responded patiently, "but you don't know how to use them properly."

Sarah spoke softly. "Wouldn't it be better if we just didn't use them at all?"

"And let the bad guys use them?" Charles asked. "No way. We have to fight back!"

"Couldn't we just stay away from the bad guys?" Emily wanted to know.

"That's easier said than done," Tracey pointed out. "I'm with Charles. We have to be prepared to do battle."

Madame was getting frustrated. "But you can't go to battle when you don't know how to use your weapons!"

Ken wanted to be a part of this argument—to listen and maybe even join in. But how could he participate when some old dead guy was yelling at him?

Listen, kid, ya gotta help me! Talk to my granddaughter— make her see some sense. If she marries that no-good scoundrel, she'll regret it for the rest of her life!

Nobody else could hear the man—only Ken. This was his so-called gift. And he hated it.

This voice was louder than most of the voices he heard. Ken thought maybe the man was hard of hearing. His own grandfather couldn't hear very well and he talked really loudly. Ken had to yell back at his grandfather to be heard.

At least with *this* old guy Ken wouldn't have to yell. He only had to think his response and the man would hear him. Ken didn't understand how this wordless communication worked. It was just the way it happened.

He "spoke" to the man. *Look, I'm sorry, but I can't help you out. I don't even know your granddaughter.*

The man replied, *I'll give you her address.*

Ken wondered if the man could hear his silent groan. He didn't know what else to tell him. With other voices he could be tough, even rude, ordering them to leave him alone and get out of his head. But how could he be nasty and disrespectful to an old man?

"Ken? Ken!"

This voice was coming from outside his head. Madame spoke sharply, and to Ken's relief her stern tone drove the dead grandfather away.

"Are you listening, Ken? We're talking about something important."

"I'm *trying* to listen," he replied.

Her stern expression softened slightly. "Is someone bothering you?"

"He's gone now," Ken told her.

"Good. Then pay attention, because this concerns all of you. Surely by now you've all realized that there are forces in this world who present a grave threat to you. Be aware. Be alert. And never, never let anyone know what you're capable of doing."

From the corner of his eye, Ken saw Amanda yawn. She politely covered her mouth with her hand, but she was directly in Madame's line of vision, and the teacher saw her.

"Am I boring you, Amanda?" she asked, making no effort to hide the annoyance in her tone.

"No, Madame. I just have something else on my mind. Something I need to tell the class."

"And I'm sure it's something very important," Madame said smoothly. "You'll be able share it with us later. Right now, I need your full attention. It's very important that you all realize how your gifts could be exploited. I don't want to frighten you, but you need to be aware of the danger. Do you understand this?"

Jenna raised her hand. "Amanda thinks you're exaggerating, Madame."

Madame frowned. "Jenna, I've told you again and again, you are *not* to read minds in this class." Her eyes shifted to Amanda. "And I am not exaggerating. Perhaps some of you need to recall some recent events. Emily? Emily!"

Ken knew Emily couldn't use hearing voices as an excuse for not paying attention. She was just daydreaming. But not like an ordinary daydreamer might. Emily's dreams had a disturbing tendency to come true.

"Emily!" Madame barked. "Would you mind not thinking about the future and joining us in the present?"

Emily jumped. "Sorry, Madame."

"Remind the class of the potential dangers they could encounter."

"Why me?" Emily asked plaintively.

"Because, if I'm not mistaken, you were the first to encounter a real threat this year."